Irish Gold

"A tale of young love and faith as modern as U2, with a cast of characters, Irish and American, that very well may open Greeley's work to a generation of new . . . readers. Yet those who have followed his works in the past will find the same storytelling mastery and the same understanding of the heart."
—*Chicago Tribune*

"May be Andrew M. Greeley's best effort yet. It has more of everything—more plot, denser character development, fresh dialogue, and a more solid *now* story line than his previous novels. . . . Gives a different dimension and personal look at Irish history and its heroes and villains . . . A first-rate adventure story with the love interest intertwined in the mystery."
—*The Baltimore Sun*

IRISH STEW!

A Nuala Anne McGrail Novel

ANDREW M. GREELEY

FORGE®

A TOM DOHERTY ASSOCIATES BOOK
NEW YORK

For the Lanes, Jack and Dani

This is a work of fiction. All the characters, organizations, and events portrayed in this novel are either products of the author's imagination or are used fictitiously.

IRISH STEW!: A NUALA ANNE MCGRAIL NOVEL

Copyright © 2002 by Andrew M. Greeley Enterprises, Ltd.

A Forge Book
Published by Tom Doherty Associates, LLC
175 Fifth Avenue
New York, NY 10010

www.tor-forge.com

Forge® is a registered trademark of Tom Doherty Associates, LLC.

ISBN 978-0-7653-6910-9
Library of Congress Catalog Card Number: 200105480-5

First Edition: March 2002
First Mass Market Edition: March 2003
Second Mass Market Edition: March 2012

Printed in the United States of America

0 9 8 7 6 5 4 3 2 1

— 1 —

WE STARTED having trouble again with our oldest child, Nelliecoyne, the day we brought her little sister home from the hospital. The difficulty, however, was not sibling rivalry with poor little Socra Marie. The problem was that Nellie heard an explosion that had occurred a hundred and fourteen years ago.

It was a lovely May day, the fourth day of May to be exact. Spring had decided that she would come to Chicago after all, against her better judgment. She had festooned our old (but rehabbed) block on Southport Avenue with delicate green lace, bright emerald lawns, and flower beds that much to their own surprise had burst into bloom.

"Isn't it a party for herself?" my wife said as I parked our ancient Benz in front of the house. "God timed spring this year just for our Socra Marie."

I knew better than to argue.

This ditsy celebration of new life (doubtless under the patronage of St. Brigid whose cross stood watch above the door of our home) matched the exuberance that the little girl's mother, Nuala Anne McGrail, and I felt. Against all odds we had brought this tiny girl child home where she belonged after one week short of three months in an NICU—Neonatal Intensive Care Unit.

Do you know how it feels to hold a six-hundred-gram neonate in your arms? Try a pound of butter that's breathing and is totally beautiful, even if she looked at the beginning like a rare species of monkey.

"She's a tough one," Jane Foley, the young resident in neonatology, whispered to me, as Nuala viewed her for the first time. "Some of them are pretty passive. This one is determined to live."

"The toughness is all on her mother's side."

"Little girls," the young woman said primly, "have a better survival rate than little boys."

"That's cause they're stronger and better," Nuala replied promptly, "just like their mothers."

Before they took Nuala down to the NICU, the resident had told us about our daughter's prospects. My wife was hurting from the agonies of birth and woozy from drugs.

"The baby is still alive, Mrs. Coyne . . ."

"Mrs. Coyne is my mother-in-law. I'm Nuala."

"Very well, Nuala . . ." the young woman said a bit primly, eager to go through her routine.

"And she's not 'the baby.' She's Socra Marie."

"Of course . . . It is very fortunate that she came at the twenty-fifth week. Her chances are so much better than if it had been the twenty-third week . . ."

"What did I do wrong?"

I started to worry. Nuala had endured a bad case of postpartum depression after our second child.

"You didn't do anything wrong, Mrs . . . ah, Nuala. Premature births usually just happen."

"I must have done something wrong."

"Stop being Irish, Nuala," I cut in. "Dr. Foley says it wasn't your fault. That should settle that."

My wife smiled faintly.

"You're right, Dermot Michael, as always."

"We're giving her increased oxygen now to help her breathing. That's why we had to take her away from you right after she was born."

Nuala nodded, though I knew she didn't understand.

"Not so long ago, we would have abandoned her as a miscarriage. Now there's a ninety percent chance you'll be able to take her home."

Nuala nodded duly.

"However, we have to be candid with you. A little more than half of our premature babies have some problems in later life, sight, hearing, speech, brain disorders like cerebral palsy. Some of these problems can be easily corrected. Others are serious, lifelong problems. She seems healthy now. We can make no guarantees."

Nuala nodded again.

"We are forbidden by law to take her off life support. However, if you wish we will put a DNR on her chart; that means 'Do not resuscitate.' You would have to sign some papers for that."

Dr. Foley was about the same age as Nuala, probably had a kid or two of her own.

"Why would we want to do that?"

"I'm a Catholic like you are, Nuala. There is no obligation to extraordinary means. What we're doing now is certainly extraordinary. The Church is more tolerant than the government. It would permit you to request that we stop trying to keep her alive. The government won't let us do that. But it will let us follow your orders not to resuscitate her if, say, she stops breathing. Then she would be with God."

My wife frowned, puzzled by the prospect that Dr. Foley was offering her. "Why in the world would we ever do that?" Nuala asked.

"There is a chance that she won't have much of a life."

Nuala cocked her eye at me. I nodded.

"Och, sure, if God doesn't mind, won't we be after keeping her?"

Dr. Foley lowered her head, to hide tears no doubt.

"Why doesn't that choice surprise me!"

So we went to the NICU. Nuala immediately went to the isolete where our daughter lay, tubes poking into her body, her eyes covered to protect her from the intense light that provided warmth, her ears covered with tiny earmuffs to protect them from the noise of the NICU. Clad only in a miniature diaper she was kicking her little feet and waving her little hands to protest the tubes

"Och, sure, Dermot Michael, isn't the little hellion here to stay? Can't you tell it by the way she looks at me and herself with fire in her eyes already?"

Socra Marie opened her eyes rarely in those very early days. However, we were assured by the nurses that she knew her mother's smell from the time in the womb. Probably knew mine too because I hung around so much.

"Can I talk to her?"

"Please do," Dr. Foley said. "The more she hears your voice, the better."

So my wife bent over the small one and spoke to her in tender and loving Irish.

"I don't suppose I could sing to her?"

"If you do it very softly, so as not to disturb the other children."

Socra Marie heard for the first time in her life—though surely not the last—the melody of the Connemara lullaby. She calmed down and stopped fidgeting. So did the children on either side of her. A kind of mystical grace permeated the NICU, for a moment moving us into an alternative world.

"You can sing louder, Nuala," Dr. Foley whispered. "All the children like it."

So we had a daily concert.

Nuala Anne was aware that it would be eight weeks at least before the tiny one saw much of anything. However, having predicted her gender and her early arrival, my wife was not likely to be wrong. She almost never is.

She accurately predicts the gender of children, not only before they were born, but before they were conceived. Nuala Anne, you see, is fey. As is our first born, Nellie. The little bishop, who knows everything, "speculates" that it is a holdover from our Neanderthal ancestors who, since they could not talk very well, needed to communicate psychically. "A neo-Neanderthal vestige," he informs us.

"Is Socra Marie fey?" I asked.

"Isn't that a terrible thing to say about this poor little tyke? She's not fey at all, at all, dear little thing that she is, but she's full of life and will lead all of us a merry chase, won't you, dear little one?"

She wept as she did often these days.

Then she sang very softly some more snatches of the Connemara Cradle Song—in her native Irish, naturally.

"Socra," by the way, is pronounced *Sorra*. You won't have the right of it, however, unless you speak it like your sinuses are packed tight with Galway fog. My wife's name is pronounced *Noolah*, with the same thick Galway mist oozing through the vowels and consonants.

The "dear little one" led us a merry chase through the first six weeks of her life, just barely surviving crisis after crisis, laser surgery on her eyes, several resuscitations, a couple of infections. However, survive she did with grim determination.

The first time Nuala nursed her, she devoured her mother's milk like she expected there to be a shortage, as if perhaps to say, "Well, it's about time!"

We spent much of our time at the hospital, "immersing" ourselves in the care of our new daughter at the suggestion of the staff in the NICU. At first that meant simply being there with her, so she could smell us and hear us.

"Isn't she beautiful, Dermot Michael?" Nuala said to me the day after the little girl was born, with very little warning.

Actually fifteen weeks early and weighing almost a pound, Socra Marie didn't look like much of anything, under the intense light which kept her warm and the Saran Wrap which kept her moist on an open bed with the blinkers over her eyes and the earmuffs over her ears and feeding and breathing tubes in her mouth and nose. Her dark brown and paper-thin skin was covered with cream (which, we were told, you could buy at the corner drugstore). She struggled violently against the tubes.

"The poor little thing," Nuala said, tears streaming down her cheeks. "There she was taking her ease inside of me and all of a sudden she's dumped in this strange place with all them aggravating things sticking inside her."

When Nuala is in her Irish country-girl mood a "thing" is always pronounced a "ding." She was very much in that modality after her little daughter was born. An African-American nurse asked if she were an immigrant. I told the truth and said that she was.

"Is all this too much for her, do you think?"

It was a perfectly legitimate question, so I withheld my amusement.

"Nuala Anne can cope," I replied. "She studied at Trinity College in Dublin."

"They have a fine medical school there," the nurse said, putting me in my place.

Eventually the staff figured out that the nice girl who sang to the babies and acted as a morale officer and chaplain for all the other mothers was *the* singer.

"Sure I do sing now and then," my wife admitted.

"Isn't her name Nuala Anne?" Dr. Foley asked me.

"Sometimes."

When other babies went home, Nuala Anne led the cheers. When some died, she led the weeping. Despite all the strain, she was remarkably patient with me.

"Wife," I said, "haven't I hinted now and again that you'd try the patience of a saint?"

"'Tis true, I would."

"'Tis not true. What is true is that you have the patience of a saint."

"Och, Dermot Michael," she said, resting her head on my shoulder, "'tis not true, but 'tis dead focking brill of you to say it."

So we were there every day all day, with only a few time-outs to return to our home to make sure that the troops were not too restless. They were, but what could we do?

" 'Tis essential for bonding, Dermot Michael, don't you see now?"

What did I know? Nothing, except that if you were a child of Nuala Anne's you bonded, whether you liked the idea or not.

There was more than a little chaos at our house for those eight weeks. We had both a nanny and a house-keeper (Ethne and Danuta respectively) but my wife is the kind of Irishwoman who has to make sure the children are properly dressed and the house properly cleaned before either of these personages appears.

The kids were restless in the midst of the confusion, though the Mick was monumentally uninterested in his baby sister once we had assured him that she would not want to play with his Tonka trucks. Red-haired Nellie (nee Mary Anne) on the other hand was fiercely impatient with the delay in the arrival at home of her little sister. "Is she EVER going to come home?" she would demand several times each day.

Finally, after the first month, when we had progressed from touching her lightly to holding her in our arms, we brought Nellie, solemn and serious, to St. Joe's for her first inspection.

By this time, Socra Marie was living in the isolete as they call an incubator these days and, wrapped in several layers of blankets, breathing on her own. She also looked pretty much like a human baby with a lovely face and her mother's fair white skin.

"She's cute, Ma, but isn't she terrible small altogether?"

"You were small once too, me darlin' girl."

"Not that small, was I?"

"Well, not quite."

"We'll have to take real good care of her, so she'll grow up big and strong, won't we?"

Nellie was echoing her mother.

"We will . . ."

Nellie and Nuala sighed in unison.

Her little sister opened her eyes then and, as she usually did, surveyed her immediate environment with intense curiosity. She seemed satisfied with Nuala and myself. Then her eyes widened as she took in Nellie's bright red hair. She paused, and then closed her eyes.

"She likes my hair," Nellie informed us. "I think we can keep her!"

Socra Marie opened her eyes again and pondered her parents and then, satisfied, closed them and went back to sleep. We touched her and caressed her for a while and spoke softly to her.

"She likes me too," Nellie whispered. "We're going to be great friends."

"I'm sure she does," Nuala Anne assured her firstborn.

"Can I touch her?" Nellie asked the nurse who was hovering over us—sensing immediately who the authority figure in the group was.

"Very gently, my dear," said the nurse, somewhat dubiously.

So our elder daughter touched her little sister's neck and murmured softly, "I love you, Socra Marie. Please come home and live with us soon. I'll take good care of you."

Everyone in the room was suddenly in tears.

With most big sisters that would have meant that Nellie would be the boss. With this sweet, loving, and very strange little kid with the haunting Irish eyes, that was by no means certain.

Our two snow-white Irish wolfhounds, Fiona and her daughter Maeveen, who did not like extra disorder in their domain, of which they assumed they were the absolute rulers, were also upset by the frantic life of our family during those long months.

Two?

Yes, two. My wife had read somewhere that dogs need other dogs to play with. Wolfhounds' notion of playing is wrestling and pretending to fight with one another and rolling around on the floor with human kids. Though they are gentle and intelligent dogs, they are also very big. Their games occupy a lot of space.

Our child could both see and hear, but we were warned that there were other possible developmental risks, though the odds were better than nine out of ten that she would survive. Cerebral palsy, for example, was always a possibility, as were recurrent lung problems. Moreover, it would take perhaps two years before her development would catch up with that of term babies, though there was a wide variation in that projection. Preemies progressed at different rates, sometimes similar and sometimes different, from those of term children.

Yet those weeks in the hospital, in which days and nights blurred into a continuous stream and the times when we weren't there seemed unreal, when the blue lights and the spanking clean walls and corridors of the hospital were like another planet, in which we belonged and the rest of the world was only a fantasy, were like a long retreat in which wonder and surprise and above all life swirled around us like a choir of softly singing angels.

One night, I woke up from the chair in which I had been snoozing to see Nuala, her face alight with a supernatural glow, bending over Socra Marie, touching her lightly and gently moving her fingers back and forth over her little arm. For a moment, just a moment, the whole universe stood still and the love from that touch leaped out of the crib scene and enveloped me. The whole world stood still. I saw how everything fit together and how the three of us, the little holy family in the neonate room, were all part of it and that all things would be well, all manner of things would be well. As I slowly eased down from the mountain I had climbed, I told myself that this was the kind of moment of grace out of which poetry was born, indeed out of which poetry ought to be born.

"You are awake are you now, Dermot Michael, and yourself should be home getting a good night's sleep and walking the dogs and getting a good run in the morning."

"I am," I admitted. ". . . Nuala, do you think God loves us the way you love Socra Marie at this moment? Does he touch us the way you touch her?"

"Och, that's a strange question, Dermot Michael, and yourself knowing that there's no point in being God unless you can do them kind of things and himself sending Jesus to tell us that, poor dear man."

Lofty praise for Jesus. Rarely was I referred to as a "poor dear man," the highest praise an Irishwoman can bestow on a member of the inferior gender.

In the confusion after Socra Marie's birth and Nuala's inability to understand why her baby was taken away from her so quickly, we forgot about Baptism. Later, she stirred out of a drugged sleep and murmured something to me about "our daughter."

"She's alive, Nuala dear. They're giving her oxygen to help her breathe. She'll be fine."

She nodded. "I know that, Dermot. Still we should baptize her just to be sure."

Neither of us believed in Limbo. We both figured that God wanted to save everyone and would find a way to do so, no matter what happened.

However, we also believed in "just to be sure."

I dashed down to the neonate room. A nurse stood guard over our little girl, who was struggling against the tubes in her mouth and nose.

"Baptism . . ." I stammered.

"No problem," the nurse said. "I poured water on her head and said the words as soon as she came in, not that God didn't love her anyway . . . Isn't she beautiful, Mr. McGrail?"

"She sure is!"

It was a story I resolved that I would tell many times to my second daughter as she grew up. Like her mother she would doubtless agree that I was Mr. McGrail.

"You shouldn't worry," a senior doctor later told us, "if she doesn't walk till she's two and doesn't talk much till she's three."

Nuala raised her eyes skeptically.

"When she does begin to talk, won't she talk up a storm just like her poor mother?"

"She might also have a hard time learning how to sit up and to crawl. You'll have to be patient with her, you know."

"Sure, won't she have to be patient with us!"

"You understand then, that you're taking a risk with this child?"

"Didn't we take a risk in bringing her into the world? And don't we all take risks in being born?"

"I understand and I admire your decisions. I merely want to make it clear that you may have to walk long miles with her."

"Aren't we Irish great walkers, Doctor?"

He sighed and looked at his pen.

"It wasn't all that many years ago that we made no effort to save children your little girl's size. We lacked the tools, the medication, the understanding. Some older men in the profession were very dubious about the progress we had made in neonatology. They said we saved children at tremendous cost only to cause many of them to live in pain and suffering for themselves and their family or to prolong hope when there were no grounds. Sometimes that is true even today, most of the time it is not. You're too young to remember the case of Patrick Kennedy, the President's third child. He died of a lung syndrome of the sort which your daughter faced. Now we have a medication that deals with the problem effectively in most cases, as it did in hers. The whole point"—he smiled self-consciously—"is to tell you that you are taking a gamble, a not unreasonable gamble, but a gamble nevertheless."

"Och, aren't we Irish the greatest gamblers in all the world, Doctor?"

We all laughed.

I favored the gamble at least as much as my wife did.

"Hasn't God been very good to us, Dermot Michael?" she said later as she rearranged the pink knitted blanket over Socra Marie and tilted the matching cap to a flattering angle.

(The knitted garments were given to the hospital by a group of elderly Jewish women who knitted them for the neonates. Nuala of course insisted on visiting them.)

"He has," I agreed.

"Hasn't he blessed us with three fine, healthy children and made the doctors smart enough to invent medicine to keep the third one alive and wouldn't poor Caroline Kennedy have a brother alive today if they had the same medicines forty years ago?"

"He has," I agreed again, wondering if the family death instinct would have extended to Patrick Kennedy if he had lived to maturity.

"So we should thank God for giving us a little challenge as well as a little girl?"

"We should . . . Nuala, my love, when you said you knew that Socra Marie would live, was that fey knowledge or mother knowledge?"

"Sure, Dermot, isn't that an eejit question? How can there be any difference?"

Anyway, despite two occasions when we were told that Socra Marie would not last the night, we were finally bringing her home in triumph.

"'Tis a brilliant day altogether, isn't it, Dermot Michael, and ourselves with this wonderful little girl child right here on Southport Avenue?"

"It is a lovely day," I agreed as I helped herself up the stairs to the entrance of our home, on the second floor like all houses built in the good old days before Chicago had modestly hidden its swampy self under many tons of earth.

"Didn't I mean the day behind the day?"

I glanced at her radiantly happy face. I was never quite sure about her excursions into Irish mysticism, in which she claimed (pretended? actually experienced?) some immediate contact with the ultimate reality—the mountain behind the mountain, the lake behind the lake, the Dermot behind the Dermot. In the last case, I was informed, that the "Dermot behind Dermot" was someone "you might call God, if you were of such a mind."

I was not sure God would be flattered and said so. She laughed, and said, "Sure, he wouldn't mind at all, at all."

Did she really emerge from Plato's cave and walk in the world of the *really* real? Or was she speaking in metaphors, something that the Irish are genetically programmed to do?

When I asked her once she had sighed loudly (the West of Ireland sigh, which at first sounded like an acute asthma attack) and informed me that, sure, she didn't see the difference.

"Was that thunder, Dermot Michael?" she asked me as we reached the door of the house.

"I don't think so . . . Maybe some angelic Bodhran drum to celebrate the homecoming of Socra Marie!"

"Hush, Dermot love. Isn't it bad luck to be blaspheming when you're bringing a newborn into the house?"

The Irish, I am convinced, make up their superstitions about bad luck to fit the circumstances.

The door swung open before I could unlock it. There were cheers and shouts and music playing on the stereo—Nuala Anne singing the Connemara Cradle Song.

In addition to Ethne and Danuta, my mother and father (a nurse/doctor combination who understandably wanted to form a discreet diagnosis of their new granddaughter) Cindasue McCloud Murphy, a Coast Guard officer and wife of Peter Murphy, and her ten-month-old daughter Katiesue were there to proclaim the tiny heroine. The neonate of the hour ignored the noise and continued to sleep, even when the two massive white canines tentatively pushed their way into the crowd of admirers, tails wagging, to sniff this new human puppy. Obviously they approved: they curled up on the floor in front of Nuala Anne on the couch as a kind of protective honor guard.

The only one who was less than ecstatic about this triumphant homecoming was our blond middle child, who continued to play with his Tonka trucks, his diaper hanging askew over his rear end as it usually did.

"No one more narcissistic," I murmured to my wife next to me on the couch, "then a two-year-old boy."

"Lest it be a thirty-two-year-old boy!"

Nuala Anne made my life difficult by pointing out whenever possible that I was "way over thirty" while, at twenty-seven, she was "nowhere near thirty."

It was the generally held opinion (even by me) that the Mick was much like his father—big, good-looking, and generally useless. The comparison caused the thunderclouds to gather on Nuala's face and her lips to tighten.

"I'll not have anyone at all, at all saying things like

that about my poor husband," she'd snap. Everyone would retreat from the comparison, afraid to ask how exactly I was different from my firstborn son.

Danuta produced a big cake, my mom offered a huge plate of cookies, and my dad began pouring the champagne. Socra Marie for her part slept on.

Her big sister stared at her intently.

"As the grandfather of this little miracle," my father began as he lifted a champagne flute, "I propose the first toast to Socra Marie Coyne, the small girl with indomitable will."

We all toasted the baby, who responded by continuing to sleep.

"I'll talk to her other grandparents over in Carraroe tonight," Dad went on, "and tell them they'll have to come over soon so they can be as proud of her as her American grandmother and I are."

"And her great-grandmother too," Nuala whispered in my ear.

Nuala claimed a special relationship with Nell Pat Malone, even though my grandmother had died before I had met Nuala.

"Wasn't she the one who brought us together?"

I wouldn't have put it—or anything else—past Ma, as I had always called Nell Pat.

"Bernie and Jackie are coming," Nellie announced confidently, and strode toward the door to admit these favorites, French musicians who played Celtic music, into the house.

"I didn't hear the bell just now," Cindasue said to me with a puzzled frown. "Does that thar' chile have hearing like to a mountain polecat?"

"Heard them on the steps, I suppose."

We had become so accustomed Nellie's anticipations that we hardly noticed them.

"Dear little Mary Anne," her preschool teacher, a woman of no more than twenty-three summers, had said. "is so sensitive and thoughtful. If one of the children is unhappy she notices it and immediately consoles the child. She leads by sensitivity and sympathy, normally pretty rare in a four-year-old."

"Maybe she's manipulating them, isn't she?" Nuala said grimly, unwilling, like so many of our kind, to believe praise of our children (and equally willing to be irate in the absence of praise).

"Oh, no, Mrs. Coyne," The teacher, unaware of the game, replied, "Mary Anne is simply adorable."

"Hmf," she muttered proudly to me as we walked across Southport, "the little brat has fooled them altogether."

"At least they haven't noticed she's fey."

"Aren't they afraid to?"

"What does Nellie think of it?"

"Why should she be any different, poor little thing, than I was at that age? She thinks everyone is that way."

Marie-Bernadette and Jacques-Yves joined the admiring throng at our house the day we brought Socra Marie home.

"Chérie," my wife asked, "did you notice any thunder when you were coming over?"

"Mais non, was not the day *très beau?"*

"Don't worry, Ma," Nellie piped up. "It was only some men setting off a bomb down at the Haymarket."

No one else seemed to notice this outrageous claim. I slipped away into our library and took down a book of Chicago history. It was as I feared. The Haymarket riot was a hundred and fourteen years ago. To the day.

My wife had heard the noise. Her daughter knew all about it.

I shivered.

Back in the parlor, Socra Marie had opened her eyes, reducing the room to silence. She did not cry out in protest against the crowd and the noise they made. Rather she carefully and thoughtfully (or so it seemed to me) surveyed the room. First of all she found her mother, who was holding her in her arms, then her eyes discovered Nellie's red hair, of which she seemed to approve, then she detected the Daddy shape, though she didn't know the word. I rated a quick glance. Then, she saw the two huge dogs. She closed her eyes as if she couldn't believe that this new world in which she had been plunged without prior consultation could possibly contain such creatures. Then she opened them again, as if reconsidering Fiona and Maeveen. Then, satisfied, she closed her eyes and went back to sleep.

"Well, she didn't reject us anyway," my wife said, kissing her daughter's forehead. "She knows she's home."

"Can I hold her, Mommy, just for a minute? I won't drop her."

"It's good crack, Nellie. Just keep the blankets around her. She likes being warm."

"I know."

Nellie held her little sister with enraptured awe, as though she were something sacred. Everyone in the room, except her mother and father, held their breath. Then carefully she gave the baby back to her mother.

"Brilliant altogether," she informed us.

("Good crack," by the way, is an Irish phrase which has nothing to do with narcotics but means something like "great fun.")

Later on that day, after everyone had gone home and all the children were in bed, Socra Marie in a bassinet right next to our bed, I had occasion to shiver again.

"Didn't Ethne tell me that someone took a shot at that gobshite Seamus Costelloe last night."

"Just as you predicted?"

"'Tis true"—she sighed—"Dermot love. 'Tis true. The mark of death is on him."

"Did they kill him?"

"They did not. Not this time. He's in hospital . . ."

That's when I shivered again. Without warning we were swept up in two mysteries. If my wife were to have her way we would have to solve them both. Naturally, she would have her way.

And ourselves with an adorable and fragile little girl in the house, a beautiful gamble.

As if to reassure me, both Fiona and Maeveen ambled into our room and snuggled up next to the bassinet.

OUR TROUBLES had started eleven months earlier in a place called Portofino on the so-called Italian Riviera. We were staying for two nights at an elegant hotel called the Cenobio dei Dogi to rest up after Nuala Anne's triumph at the Celtic music festival in Milano, a city which is heavy into festivals but had only recently taken seriously the truth that its heritage was more Celtic than Lombard.

"Dermot Michael," Nuala Anne whispered in my ear, "you're not asleep, are you?"

"Woman, I am not!"

Only about 95 percent asleep after a bout of very satisfactory lovemaking. My wife, playing the role of the poor, shy Irish countrywoman, was clinging to me as though she had to absorb my protection after the outrageous behavior in which she had enthusiastically engaged.

"Wouldn't they be not so far from wrong who said that it would be a mistake for us to have another child just now?"

That's the way the Irish talk. Three or four negatives wrapped together in the same convoluted sentence.

I was instantly alert. We were about to have a serious discussion.

"I've always thought meself, uh, myself, that the person who should make that decision is the one who will bear the child and nurse him."

"Her," she said firmly.

Ah, the gender of the yet unconceived child had already been determined.

"Sure," she continued, "isn't it the truth that the father should have an equal vote?"

"No," I said firmly. "Fathers never get an equal vote."

"But we have to pretend they do, don't we now?"

"So long as everyone knows we're pretending."

There were a number of reasons why we were not quite ready for a third child. Nuala's first two pregnancies and deliveries had been extraordinarily difficult. The second had plunged her into deep, if, as it turned out, temporary depression. Even though we could, thank the good Lord, afford help (through my luck and her talent), my wife was a responsible parent to the point of obsession. While she had learned to be a little more laid-back in her assumption of total responsibility, she still could be very hard on herself if, for example, one of the kids came down with a cold.

Moreover, she had become, as her triumph in Milano had shown, an international celebrity. Although at first she had dismissed the invitation to the *Festival di musico Irelandese e Celtico,* as a serious temptation to grave sin, she had finally succumbed to my mom's insistence that she and Dad would enjoy hosting the kids and the hounds for a week or so. It would be good for us and for the kids if we got away.

Thus Mom, who knew all about compulsive Irish matriarchs, had trumped one moral responsibility with another.

"Besides," she added, "it would be good for those Italians to know that Ireland was a civilized country long before they were."

The claim was dubious historically, but any appeal

to Irish national pride in these days of the Celtic Tiger, struck a responsive chord in my wife's heart. The Irish were no longer a poor people and no one, save some of the Brits, thought they were uneducated or uncivilized. So we had to drive the truth about Ireland home to everyone, didn't we now?

A minor problem was that Nuala Anne was Irish and a singer, but she was not exactly an Irish singer. Quite the contrary, she sang anything and every-thing—Protestant Gospel hymns, blues, American folk songs, English language and Latin hymns from the "old church." She probably knew more Irish-language music than anyone of her generation, but she did not consider herself a specialist. Hence we had to suffer through a lot of practice to make sure that we'd do it just right.

I've often said that I sleep with many different women and my wife is all of them. Though she had majored in accounting, Nuala Anne had hung around the theater group at TCD where she had found justi-fication for moving from role to role to role in her com-plex personality. She could board an airplane as a sophisticated woman of the world who had been everywhere and seen everything and was impressed by almost nothing and certainly no one.

Or she could be the shy Galway peasant, frightened to be out of the familiar context of Carraroe. Some-times, when we traveled, she insisted on talking to me in Irish, a language of which I knew hardly more than a dozen words

"Och sure, Dermot love, don't you know what I'm saying from the tone of me voice and the expression on me face?"

I didn't argue.

The Irish peasant lass appeared frequently on our quick trip to northern Italy as me wife decided she did not want to be an international celebrity—as if that were possible after her Christmas programs, which were now broadcast all over the world. People would think they recognized her, but the young woman seemed so shy and spoke neither English nor Italian and babbled in some strange, if musical language, so it couldn't be her.

Her voice was sweet and beautiful and now, thanks to my insistence, well trained. It is the kind of voice that if you listen to it closely, you can hear the sound of church bells ringing over the bogs on a day when the mists and the sunshine alternate with one another. She had wonderful stage presence and could get inside any song she tried. She would not be much of a threat, however, to the divas at the *Teatro a la Scala*. They, however, had not become part of Christmas around the world, a role which my wife would vehemently deny whenever it was suggested to her.

Nuala Anne is tall with the firmly disciplined body of a woman athlete, long and lustrous black hair, and a slender and expressive face that would remind one of an Irish goddess, not that I have ever met another Irish goddess. She's the kind of young woman they put on the cover of the Irish travel magazines, save that those young women, gorgeous as they might be, cannot reveal a face whose expressions change by the second and half the time is filled with the light of pure mischief.

"Nuala Anne," I said to her shortly after we were married, "you are a shit-kicker."

"Am I now?" she said, grinning at the prospect of another argument.

"Woman, you are."

"Well, now wherever in the world do I kick shite?"

"Wherever you find it."

"Do I now?"

"You do. You come into a situation where you notice a pile of shit in the corner. You walk over to it to test it delicately with your foot to make sure that it's high quality. Then you kick it around until the whole place is covered with it, all the time pretending that you're not at all responsible for starting the argument."

She threw back her head and laughed joyously.

"Dermot Michael Coyne," she said, pretending to outrage, "I'd never do anything like that . . . and isn't it yourself, poet that you are, who has a fine sense of metaphor."

Then she hugged me fiercely.

Her denial didn't indicate she was about to give up the habit. On our quick trip through northern Italy her premise was that she could find nothing there, at all, at all, which did not compare unfavorably with the County Galway.

The Duomo in Milan: "Sure isn't St. Nicholas Collegiate Church a better example of late Gothic?"

The Piazza di Duomo: (With a sniff) "It can't compare for elegance with Eyre Square in Galway Town."

The Riviera "beach" at Portofino with its black gravel: "Don't we have a dozen beaches on Galway Bay that are nicer?"

To which I replied, "I admit that Inch is incomparably better."

She replied with an angry frown: "That's a beach in Kerry. Kerrymen are sheep thieves."

Venice (we're standing on an elevated platform waiting single file to enter San Marco as a foot of Adriatic water covers most of the Piazza): "This place is a friggin' sewer. They say Galway Town is the Venice of Ireland. Sure, doesn't our County Council have grounds to sue?"

She doesn't mean any of this shite, you should excuse the expression. It's all part of the game. Does the game ever grow dull?

She keeps people laughing with it even when they're not hopelessly in love with her like I am.

There was an incident in Venice that showed another side of my wife.

We had wandered out of the Danieli after having a Bailey's Irish Cream nightcap and were strolling along the bank of the Grand Canal, to which the Adriatic had receded when the tide went down. We heard a soprano voice singing Schubert's "Ave Maria" and Gonoud's "Panis Angelicus," for which liturgical chestnuts elderly Irish and American tourists are suckers. There's always music around the Piazza, string groups playing melodies from my parents' era like "Fascination" and "Always," and "Dancing in the Dark." Nuala knew the lyrics and sang the tunes softly.

She hummed along with the "Panis Angelicus" soprano and grabbed my arm. "Dermot Michael, that child has a beautiful voice."

"How do you know she's a child?"

"She's better than I am."

A crowd had gathered around the Palazzo di Dogi (under repair) to listen. Nuala was right, the pretty young woman, who sang with hands behind her back, was indeed a child, as was the man who was accompanying her on a guitar. She paused and bowed her head politely to the applause. The crowd added lire to the small box in front of her mike. A group of Italian naval cadets were especially generous.

The singer then turned to Mozart, chestnuts which were not quite so well known to the tourists. Next to me, my sentimental wife was weeping. I knew what would happen next and was already proud of her.

After a couple of Mozart pieces, they paused again. Nuala slipped up to them, put a 500,000 lire note in the box (two hundred dollars) and then purchased one of their CDs. She chatted with them for a few moments, wrote down their address on a used Vapo ticket, and gave them her business card.

(A plain white card which said simply *nuala5@-aol.com.*)

They would almost certainly be on her next Christmas show. Or the one after.

"'Tis not fair," she said to me as we resumed our stroll, tears streaming down her cheeks.

"What's not fair?"

"That they have to be street musicians to stay alive and meself pretending to be a great Celtic singer over in that town with the awful cathedral."

"I bet they earn a very good living," I replied. "There's a new crowd of tourists walking the Grand Canal every night of the year."

She sighed, her saddest West Galway sigh. "Still it's not fair at all, at all."

She had already adopted, with some help from the little bishop, Marie-Bernadette and Jacques-Yves. My Nuala Anne had a heart as big as all outside.

SOMEDAY YOU'LL GET TIRED OF HER, the Adversary whispered in my ear. ISN'T SHE TOO MUCH ALTOGETHER.

"Don't pretend to talk Irish."

YOU DO IT ALL THE TIME.

"Regardless."

SOMEDAY YOU'LL GET TIRED OF OGLING HER BREASTS AND REALIZE YOU MADE A MISTAKE. ISN'T SHE ROUND THE BEND ALTOGETHER?

The Adversary is a voice from the subbasement of my soul who often complains about me. I am no more responsible for what he says than I am for what my wife says.

Nor would I ever grow weary of her breasts no matter how old we might be. Elegant, graceful, inviting, they challenged me, even when they were completely clothed.

Which brings me back to the scene in the bedroom in Portofino. I chose my words very carefully because I knew they would be stored up and used against me if the occasion warranted.

"Well," I said as if I were discussing an interesting if abstract philosophical principle, "I suppose that the only thing the father might have a right to say is that he would have no objection to a new rugrat around the house, so long as the child's mother would try hard not to be so obsessive about being a perfect mother."

Dead silence. I had touched a sensitive point.

"Well, now"—she had adopted her philosophy debating voice—"sure, after a woman's had a couple of small ones, shouldn't she know enough not to be obsessive anymore?"

"She should," I agreed.

Another long silence.

"And I suppose," she said cautiously, "I suppose the father would be the one that would decide whether she was being obsessive or not?"

"Who better?"

She sighed loudly, a sigh that indicated that the conversation was over and I had, for the moment, won the point.

You won't have the guts to stick to it.

I ignored him. I knew that I had better or I would not be a very good husband.

Then, as I was falling into the sleep of the just man who had won part of an argument with his wife and had a very pleasant time loving her, she whispered, "Won't we call her Socra Marie?"

That settled that.

I thought we'd probably conceive Socra Marie before we had returned to Southport Avenue. However, that would happen only on or about the Labor Day weekend at Grand Beach.

How do you keep a mother from obsessing about a little girl, of whom a senior neonate consultant had said, "I don't think we should make any special efforts to save her, Mrs. McGrail(sic!)" he had said. "She is likely to grow up with some severe damage to her system. It would be better to let her go and try again sometime in the future. I don't think there would be much quality of life for her."

I held my breath, expecting an explosion.

All she said was, "There's nothing wrong with the poor little thing. She will live and be fine, no matter what you say."

That was that. Dr. Foley, careful not to disagree explicitly with the great man, just nodded. God knows a lot of special efforts were necessary, especially with membranes in her lungs. Yet, at least as stubborn as her mother, "poor little Socra Marie" survived.

A pediatrician confided to us, "There's nothing wrong with her. She just has to catch up. When she does, she'll be as healthy as her brother and sister."

"Didn't I know that all along?" Nuala beamed radiantly.

Then to me she whispered, "I knew it, Dermot Michael, yet I really didn't know it, if you take me meaning?"

I did indeed take her meaning. When you have someone as precious as a tiny girl child, you don't completely trust your fey insights.

Anyway, the day after I was told the name of our third child, we met the Costelloe family at the swimming pool at the Cenobio dei Dogi, our hotel in the town of Camogli on the Portofino Peninsula.

"Not much of a view, Dermot Michael, is it?" she complained, as we walked out to the pool, at the top of a sheer ledge above the Ligurian Sea. "Nothing like Galway Bay?"

"Not quite up to the Cliffs of Maher," I agreed.

"That's in Clare," she protested. "Wasn't I thinking of the Aran Islands?"

"Ah," I said . . . "Nuala Anne, the water is freezing! This pool isn't heated!"

She dipped her fingers into it.

"Isn't it grand, Dermot love, just like Galway Bay this time of the year!"

She tossed aside her robe, paused briefly (in her skintight maillot) and then dove into the pool.

Nuala, I should note, resolutely rejects the notion

that pregnancy should interfere with the shape of her body. Diet, exercise, and grim determination seem to work for her. "I'm not doing it for you, Dermot Michael Coyne, I'm doing it for me own self-respect."

"Not even a little bit for me?"

"Maybe a tiny bit," she admitted grudgingly.

"What percent?"

"Well," she considered the question, "no more than 90 percent."

I love her, as you have probably gathered. Each day more than ever.

A family group at the side of the pool watched her dive. They looked like folks who might have stepped out of an Addams' family film—better-looking than that crowd but not exactly the kind of folks you'd want to mess with. The father was a big man with a large bald head on top of a large body, more solid muscle than fat, and a frown on his square face that suggested a major grudge against the world. Since it was northern Italy, I thought, giving full rein to my ethnic prejudices, he was probably a crooked industrialist instead of a mafioso.

My wife's dive was graceful, as was everything she did. She splashed a little water several feet from this crook and his family.

"Jesus Christ, you little bitch," he shouted, his face turning crimson, "watch where you're splashing the goddamn water!"

Are you going to let him get away with that?

"No way!"

The man had recoiled as though some of the water had actually fallen on his well-oiled body, which it hadn't.

The woman who was presumably his wife, a skinny artificial blond with a frown that matched his, glared contemptuously at my wife and muttered something that had to be obscene. The four younger people, children and children-in-law probably, all of whom looked like skimpily dressed, hardened criminals, shifted on their lounges and began to reapply their oil.

I wandered over casually. I played linebacker at Notre Dame before I flunked out despite the fact that some people claimed that I would have been an all-American. I haven't put on any weight since then, mostly because of Nuala's good example. Unfortunately, my blue eyes and blond hair and dimpled chin made me look harmless, which in truth I usually am, a pleasant, good-natured lout.

"My wife," I informed this crowd, "is an innocent peasant girl with a delicate sensibility. I'd ask you to watch your language when you're talking to her."

Prig. Liar too.

"I am not. She doesn't like to hear the Lord's name taken in vain."

The big guy looked up at me.

"Fuck off!"

He talked like Chicago. Flat A. Personal injury lawyer, I decided. I noted that the son and the son-in-law, as it seemed, were also big guys, but going toward flab. Not a problem.

Nuala Anne, who had heard his shout, ignored it and swam to the other end of the pool, returned—perfect Australian crawl of course—thunderheads marring her lovely face.

"Leave the focking eejit alone, Dermot Michael," she screamed at me.

"Jesus Christ, twat," the man yelled at her, "you have a goddamn filthy tongue in your mouth."

He looked up at me and grinned. He was pleased with himself. He had made his point.

Someone else took over inside me and it wasn't the usual adversary either.

I lifted him out of his chair and tossed him into the pool, knowing full well I'd catch hell from my wife for doing it. He kind of bounced when he hit the water and yelled with pain. He was not used to swimming in Galway Bay.

Then things began to get weird. I mean really weird. I was more or less prepared to throw the two young males in the pool when they came after me. Instead everyone in his entourage convulsed in laughter.

"Serves you right, asshole!" The good wife led the laughter.

"Got what you deserved," a young woman who was just bitchy enough to be his daughter chortled.

In the pool, the big guy was laughing himself.

"Didn't you play linebacker for Notre Dame?" he demanded, trying to pull himself out of the pool.

"Gave it up as a bad business," I said, extending a hand to help him. "Not mean enough."

"Couldn't prove it by me," he said lunging onto the deck.

"You looked like a beached whale," the wife said without much imagination, but with some accuracy.

"Dad," said a kid whose square face, like his father's, had been hacked out of stone with an axe, "you'll never learn to keep your mouth shut."

"Gimme a towel."

His wife negligently tossed him one.

"A dry towel, goddamn it!"

I gave him mine.

"Yeah, thanks. When did you play at the dome?"

"Twelve years ago."

"Bad time to be on the team, asshole for a coach."

"Last good one was Ara."

"Goddamn right! I played for him."

"Excuse me," I said, "I have to run after my wife. She thinks I disgraced the family."

The only remaining question was whether this loudmouth braggart who was a lawyer in tort practice had also been a Marine. At least he wasn't from Texas.

When I cautiously entered our neat, airy room overlooking the Ligurian Sea, I might have encountered Nuala Anne crying. Then I would have had a chance. Instead she had turned into a banshee, her lovely face twisted into an enraged grimace, her gorgeous body tense with rage.

"Dermot Michael Coyne," she said softly, "how many times do I have to tell you that I don't need you to protect me? I can take care of myself."

Old fight.

"You've made the point before," I temporized.

"You still think you're my big tough, testosterone hero who has to fight other males for me."

The Galway brogue had vanished. This was good, old-fashioned plain American talk.

"You usually make the point," I observed, "that we don't have to fight off the Vikings anymore and even if we did you could dispose of a half dozen of them poor fellas."

"Don't try to laugh me out of it. You had no right to throw that poor man into the pool and himself with the mark of death on him."

He had insulted my wife and maybe I did have some right to throw him into the unheated waters of the Ligurian Sea. However, mark of death . . .

"I didn't see any mark on him . . ."

"Of course you didn't. I did. That's why I told you not to fight with him."

"I missed that nuance."

"You weren't listening."

"That's an unreasonable remark, Nuala Anne. I'm not fey."

"I know THAT!"

The phone rang.

"Mr. McGrail? I'm Seamus Costelloe, the lug you threw into the pool. I wonder if you and your wife would have supper with us tonight. There's a nice place down the beach. We could make peace. Domers have to stick together. We'll watch our language."

I was not a Domer. I had flunked out of Notre Dame because it was interfering with my education.

"I'll check with my wife."

"'Tis the poor gobshite and himself wanting to make peace and himself thinking it was a big joke and meself not having to be fey to figure that out. Tell him that we Irish always believe in peace."

She wasn't smiling yet, but the worst of the thunderstorm had passed.

"After a good fight."

"'Tis true."

"Fine," I told Seamus Costelloe. "I'll try to keep her language under wraps too."

She grinned faintly.

"Maybe you'll go back and swim?"

She looked out the window.

"Only when they're gone. I'd die of shame . . ."

"Does he have some kind of sickness . . . Heart, cancer?"

"No, of course not," she said impatiently. "There are people who want to kill him."

"Will they?"

"How do I know!"

She sighed loudly.

"And Dermot Michael, I'm sorry I acted like such a terrible witch. I didn't want you to be the one who would kill him."

I shivered, as I usually do when I encounter whatever powers intermittently take possession of my wife.

"I'd say banshee."

She grinned crookedly.

"Maybe that's what I am. A spirit howling at the time of death."

I shivered again.

She stood up, put her arms around me, and rested her head on my shoulder.

"And now," she whispered, "don't I need a lot of protection altogether?"

It's always a surprise to me to discover that this beautiful, talented, and brilliant woman loves me. She claims that she fell in love with me the first night we met at O'Neill's pub down the street from College green in Dublin.

"Sure," she says, "wasn't it the great pools of kindness in your pretty blue eyes?"

Male of the species, I'm a sucker for that kind of line even if I only half believe it.

"Did you now?"

"And wasn't that the night I gave up smoking because I said to meself, you friggin' eejit your fella isn't going to tolerate smoking and yourself ruining your voice?"

In the Irish ethical system there is always room for a bit of exaggeration to make a point.

"I didn't know you smoked, Nuala."

"Och, did I ever! Not when I lived out in Carraroe of course. Wouldn't me ma and me da be terrible disappointed in me? But when I came to Dublin everyone else was smoking and I reckoned I was never going to be a singer anyway."

"Was it hard to quit?" I said, full of the virtue of a man who had smoked but one cigarette in his whole life.

"Not when I was doing it"—she grinned shyly—"so that my fella would love me!"

I had tried to run away from her in Dublin, small chance of getting away with that. Then or ever.

We had eaten supper with the Costelloes that night in Camogli at a lovely little place called Ditte Ristoránte on the street above the beach. A man played the accordion. Nuala led the house in singing "Santa Lucia." Vacation in Italy kind of movie.

Seamus was loud and often vulgar, but, oddly, good-hearted and very funny. As my mother, a tolerant woman usually, would remark of the South Side Irish, "They're all right once you get used to the noise they make."

Sometimes she would add, "They could do with a little refinement."

Seamus told wonderful if improbable stories about the practice of tort law. He lectured on apparitions of the Blessed Mother—Lourdes was the only one he believed in "because of that little girl. Her answers to the bishop reminded me of Jeanne d'Arc." He talked about his favorite charities in Chicago, Angel Guardian Orphanage and Maryville Academy, which he pronounced far better run than the Archdiocese. Nuala Anne sang without being asked, which proved she was in an excellent mood, even if she was convinced that her children did not miss her at all, at all. I would not say that the rest of the Costelloes were fun dinner companions. They were not obnoxious, only kind of dull, collections of South Side Irish clichés. Diane Costelloe and her daughter Lourdes talked about the fashions in Milano. Andy Costelloe made sweeping predictions about the American stock market which seemed to me, lucky failure at the commodity exchanges that I was, to be so much nonsense.

Lourdes's husband, Patrick Loftus, was a quiet sort of dolt, who joined the conversation only when the subject was football or golf. He repeated frequently that Tiger Woods was a passing phenomenon and would not survive the tournaments next year. Andy's "finance" Sonia's high cheekbones and long blond hair, tied in a determined knot, suggested Eastern Europe as did her slightly hesitant speech. Not Poland. Maybe Lithuania. She was the only one in the family who appeared to be as tough as her future father-in-law. She also seemed bored.

I consumed two helpings of pasta with Genovese pesto sauce and two glasses of Barolo wine and generally kept my mouth shut (which I can do quite easily, especially when distracted by good food and drink and my wife's smile.)

She was determined to win all the Costelloes to her

side, turning on all of her West of Ireland charm mixed with an overpowering "woman of the world" sophistication. It is a very dangerous combination as I had come to realize early on in our relationship—and from which I tried to run away when I dumped her at the Dublin Airport.

Under the influence of such womanly charm, Seamus Costelloe became a seanachie. He told stories about his dealings with Cardinal Cody as a young lawyer ("Nuttier than a fruitcake and a poisoned fruitcake at that"), about Notre Dame football legends, about multimillion-dollar P.I. settlements which he had earned with brilliant courtroom tactics, about criminals for whom he had won acquittals, mostly because of the stupidity of government attorneys.

The stories lost nothing in the telling. Moreover, lest he offend Nuala Anne's pious ears, his stories were free of scatological and obscene and blasphemous language.

One of the more interesting was about the trial of a Mafia hit man who had shot scores of people and whom the police had trapped in a setup after he had gunned down an important Calumet City crime boss.

"The State thought it had a good case against him. The media treated him like he was a goon, a psychopathic killer, who belonged in the electric chair—which he probably did. However, the State's witnesses were even dumber than Testa—my man. I tied them in knots. I told the jury that Ernie Testa was a bad man, but that even bad men had the right to be presumed innocent until they were proven guilty, that his freedom was their freedom, all that ACLU bu, uh, baloney. They bought it. The guy walked out of the courtroom, all dressed up in expensive Armani suits with his jewelry rattling, like he was the King of Sicily. My last words to him were, 'Ernie, be careful and get out of town, there are some people who want you dead.' Well, before the editorials could attack me the following morning he was dead. Gunned down in a Rush Street bar. The cops knew who put out the contract, but they didn't have any proof and the hit man, a lot smarter than Ernie Testa, disappeared. *C'est la guerre.*"

"You knew they'd get him?" I asked.

"Sure. He was too dumb to live in that world."

"And he didn't live to pay you?"

"He wouldn't have been able to pay me even if they hadn't put him down."

"Then why bother?"

He shrugged indifferently. "Because it was fun, because they didn't have a good case against him, because that's what lawyers are for, because next case I take there's a big fee up front, because I gotta do something."

"Is not it wrong for a guilty man to go free?" Sonia asked suddenly.

"Only if his guilt has been proved beyond a reasonable doubt. That's the way we do things in this country, Sonia Babe. Better that ten guilty men go free than one innocent man be convicted and maybe die in the electric chair. We presume that a man like Ernie Testa is innocent until the State proves him guilty. They didn't. Next time maybe they'll be more careful about collecting evidence."

Sonia shrugged as though Americans were a very strange people.

Not Lithuanian, I thought. Russian.

"Besides," Diane drawled, "you didn't like the State's Attorney very much."

Seamus chuckled and filled my wineglass, "This Barolo stuff is good, Dermot. Glad you told us about it."

That's when the accordionist began "Santa Lucia" and Nuala Anne led the restaurant in singing it.

"Your man is complicated," Nuala said later as we were undressing—a process which for her sometimes was long and languid.

"Is he now?" I said, admiring her disrobing sequence.

"He is. I had a few words with his wife. She really loves the poor amadon. Says he's very gentle and kind and that he has a loud bark, but no bite at all."

"Does he now?"

"Dermot Michael, stop staring at me like you're a hungry wolfhound!"

"Woman, I will not!"

"I wonder who wants to kill him."

We had turned off the lights in the room, because the moon, hanging over the Ligurian Sea, provided more than enough light to see my wife's black hair as it fell over her pale white shoulders.

"Woman, you're deliberately tormenting me!"

"Good enough for you, Dermot Michael, and yourself filled with lascivious thoughts!"

"I don't want to talk about Seamus anymore," I said as I captured her in my arms.

"The woman adores him," she said, slipping out of my arms and walking to the window to stare out at the black sea. "He can't be all bad, maybe just a little daft."

I recaptured her, this time pressing her breasts against her ribs.

"Is it yourself that wants to make love? Sure, I never would have guessed."

I wanted to forget about the Costelloes when we returned to Chicago. Herself wouldn't hear of it.

"Maybe we're supposed to save the poor man."

Right!

So there we were on May 4, a fragile little girl in our house, a loud and sometimes obnoxious lawyer whose life we were supposed to save, and the Haymarket bomb alive in our midst.

$$-3-$$

 AT THE Chicago Historical Society I found a book on Haymarket which had the clip of a story in the *Chicago Daily News* of May 1886, written by our old friend Ned Fitzpatrick, whose diary had recounted the story of the Maamtrasna murders and of the hanging of six innocent men for the crime.[1] It had also told how Ned had married the young widow of Myles Joyce, a clan leader who, in a free Ireland, would have been a king.

QUIET MEETING TURNS BLOODY

Special to the Chicago Daily News
By Ned Fitzpatrick

May 4

A quiet protest on Desplaines Street last night turned into a bloody riot as police clashed with the remnants of a relatively quiet anarchist protest. Seven people were killed, six of them police officers.

There was supposed to be great rage among this city's workers because of the shooting yesterday over at the McCormick Works on Black Street. This

---

[1] See *Irish Love*

rage was not visible, however, on Desplaines Street between Lake and Randolph early in the evening, a gentle touch of spring in the air. A crowd of perhaps a hundred and fifty people milled around like sheep without a shepherd until August Spies appeared. He was plainly shocked that there were no speakers.

"There are no speakers," he said to me at my outpost in Crane's alley. "We distributed twenty thousand broadsides and we have no speakers."

"You're a speaker," I replied.

"I am supposed to speak in German at the end. Were there more people here before I came?"

"No."

"People do not care about the innocents killed at the McCormick Works." He sighed.

Spies had spoken in German to the workers at the Lumber Shovers strike the day before. Some of his listeners rushed over to McCormick to join the strikers there in heckling the scabs. There was no violence until the police appeared with guns and clubs and killed two workers.

Spies, the editor of the *Workers Times*, a German-language newspaper, is better-looking, better-dressed, and more articulate than most Chicago journalists. He does not act like a revolutionary. Most of the so-called Anarchists in Chicago appear to be respectable German bourgeoisie, far less dangerous than their Irish counterparts you might encounter in the local saloon. Until they start to talk, especially with strong German accents. Then in a city wracked by labor strife, beset by violence, and fearful of "foreigners," they appear to be very dangerous indeed.

Organizer that he is, August Spies found a wagon on Desplaines, just above the Haymarket, which he turned into a speakers' platform. There would be no obstacle to the streetcar that came through the Haymarket, hardly a consideration which would have troubled a real revolutionary.

Spies cried out against the terrible oppression of the workers by the "slavemasters" of the giant companies like McCormick. Yet his rhetoric was extremely mild, compared to what more radical Anarchists around the city were saying.

"Not very strong, is he, Ned?" Mayor Carter Harrison whispered to me.

"He never is, sir."

"Looks like a peaceful night."

"It usually is, sir, until Black Jack shows up with his cops."

"Whose side are you on, Ned?" he asks me, puffing on his cigar.

"The Constitution, sir."

"I'm glad to hear that."

"I'm told Black Jack has summoned in cops from all over the city."

"Oh? I was unaware of that . . . Well perhaps while I'm riding back to Union Park, I'll stop by the station down the street and have a word with him."

"Yes, sir."

He waved his cigar at me and slipped off into the darkness.

Albert Parsons replaced Spies on the wagon, his rich Texas accent in sharp contrast to Spies's heavy Teutonic sound. Onetime secretary of the Texas Senate, onetime employee of the Grant Administration, firm believer in the eight-hour working day as a solution to the problems caused by the Panic of 1873, he sounded even more harmless than Spies.

I noted that his wife and two children were waiting for him in a carriage behind the speakers stand.

The crowd cheered for Parsons's tightly packed logic, but not very loudly.

An anticlimax, I reasoned. Everyone is tired of the violence and the inflammatory rhetoric.

The wind changed. A cold chill crept down Desplaines Street and with it the smell of rain.

Young Samuel Fielden was talking, a burly, bearded young Englishman who was once a Methodist preacher. He didn't have much to say, but he said it beautifully. The diminishing crowd yelled its appreciation.

Then Black Jack Bonfield and a hundred and seventy-five cops appeared out of Waldo Court next to the police station a block away and, their way illumined by torchlight, marched heavily up the street. Bonfield had waited till he was certain that Mayor Harrison had left the scene before he disobeyed orders. There were as many police as there were protesters. The police held pistols in their hands. Black Jack trailed behind the leading rows of police.

In the front row, Captain William Ward, Black Jack's stooge, shouted, "In the name of the people of the state of Illinois disperse, immediately and peacefully."

"Why, Captain," the sweet-tempered Fielden replied, "this *is* a peaceful meeting."

Willy Ward, perhaps the least intelligent cop in the city, repeated the order. His men shoved most of the crowd up Desplaines and now behind the speaker's wagon. Fielden climbed down off the wagon.

Then it happened.

I heard someone running behind me in the dark of Crane's alley. A tall, strong man, heavily cloaked, pushed me out of the way. I thought I knew him. He had something in his hand, about the size of a baseball, with a sputtering fire on it. For a moment he stopped in the gaslight of Desplaines Street. Then he hurled the bomb into the crowd and turned to run back up Crane's alley. I lunged at him, but he brushed me aside.

Then the bomb exploded with a deep, wrenching roar and dark orange burst of flame in the midst of the police. I saw a man collapse, his leg torn open. Shocked by the sound and paralyzed by the carnage, I was surprised that the bomb had hit the police lines. Only a moment before the protesters had stood on that spot.

Then the police began to fire their guns at the crowd. And at one another. They fell over like ninepins.

No discipline, I thought. They panicked.

Who wouldn't panic under such circumstances?

The shooting ended. Bodies littered the streets on both sides of the speaker's wagon. The crowd had disappeared. The police did not pursue them. Instead they gathered their dead and wounded and carried them back to the police station.

In the station the large room on the first floor was a scene of chaos and carnage. The dead, the dying, the wounded, the maimed were scattered about on the floor. Other officers were slumped against the wall, heads buried in their arms. Doctors were already at work. Some men were carried out on their way to County Hospital or to the morgue. Father Galligan, the handsome and popular young pastor from St. Patrick's down the street, stole around his neck, was rushing from one dying man to another. I tried to answer his prayers.

I knew most of the men, some of them from my parish—Barrett, Flavin, Sullivan, Sheehan, Degen. Irish cops caught between the German Anarchists and the English titans of business.

"Don't worry, lads," Bonfield yelled. "We'll get them, every last one of them!"

No one cheered.

"They're cursing the Germans," the priest said to me. "Why blame a whole group for what one man did?"

"All but poor Matt Degen were shot by frightened police," I replied.

Willy Ward wandered about in a trance, muttering over and over again, "It almost hit me! Degen saved my life!"

Not intentionally, I thought.

"What happened, Ned?" Father Galligan asked me.

"I don't know," I said. "I don't think I'll ever know. None of us will."

4

NUALA ANNE had warned me when we left Ireland that we had not seen the last of Edmund "Ned" Fitzpatrick. As always, she was right. I folded the xerox copy of Ned's article and slipped it into my jacket pocket. I would have known it was his work even if it had not carried his by-line.

Strange that the *Chicago Daily News* had carried his kind of report of the Haymarket Riot the day after the event, when the cops were rounding up every alleged radical and socialist in the city. Strange too that he had the right to express his emotions and his sentiments so strongly in a paper that, like all the others in the city, was howling for the blood of the Anarchists.

Apparently Ned had built up a journalistic reputation that protected him. Others who expressed sympathy with the Anarchists were promptly arrested by the police.

Who was the man who threw the bomb, a man whom Ned in a brief hint thought he might know? Had Ned eventually figured that out?

Had he kept a diary after he returned to Chicago with his bride Nora, the widow of a clan chieftain the British had unjustly hung?

I left the Chicago Historical Society with a briefcase full of books and xeroxed pages, the beginnings of my research on Haymarket. I would walk over to the Inner Drive and down Michigan Avenue to Northwestern Hospital to visit Seamus Costelloe. The Historical Society and the hospital were both assigned to me by Nuala Anne, who couldn't possibly either leave the baby home or bring her along, surely not to a musty Historical Society or a germ-filled hospital.

The little lass herself continued to sleep and eat and defecate.

When not across the street at preschool, her girl sibling would sit next to her cradle for hours and rock her gently back and forth as she hummed tunes I had never heard before.

I wondered if Nellie had figured out a way to communicate reassurance and love to the small one's consciousness.

"Some babies die," my father told me. "Most don't anymore, thank God. No pediatrician dares to provide absolute guarantees. Socra Marie is at risk, more at risk than any new term baby. At so much of a risk that you should have let her die? That would have been ridiculous!"

I nodded solemnly.

"Nuala Anne says she'll be all right."

"All mothers would say that."

I didn't explain to him that his daughter-in-law seemed to have access to special information.

Before I had set off for the Historical Society, we began our research. First of all herself called Commander John Culhane of the Sixth District.

"I hear there's a new little one in the house," he began genially.

"The sweetest little thing in all the world, Chief Superintendent. She sends you her very best."

My wife always calls the Commander by his more or less equivalent title in the Garda, even though she knows better. See what I mean about kicking up the shite, er shit?

"I hope we don't have to open a file on her like the one we have on yourself."

"That was when I was a callow greenhorn . . . But tell me, now, whoever was it that took a shot at your man the attorney?"

"You mean Seamus Costelloe?"

"Didn't I say that?"

She grinned impishly at me.

"I didn't know he was a friend of yours."

"Haven't I learned since I've come to this brilliant city that even the South Side Irish have souls, even if they're White Sox fans?"

Ah, how quickly the peasant child from Galway had learned to be a Chicagoan.

"Maybe he does," John admitted grudgingly. "You'd have a hard time persuading insurance companies of that."

"Och, now, didn't me husband tell me that in this country a person is innocent until proven guilty! Then what does he know?"

"All right, all right . . . He came out of his office in the IBM Building late at night, walked to the elevator, someone called his name. He was smart enough not to look around since he knows that's a hit man's ploy, but ducked around the corner. He took a twenty-five slug in the shoulder. Just then a security guard got off the elevator and the shooter, wearing a Bill Clinton mask, took flight. The guard had the sense to call for an ambulance instead of chasing the shooter, who disappeared down the stairway—twenty stories up."

"No description?"

"Black clothes besides the Clinton mask."

"How did he get out of the building?"

"Grabbed a service elevator to the parking lot, we think."

"You'll find him?"

"Professional, not much of a chance."

"A professional who missed?"

"They do sometimes."

"Who do you think put out the contract?"

My sweet little wife had all the lingo down.

"Maybe someone whose case he lost. Or someone whose case he won that didn't like his 40 percent take. Or a lawyer that he beat. Or a judge whom he bribed and wants higher office."

"You don't know?"

"You got it, Nuala Anne. I am, however, delighted that you're going to find out for us. Give my best to the new kid."

"Not much help," she sniffed. "If someone had shot down a prominent solicitor in Dublin, wouldn't we have the whole Garda out on the street? . . . Well, Dermot Michael, what are you waiting for and yourself knowing whom we call next?"

So I dialed the Reilly Gallery, which was also the headquarters of Reliable Security and its president Michael Patrick Vincent Casey.

"Reilly Gallery, Annie speaking."

"Dermot, Annie."

We had called her husband so often that she would surely know my voice.

"Dermot! Congratulations on the little one! I hear she's gorgeous like her mother."

"Certainly doesn't look like me . . ."

"You want to talk to himself, I suppose?"

"If I may . . ."

"Dermot, what's up?"

"Seamus Costelloe, how bent is he and who shot him?"

Mike the Cop, as his family calls him as though there is another Mike in the family when in fact there is not, chuckled.

"That *fairie* woman is at it again, isn't she?"

"Is there a conflict of interest?"

"Not yet. Diane Costelloe wants him to hire Reliable as bodyguards. He's not having any of it."

"What's his story?"

"Very high-priced and very successful tort lawyer. Strange personality. Devout Catholic with a foul mouth and reputation for corruption. Made a lot of money and a lot of enemies, including lawyers who have been his partners."

"So?"

"He dumped Helen O'Leary, who was his partner in the firm. He replaced her with his son, Andy, who is somewhere between beta and gamma on the brains, a nice but harmless kid. Helen turned around married Len Shepherd, the other top personal injury lawyer in town and Seamus's arch enemy. She is a hater and, if you believe the rumors on the street, was 'involved' with Seamus before she married Len."

"Seamus fools around?"

"So it is said. Not as much as do some of the hotshot P.I. guys. Is a Catholic of a sort, active in charity work, big guilt feelings maybe. Loud and obnoxious, takes too much of the creature but is not a drunk, likes big stakes card games, and Calcutta tournaments at the country clubs. Not in debt. Not in trouble with the Feds though they sniff around periodically."

"Family?"

"None of them very bright, take after their mother, it's said. No records for anything—gambling, drugs, fooling around. Ciphers. Kind of likable in a shallow way. Lapdog types."

Mike had obviously been collecting data in case Diane Costelloe hired him.

"Mixed up in Irish stuff?"

"Plays golf over there every year with a bunch of Notre Dame cronies. I don't think he's connected to the lads."

"That would be very dangerous."

"You're telling me."

"Why doesn't he want any security?"

"Says they won't try again."

"Why does he think that?"

"I suspect he's paid someone off."

"We should probably keep our noses out of it?"

"Absolutely—and you tell that to your wife and the next thing would be to tell the sun to stop rising in the morning."

Mike knew Nuala Anne pretty well. Whenever something fey happened, we had an obligation to protect someone, whether they wanted to be protected or not.

"Outfit hit?" I asked, referring to the Mafia who are never called that in Chicago. "Outfit," "The Boys," "Our Friends on the West Side" are the preferred euphemisms.

"The word on the street is that the Council did not approve of the hit or even know about it. Independent operator. The boys don't like that, but they're not about to provide the cops with any information. If they find out who did it they might or might not take their own measures."

"Why do you think he doesn't want any personal security, Mike?"

"How well do you know him?"

"Not too well. Had dinner with the family a couple of times."

"Loudmouth braggart, right?"

"I won't argue the point."

"He ever tell you about the DSC he won in 'Nam?"

"He never mentioned that he'd been there."

"Marine of course, fresh out of Notre Dame with an ROTC commission. First month in combat he leads a whole platoon out of a trap. Saves a lot of lives. Badly wounded."

"Brave guy."

"And maybe dumb, but certainly brave."

"Uh-huh."

"Unless he paid someone off, I suspect that he knows who put out the contract on him and has put out a return contract with the warning that if anything happens to him or to his family the contractor is a dead man."

"Tough guy."

"Guy that believes he lives in a jungle or a war zone. Too many tough criminal cases or P.I. cases to trust the police to take care of him or even Reliable."

"So he doesn't need any security."

"I didn't say that. I don't know who's behind the shooter. I'm just saying that he thinks he's safe."

"Thanks for the information, Mike."

"I'll stay in touch."

"Do that . . ."

"And, Ms. McGrail, I know you're listening in, so congratulations on the new daughter."

Nuala stuck her nose skyward.

"I'm not listening at all, at all," she informed him.

Mike laughed and hung up.

"Male detectives," she protested, her face crimson, "think they know everything!"

"So what do you think?" I asked her.

"I think you should visit him at Northwestern Hospital and find out who he thinks hired the shooter."

"That's all?"

"Something even an amadon could do! . . . Don't I have to stay here and take care of our daughter?"

Socra Marie was sleeping peacefully on her mother's lap with Maeveen standing guard. No need to keep the poor father around.

I had written a sequence of poems about our weeks of immersion in the hospital. I needed time to revise them before I sent them off to *Poetry*—which probably would not accept them anyway. The task could wait.

We had supper with them a couple of times after our return from Italy. They summered at Lake Geneva and we at Grand Beach so we didn't see much of them in the summer. Seamus talked at great length about the superiority of Lake Geneva over the Dunes.

"I see your point," I agreed. "There are a lot of West Side Irish up at Geneva. Civilizing influence."

For a moment he looked like he might begin a long argument. Then his big, flat face, cracked open in a grin.

"Touché! Dermot . . . The problem with them is that they're no fun. Terribly dull. You're lucky down at the Dunes, you have a lot of South Siders around down there, so you have lots of fun."

"I do not understand this West Side/South Side material." Sonia protested sternly.

"'Tis all nonsense, dear," Nuala Anne assured her. "But they have fun with it."

That was about as lively as the conversations ever became.

Then, with Nuala's pregnancy, we drifted away from them, though I was sure she called them regularly. We were still responsible for keeping this awful man alive.

Michigan Avenue was awash in color from Mayor Daley's gardens in the parkways and on the median. Spring dresses had blossomed on young women. People were smiling at folks they did not know. Spring, as the song said, was busting out all over in honor of our daughter.

The Chicago skyline, pastel in morning mists, loomed up like a mystical fairyland or a scene in Coleridge's poem.

My cell phone rang.

'TIS HERSELF.

"Who the fuck else would it be?"

TEMPER!

"Dermot Coyne."

"And me expecting Dr. Watson?"

"Nuala Anne!"

"I suppose you're not interested in a report on your children?"

She was up to something. This was merely a dodge.

I leaned against the red wall of the Nieman Marcus building—Needless Markup as everyone calls it—and waited for her to spring the trap.

"Tell me about them."

"Well, your elder daughter didn't want to cross the street for school this morning. Wanted to stay here and help with her little sister. We were having none of that, though I did promise her that when Socra Marie was a little older I'd walk over and show her off to the other kids."

"Wise decision."

"Your son and Ethne are playing with his trucks in the family room and he comes out every half hour to kiss the baby and offer her a truck. He's delighted when she doesn't take it. He's trying, Dermot."

"I'm sure he is."

"Maybe when you come home, you could spend a minute or two playing with him."

She meant at least a half hour.

"I'd been planning to do just that."

LIE.

Well, I'd thought about it.

A COUPLE OF DAYS AGO.

"And meself and herself and themselves are sitting here in my office and ourselves listening to Mozart.

That sentence was phony Irish. Nuala was putting me on.

"And you all like old Wolfgang Amadeus?"

"The poor dear man was only two years older than you when he died. Our younger daughter seems to enjoy him. Isn't she right here in me lap, all wrapped up the knitted blanket that arrived this morning from Carraroe and meself already calling me ma to thank her for it."

"Annie is well?"

"You'd think that Socra Marie is the only baby in all the world to hear her talk and herself not even seeing the lass yet save on our e-mail picture."

"She is the only baby in all the world."

"Sure, Dermot, you always know how to say the right thing."

"What's our new daughter doing?"

"When she's not eating, she's checking out themselves. I don't think she can quite believe that such creatures exist. She seems to like them though."

"I'm glad to hear that."

" 'Tis true. She'll have to learn to live with them . . . What have you found out so far?"

"I discovered a vivid description of the riot in an article in the *Chicago Daily News* by our old friend Ned Fitzpatrick."

"Did you now? Wasn't I saying we weren't through with that young fella yet."

"I hope he kept a diary of the whole story."

"He's the diary-keeping type."

" 'Tis true."

"When you see your man in the hospital, you should ask him outright who the fella is that he put out the countercontract on. You might startle him into an answer."

"I doubt it."

"No harm in trying. Let me know what happens."

"Okay."

I had been Nuala Anne's spear-carrier for seven years now. I was used to doing what I was told.

"Thank you, Dermot love."

I walked down to Superior Street and turned toward Northwestern Hospital. The cell phone rang again.

"Still Dermot Coyne."

"Is it now?"

Different woman altogether, shy, vulnerable, even fragile.

"Didn't I forget something the last time?"

"Did you?"

"I said I did."

Fragile indeed but still a touch of the woman leprechaun. It would do me no good to be impatient.

"Was it important?"

"Not at all, at all."

Which meant very important.

She said something but static interrupted it.

"Lost that, Nuala."

"I saw your man at the hospital yesterday when we picked herself up."

"Ah."

Who was me man, er, my man.

"And you know what he told me?"

"No." ·

"You do. You're just having me on."

"I'm not."

"Och, Dermot, you are terrible dense sometimes."

"Well, who was me man, er my man?"

"Wasn't it the OB doctor?"

This in a tone of voice which implied that I was a friggin' gobshite for not knowing that.

"Ah."

"And you know what he said?"

"I'm still dense."

"Well," she hesitated as though she were embarrassed which she may or may not have been, "didn't he hint that it might be all right if we resumed normal sexual relations?"

My heart missed a couple of beats and my loins reacted appropriately.

"Did he now?"

"He did."

"What did he mean by normal?"

"I didn't ask the man. Would you think we were ever normal, Dermot?"

"I think I may have forgotten how."

She laughed, with just a hint of lasciviousness in her voice.

"I'd be thinking that you'll remember quickly enough tonight."

"Maybe I will and maybe I won't."

"That's the way I talk, Dermot Michael Coyne. You shouldn't do it at all, at all."

She hung up.

Sex with Nuala, I told myself, as I floated down the street toward the hospital was never normal, thank God.

5

"YOU LOOK fine," I said to Seamus Costelloe in his room in the massive new hospital building. It reminded me of a room in the Ritz-Carlton Hotel, and probably cost his insurance carrier a lot more.

He grinned and reached out to shake hands with me.

"Going home tomorrow, just a scratch really. Hey, congratulations on the baby. I bet she's a beauty."

His geniality was pure South Side Irish, maybe phony, maybe not. He'd practiced it so many times in so many locker rooms, courtrooms, law offices, and rectories that he himself probably no longer knew how authentic it was.

"Looks like her mother."

"So she has to be. It's wonderful what they can do with preemies these days. We lost one. Hell on poor Diane."

Dumb statement.

Sonia, who was sitting in a chair reading Trollop, looked up from her book and frowned at him. He missed it completely.

"Cops know who took the shot at you?"

"Naw! Cops don't solve crimes. They only make arrests. I could probably get the guy off on a motion for summary judgment."

OK, Nuala Anne, here I go.

"Well, you know who put out the contract, since you put a countercontract on him."

"Whadaya mean?" he said, his face turning dark red and his immense jaw tightening.

"Come on, Seamus, we're both grown-ups. You warned the guy that if anything happens to you or your family, he's a dead man. Maybe his family is dead, too. He knows you're tough enough to do just that. Maybe you have put out a provisional contract and maybe not, but he can't afford to take the chance you haven't."

His eyes narrowed into hard little emeralds.

Sonia closed her book, finger in the page, and watched her future father-in-law intently.

"Ya don't know whadyatalkinbout."

"Seamus, I've been around this city long enough to know that some really tough people play it that way. Your friend the restaurant owner, for instance . . ."

I suddenly remembered that guy. The Boys tried to blow up his place and missed. He warned them that the whole bunch of them were dead if they didn't lay off. The Boys, who did not like intimidation, nevertheless backed off.

"The cops tell you this?"

"Cops don't tell me things," I said, a half-truth at best.

"You just figure it out?"

"I write novels, Seamus. It's my job to figure things out."

He relaxed and grinned.

"Well you got a good imagination, I'll say that for you. Have you imagined who it is?"

"One of your former law partners whom you're threatening with blackmail!"

IDIOT!

Seamus threw back his head and roared with laughter. Then he coughed and grabbed his shoulder. Sonia put aside her book and firmly rearranged him on the bed. She too was laughing.

"My future daughter-in-law was a nurse," he gasped, "and I think a concentration camp guard."

She stopped smiling and returned to her book.

"Well, nice shot anyway, Dermot. You stick to your novels and leave the detective work to others."

Little did he realize that the detective work was left to either the best or the second-best detective in the city—depending on how you ranked Nuala Anne and the little bishop. (She put him in first place, probably correctly, but he wasn't fey.)

"Hey, when you gonna pour water on the little tyke?"

"She was baptized in the hospital of course, but we're going to do the rest of the ceremonies next Sunday at St. Josaphat's."

"Where the fuck is that?"

Sonia frowned. Given half a chance she might restore some sanity to the Costelloe clan. Good luck to her.

"Southport Avenue."

"OK, some of us will be there."

DELIGHTFUL.

I was thinking the same thing.

Outside the hospital, I phoned Ms. Holmes.

"Mr. McGrail here, aka John Watson, M.D."

"How do you spell that name?"

"The right way M-c-G-r-a-i-l."

"Good on you . . . what did you find out?"

"Well, you were right. He's put out a countercontract."

"On whom?"

"I tried a stab in the dark and it didn't work."

I recounted my effort and the reaction.

"Och, Dermot Michael wasn't that a brilliant idea!"

In Irish talk the adjective "grand" is a mild way of saying "super" and if you want a really grand and super word you say "brilliant."

"Was it now?"

"Maybe not a law partner, but some kind of business

partner. You came close enough to scare him; otherwise, he wouldn't have laughed so hard."

"Maybe . . . Everything still peaceful?"

"Dear sweet little Mary Anne is home from school and she sits and stares at her little sister. I think she's communicating with her."

"She's not!"

"Can't stop her and herself sending reassuring messages of love if she's doing anything."

What does a baby think when some other being intervenes in her head? Probably figures it's all part of the package.

"Better send her out to play with the dogs."

"Wasn't I after thinking that very thing meself?"

("dinkin' dat very ding").

"I'm stopping at the Hancock Center for a swim. Gotta get myself in good shape for normal sexual relations tonight."

"Who ever said tonight?"

I hung up on her.

I used to live in a one-bedroom at the Hancock Center. We hung on to it after our marriage because it was a great investment with a great swimming pool. Also a nice place for a secret rendezvous with my wife.

At home, only Danuta was visible—polishing silverware, a weekly task by her definition.

"Ethne and girl in yard play with dogs, boy play with trucks. Missus and baby nap upstairs. Need naps."

When she had turned her back, I sneaked upstairs and peered through the slightly open door to the master bedroom. My wife and my daughter, breathing contentedly, were both sound asleep. Beautiful women.

Don't take her away from us, I begged God, we love her so much.

Then, because my mother had always warned me about being too insistent, I added, it's up to You of course.

DON'T EVER FORGET TO SAY THAT.

As I admired them, my hungry body filled up with lust for my wife. It had been a long time. I wanted her desperately.

YOU'RE A HORNY BASTARD. SHE'S A NURSING MOTHER WHO HAS JUST SUFFERED THROUGH A TERRIBLE CRISIS WITH A PREMATURE BABY.

"She suggested sex."

BECAUSE SHE KNOWS WHAT A HORNY BASTARD YOU ARE.

I went out into the yard where Ethne and Nellie were rolling around with the inexhaustible wolfhounds and the Mick was playing with his trucks. I joined him, much to his delight. I was filled with the virtue of a man who knew he was being a good father.

"Time for baths," Ethne announced as she gasped for breath.

Obediently the two kids followed her into the house. I picked up the Tonka trucks. The two dogs assaulted me. I was only a poor substitute for the kids, but in a pinch I'd do. So I wrestled with them for a while and then, despite their efforts to prevent it, slipped in the back door.

Nuala was not in the parlor or her office. A long nap in preparation for the evening's amusements.

I withdrew to my office down the hall, turned on my computer, and opened the file of my new novel—all twenty pages of it.

An hour later, when Nuala entered in jeans and a bright Chicago Bears sweatshirt, carrying Socra Marie in a matching sweat suit and an orange Bears blanket, there were twenty-one pages in the file.

I am a fastidious writer.

Or so I tell them.

"Bear down Chicago Bears . . ." My wife sang the Bears fight song. In May.

"Doesn't she look wonderful?"

"She does indeed. She also looks like she'd rather go back to sleep."

"She just woke up and she's not sure she likes the idea . . . Here, Socra Marie, Daddy wants to hold you. He's not doing any work on his friggin' novel."

So I took the little mite into my arms, tucked the navy blue-and-orange blanket around her, and regarded her with something like worship.

Her eyes tried to focus on me, failed for a moment, and then succeeded.

"Dada person," I said.

She continued her close inspection of my face.

"Did the other two explore so seriously?"

"Not at all, at all. The poor little tyke has had so many sensations she just wants to figure some of them out. She's made up her mind about her sister and us. Doesn't know yet that her poor brother exists . . . You did play with him, didn't you, Dermot Michael?"

"Of course."

"May I read Neddie's story?"

"It's on the desk."

I continued to hold our four-pounder. Nuala sat on an easy chair next to the desk and read the xerox quickly. Then, as was her custom, she reread it, this time very slowly and carefully.

"The ma is thinking," I said to our child.

"She knows *that*," Nuala frowned.

The little girl snuggled close to me . . . Well, she really didn't but I liked to think she did . . . and continued to study my face.

"Well . . ." The child's mother sighed loudly. "Deep waters, Dermot Michael, aren't they now?"

"I wonder if he kept a diary of the Haymarket story."

"Sure he did. Wasn't he a diary-keeping man?"

"I wonder where it is."

"Where was the one about the Maamtrasna murders?"

"In the rectory in Clifden."

"So?"

"Maybe in a rectory here?"

"And which one?"

"What was his parish here?"

"Immaculate Conception on North Park."

"And who's the pastor there?"

"My brother George the Priest."

"I thought so."

George was utterly unlike me, medium height, straight brown hair, deft, supple, smooth, charming—the perfect cleric. Nuala Anne, mostly to aggravate me, treated him with enormous respect.

She picked up the phone and punched in a number.

"Good afternoon to you too, young woman." The thick Galway accent took over. "This is Mrs. Coyne, his riverince's sister-in-law. Would he ever have a minute for a brief word with me . . . ah, Father, how you keeping now? Wonderful! We're looking forward to the Baptism too. Sure, isn't herself a picture of health and contentment and resting in her father's arms, not sure who he is at all, at all . . . You have all those important historical documents down in your cellar, don't you? Well, I want one of them. The Haymarket book by Edmund Fitzpatrick, the great journalist . . . Of course it's there . . . Just curious, that's all . . . Could you bring it along on Sunday . . . Ah God bless you now . . ."

She hung up, a beatific smile on her face.

"Isn't he the nice priesteen?"

"You have him wrapped around your little finger."

"That's a terrible, terrible thing to say, Dermot Michael Coyne," she said complacently.

Then she sighed.

"Don't we have enough to do with this little hellion"—she removed Socra Marie from my arms—"without worrying ourselves about mysteries from a hundred and fourteen years ago?"

"And mysteries today too."

"You have the right of it, Dermot Michael . . . Well, come along little hellion. You need a bath and a clean diaper and your supper."

After the kids were in bed, protected by the wolfhounds, and Danuta and Ethne had gone home, we had a leisurely dinner by candlelight, roast beef and the best Barolo and herself in an off-the-shoulder dress. Then we walked up to our bedroom, hand in hand.

Socra Marie was sleeping soundly and peacefully. Fiona, who was on duty in our bedroom, acknowledged our presence with a briefly opened eye.

Nuala let the gown fall off her body.

"A nicely orchestrated seduction, my dear," I said.

"I thought so too, if I do say so meself."

A few more deft moves and she was naked in front of me, her hands behind her back, her face glowing with anticipation.

Another wedding night, I thought. Only much better, because we know each other's moves.

Our love was tender and leisurely, healing and renewing, a symbolic turning point that in the last few moments culminated in astonishing ecstasy.

So noisy was that conclusion that Fiona, who usually ignored human couplings, stirred from sleep and glared at us. Socra Marie, for her part, actually opened her eyes and closed them promptly.

Nuala usually wanted to talk after lovemaking. So we talked.

"You didn't forget how to do it, Dermot Michael," she murmured.

"I'm glad to hear that."

"Didn't I say to meself that night in O'Neill's pub, sure, the man is a bit of an eejit but he's probably pretty good in bed?"

"I don't think you said that at all, at all."

She giggled. "I did so . . . Dermot love . . ."

"Uh-huh." I drew her close so that our bodies touched from head to toe.

"That's nice . . . I'm afraid I haven't been a very good wife all these months."

She meant it.

"I think you've been wonderful."

"And meself promising you by that awful black gravel beach that I wouldn't be compulsive about this child."

"I don't think you've been compulsive about Socra. You responded appropriately to a major challenge in our lives."

"I didn't really . . ."

"You did too really."

She paused to consider that.

"A little better maybe."

"Nuala Anne, you have been incredibly mature through this whole crisis."

A bit of an exaggeration maybe, but close enough to the truth.

"You mean I acted like a grown-up?"

"At least as grown-up as I did, which maybe isn't saying all that much."

She kissed me gently.

"We've done fine so far with this little imp and herself so serious."

"She's just trying to figure out what to laugh at . . . and whom."

"Ay, you have the right of it."

Silence.

Then, "Och, Dermot Michael, aren't there so many things for us to worry about?"

"Worry?"

"Well," she said, sighing as though she were preparing a list, "we have to stew about poor Socra Marie and herself not coming down with cerebral palsy, and the Mick that he doesn't feel left out, and Nellie that she doesn't become too serious, and Neddie and his wife and the Haymarket Riot, and Seamus Costelloe and that strange crowd of his, and Marie-Bernadette and Jacques-Yves and their career, and not forgetting about our own love . . . And all the other things."

I really didn't want to know what the other things were.

"That's what we have wives and mothers for, Nuala Anne McGrail. They're the professional stewers in the family. If they're Irish it's Irish stew. Your Irish mothers are really good at Irish stew."

"Is that all I'm good for, Dermot Michael Coyne?"

"I didn't say that . . ."

My fingers began to explore her body again, followed by my lips.

She sighed contentedly.

"We mustn't wake Fiona and Socra Marie this time."

I don't know whether we did or not.

—6—

 "CONSIDER THIS wisp of humanity," the little bishop said, "called Socra Marie Coyne, whom the Church welcomes today with noisy and indeed solemn high celebration."

Our daughter shifted her gaze, which had been focused on Cardinal Sean Cronin in his crimson robes to this unobtrusive little priest.

"She is examining us very carefully, as if to make up her mind whether we really deserve her attention or she should apply for another venue. All babies do that, you know. They don't make up their minds about those of us who welcome them until we have proved that we deserve them. Fortunately for the continuity of our species they generally decide that those standing around the baptismal font with them are on the whole no worse than other prospects."

Nelliecoyne giggled, as she usually does when she encounters the little bishop.

"A tiresome English poet thought that the glow in a baby's eyes when she comes into the world is a hint of her contact with God, a memory of which never fades away. My own feeling is that the child is smirking because she knows that she's God's hedge on the future of the Church and indeed of the species. In the ordinary course of human events she will still be alive when all of us are dead. She will see to the continuation of the Church after our own efforts have become superfluous. We can face that lamentable if inevitable fact with some confidence because we know that life is stronger than death, not only in the resurrection, but also in the birth of a new child, an event which is a cognate, a hint, a promise of the resurrection. Because of people like Socra Marie and because of the God who sent her to us to delight our lives, we know that death finally will have no power over us and we even cry out with St. Paul, if we are in such a mood, 'O death where is thy victory! O death where is thy sting!'

"Small wonder that the tired, weary old church goes crazy with joy on a baptismal day. We may have lost many times and we still continue to lose. However, as long as there are small children like Socra Marie whom we can eagerly welcome into our band, then we will never lose completely.

"Therefore the Church makes exuberant promises today. It tells us that the waters of baptism are a down payment on resurrection. It assures Socra Marie that we will never let her go, and that we will always be around to help and support her, at the risk of on occasion seeming pushy, even obnoxious. Small child, I repeat, we will never let you go."

George the Priest, with a touch of impatience, continued the baptismal ceremony. However, my daughter continued to stare at the funny little priest (whose staff had found him a clerical collar and his lovely silver St. Brigid pectoral cross). Perhaps, like all little kids, she already had found him cute.

It was a solemn high Baptism, though not in the old sense of the word, even if we had three priests (and a fourth if one included the pastor who observed from a distance, intimidated as he was by the presence of a cardinal and a bishop). However, the solemnity of the event was not created by the three priests, however impressive the cardinal's robes might have been. Rather it was created by the mother of the "wisp of humanity," who had arranged for Marie-Bernadette and Jacque-Yves to provide violin and viola music, had led the singing of the music from Liam Lawton's "Mass for Celtic Saints," and who herself had interjected several lullabies mostly in Irish.

Her parents had showed up at O'Hare the night before as had some of her American nieces, siblings, and cousins. All of my siblings were present as well as their own broods, many of whom actually did not run around the church during the ceremony, as did Micheal Dermod. My sister Cindy and her husband were the sponsors. However, the most careful watcher at the ceremony, squeezed in between the two godparents, was Nelliecoyne, who didn't miss a thing.

I was a supernumerary, of course, which is my role in such events, the big lug whom Nuala and the children tolerate. Good enough for me!

SELF-PITY.

Shut up.

Socra Marie seemed quite relaxed through the ceremony, almost as though she were enjoying the entertainment. However she had been restless and irritable (for her) during the last couple of days. The polite and plaintive little cry with which she demanded food and wiping in the middle of the night sounded more frequently. Nuala was feeding her every two hours. If she didn't wake up to meet this schedule, our daughter registered strong displeasure.

It is an interesting kind of epiphany to open your eyes and see your naked wife, whom you have only an hour or two ago pleasured, nursing a frowning little kid.

I don't resent the child all that much anymore, yet I have not been able to capture that epiphany in a poem. Can't find the key metaphor.

I also worried because Nuala had reported to me

that Socra Marie had not gained a "single ounce" since she had come home from the hospital. So I stewed too. The doctors had told us that it was most unlikely that she would show signs of cerebral palsy, but what did they know?

George the Priest summoned the little kids to touch the baby gently on the forehead to welcome her into the Church. They did this with great reverence and awe—under the gimlet-eyed supervision of the baby's big sister.

Then the moment everyone was waiting for. With the kids peering eagerly, George the Priest poured an inordinate amount of water on my daughter's head and informed the world in a loud voice, "Socra Marie, if you have not already been baptized, I baptize you in the name of the Father, and of the Son, and of the Holy Spirit."

The daughter blinked at the water, but didn't seem greatly displeased.

Then, after George had wiped her with oil and put on her long white robe and offered Nuala Anne a candle, he held her up to the crowed, which cheered lustily.

"Don't drop her," I muttered sotto voce so Nuala wouldn't hear me.

Like a reigning monarch, the daughter accepted this acclamation as if it were a matter of right.

I sought out the pastor in the sacristy.

"A bid of a crowd, Father."

He smiled. "At least you didn't bring the dogs."

"I won that fight at the last minute."

I slipped a thousand-dollar bill into his hand, and said, "For the remodeling fund."

"There was a time," my mother said when I responded to her question about whether I had given anything to the pastor, "when a dollar or ten at the most would have been enough for a priest."

"Inflation."

"Didn't his rivirence do a wonderful job?" my wife gushed as we walked across Southport.

"The nurse at the hospital did it when it counted."

"Och, Dermot Michael Coyne, give over. For a poet, you sometimes have no soul, at all, at all."

At the end of the party, which went on for hours with no regard for our daughter sleeping upstairs (guarded by Fiona and Nellie), George handed my wife a slim, dusty volume. The faded label on the cover said simply, "Haymarket 1886."

"The least he could have done," I observed, "would have been to clean off the dust."

Then I added, "Good job today, George."

"Thanks, little bro. It's kind of hard not to be up-staged by those two successors of the apostles."

"Why would anyone want to call themselves successors of the apostles?" my wife demanded. "And themselves liars and cowards and thieves."

— 7 —

May 5, 1886.

The police came to our house on Dearborn Street tonight as I was sitting before this blank book, wondering how to begin. The General had warned me at lunch that they would come. They were arresting "Anarchists" and "radicals" all over the city, hundreds of them. They're trying to terrorize everyone, he said. They don't like you, naturally enough. But they wouldn't dare arrest you. Even if they were not afraid of the Chicago Daily News, they'd be afraid of me.

I knew he was right. Yet, the least brave of men that I am, I was momentarily frightened when Nora came into my study and, her face pale, her eyes dark with fear, gasped, "The police are here, Ned."

The police in Galway had come for her first husband, a police no worse than the Chicago police for a man no more guilty than I. He had never returned to their cottage and now his bones had dissolved in limestone in Galway Prison.

Suddenly I was more furious than frightened. Anger gives even weaklings courage.

I strode into the parlor and encountered Captain Michael Schaack, the most crooked police officer in

Chicago. From his fortress at the Chicago Avenue Police Station, just off Dearborn Street, he had stormed around the city, dragging innocent men and women out of their beds and herding them into jails.

"Get out of my house!" I ordered him.

"I am Captain Michael Schaack."

He is a big man with broad shoulders, a long handlebar mustache, and a shaven head. He carries a long billy club which he caresses affectionately. A .45 caliber revolver is strapped to his belt. He might well be one of Genghis Khan's viziers.

"I know damn well who you are. I do not want a parasite who lives off money stolen from prostitutes and saloonkeepers frightening my family and befouling my home."

My beautiful young niece Josie had pressed herself against the wall of the parlor and, eyes filled with hate, was glaring at the Captain and the three cops, all clearly Irish, as they stood just inside the doorway. She remembered the arrest of her uncle too. When Josie stares that way, one could think she was putting on a hex. I was never quite sure myself.

The police had all taken too much drink.

"Six police officers were killed last night by Anarchists," Schaack began.

"All but my neighbor, poor Matt Degen, were killed by other police whose discipline collapsed at the sound of gunfire."

"That's what you say."

"Get out," I repeated my order. "I will have nothing to do with you."

"You said in your story that you knew who the bomb thrower was."

"You misquote me. Get out!"

"We want to question you."

"Do you have a warrant?"

"We don't need a warrant."

"Yes you do!"

"We want you to tell us who threw the bomb!"

I sensed my terrified Nora behind me.

"If I find out who it was, you'll read about it on the front page of the Chicago Daily News. Now for the last time get out before I throw you out."

I'm not a large man like my father the General. However, I have some small and undeserved reputation as a boxer. Whether I would have hit Captain Schaack or not I don't know. Probably not. If I had, he would have fallen with one punch. Fortunately, muttering unimaginative curses, he and his cronies departed.

"Good on you, Uncle Ned," Josie cried out.

"I think they were more afraid of your hexes, Josie, than of my fists."

She laughed as she always did when I alluded to her fey propensities.

When I had carried off Nora and Mary Elizabeth, her daughter by the murdered Myles Joyce from Ireland, I also invited Josie, at that time a thinly clad, dirty-faced urchin to join us. I came home therefore with a family, to which we soon added our own daughter Grace. All these women in the house overwhelmed me.

Standing behind me, Nora wrapped her arms around me. I turned to mush as I always do under such circumstances.

"Will they be back, Ned dearest?"

"No, Nora." I sighed. *"They won't. They're afraid of the* Daily News *and of the General."*

"And of your fists," she said, burying her face in my back.

I didn't deserve her worship. I never have. However, at that moment, as at many other moments in my life, I gladly accepted it.

As soon as I finish this first entry, I will join her in our bedroom.

I had lunched with the General at the Union League Club, a place at which neither he nor I would be wel-

come but they couldn't keep him out. If he wanted to eat lunch with his son there, no one was likely to stop him, even if the son was nothing more than a lowly journalist.

At nineteen, my father, a raw and very strong immigrant from County Mayo, enlisted in the Union Army, married the seventeen-year-old down the street, and went off to defend the Union. Having come back twice on sick leave and sired two children, myself one of them, he fought from Fort Donaldson to Appomattox Courthouse and risen to the rank of Lt. Colonel. He marched in the victory parade in Washington, was mustered out, and walked home to us. He stayed on as a member of an inactive reserve regiment and rose to the rank of general and became a lawyer by sitting in a law office for a year. At forty-five, a big, handsome man with a strong Irish brogue and powerful intellect, he was one of the most important members of the Illinois bar and if not exactly rich, wealthy enough.

"I don't sit down at the table very often with Cyrus McCormick or Potter Palmer," he said once, "but they listen to me when I do. Then I go out and wash my hands to get rid of their dust."

My father and mother were both just a little bit daft and viewed me as kind of an anomaly—a white sheep in their daft family, a quiet, sober and responsible young man. They modified their judgment somewhat when I brought Nora and Josie and Mary Elizabeth— Myles Joyce's daughter—home from Ireland with me. They love me greatly and are proud of me for my work, which isn't all that much.

"Great story!" the General bellowed as I joined him at the lunch table. "That'll show them!"

His blond hair was now tinged with a little gray but it was wild as ever in contrast to my carefully pasted-down and short-cut blond hair.

It wasn't clear to me whom it would show, but I did not pursue the subject.

He ate a hearty meal. If he noticed I was only pick-ing at my roast beef, he did not comment.

"What's happening?"

The General rarely gave a straight answer to any-thing, which may have been why he was such a good lawyer. Rather he approached any and every subject in an indirect and roundabout way, during his walk on which he would provide background for what he was about to say.

"Do you know what proportion of Chicagoans are immigrants, Neddie?"

"Half?"

"Seventy percent. Now if you're good Yankee stock like Potter Palmer or Marshall Field or Cyrus Mc-Cormick think they are, that scares you. These immi-grants talk strange tongues, look sneaky, and glare at you. They remember what the Communards did in Paris fifteen years ago and have anticipatory pains in their necks."

"The government murdered most of the Commu-nards."

"Indeed they did, but a few wealthy people were guillotined too. So the powerful in this city live in mor-tal terror of bomb-throwing Anarchists and their hordes of followers."

"The local German Anarchists are harmless, sir. They make a lot of noise and even talk about bombs, but the only one I know of who makes them is a young organizer for the Carpenters named Louis Lingg."

"I take your word for it, Neddie. My point is that the plutocrats in this city are afraid of them. They think the Germans will lead the Poles and the Italians in an up-rising against them. They see this 'riot' as an excuse to get rid of them."

"I understand, sir."

I tried a bite of potato and gave it up.

"Their second fear is unions. They've won every

battle so far. They are afraid that in the long run Chicago will become a union town."

"That's impossible, sir!"

"No, it's not, Ned. Once the Irish take some time off from scheming against England, they'll organize the city. It may take years, but it will happen. There's just too many workers in this city. Anyway, the people around us here in this dining room also want to throw a spoke into the union wagons. Kill off a bunch of Anarchists and that will happen too or so they think."

"I agree that the strikes will continue."

"Then there's the police," he said, ticking off the count on his strong, workman's fingers. "Their bosses generally do what the wealthy want them to do. Now the ordinary cops want revenge."

"They've already arrested poor Lucy Parsons, who was sitting in a carriage with her two children behind the speaker's stand when the bomb went off."

"That's the former slave?"

"I doubt it. Like her husband she's from Texas. More probably Mexican and Indian as well as some Negro."

He nodded.

"Kind of woman cops love to abuse . . . Her husband's gone into hiding, I understand."

"He's a tough man, sir. Not a killer, not with his wife and kids near the bomb."

"Ned, men are going to die for this, most likely innocent men because the powerful people in Chicago want them to die."

I nodded.

"I see your point, sir, and don't dispute it. Just like Nora's husband, Myles Joyce, died in Ireland."

"That's right, son. Just like Myles Joyce. Right here in Chicago and the United States of America and only after the rich and the powerful and the ambitious have made of the affair all they can."

"It wasn't even a major riot, Dad. A man threw a

bomb. It blew open the leg of a man I consider a friend and a neighbor. The cops lost their heads and fired their guns, killing one another. It was all over in a couple of minutes."

He shook his head sadly, his solid, honest face sad for a moment.

"I read your story, Ned. Most people around the world won't read it. The Haymarket in Chicago is the place where the Anarchists threw a bomb which killed a half dozen police."

"Most of them Irish at that."

He sighed loudly.

"I know that, Ned."

We were both silent for a moment.

"I assume," the General renewed the conversation, "that you will continue to write your version of events."

I looked up surprised.

"Of course, sir."

"More power to you . . . Will your editor support you?"

"He will. He likes me. My stories stir things up. That sells papers. He likes that too."

The General pondered for a moment.

"The police will leave you alone for the most part. So will the prosecutors. They will fear the Daily News *. . ."*

"And they will fear you too, sir."

My father grinned broadly. "Well they might, Neddie lad. Well they might."

"I appreciate your support."

"And if ever there is any threat against that family of yours . . ."

"You will break the necks of those who make the threats!"

"Something like that."

The General always astonishes me. In effect he had told me that I was to have free rein in pursuing the truth of the awful affair with his guaranteed protection.

"It was awful last night," I continued as they brought the bowls for us to cleanse our fingers. "During the war did you ever get used to seeing men die violently?"

"Never, Ned. Never."

So I walked home to North Dearborn Street and was morose and solemn at the dinner table. Nora and Josie knew why and tried to keep Mary Elizabeth and Grace Ann quiet. What a trial I am to the women I love.

Then I went to my study without much of an explanation and the police arrived.

Well the fight has begun.

May 7, 1886.

Having attended Matt Degen's wake last night I took the carriage over to St. Patrick's for the funeral mass of two other policemen. The parish has slipped since the days of the Great Fire. There are still some elegant homes over on Jackson and Monroe but on Desplaines Street there are factories and warehouses, including the area where the "riot" occurred. The rich Irish have moved farther west to Our Lady of Sorrows, where my parents and brothers and sisters live.

The church was filled. Both policemen were young and their widows and children are young. The anger among the police officers in church was palpable. They wanted to get out of the hot and cramped building and continue on their quest for revenge.

Under the circumstances, Father Galligan acquitted himself well. There was no place, he said, for vengeance in the hearts of Catholics. We mourn those who are gone. We expect to see them again. Though we pursue justice, we strive to do so with calm hearts. We leave it to God to punish those who are to blame. Vengeance is mine, He has said, I will repay. He meant that, Father Galligan insisted.

Some of the police officers seemed thoughtful, his words having hit them hard. Most squirmed in their seats, eager to be out on the streets tormenting union leaders and Germans.

I wrote an incendiary piece in which I described the grief of the widows, the Catholicism of the sermon, and the responsibility of men like Captain Bonfield and Captain Ward who marched into a dispersing crowd where their presence was not needed and against the explicit orders of Mayor Carter Harrison.

My editor grinned happily after he had read it.

"There'll be hell to pay over this one, Ned. Cyrus McCormick will send his footman over with a strong note."

"Which you will publish!"

"Certainly! To tell you the truth, Ned, he's not the writer you are."

"That's hardly a compliment."

Then I went up to Lucy Parsons's house on Larrabee Street. She had just been released from jail, but not for long. The police were hoping she would lead them to her husband.

They did not know Lucy if they believed that.

She peeped out of the corner of the door, saw me, and opened it.

"Ned," she said, "it is good to see you. Please come in."

Their apartment was no more than a couple of bare rooms with a few sticks of old furniture. The Parsonses, a man and woman of considerable intelligence and industry, lived in abject poverty.

Lizzy Holmes, her good friend and ally in the Seamstress Union, was with her. Her two little children, dark and lovely but haggard and undernourished, sat quietly in the corner.

"Albert is not here." She sighed. "He thought it best to go into hiding temporarily. He expects there to be battles in the street."

"Do you?" I asked gently.

"I don't think so," she said. "Ned, would you please put to rest the rumor that we plan to blow up St. Michael's Church. The story is designed to turn German Catholics against us."

"I'll do what I can . . . This is a difficult time in Chicago for the Germans."

"I understand."

Lucy Parsons is a beautiful woman, dark and exotic with a lovely body and bright eyes. She's in her early or middle thirties. I don't know what blood is in her veins and I don't care.

"Would it be possible to interview Albert?"

She shook her head vigorously.

"I'm afraid not, Ned. We trust you, of course. Everyone in the labor movement does. The police are outside now watching my every visitor. They will follow you, hoping you will lead them to Albert."

"Is he safe?"

She sighed. "For the moment. We hope he can move shortly to a safer place where Captain Schaack will never find him."

"That is very wise. I hope he stays there. They are looking for men to hang."

"If others are to hang, he will insist on hanging with them. The working class must stand together against its oppressors."

"The city is hysterical now, Lucy. The hysteria will pass eventually. People understand there was no conspiracy, especially not from a man who had brought his wife and children in harm's way. It will be safe then for him to return and he can resume his work."

"Who will they want to hang?"

"Lingg, certainly. They have bomb materials in his room. Spies probably and Fielden because they were there . . ."

"And hence targets for the bomber and the police pistols?"

"They'll probably pick up a few more harmless innocents."

"And Albert? If he should return to Chicago?"

"He's been too articulate, too prominent, just the man they're looking for as the ringleader . . . Lucy, don't let him return."

"We have often spoken"—she pursed her lips thoughtfully—*"of the possibility of death. In our work it is always a present reality. We have agreed that if necessary we would find it an honor to die for our cause. Our blood would win thousands to the cause of workingmen and -women."*

"Blood of martyrs the seed of the faith," I mused.

"Who said that, Ned?"

"St. Augustine, I think."

"For Albert and me, the only God we can worship is humanity itself. Willingly we would die for that God."

The humanity which wanted to hang her husband just as it had hung Myles Joyce in Galway Prison.

The rich and powerful in Chicago wanted blood. So did the Anarchists—their own.

"Perhaps, but only if there is no other way. Both of you will do more for the workingmen and -women alive than dead."

I was not sure of that. Yet I had to say it.

"As you say, Ned, perhaps."

"At least tell Albert my opinion."

"Naturally. However," she said, her eyes shining even more brightly, *"I must inform you that Albert will not let others die alone."*

"I do not question his courage," I managed to say.

"I know you don't, Ned." Tears formed in her eyes. *"Please continue to report the truth about the oppression of the workingmen and -women of Chicago, in your ironic Irish way."*

I promised I would, not altogether sure that her description was accurate.

Brave people, I thought as I left their old house

which had somehow survived the Fire. Foolish perhaps but brave.

Outside rain clouds were gathering. Two policemen across Larrabee Street glared at me suspiciously. I was so angry that I almost started a fight with them. There would be some relief in knocking them both down. Since I was General Fitzpatrick's son and a reporter for the Chicago Daily News, I could get away with it.

Naturally I did not do so and indeed feel ashamed of myself for the thought.

Tomorrow I will write a story about Lucy and Albert Parsons. I will try to present them for what they are—a dedicated man and woman who would not step on an errant ant. In the temper of Chicago today it would do little good. Yet one must do what one can.

I wanted desperately to return to our comfortable home on Dearborn and bask in the warmth of my wife and family. There was, however, work to be done.

At North Avenue and Sedgwick I entered Laddy's Saloon, a gathering place for the working-class Irish—teamsters, sewer diggers, sailors, longshoremen, boatwrights from the yards on Goose Island, where they were still building schooners. My elegant white clothes and bowler hat were utterly inappropriate for such a place. Yet I was always welcome, whether because I was the General's son or a reporter I do not know.

I found myself at a table with some of the men from Goose Island who told me that plans were being made to build "iron" boats with steam engines there, yet another revolution in the always dangerous Lake shipping trade. I let the conversation drift to the "riot."

What do I think? I was there. The meeting was over. People were going home. Bonfield sent in his police looking for trouble. Someone threw a bomb which killed a policeman who was a friend of mine. The police panicked and killed one another and a few of the *protesters. It was all over in a few minutes. The term riot doesn't apply.*

"Do you know who it was, Ned?"

"No, he came rushing out of Crane's alley, pushed me aside and threw it. It was a long throw. Only moments before the protesters were there. My guess is that he wanted to throw a bomb and didn't much care who it hit."

Silence around the table and indeed around the whole saloon as they listened to the journalist tell his tale.

"Would you be thinking, Neddie lad," *a young red-haired giant asked with a wink of his eye,* "that Bonfield and Ward and Schaack were looking for a little riot bloodshed."

I stared into the darkness of my beer.

"That's certainly possible. Yet why march your own men into it? They could have waited fifty yards back."

"What was the man like?"

"Big fellow, shrouded, strong. In a great hurry. There was only the one gaslight at the corner of the alley. He didn't take time to aim. He just threw."

"Crazy man?" *a little sail rigger named Higgins asked.*

"I've thought of that. His behavior certainly seemed crazy. I don't think he cared whom he hit."

"They're out to hang them German Anarchists, ain't they Ned?"

"They're saying there was a conspiracy. That's complete nonsense."

"They'll swing anyway, won't they?"

I nodded solemnly.

"The papers want it, the rich people want it, the police want it. Innocent people will indeed swing."

"That ain't fair," *the big redhead said. Everyone around the table murmured agreement.*

The Irish working class would not rise in the streets

to save the Anarchists, much less to punish the police force on which many of their fathers and brothers and cousins served. They could, however, recognize unfairness when they saw it.

Then one of our regulars came in. He limped, his eyes were black, his face swollen.

"Vaclav! Who hit you!"

"Cops come to my house in middle of night, screamed at me and wife, hit us both, woke kids, ransacked house, tore bed apart, dragged me to Chicago Avenue station, choked me, kicked me, beat me, clubbed me. I ask what I do. They said I part of conspiracy to kill cops. I say I'm just working stiff in yards, no Anarchist. They tell me I turn state's evidence against Anarchists they let me go. I say I don't know nothing. They beat me some more and then let me go."

"Bastards!" one of the lumber shovers shouted.

"Maybe the Anarchists are right!"

"Maybe we should hang the cops!"

Perhaps, I reflected, the situation is more volatile than I thought. The denizens of Laddy's were not revolutionaries. However, they hated the bosses and the rich. It would take more than a spark to bring them into the streets. Still it could happen. Then the city would have a mob on its hands far more dangerous than a few German theorists.

As I left Laddy's a big, solid, bearded man ambled out with me, probably a stevedore from the river docks. His face was hidden by a cap.

"Aren't there some folk saying, Ned, that it was all a balls-up?"

A Mick.

"Are they now?"

"They're whispering that no one who died was supposed to die, if you take my meaning."

"Ah."

"*I hear that they're saying the amadon that threw the bomb panicked and threw it at the wrong time.*"

"*Very interesting . . . An Irishman threw it?*"

He laughed.

"*I'm not saying that he did and I'm not saying he didn't. I'm only saying that you shouldn't believe everything you hear.*"

"*I usually don't.*"

"*This time, don't believe anything you hear.*"

He turned away and walked up Clark Street.

There were perhaps fifty Irish groups in the city dedicated to the expulsion of the English from Ireland, some of them armed, and some of those more than a little daft. Why might they get in a fight between the Anarchists and the police?

The man who had spoken to me was trying to influence what I wrote tomorrow. Maybe he was merely throwing sand in my eyes and in the eyes of the police. I could write about rumors without playing the game of those who wanted to create more confusion. I might learn something more.

I did not, however, think that would be the case.

Nora hugged me when I came in the door of our house, her radiance banishing some of my gloom.

"*It was only one beer, Mrs. Fitzpatrick.*"

She laughed enthusiastically.

"*The last thing I fear is that Mr. Fitzpatrick will ever become a drunk.*"

"*I think Uncle Neddie would be very funny as a drunk,*" *Josie observed.* "*He'd cry a lot because he's such a sentimentalist.*"

"*We should have left you on that hill, young woman!*"

"*And you would have if you didn't know that she wouldn't come along without me.*"

We all laughed. The truth of the matter, however, was that when God (or some good angel) inspired me to say that of course Josie would come along, Nora decided to surrender.

My wife put her arm around me as she led me to the dining room.

"When you do that," I said, "I melt."

"That's why I do it."

Here in my study, where I try to make sense out of this dark and terrible day, I think of Lucy Parsons and Nora Joyce. Like Nora, Lucy would lose her husband to the gallows, a victim of the gross miscarriage of justice. There would, however, be no one to save Lucy because she would not want to be saved.

Where should I be in all this? I play a coward's role, that of an outsider who reports and comments on the struggle between the workers and the bosses. I am not part of the struggle despite my sympathy for the workers. I tell myself that now is not yet the time, that anarchy will not work, that when this vast immigrant population of our city begins to vote, there will be change. Until then, however, people will live in misery and injustice and brave men and women like Albert and Lucy Parsons may lose one another just as Nora and Myles lost one another.

It is raining hard now, perhaps washing away some of the blood on Desplaines Street. A chill in the air. I am tired. I cannot answer my questions. Nora waits for me in our bedroom.

"IT'S TERRIBLE altogether"—Nuala Anne sniffled as she dabbed at her tissue— "but, sure, isn't our Neddie growing into a wonderful young man."

We were in her office with the child and the hounds, the latter curled up in opposite corners watching the former intently.

"Sounds like he's a mere plaything in that woman's hands," I said.

"Isn't that why he married her? And himself a boxer!"

"That's worse than being an overgrown linebacker!"

Nuala lowered her reading glasses, which she had to use with Ned's script and glanced over them at me.

"'Tis not! Aren't both fine manly exercises, so long as the man . . ."

"Does what his wife tells him to do?"

"Me very thought!"

Socra Marie was in a crib at her mother's feet, kicking her legs up and down with great glee, having just discovered that she could do it.

"I'll admit that he has become a tough and sensitive journalist. He still has to get over his feeling that he's inferior to that wild man who is his father."

"I think the General is cute! I can hardly wait to meet the mother, can we, Socra Marie?"

The child stopped kicking her feet when she heard a familiar sound. However, she didn't identify it with herself and went back to kicking.

She couldn't possibly have cerebral palsy, could she?

"Well, we'll just have to plow through this won't we? Didn't his rivirence say that he thought there were some other copybooks around his basement?"

"He should call in the Chicago Historical Society and have them archive the place."

"'Tis true . . ."

She put her glasses back on and began her second reading.

"Well, at least he's learned how to be a strong husband," she mused, "and himself not really knowing that yet."

"Oh, he knows."

She looked over her glasses at me, as if reflecting on a serious issue instead of a marriage, both partners of which were now in heaven.

"Och, Dermot," she said, deciding that it was time for a serious answer, "don't you have the right of it again and herself a very lucky woman."

She averted her eyes and her face slowly turned crimson.

You won that.

I offered Socra Marie my finger. She considered it and then grabbed it . . . Something nice to hold on to.

"How did you think Seamus looked at the Baptism?" Nuala asked as she continued to read Ned's manuscript.

"Pale and worried."

"I thought so too . . . Why don't you give your man a call?"

I punched in the number of the Reilly Gallery with my left hand since my daughter showed no intention of loosening her grip on my right hand.

"His son's fiancée—marriage set for next month—called me this morning," Mike the Cop began. "Russian woman. Pretty tough. She wanted to know the details of our protection. If she makes up her mind that Seamus needs security, then we'll have a client. She'll be good for that clan."

"I think so too."

"I have a lot more information about him, if herself is still interested."

Nuala Anne smiled benignly over her phone.

"Herself is always interested."

"He has had a lot of business interests, most of which have ended in conflicts that he's won. Two of his former law partners sued him last year on the grounds that he defrauded them of their share of a settlement of a P.I. suit, Messrs. Kevin McGinty and Brian McGourty. Over a million dollars involved. He is majority owner of a string of profitable high-class suburban restaurants called Elegance Incorporated. He shoved out the founder and general manager of the chain, a certain Nick Papageorgiou, and charged him with inadequate financial reports. Then there is a developer named Jim Gigante, alias Jimmy the Giant, who planned a multiuse project out west on Ogden Avenue. Seamus funded him and then dumped him when the man couldn't launch the project. Somehow Seamus was able to clear all the legal hurdles and is going ahead with it. It's a high-risk venture, but he could make a bundle out of it."

Nuala was busy jotting down names, probably misspelling them.

"He enjoys fights, I suspect, more than just winning.

"Doesn't he like to win too? . . . Any of them fellows the kind that would put out a contract on him?"

"None of them would profit by his death, but all are very angry. Papageorgiou is in a business where, one hears, contracts do happen."

"Never get a Greek angry at you," I observed, "or a Mick either. Both have long memories. Who does stand to benefit if he should die?"

"If you order the suspects by the amount they would inherit, the prime suspect is one Cardinal Sean Cronin, Archbishop of Chicago."

Nuala covered the phone and giggled.

"You never can trust those cock robin fellas."

"Or those little auxiliary bishops with Coke-bottle glasses . . ."

"The money that's not left to the Church, in his various different manifestations, goes into family trust funds for Diane, Lourdes, and Andy. Diane likes to shop, has more shoes they say than Imelda Marcos. Lourdes's husband lost his shirt in a dot com start-up last March. Seamus supported that game and won't support another. Andy blew his capital at the Merc and is now nothing more than a low-paid law clerk in Seamus's firm, which by the way is still known as Costelloe and O'Sullivan."

"Who's O'Sullivan?"

"Got out long ago. Bad stomach.

"No Jewish names?"

"Find me a Jewish lawyer who's dumb enough to get mixed up with Seamus."

When we had hung up, I tried to recapture my finger from Socra Marie and instead hoisted her out of the cradle.

"Dermot Michael Coyne! Stop that!"

"She won't let go!"

I lowered the child into the cradle.

"Well!" her mothered towered over us. "Won't you just have to sit there until she goes asleep!"

She folded the child into her arms. Smelling Mama, Socra Marie promptly lost interest in Dada.

"Is Da being silly?" Nuala cooed. "He's a little kid just like you!"

She began to sing.

The October winds lament
Around the castle of Dromore
Yet peace lies in her lofty halls

My loving treasure store
Though autumn leaves may droop and die
A bud of spring are you

Our daughter closed her eyes contentedly. If the strange world into which she had been plunged had such nice sounds, it must be all right.

Nuala sang again

Lullaby, lullaby,
Sweet little baby,
Don't you cry
I'd rock my own little child to rest
In a cradle of gold on the bough of a willow
To the shoheen ho of the wind of the west
And the lulla low of the soft see billow
Sleep baby dear
Sleep without fear
Mother is here beside your pillow.

The small one was now sound asleep, doubtless with peaceful dreams of the sort we could not imagine, though I would have wagered that the wolfhounds were in them.

"WELL," my wife exclaimed. "Da's foolishness didn't upset our little angel because Ma was right here to sing to her, wasn't she?"

"The little brat wouldn't let go of my finger!"

Ethne knocked at the doorjamb.

"There's a foreign woman here to talk to you, Nuala Anne."

Ethne, with her thick West Galway brogue, would not have for a moment thought of herself as a foreigner.

"Did she say who she was?"

"She said her name was Sonia and you'd know who she was."

"A blond is it now and pretty in a Russian sort of way?"

"You have the right of it, Nuala Anne."

"Ask her to come up."

"Nice doggies." Sonia hugged both Fiona and Maeveen, who rose to greet her. "Good, good doggies!"

A stranger walks into your office where the hounds are supposed to be standing guard and they promptly make peace with her because she likes them. Fierce guards, aren't they now.

"Pay no attention to them," Nuala insisted. "They think they're the owners of the house . . . sit down the both of youse!"

The dogs sat down, their tails still wagging.

"Will they let me look at the baby, Nuala?"

"As long as I show her to you."

Nuala lifted the sleeping child out of the crib. The two women mumbled approving sounds. The dogs joined the circle. Da was completely out of the picture.

Naturally.

"So pretty." Sonia sighed. "So tiny and so pretty. Beautiful curls. I did not see her close yesterday."

"She's a feisty little one," Nuala said proudly. "Determined to live."

"One sees that."

Nuala returned Socra Marie to her crib. The two women sat down on either side of her. The hounds reluctantly retreated to their sentential posts.

"Dermot love," my wife said in her Holmes to Watson tone, "would you ever put on the samovar for us?"

I took the hint and slipped away.

Samovar indeed! She'd been reading Tolstoy again.

When I returned with the teapot and the cozy, the cups and the milk and sugar, Nuala and Sonia were chattering like lifelong friends.

"I'll pour the tea, Dermot love."

"Grand," I said.

"Doesn't Sonia want us to find out who's trying to kill your man and Commissioner Casey telling her that occasionally we solve a small mystery?"

"Ah," said I.

"I love Andrew. Good man. Father too much for him sometimes. Father good man too. Mother weak. Must keep family alive."

That seemed to say it all.

"Indeed yes," I said at my Watsonian best.

"I tell Seamus. He say hokay."

That I thought was a little strange, but I let it pass.

"Seamus think Greek man put out hit. Tell Greek man he do it again he die. Greek man plenty scared. Beg mother she tell Seamus he didn't do it. No one talk to police. Commissioner Casey do security now."

"The best there is," I said, trying to sound reassuring.

"You and Nuala solve mystery?"

I caught my wife's amused eye. Poor Sonia thought that my wife needed my permission. Is to laugh!

"We'll certainly try."

"I talk to Greek man. Very bad man. Greeks all very bad. He talk to you."

Nuala nodded imperceptibly.

"We'll do whatever we can," I said cautiously.

"Good." Sonia relaxed, her task successfully accomplished. She scratched the head of the good Maeveen, who had cautiously slipped across the room. "Good doggie!"

"I talk to anyone. Tell them talk to you."

"Fine," I said, suppressing a sigh.

"Well?" Nuala asked after I had returned from escorting Sonia to the door. The dogs had accompanied me. It was, after all, their house wasn't it?

"Should we trust her?"

"Fiona and Maeveen trust her, don't they now?"

Wolfhounds are the friendliest canines in the world, but they can sniff a phony from across the bog.

"That makes it official."

"There's something strange going on, Dermot Michael, very strange. Dark."

She passed her hand across her forehead as if to banish the darkness.

"You don't like it?"

"Not at all, at all, and himself such a difficult, contentious man, leaving enemies behind his path like a cow leaves manure."

Nice metaphor.

"I'm supposed to interview this Nick the Greek person?"

"You certainly don't expect me to take this poor little tyke into a Greek restaurant, do you?"

I could have pointed out that the restaurants were not Greek, only the former manager. However, that would be a waste of words.

I met Nicholas Papageorgiou in Elegance Mount Prospect, a tasteful imitation French bistro in a shopping mall on Busse Road. Apparently he was still welcome in the restaurant, though he didn't own or manage the chain anymore. The hostess, the waiters and the buspersons treated him with respect and affection.

Such are the power of stereotypes, I expected to encounter Anthony Quinn playing Zorba the Greek, a big uncouth man with dark skin, a thick accent, and a sinister mien. Instead Nick was a short, slender man with light skin, delicate features, and razor-cut black hair. He wore a navy blue Italian suit and a custom-made white shirt, with ebony cuff links. His gestures were neat and economical, his voice soft, his eyes sad, a man who had perhaps just lost his fortune at Monte Carlo. The food was excellent, as good as one would have found downtown, and at half the price.

"I have a young wife," he said, as though this were a tragedy, "and two beautiful children. If I should die, they would be virtually penniless. Mr. Costelloe has warned me that if anything happens to him or to anyone in his family, I will be killed and they will be left to starve or maybe he kill them too."

Real sweetheart, our Seamus.

"Why does he think you were responsible for the attempted assassination?"

I nursed my white Rhone wine carefully. I did not want to ride back down the Kennedy Expressway at rush hour with a light head.

He sighed, as he often did during our conversation.

"This chain of restaurants was my concept. I put all my money into it. Mr. Costelloe ate in one of them one night and called me to praise it. He offered to invest in it. I thought God had sent him to help me."

He made the Greek sign of the cross, the wrong way as we Romans think.

"We were very successful. He was pleased. I . . . I have no head for business. I am an artist, you see, not a thug as Mr. Costelloe seems to believe."

His cell phone rang. Nervously he flipped it opened and spoke tersely, then angrily in a foreign language that I assume was Greek.

If I were a real detective in a real mystery story, I would be able to speak Greek and know what he was saying to his wife.

The tones were of the sort of impatience that a man uses with his wife if he can get away with it. I have never dared to use such tones because I know full well that I wouldn't get away with it.

"My wife." He waved a dismissive hand. "She is an immigrant from Greece. She is very anxious."

My wife is an immigrant too, but patently of a different sort.

"So what happened to his successful business arrangement?"

He waved dismissively again.

"As I say, I am an artist who specializes in food and restaurants. I am not a bookkeeper. I hired my brother Hector to keep the accounts. He is very clever, very skillful. He showed that we made a nice profit. I do not know why Mr. Costelloe was so upset."

"He did not think it was a nice enough profit?"

"He accused Hector of stealing from the company."

"Did he?"

He shrugged as if it were an unimportant matter.

"I do not know. I am not a bookkeeper. Hector had a few unfortunate reverses. He may have borrowed some money. He would have returned it."

I bet.

"I see . . . How much money did Mr. Costelloe claim he took?"

"Several million dollars. I do not believe this. However, I had no choice."

"No choice?"

"If I did not turn the whole business over to him, he would see that both Hector and I would go to jail for long terms. It would kill our mother."

Did Seamus pick up such losers and then put them out of business deliberately? Or was he being generous to people who belonged in jail?

How dumb did you have to be to think you could cheat Seamus?

"Is the matter settled?"

"Do you mean does he now own the whole company? Oh, yes, he bought my share for a half million dollars. It was worth much more, but we did not dare challenge the arrangement. But, you see, we would have nothing to gain by killing Mr. Costelloe. We would not get Elegance back."

"He is convinced, nonetheless, that you are responsible for the attempt on his life?"

Nick's eyes flicked nervously from side to side, as if Seamus Costelloe's hired guns were lurking somewhere in Elegance Mount Prospect.

"He sent a message from the hospital saying that he had put out a contract on Hector and me and our wives and children. It would be carried out automatically if any further attempts were made to kill him. He has made this threat, it is said, to others who tried to eliminate him."

"How was the threat made?"

"A man with a mask came to my home when we were having dinner with our families. He made the threat and then left. Our wives became hysterical."

Five would get you ten, or perhaps I should say five thousand would get you ten thousand, that Seamus was bluffing. He knew he was dealing with cowards. You could scare them out of their minds by a threat.

"The police?"

"How could we go to the police? They would begin to ask questions about the business . . ." He shrugged helplessly. "We are at his mercy and the mercy of whoever tried to shoot him the first time. I beg you in the name of my innocent wife and children, Mr. Coyne, tell Mr. Costelloe that we had nothing to do with that attempt. We are only poor people who have no money and no future."

"Don't you have the half million Mr. Costelloe gave you for full ownership in the firm?"

"We cannot use it for two more years. That was part of the agreement. He did not want us to begin other restaurants until he had full control of these. We had no choice . . ."

I decided that I liked neither the whining nor the whiner. I didn't much believe him either.

"Your brother's debts were from gambling?"

"Yes, I believe so. Racing and such matters. I did not want to know about them. He behaved very foolishly. If it were not for him, we would not have these troubles . . ."

His cell phone rang again. He opened it, listened for a moment, muttered a word, and then snapped it shut.

Poor wife.

"Yes," he continued, "my brother is responsible for all our troubles. What can I do? Our poor old mother worships him. She would die if anything happened to him. We must protect him."

"Where is he now?"

"He has gone away for a few weeks until matters settle down. Then he will return. I do not know where he is. I do not want to know."

"I see."

"It sounds like a crock of shite to me," my wife announced later when I had finished the story.

She and Nellie and the hounds had taken Socra Marie out for a walk in the stroller. The child had enjoyed it very much. She was sleeping soundly. And why hadn't I phoned to find out how she was? I argued that I had been working and that I assumed I would hear if there were any bad news.

Nuala sniffed. My explanation was inadequate. Naturally.

"Next time, call!"

"Yes, ma'am."

"Well," she asked after I had finished my report, "what do you think?"

"I quite agree that the man is a gobshite. I'm sure Seamus suspects the two brothers, probably because no one else is unbalanced enough to try such an idiot trick. I also think he's bluffing about killing their families."

"What would be their motive for trying to get rid of the poor dear man?"

"Beats me, Nuala. Maybe they think that if Seamus is out of the way they can try to void the agreement giving him control of Elegance."

"The name was accurate?" she asked.

"It was indeed."

"I don't think I'll ever want to eat there . . . How could they void the contract without revealing their embezzlement?"

"I don't know. My impression is that they're both a little mad, Hector more than Nicholas. They're not clever plotters, but impulsive, madcap schemers. They get a nutty idea and act on it without thinking about the consequences. They're negative on both emotional and intellectual resources. I sort of believe

Nick, however, that most of this trouble would not happen if it weren't for the brother."

She nodded.

"Sonia said that this man Gigante will talk to you tomorrow."

"Everyone's eager to talk."

"You might stop in to visit your man tomorrow and see if you're right about his actually putting out the contract on the Papageorgiou family."

"I might indeed."

"And, Dermot love, I'm sorry for snapping at you when you came in. I guess I'm doing more stewing than I thought."

"I should have called."

"I should have kept me big mouth shut till later, but you know how hard that is for me."

She brushed her lips against mine and all was once again right with the world.

That night St. Ignatius College Prep was playing Fenwick. Nellie Coyne, five feet nine with a comet's tail of red hair behind her was still power forward. However, there was a new point guard, a tiny unsmiling freshman with a ring of thick black curls, who dominated the floor and fed the ball repeatedly to her big sister. St. Ignatius was about to drive Fenwick from their own gym in defeat when the stands collapsed from under me, the team disappeared in the terrified crowd and someone shook me out of my sleep.

Nuala Anne, full-dressed, and eerily calm.

"The little one is terrible sick, Dermot love. Ethne is coming over to watch the others. I'll take the Chevy. You follow over in your Benz when she comes."

She was wearing jeans, her "Galway Hooker" tee shirt, a white windbreaker ("Chicago Yacht Club") and running shoes without socks. Where was she going dressed so carelessly at this hour of night?

The hounds were prowling around. Nellie was

screaming hysterically. The baby was crying too, desperately it seemed.

I tried to shake sleep out of my head, still thinking I was in a nightmare.

"What's the matter with her?"

"She can't breathe and she's burning up with fever. I suppose it's pneumonia."

Only then I see the little wisp of a child in her arms. She was turning blue.

I stumbled down to the door with my wife. Doll in one hand, Nellie followed us, still screaming.

"Hush now, child," Nuala Anne said calmly, "your sister will be all right once we get some oxygen in her. Daddy will bring you over tomorrow . . . Hold the poor thing, Dermot love."

Nuala, babe in arms, rushed down the steps, piled into our old Chevy and drove off into the night. I held the hysterical little redhead in my arms and kept repeating the mantra, "She'll be all right, Nellie. She'll be all right!"

— 9 —

 FROM NED FITZPATRICK'S DIARY:

PARSONS RETURNS TO STAND TRIAL WITH "COMRADES"

By Ned Fitzpatrick

Albert Parsons, the union printer who is accused of being the mastermind of the Haymarket riot last month has returned to Chicago to stand trial with his comrades. Parsons was once the Secretary to the Senate of the State of Texas and has also spoken before the Congress of the United States. A slight man, he left a train at Kinzie Street this morning, falling as he jumped from the train. A passerby helped him back to his feet, not seeing in this frail little man in farmer's garb a dangerous Anarchist, accused by a Cook County Grand Jury of murder.

Parsons was greeted in the rail yard by his wife Lucy, his small children Albert Junior and Lulu and a number of friends. He was returning from a safe hiding place some distance from Chicago to an uncertain fate.

Parsons and his wife understand full well that the drama about to be enacted farther down on Illinois

Street in the Cook County Courthouse could lead to his hanging in the alley behind the courthouse. They realize that by returning to face trial with his colleagues he is risking almost certain death. Yet they also realize that the trial will make headlines around the world. They believe that it will become a great drama in an ongoing conflict between good and evil. Even if they lose in the trial, as they probably will, they feel that they will win.

One does not have to share either their anarchist convictions or their faith in the eventual triumph of their cause to admire their courage.

After hundreds of arrests by the police and massive beating and torture a carefully chosen grand jury has indicted eight men and charged them with the murder of police officer Matthias Degen on the night of May 4.

They are a disparate lot. Four of them—Parsons, August Spies, Fielden and Engel were present at the explosion. There is no evidence that any one of them threw the bomb. Indeed they could not have thrown it because they were in plain view of the police who, with drawn pistols, were driving the small crowd of protesters away from the speaker's stand.

Yet they are accused of being part of the "conspiracy" to murder Patrolman Degen. In fact, the charge against them is that they are all Anarchists. That is certainly true, but that is not of itself a crime in this country.

According to courthouse observers Judge Joseph Gary and State's Attorney Julius Grinnell will almost certainly get a conviction because the jury will be stacked with citizens who think all Anarchists should die. This reporter has seen judicial murder committed by the English government in Ireland.

He does not want to see it in Chicago.

Note later:

My editor looked at me skeptically after he had read the above story which I have pasted into this book.

"Pushing it, Neddie boy, aren't you?"

I shrugged indifferently. He would use the story but he had to object.

"Anytime you want me to cut off my contacts with the defendants, just tell me. I'll report on what Captain Schaack has to say."

"No"—he pretended to ponder—"that wouldn't be a good idea . . . This is a scoop about Parsons returning. Keep up what you're doing."

"Yes, sir."

"Are these Parsons people a little crazy?"

"More than a little, sir."

"What do they hope to accomplish?"

"They see the trial as a stage for a great drama in which they can speak to the world about their beliefs."

"Do you think they're right?"

"That it will be a great drama that the whole world will watch? Sure!"

"That it's worth dying for?"

"My father thought the Union was worth dying for."

The story was a huge success. The headline, **"Parsons comes home to die"** *was plastered all over the city. It also brought my family into the drama in a way I never intended.*

While we were eating supper that night ("tea" as Nora calls it), Annie, our Irish serving girl (who aligns herself with the other women of the house against me) rushed into the dining room and cried, "There are men outside shouting things."

I folded my napkin with deliberation that I did not feel and said, "Thank you, Annie. I'll see to it."

I walked as calmly as I could into the parlor, drew back the drapes, and glanced out the bay window.

"Be careful, Ned," Nora warned, as any sensible wife would have warned me.

A dozen or so thugs had arrayed themselves on Dearborn Street. They were shouting curses, warnings, and obscenities. Schaack's men undoubtedly. They had the right to protest if they wished. I would not play the Cyrus McCormick game of denying their freedom of assembly and freedom of speech. As I watched one of them picked up a rock from the street and threw it at the window. Involuntarily, I pulled back. It was well that I did. The rock shattered the window and fell at my feet.

I looked down at the rock and the broken glass. I confess that my self-control collapsed. That rock might have hit one of our little girls, Mary Elizabeth or Gracie. I picked up the rock, strode out the door, onto Dearborn, and up to the thug who had thrown the stone—a large and bearded Irishman.

"I believe this is yours, sir," I said, dropping the rock at his feet.

"And if it is?"

I hit him twice, once in the jaw and once in the stomach. He folded over and collapsed into a pile of horse manure.

"Is there anyone else who has problems with what I write?"

No one replied.

"Then get out of here and don't come back."

"Begone, you worthless blatherskites," a familiar womanly voice screamed behind.

The good Josie Philbin, Nora's niece and now mine. Her next words could well be a curse. I turned to restrain her.

Our golden-haired Gaelic warrior queen, her face glowing with wrath in the pale gaslight, was brandishing a large poker. At the slightest provocation she would dash into the mob and batter them with her poker. Next to her my good wife Nora was clutching a shovel, also ready to charge into the fray.

The mob drifted away quickly, more intimidated, I daresay, by the weapons of my women than by my fists.

"Nora Joyce Fitzpatrick, Josephine Philbin, just who do you think you are?"

"The First Illinois Infantry!" Nora informed me, her eyes tight with fury.

I bowed respectfully—what else could I do?

"I think, gallant allies, that the enemy has retreated. Might I suggest we finish our supper."

"Tea," Nora corrected me.

An hour or so later, we were sitting in the parlor, each of us with our own book.

"The General is coming," Josie informed us.

I heard no hoofbeats but I did not doubt it. Josie has a sense for these things.

A few moments later, a small cavalcade came down the street, all the men in uniform. My father led them, of course, his white charger and his blue uniform and his silver-and-gold hair shining in the light of the rising moon, brave Fenian men, I thought remembering the song. Except the General was hardly a Fenian.

It was the kind of dramatic entrance that the General loved.

"I think we might be spared the sabre, sir," I said lightly, "my gentle and docile niece and my modest and respectable wife frightened off the Rebs with a poker earlier this evening."

I knew that Nora was blushing—proudly—behind me.

"My compliments, ma'am," the General saluted her. "May I say that I'm not surprised?"

"My husband," she replied smugly, "rendered the ruffian who broke our window unconscious with a single punch."

"May I say, ma'am, that I am surprised?"

"Sir, I am not."

"If you two don't mind," I muttered, "might I suggest we go inside and have a small sip of Irish whiskey."

The General helped himself to several sips, cursed Captain Schaack for risking the life and health of his granddaughters, promised us that two of his "troopers" would stand guard at our house "as long as necessary," and took his leave, having hugged his grandchildren and kissed the hands of Nora and Josie.

"The man is too much," I protested, as he rode off into the moonlight.

"Isn't he splendid!" My wife seemed to think she was agreeing with me.

Now I sit in my study, this book open in front of me and wonder whether in my own way I really am the General's son, quite as mad as he is.

The thugs apparently did not have guns. However, while I might have expected that, I did not even think of it when I charged out of the house to dispose of the man who had threatened my children.

I should have known that Nora and Josie would follow after me, armed for battle. Yet I did not order them to remain in the house. On reflection, they might have ignored me. If I had lost my mind, was it not their right to do so too?

The basic problem, however, was more serious. Albert Parsons had chosen to endanger the life of his wife and family for what he considered to be a sacred cause. I was now endangering my family for much more frivolous reasons, for the emotional satisfaction of writing stories which would goad men like Cyrus McCormick and Marshall Field.

No one would complain if I changed my tack, if I wrote a little more cautiously and carefully.

Would it not be wise if I sent my family to Geneva Lake during the trial? Perhaps I could spend time with them up there, away from the perfervid atmosphere of Chicago?

As I wrote those last words, Nora entered my study in her robe, both highly unusual events.

"Don't even think of it, Mr. Fitzpatrick."

"What should I not even think of, Mrs. Fitzpatrick?"

"Of sending us to Geneva Lake before the time we are scheduled to go there!"

She stood above me, arms crossed, a deep frown on her face, a warrior goddess of Irish antiquity.

"Oh?"

"Or of curtailing what you write because of us!"

I might have argued with her, as I have done before. I would have lost as I have also done before. My wife knows how to be submissive at the proper time, as when I carried her off from the hovel in which she and Mary Elizabeth would have certainly died. At other times, however, she does not know the existence of the word.

I knew who and what she was when I married her.

"Yes, ma'am," I said, saluting her as the General had done.

She smiled triumphantly and then bent over and kissed my lips, with what I must confess was devastating impact. I had no choice about what followed.

— 10 —

"JESUS," SAID the little bishop after the fundamentalist minister had left, "was a very difficult man."

The sun had risen, so it was morning. We were back in the neonatology ward. The most that could be said about Socra Marie was that she was breathing somewhat more easily and her temperature was down to 102–from 106. The antibiotics, we had been assured, would take effect soon and rout her pneumonia. She was screaming only some of the time, but continued to fight the various tubes which protruded from her tiny body.

My wife and I were beyond exhaustion, too worn to wonder how our child could come down with pneumonia so quickly or to worry about the chaos at home. Nuala had remembered that her ma and her da were in town and had called them as the sun appeared in the sky to plead for help.

Then the minister had entered the ward, Bible in hand, and offered to pray over our daughter. We figured that we should welcome prayers from anyone and everyone and readily agreed. He had prayed and read the Bible over Socra Marie and then over us. Not content with these rituals he asked us if we had yet been converted to the Lord Jesus.

Hell, we were both Catholics. Wasn't that enough?

Apparently it was not. We would not be saved unless we were converted. Perhaps our little girl's pneumonia was a warning from Jesus. Perhaps we should convert now to save her life.

At this point the little bishop had appeared, in his usual windbreaker (White Sox this summer) and clerical shirt with the Roman collar missing. As usual he was practically invisible. The preacher certainly did not notice him. He listened silently to what was being said. Somehow his presence prevented us from assaulting the poor preacher.

"I will pray to the Lord Jesus for you," he said, as he left, "that you may find him and salvation."

The little bishop may have muttered something about praying to his mother too because she had a lot of experience finding him.

Or maybe I had only imagined that.

"Jesus," he continued to us, "had a very bad habit of refusing to fit into anyone's paradigms. He learned a lot from the Pharisees, but He wasn't one of them. He may have hung out with the Essenes, but He was not a compulsive hand-washer. He was surely a Jew, steeped in the Torah, but He put a very different spin on it. He was charming and even witty and told wonderful stories but He refused to be a celebrity. He dealt politely with those in authority, but did not sign on with them. Half the time He reassured people and the other half of the time He scared them. He told all the old stories but with new and disconcerting endings. He was patently a troublemaker. Which is why they had to get rid of Him."

Nuala and I listened.

"It's been that way every since. Everyone claims Him for their own. He's on our side. He's doing things our way. He confirms what we say. Then when we think we've sewed Him up, He's not there anymore. When we have domesticated Jesus, we may have a very interesting person on our hands, even a superstar

maybe. Alas, it is not the real Jesus. He's gone somewhere else, preaching His contradictions about His Father's kingdom and stirring up His kind of trouble. A
Jesus who does not disconcert and shake us up is not
Jesus at all."

"What does He say about our little wisp of humanity?" I asked.

"Well, He might say that you're lucky to have her
and she's His child more than she's yours and if He
wants to call her home early that's His privilege. And
He might say that He loves her more than you do and
that as a good parent He suffers with her, even more
than you do. When she cries, He might insist, He
weeps. He might say that He agrees with the doctors
that the antibiotics and the oxygen will bring her around
and you'll take her home in a day or two and that you'd
better take care of her. He might say that she's always a
gift and you should never be possessive. But then He
might not say anything at all. He might just smile and
touch her hot little forehead and slip away."

"'Tis true." Nuala sighed. "'Tis true altogether."

"But then"—the little bishop sighed, almost as
loudly as my wife—"what do I know?"

He blessed Socra Marie and us and promised he
would stay in touch.

We didn't ask how he knew we were back in the
hospital and why he had added us to his morning hospital calls.

Nuala put her Rosary aside, having fingered it all
the night, and picked up Ned's diary.

"I'm letting Jesus worry about her for the moment,"
she informed me.

Before she could tackle that scene on old Dearborn
Street in the moonlight, there was a knock at the window of the nursery—Annie McGrail and her red-
haired granddaughter.

Nellie, grimly serious, stared at Socra Marie

through the glass, once again as if she were communicating with her little sister.

I walked outside and hugged my mother-in-law and my elder daughter.

"The poor little thing doesn't look very happy," Annie said tentatively.

"A lot better than last night. Her fever's down, she's breathing better, and she's a little less restless."

"She doesn't like those tubes," Nellie informed me. "Not at all, at all."

"They keep her alive, Nellie."

"I know THAT, Da."

I changed places with Nuala.

When she returned to the bassinet, she said, "Me ma says that everything's fine at home. The lad is playing with his trucks, the dogs are chasing one another, and Nellie went to school this morning and asked everyone to pray for her little sister."

"Your ma has a way with kids."

"And meself knowing that."

She sat down in her chair and listlessly picked up Ned's manuscript. She glanced at Socra Marie.

"Dermot, isn't herself resting a little more easily?"

Nervously I glanced at the monitor over the little bed. Her temperature was down to just under a hundred. All the other vital signs looked OK.

"She is indeed!"

"You know what the other one told me out there?"

"Nothing would surprise me."

"That she was going to tell Fiona and Maeveen that Socra Marie was getting better."

"Sometimes the kid scares me, Nuala," I admitted.

"And herself scaring me all the time!"

Then Jane Foley appeared and smiled happily.

"The little girl is much better, isn't she?"

"Och, weren't we hoping it wasn't just our imagination?"

"No, there's been a steady decline in temperature and improvement in breathing. As I told you before, she's a fighter. She wants to live. She also probably wants to go home."

"Ah, no," Nuala relaxed. "Don't her da and her ma just love the hospital?"

"Nuala Anne?" I asked when the resident had left the room.

"Dermot love?"

"Did you talk to babies and animals when you were a little girl?"

"Dermot Michael Coyne! I did not!"

I had learned to tell when me wife, ah, my wife, was fibbing.

"Not ever?"

"Well not exactly talk to babies, animals maybe a little if you take me meaning . . ."

"Did they talk back?"

"Not to say talked back exactly, because they can't talk. But I knew they heard me."

Scarier and scarier.

"You don't do that anymore, do you?"

Silence.

"Nuala Anne!

"Sure sometimes when the dogs are making too much mess and noise, don't I kind of think, 'Cool it, girls.'"

"And they do?"

"Naturally."

Yeah, naturally.

Later the resident said Nuala could nurse her daughter if she wished. She wished of course. The young 'un's appetite returned with a vengeance.

When Nuala had accomplished this maternal task, she went out into the corridor to call home.

"Me ma has everything under control. Nellie's out jumping rope with the other little girls. The Mick is watching *Tarzan* again. The girls are wrestling with each other in the yard . . . And wasn't it a wonderful idea for finding someone for Fiona to play with?"

"It was," I agreed.

Actually, I didn't have the opportunity to vote on whether our home should be converted into a kennel.

"Nuala Anne?"

"Dermot?"

"You don't get inside of people's heads, do you?"

"I'd be afraid to," she said seriously. "Besides, people have free will, don't they now?"

"They do."

"Well . . ."

"Well?"

"*Well*, this one time wasn't I sitting in O'Neill's and meself studying for an exam and didn't this gorgeous boy with the kindest blue eyes come in and wasn't I afraid to look at him, but didn't I kind of suggest that maybe he'd look at me?"

"Did he?"

"I don't know and himself sitting down at the same table I was and ogling me boobs when I sang me song."

She didn't look up at me when she told this part of the story. It was probably true. She had always claimed she fell for me that first foggy night in Dublin. Besides I would have to have been deaf and blind not to notice her.

Still . . .

"I didn't have much of a choice at all, at all, did I now?"

"God's truth, Dermot Michael Coyne!"

"You don't do that to me anymore, do you?"

"I never do it!"

"Except once in a while."

"Well, now and again when you're after not really listening to me . . . Now stop all these silly questions. I have to read what Ned is up to."

She read through the episode I had copied, hurriedly at first like she always does.

Then she looked up at me, her eyes wide.

"Dermot Michael, these people are around the bend altogether!"

We, on the other hand, were perfectly normal. Just like everyone else. We dialogued with animals and sent unconscious messages to potential lovers.

I shivered, not that it would do me any good.

"I COULDA been a rich man," Jimmy Gigante said to me. "And I coulda had something to look at and be proud of. I could say, 'That's mine. I put it up myself.' That son of a bitch stole it from me."

We were sitting in a small construction yard at one end of Cicero. A couple of front loaders, some trucks, a few workers polishing equipment, some lumber and bricks, not much else.

Nor did there seem to be much in the way of paperwork on Jimmy's desk in his cubbyhole office inside a mostly empty warehouse. The Giant Construction, as he had called it, had been knocked off its beanstalk by a Jack named Seamus Costelloe.

"And now he's going to make a fortune on it?"

"Can't tell." He ran his fingers through thick wavy hair. "It was a risk from day one. I'd had my eye on Ogden Avenue for years. I knew that gentrification was going that way and wouldn't stop till it got to Hinsdale. Timing is everything."

Jimmy Gigante was a genuinely handsome man, probably in his late thirties. He was not cute, not, heaven save us, pretty like the current chick-flick movie stars, but good-looking in a strong masculine style—lean, taut, athletic with long black hair and the face of a Roman prince or a character out of a Fellini film. He wore a gold bracelet and a gold necklace set off by a hairy chest. His formfitting black jeans and sport shirt completed the Hollywood effect.

"I owned the land. I had to wait till the right time. I moved a little too soon. Put all my money into it. Played golf with Seamus at the club. He asked me how it was coming. I told him fine, but I needed some cash to jump-start it. He bought in right away. He said that he found the combination of high-class stores and homes and cultural centers appealing. He even talked about launching a symphony orchestra."

"Do you think he led you on so he could take over the project?"

Jimmy drummed his fingers on the torn desk blotter. "I don't know. Maybe he's a predator who goes looking for projects that need money like the Elegance chain, gives them enough money to keep them going, and then moves in when the guy whose idea it is runs out of money. Or maybe he just picks out losers. Who knows?"

"You figure you're a loser?"

"Sure looks like it, doesn't it? I guess he saw me coming."

"Isn't he stuck with a potential white elephant now?"

"Maybe he is. It would serve him right. But Seamus Costelloe always comes up smelling like roses. He's got contacts, big contacts. He won't be so eager to get their money that he signs contracts like I did. Seamus is a winner, I'm a loser. That's the difference."

"If he were dead, would you get the development back?"

"No way. His heirs might figure it's a lemon right now, sell the land and the infrastructure development we did, even sell it cheap. No way I could find the money to buy it back even at ten cents on the dollar."

I wondered about that. The world was awash in venture capital. Still, would not the police suspect that

Jimmy was involved in the murder, especially if the word was out that he was planning to buy the development back from Seamus's estate.

"The police hassle you?"

He threw up his hands in dramatic protest.

"Sure they did. Look at me! I'm Italian, right. I'm a developer, right? So I have to be connected, right? I can find hit men, by picking up a phone, right?"

"Are there any grounds to think you're connected?"

"My family was from Lucca. That's northern Italy. The Boys spit on us. My operation is too small to interest them anyway. I don't know any of them. I don't think any of them could care less about me. I have four kids to send to college and the cops think I'm putting out contracts! Go figure!"

"What do you do for a living?"

"At first Seamus kept me on as manager of the project. I fought with him because I didn't like him. My wife works, I do a few small jobs. Now he threatens to kill me."

"What!"

"He sends a goon to warn me at the Baptism of my youngest kid that if anyone shoots him again, we're all dead. Not only me, the whole family. I had nothing to do with the shooting. Now my life and my family's lives are hostage to some idiot that wants Seamus dead."

Bluff, I thought. Seamus is scaring all his enemies, figuring one of them is guilty. Does he plan mass murder or is he playing games with them all? The latter seemed to be a reasonable explanation, the kind of practical joke Seamus would love.

"Did you complain to the cops?"

"Sure. They just laughed. Said I was trying to embarrass Mr. Costelloe. One cop said he didn't blame Mr. Costelloe for investing in a little insurance."

There are bent cops in every police department. Yet

I didn't think a typical Chicago cop would have much love for Seamus Costelloe or make such a dumb remark. Jimmy Gigante was holding something back.

"Look, Mr. Coyne, I'm broke. If this goes on much longer I'll lose my home, maybe my family too. I can't afford an expensive lawyer or security protection. There's not much point in staying alive. I've got a lot of insurance. I'm worth more to my family dead. Then they'd be safe if some goon took a shot at that son of a bitch."

Did Seamus Costelloe know that his about-to-be daughter-in-law was setting up interviews with men who would report his threats to have them and their families killed? Was he sharing a huge joke with us? Or didn't he care who knew that he was joking? Or was he really joking? Had he laid plans for an elaborate bloodletting if there was another attempt on his life? Strange man that he was, Seamus didn't seem capable of that kind of evil.

Yet was it not evil to be tormenting weak and ineffective men like Gigante and Papageorgiou with terrible vengeance against their wives and children?

"Do your wife and children get to vote about your suicide?" I asked Jimmy Gigante.

He slumped in his chair and buried his head in his hands.

"I haven't told Marci that I'm thinking about it. She'd become hysterical. Yet she didn't know she was marrying a loser. She's young enough and gorgeous enough to find herself another husband."

"Would Seamus give you back the job if you asked him for it?"

His face still covered by those strong, manly fingers, he shrugged.

"I donno. Maybe. Certainly if Marci asked him. He likes it when women beg him. I'd rather die than have her do that."

As I drove back on the Congress Expressway (as Democrats still call it), to our neighborhood I was afraid that I might have missed a question Nuala would have wanted me to ask. I couldn't think of anything else. I had better be prepared for the accusation that I was a friggin' eejit.

However, what do you expect from Dr. Watson?

Hey, I'm beginning to sound like a loser too.

IT'S ABOUT TIME YOU REALIZED THAT YOU ARE A LOSER.

No one who sleeps every night with a woman like Nuala is a loser.

THE KIDS ARE MORE IMPORTANT TO HER THAN YOU ARE. YOU KNOW THAT. ADMIT IT.

"I won't."

Our house on Southport was remarkably quiet. Danuta was polishing the silverware, which she did every week though Nuala had told her that once a week was too much.

"Silver not wear out," Danuta had responded.

There were times when even Nuala was a loser.

"Mother nap on couch in office. Baby nap too. Redhead out jump rope. Boy in park with nanny. Dogs chase each other in yard. Never get tired."

I tiptoed up to my wife's office.

She was curled up on the couch, Ned's diary on her belly, her sweatshirt cast aside, so she would be ready to feed Socra Marie as soon as she demanded food. Spoil the little monster. In repose her face revealed exhaustion that her always mobile waking face covered up.

I thought my heart would break. Couldn't Ned's story wait a little longer? Why were we messed up with Seamus Costelloe? We didn't need a sick mother around the house.

In the bassinet next to the couch, the cause of my wife's exhaustion was whining softly, the delicate cry that meant would someone please wipe the shit off my ass and give me a clean diaper.

OK, Dada, time to show once again that you're a card-carrying feminist.

So, I said to her mentally, you are a troublemaking nuisance. You wear out my poor wife, you put me in a foul mood, you cause your big sister to act like a witch, you threaten your big brother, you upset the poor hounds, you disrupt the life of our family, and you lie there like all the attention is yours as a matter of right. You'll be nothing but trouble for the next two years before you'll catch up developmentally, then you'll make up for lost time by becoming a terrible two. You'll fight with poor Nellie and your dumb brother. You'll drive your mother up the wall. You'll try to manipulate me like you're doing now and you'll probably get away with it. Then you'll become a teen and rebel against us and then go off to college, marry some jerk from across the continent and visit us maybe once a year. And all the time we'll have to love you because we're hard-wired, like my brother says, to love our children even when they don't earn it, which they never do.

She grinned at me.

I know babies don't grin, not for a couple of months anyway. Nonetheless, the little brat did grin at me as I put her back in the bassinet and tucked all the swadling clothes around her.

Already she was laughing at Da.

I admit that I grinned back.

Don't worry, I won't tell the ma that you smiled at me first.

A herd of thundering elephants rushed up the stairs and barged into Nuala's office, which they were strictly forbidden to do without first receiving her permission. They sniffed my sleeping wife, presumably to make sure she was still alive and then sniffed the child who had closed her eyes once back in her bed, clean till the next defecation.

Nuala shifted on the couch, sighed, and murmured, "Dermot?"

"'Twas the beasts," I pleaded.

She opened her eyes and saw Fiona's face a few inches from hers.

"Fifi, girl, you really shouldn't be in here." She scratched the comically outsized head. "I love you anyway . . . Dermot! The baby!"

She sat up, startled and wide-awake. Ned's book fell to the floor.

"Sleeping peacefully, despite Hannibal's army invading us."

"Her diaper!"

"Clean and fresh!"

"Och," she said, collapsing back to a prone position on the couch, "brilliant altogether!"

She closed her eyes.

"Aren't you the best husband in all the world?"

"Woman, I am!"

"What did your man have to say for himself?"

I sat on the edge of the couch and held her hand.

"He said he was a loser and he might commit suicide so that Seamus wouldn't blame him if there's another attempted hit. Figures that he'd save his wife and four kids from Seamus's avenging hit men."

"Will he kill himself?"

"No. Doesn't have the energy."

"Seamus is threatening everyone, is he now?"

"Same technique. A hooded goon shows up at a family gathering and makes the threat."

"He's bluffing, isn't he?"

"Probably."

"He knows how to pick his victims doesn't he?"

"I think he puts money into things like Ogden Town and Elegance because he likes the ideas. Both of them seem pretty classy. Then he finds out that the guys behind the ideas are incompetent and weak. He has to get rid of them to protect his investment. Nick Papageorgiou doesn't want to break his mother's heart by dumping his crooked brother. Jimmy Gigante thinks he's a loser and is too busy feeling sorry for himself to organize the development."

"Umhum . . . How did we get mixed up with this Seamus Costelloe anyway?"

"A woman I know saw the mark of death on his forehead and figured we had to save his worthless life."

"Friggin' eejit . . . Well, I think we ought to look at the sex issue, don't you? This O'Leary woman should probably be next on our list, shouldn't she?"

"You going to trust me with a temptress?"

She laughed at me.

Our daughter stirred again. Nuala sat up, unhooked her nursing bra and reached into the bassinet.

"Hungry again, are you now?"

I noted with interest that Socra Marie did not grin at her.

After the child had been fed, appropriately burped, carefully wrapped up, and placed back in her bassinet, Nuala collapsed back on the couch. The wolfhounds, apparently in response to a silent signal, obligingly left the room.

"Dermot Michael, I'm so tired," my wife murmured as she closed her eyes. "This little wisp will be the death of me."

I closed the blinds, retrieved a coverlet from behind the couch, and wrapped it around her. She was already asleep. I kissed her forehead, glanced at Socra Marie to make sure she was still breathing (she was!), and slipped quietly out of the room.

"Your ma is taking a nap," I told Nelliecoyne, who had appeared on the stairs.

"I wish that baby would stop crying all the time," my elder daughter replied without a trace of sympathy for her sibling. "Doesn't Ma have enough to stew about?"

—12—

July 1886.

*I must note in my diary that I'm spending
more time at Laddy's Saloon these days.
The reactions of the Irish workers persuade me that
they are by no means unsympathetic to the plight of the
Anarchists. They all know that the bailiff, John Ryce,
who collected the jury panel, has bragged that every
one of the potential jurors is determined to hang the
Anarchists. They also know that the prosecutor, Julius
Grinnell, told the police the day after the explosion,
"Forget the law. Make the arrests and we'll worry
about the law later." They also know that Judge Gary
has bragged to his cronies that he will destroy anarchy
in Chicago forever. They also know that Marshall
Field has contributed some four hundred thousand
dollars to support Captain Schaak's reign of terror, all
of which has gone into the pockets of the captain and
his principal flunkies.*

*They know all these things, because they have read
them in my stories. They trust me because the story of
my fisticuffs on Dearborn Street have become a legend, as well as the performance of the armed women
in my family. The legend now claims that our two little
girls armed with large sticks stood at the doorway in
their nightclothes ready to rush into the fray.*

They didn't, as far as I know. It is possible that their mother chased them back into the house before I turned around. I have not asked Nora because I think I am better off not knowing.

Everyone is interested in Josie, the golden-haired young woman with the poker. I tell them that she's dangerous. This is true in the sense which I say, but not true in other senses.

What's happening down there in the courthouse? They ask me when I entered the humid darkness of Laddy's.

"Still selecting a jury. It will take another couple of weeks. The Judge is interfering constantly with Captain Black's questions. The Captain is fighting for justice, like any good lawyer would. Judge Gary wants a quick trial and a quick hanging, before the year is over."

"Will they all hang?"

"I don't think so. By letting one or two of them off, the court will try to make itself look just and fair, which it isn't. Oscar Nebbe probably. Even Grinnell has admitted that there's no evidence against him."

"They wouldn't do that to us, would they?"

I sipped on my whiskey. Scotch. Vile stuff.

"If someone who was a friend of yours and committed a terrible crime, Captain Schaack might arrest you on the grounds you were a coconspirator even if you were in New York the night of the crime. What they are doing to the Anarchists they would do to you. You'd be guilty till you're proven innocent and they wouldn't let you prove yourself innocent, especially if you're a union member as I know many of you are."

"We're not bomb throwers!" a good-looking kid of maybe eighteen protested.

"None of these men are either. They have talked about bombs a lot, that's part of their rhetoric, but the only one at whose residence they found bombs was Lingg. He's a little crazy and maybe knows too much.

He's younger than most of you, outspoken, contemptuous of the court. Short of a miracle, he will hang."

They were all silent.

"This fellow Parsons, does he really want to die?"

"He's the only American-born of the lot, a brilliant man who worked for the Grant Administration and testified to Congress. The more he saw how bad the plight of the workingmen had become since the war, the more radical he became. He would be happy to die if it would dramatize the sufferings of poor people in this country."

"No wonder the bosses want to get rid of him."

"Gus Spies?"

"He's doomed too. He's too smart for the bosses and the wealthy. He edits a newspaper. In person he is the most gentle man you'd ever meet. I don't think he'd be happy to die like Al Parsons would. But he is a man of strong principle. If he must die, he too will use his death to prove how corrupt the bosses and the cops are and how much you and other workers deserve an eight-hour day."

"We'll never get it!"

"Yes you will. The trial will set the labor movement back for a while, even though union leaders like Sam Gompers of the American Federation of Labor and Terry Powderly of the Knights of Labor are not allied in any way with the Anarchists and are furious at them for stirring things up too quickly and with too much incendiary rhetoric. Pullman and Field and McCormick want to put the whole labor movement on trial."

"They're a bunch of fucking Krauts!"

"All but Fielden and Parsons. So that makes them foreigners. The bosses don't much like foreigners, especially when the foreigners are smart."

"Are we still foreigners?"

"Damn right and the worst of the foreigners too because, being Irish, you'd never call attention to yourselves by spreading around pamphlets about vio-

lence when in fact you lack the stomach for blowing up people."

"The trouble with your Germans is that they're too logical."

General laughter.

"Parsons and Spies are certainly logical men, though Al is from Texas, too logical for their own good."

"The others?"

"Engel owns a toy shop, Fischer a shoe store. Does that sound like the kind of men who would throw bombs? They arrested Schwab because they found a pistol and a red flag in his house. Are these crimes?"

"How can there be a conspiracy," the young lad asked, "when they don't know who threw the bomb?"

"What's your name, lad?"

"Timmy Hardiman, sir."

"Timmy Hardiman, that is the question which the defense attorneys keep asking. It is the obvious point in law. Judge Gary, who knows less law than any judge in Illinois, either does not or cannot answer it. He is content with the observation that these men are the leaders of the anarchist movement and hence are responsible for whatever any Anarchist does."

"Is that not reversible error, sir?"

Timmy Hardiman would not spend all his life working as a lumber shover on the banks of the Chicago River.

"In a court of justice, it would be, but not in the Illinois Supreme Court as it is now constituted.

"What's it like down there at Michigan Street[2] and Dearborn, Ned?"

"Imagine your worst pictures of Purgatory. It is unbearably hot. The humid air is laden with all the aromas which sweaty human bodies produce, smells which would make the Union Stockyards seem like a

---

[2]Hubbard Street today. DMC

perfume store. There is a constant hum of gossip among the spectators who are interested only in being there and have no interest in the trial itself, Judge Gary on the bench canoodling with pretty young women, the prosecuting attorneys telling one another jokes and poking fun at the defendants, who are solemn, serious, and sober as befits both their passion for justice and their German sense of propriety, gross and vulgar journalists straining for a tidbit of gossip or for a possible headline which might persuade an editor to give them a raise. It would physic a rat—and there are plenty of human rats in the building."

"Makes the shipyards look easy," said one of the workers.

"Everyone knows that it will be the trial of the century so they want to be able to say they were there. Most don't realize that this travesty of justice will disgrace Chicago for at least a century."

"They're not really our kind of people," a stevedore sad softly. "Still they want for us what we want too. So they really are our kind of people."

That was the raw material for my headline: **Anarchists our kind of people: Stevedore.**

It was time to go home, lest I miss the family supper, only a venial sin perhaps but Nora's unhappy frown always troubled what was left of my conscience.

Timmy Hardiman left Laddy's with me.

"Could I ask for a favor, Mr. Fitzpatrick?"

"You can surely ask, I make no guarantees."

"Would you ever consider introducing me to your niece Josephine?"

I was too young to face the problems that a daughter like Josie would create for us.

"No, Timmy Hardiman, I will not do that."

"Why not, sir?" he said, as if his world had suddenly come to an end. "I mean no harm to her."

"Why do you want to meet her?"

He gulped.

"*I love her, sir.*"

"*I thought as much.*"

"*I watch her at Mass every Sunday. She is so beautiful and intelligent and so virtuous. I'm a student at Notre Dame. I'm only working as a lumber shover during the summer to meet the costs of my tuition.*

"*When you have daughters her age, Timmy Hardiman, never make the mistake of seeming to support the suit of a male for her favor. It is the kiss of death.*"

"*I see,*" he said grimly.

"*You have no choice but to address her yourself. Ask her, for example, if she always carries that legendary crowbar except when she's at Mass.*"

"*I could never say anything like that to her, sir.*"

"*Then forget about your love for her. Josie is a vigorous and arguably even dangerous woman. Only a remark like that will arouse any interest in her.*"

"*I see . . .*" he said.

However, he really did not.

Would he do for Josie, not now indeed, but in a couple of years? My vote would not count of course, but Nora's would. My wife, I suspected, would soon be very fond of this boy, if he had the courage to approach the family properly—after Mass on Sunday of course.

"*If she mentions you to me, I will say some nice but not imprudent words of praise . . . And, oh yes, I wouldn't mention Notre Dame du Lac until she gets to know you reasonably well. Right now she holds the position that all boys who attend that school are toads.*"

"*Oh.*"

"*The fact that you are a lumber shover, though a polite and respectful one, will be counted in your favor. Just now Josie is a strong supporter of the working class. She periodically threatens to attack Judge Gary with her magic poker.*"

"*Really?*"

"*Really.*"

He drifted away from me, a lot on his mind. In fact, I had exaggerated somewhat Josie's animus towards Judge Gary. She had never picked up the poker again after the Battle of North Dearborn. She had, however, expressed a desire to assault him, more as a jest than anything else.

"It will catch up with him anyway," she said.

I did not want to know how she knew that. Shrewd political instincts, perhaps. I hope.

As I was turning off North Avenue onto Dearborn, the same tall man, with his jacket turned up this time, joined me. He was not, I judged again, the man who had rushed past me from Crane's alley.

"How you keeping, Ned?"

"Reasonably well."

"Are they going to hang those poor men?"

"Some of them anyway."

"They're all innocent."

"Is that a question or an allegation?"

"A statement of fact. As I told you before the job was bungled badly."

"I remember what you said. I confess I could not interpret it."

"You're a smart one, just like your dad. You should be able to figure it out."

"I continue to try . . . Are the Fenians involved?"

"I'll not say that they are and I'll not say that they aren't."

Another obscure, riddlelike hint.

"I'll need more than that to save the lives of the accused."

He sighed. "I know that. They're dead men . . . They won't hang them all, will they?"

"I doubt it."

"Maybe later it will help them that are still alive."

"Can't you help me prevent the murder of these innocent people?"

"Ned, even if you figure out what I'm hinting at it wouldn't help now. Eventually it might."

He turned around and drifted away into the hot summer darkness.

Sunday.

Timmy Hardiman worked up the courage to address my niece briefly after Mass this morning at Immaculate Conception Church. He and Josie spoke for a few moments. Then she dismissed him with a wave of her hand. From my distance it seemed like the dismissal was without prejudice.

"Josie," Nora asked, pretending indifference, "who was that nice boy I saw you talking to this morning after Mass?"

"He's not nice. He's a toad."

"He didn't look like a toad."

"He asked me whether I really intended to go after Judge Gary with my magic poker."

Perhaps the poor lad should not have quoted me quite so literally.

"And what did you tell him?"

"I told him that I turned the poker into a broom stick and followed the Judge home every night to his home over in Union Park. Some one of these nights I would turn into a black cat and scratch his eyes out. Then I said to Timmy Hardiman he was next on my list and I'd chase him around Chicago and scratch his eyes out."

Ah, Timmy's first venture was not a complete failure by any means.

"He seemed to be a very polite boy."

"I don't like polite middle-class boys."

"Do you know anything about him, dear?" Nora asked.

"Who?"

"The boy Josie was talking to after Mass, a certain Timmy Hardiman."

I folded the Sunday paper thoughtfully.

"Hardiman? Let me see . . . Brown hair, freckled face, twinkling eyes?"

"I wouldn't describe him that way," Josie insisted. *"He's a toad."*

"I think I do know him," I mused. *"He hangs out at Laddy's sometimes. He's a lumber shover down by the river, a little young for Laddy's but everyone likes him. On our side in this case, like everyone at Laddy's."*

"He doesn't look *like a lumber shover,"* Josie muttered indifferently.

"Probably because he's too young to have that terrible occupation ruin his health."

"Hmn . . ."

Well, Timmy Hardiman, I've done my part. Now it's up to you. She's fey. She'll figure out soon that you go to college. Let's see how you handle that.

July.

I append some of the transcript of my testimony as a witness in the Haymarket trial. I assume that Julius Grinnell permitted me to appear because he wanted to intimidate me and thus discredit me.

Insofar as one can find a theme in the prosecution's case, it is that Gus Spies and Michael Schwab schemed at a meeting in Zepf Hall and that Schwab asked his brother-in-law, a certain Schnaubult, to prepare the material for the bomb and then he and Spies put it together at the protest rally. My story clearly refutes that line.

Schnaubult had been arrested and then unaccountably released. He left Chicago and, unlike poor Albert Parsons, he has not returned and probably never will.

It is a very thin case. Grinnell doesn't seem too worried about it because anarchism is on trial and all these men are admittedly, indeed defiantly, Anarchists.

As I walked to the witness stand I saw my womanly claque in the courtroom—mother, wife, and niece. The General was on one side of them and, surprisingly, Timmy Hardiman on the other.

Judge Gary, a slippery, greasy, fatuous man, loved to ingratiate himself with women, or to seem to ingratiate himself with them, began, "I am very happy, Mr. Fitzpatrick, to see that your lovely mother is gracing my courtroom today."

"If you knew what I'm thinking about you, gombeen man that you are, you wouldn't be so happy about it."

That's my mother, whom I have kept out of this account, perhaps unfairly. To say that she is larger than life is to understate the matter, much larger even than her husband. Not physically by any means, but personally. She was wearing a snow-white dress with silver trim, her flaming red hair piled on her head in a vast crown. One would have thought that instead of a once illiterate milkmaid and servant girl from West Clare, she was a grand duchess and one with a brogue at that. My mother is a beautiful, outspoken, passionate, determined, and frequently inconsistent woman, save on the subject of the excellence of her husband and family. When that is the issue she is remarkably consistent. Poor Nora was frightened of her when we came to Chicago from Galway as husband and wife with a ready-made family of daughter and niece. I told her she need not worry.

"Even if you weren't the perfect wife for me, she would decree that you were because of the fact that I had chosen you and I can do no wrong."

And so it was.

I was grateful that Mother had not used any scatological language in her assault on Judge Gary.

"And, Mr. Fitzpatrick, those two other lovelies are

your wife and your daughter," Judge Gary continued his *insinuating prattle.*

"They are the three warrior goddesses of ancient Ireland, Your Honor. Boyne, Shannon, and Erin. They are very dangerous women. The old man with them is only the Archangel Michael."

My mother brings out the worst in me.

Laughter swept the courtroom. Even the soberly dressed, respectable-seeming defendants smiled. I noticed that they were all wearing flowers in their lapels just like the judge and the lawyers. Poor men. They knew that they were doomed. They knew that the jury of clerks and salesmen had already made up their mind. Yet they still hoped that they might win, even those like Parsons and Spies, who wanted a drama to the death.

Judge Gary ostentatiously took out a stack of daily papers and began to read them during my testimony.

Under questions from Captain Black, I retold my story of that night, stressing the small size of the protest, the massive phalanx of pistol-pointing police, and the man appearing from behind me in Crane's alley.

Then Julius Grinnell took over the cross-examination.

JG: Mr. Fitzpatrick, surely you saw defendants Schwab and Spies make the bomb behind the speakers' wagon?

EF: No, sir, I did not.

JG: You are aware that another witness has testified that he saw them engaged in that activity?"

EF: Yes, sir.

JG: How do you explain this discrepancy.

EF: Your other witness perjured himself, as have many of your witnesses.

JG: Your Honor, I ask that the witness's comment be stricken from the record.

Court: Strike it from the record! Let me warn you, young man, that you are under oath.

EF: You are under oath too, Judge Gary!

(Laughter in the court)

JG: *How do you know that defendant Spies was not behind the wagon making the bomb?*

EF: *Because he was on the wagon speaking.*

JG: *Now you claim that a masked man ran from behind you in Crane's alley and threw the bomb at the police.*

EF: *No, sir, that's not what I reported.*

JG: *(impatiently) Then what did you say?*

EF: *I said that he threw the bomb. I did not say that he threw it at the police. He did not seem to be aiming it at anyone.*

JG: *But the bomb hit the police and killed seven of them.*

EF: *No, sir, it did not. It hit Officer Degen, who later died. Everyone else, as you well know, was killed by undisciplined police fire.*

JG: *Your Honor, I object!*

Court: *Sustained, strike it from the record.*

JG: *Did not the man you claimed to see take careful aim?*

EF: *I don't think so. He was in the street in a matter of seconds.*

JG: *You did not try to apprehend him.*

EF: *No, sir. As he ran back into the alley I tried to stop him. He brushed me aside.*

JG: *You must not have tried very hard.*

EF: *He was a big man running at full speed.*

JG: *A weak excuse, Mr. Fitzpatrick, a very weak excuse.*

EF: *If you say so, sir.*

JG: *So, now you admit that the bomb thrower was aiming at the police?"*

EF: *I don't admit that, sir. When I heard him behind me, the police had driven the small group of protesters together in front of Crane's alley. When I turned around to see him throw the bomb I thought at first that it would hit the protesters. However, in the few seconds, the protesters were behind the wagon and the police were where they had been.*

(Stir in the courtroom)

JG: *(Astonished):* *You are trying to tell the court that the Anarchists were trying to kill their own people!*

EF: *I raise the possibility that someone was trying to kill the Anarchists!*

JG: *You must think us all fools, sir! No one has advocated the use of bombs against Anarchists!*

EF: *Surely you are aware that many editorial writers in this city have advocated such measures, even before the incident on Desplaines Street!*

JG: *Your Honor, I move that this whole testimony be stricken from the record!*

Court: *Strike it from the record.*

JG: *I also move that the witness be excused from further testimony.*

Court: *The witness is excused from further testimony.*

BB: *One minute, if it please the court, I have the right to redirect examination of the witness. He is my witness after all.*

Court: *Overruled. The witness may step down.*

The witness did step down, neither surprised nor frustrated by the experience. The judge and jury had continued to read their papers. Even the defendants seemed surprised at my suggestion that they were the targets of the bomb. I walked over to them and shook hands with each of them, a totally unnecessary act of defiance. Only young Louis Lingg, a proven maker of bombs, ignored my hand. A couple of my professional colleagues grinned at me, not displeased that Ned Fitzpatrick had looked silly.

My mother had risen from her seat and, followed by the rest of the family, swept out of the court. That conclusion of the scene was far more dramatic than my testimony.

Grand Duchesses have a way of doing that. In the

hallway I was hugged and congratulated, as if I were a hero.

My editor was greatly pleased too.

"Splendid, lad, splendid. More excitement than this court has seen all summer! Write it up for us!"

"Write up my own testimony?"

"Why not? Everyone else will!"

At least I was contributing to the sale of newspapers in Chicago.

I wrote about the Judge and jury reading newspapers in courtroom and suggested that the Judge had failed to entertain the court by bringing lovely young women to the bench.

HAYMARKET JUDGE REPLACES LOVELY WOMEN WITH NEWSPAPERS!

"Good on you, Ned," my mother proclaimed at supper that night at their house on the other side of Union Park, down Ashland Avenue from Mayor Harrison's home. "You showed that stuffed shirt, didn't he, Nora?"

My wife smiled proudly.

"I think Ned's right. The police were not the target."

In Nora's eyes, I'm always right, save when I disagree with her. Even on those rare occasions she will sometimes concede a remote possibility that I might be right.

"Who, Ned?" My father frowned. "I admit that in your description it was a strange event. Who would want to throw bombs at the protestors?"

"Marshall Field, Cyrus McCormick, George Pullman, Gustavus Swift, Potter Palmer, Joseph Medil, my editor, even Captain Jack Bonfield himself."

"But Uncle Ned, why would he risk his own men?" Josie asked.

"He made a mistake, a big mistake."

I noted that Timmy Hardiman was absent. Too early

in the relationship to bring him to the family dinner on elegant Ashland Avenue. Might scare him away. However, he had been dismissed again without prejudice.

"Did you notice poor Miss VanZandt in court?" mother asked.

"Who?"

"Nina VanZandt, that pretty girl sitting with the defendants' families," Nora explained. "She's fallen in love with Mr. Spies. Because she's not part of his family they won't let her visit him in jail."

"Poor dear man," my mother observed. "He's so gentle and sweet."

"That's all we need," I said in outrage, "for this cheap drama, a love affair. Maybe it could be set to music and performed at the Auditorium if it's ever finished!"

"Perhaps they do love one another," Josie argued. "I never have and never will, but people do fall in love, Uncle Ned."

"She's there every morning and afternoon," Mom observed, "and wears a different dress each time she comes. That must mean love of some sort."

"Or wealth of some sort," I said grimly.

"She went to Vassar," Nora added. "They say her aunt will leave her a half million dollars."

I had lost my appetite for both food and conversation. When we were back on Dearborn Street, I went for a walk along the Lake in the stifling heat, pleading that I needed a cool lake breeze to clear my head.

"Taking your ease, Neddie?" said my mysterious friend, his cap pulled down over his face.

I looked away from him. I did not want to know who he was.

"Clearing my head."

"You do look a little peaked, don't you now?"

"These are very difficult days."

"You had the right of it today, didn't you?"

"If you say so."

"I do say so."

"You mean that the bomber wasn't aiming at the police?"

" 'Tis true, in a certain fashion."

"How do I prove that."

"You don't, not now anyway."

"So you've said . . . He was throwing the bomb at that pitiful band of protesters?"

"I didn't say that . . . Well, Neddie, I'll be taking my leave now."

He slipped away down the beach.

I returned to my home more confused than ever.

July

We attended Mass this morning at St. Patrick's. The Protestant ministers in the city had been denouncing the Anarchists as "godless pagans," forgetting perhaps that the problem with pagans was not that they had no god but too many. The papers had been writing stories on the religious beliefs of the defendants. My colleagues in the press had expressed surprise and horror (feigned of course) that none of the Anarchists believed in God.

This led to a characteristic letter from my friend Al Parsons to the Chicago Tribune:

"To settle a dispute concerning my religious belief, which will doubtless arise after my judicial assassination, when it will be beyond my power to speak, I desire to say that religion in the sense now understood and practiced by those who profess it is merely a blind faith of the honestly superstitious or a cloak of designing knaves.

"If there is a Supreme Being or Almighty God, who rules the universe, the sphere as well as the actions of puny men, then why do those who profess allegiance to Him cast aside and violate His laws and impeach His

integrity and insult this beneficence by erecting man-made governments and enacting man-made laws and use the bloody weapons of war to prop up and maintain these man-made laws and government?

"My religion—if it can be called such—is viz: Who lives right, dies right. There is but one God, Humanity. Any other kind of religion is a mockery, a delusion, and a snare."

One could have made a case that Albert was preaching pantheism, an ancient and honorable faith. One could also have argued that he identified religion with the hypocrisy of many believers, which lacked a certain logic. However, his cry for justice and peace was grist for the mills of the editorial writers and the Protestant clerics.

"Why does he write things like that?" I said to Lucy. "They don't help. Most of the workers in Chicago are believers. They are his potential allies. It doesn't help to insult them."

"We must teach them that religion is on the side of the rich and powerful, not the poor and the oppressed."

It was an answer that I might have expected. Lucy and Albert knew he was doomed. They were preaching the truth, not trying to win converts.

Monsignor Dunn, the Chancellor of the Archdiocese, had sent word to me that Father Galligan was going to preach on the rights of the workers at St. Patrick's that morning and that I might find his remarks interesting. Most Catholic priests in the city had remained silent during the trial. They didn't like the Anarchists, but they didn't like the bosses either. While their own people were rarely Anarchists, most of them were laborers, overworked, poorly paid, and without hope. It was not an accident that most of the union leaders in Chicago were Irish.

Timmy Hardiman was ushered into our carriage as if he always went to church with us.

"Mr. Hardiman attends the University of Notre

Dame du Lac, Uncle Ned," Josie explained to me as if this were a passport into our four-in-hand.

"I thought all boys from that institution were toads, Josie."

"I never said that," she insisted with a guilty giggle.

The night I returned from my walk along the Lake, my wife was waiting for me in my study, an unheard of event. (Mind you, I had never established any rules about access to the room. They were all in her mind.)

"You are coming up to the camp at Geneva Lake with us next week, are you not, Ned?"

I gulped and found my chair with some difficulty.

"If you dress like that up there, I don't see how I can resist."

She was wearing a thin shift which deprived me of my power of thought.

"It's a very hot night," she said sternly, as a flush crept over her face and down her shoulders.

"Very hot indeed."

"Your mother and I agree that you look peaked. We also agree that you need a rest in a somewhat cooler place."

"Then you won't dress like that at Geneva Lake?"

"Neddie," she said, trying to sound displeased with me, "we are not talking about my shift."

"I was."

"That's not the issue."

"It is too."

"All right, it is the issue."

She bowed her head and looked away from me.

Everyone else in the house was asleep. The door to my office was closed. There was an unused couch against the wall.

I did need a vacation. Indeed I had already made up my mind that I would join the family at our Geneva Lake camp. I would admit that now, however, only if I were a fool.

I had been husband to this woman for four years,

happy years I would have thought, though she was still a mystery to me, more than ever. I had tried to blend gentleness and firmness in our love, without ever knowing how appropriate my efforts to be a good husband were.

I rose from my chair and took her hand to lead her to the couch.

"You win, Mrs. Fitzpatrick, as you knew you would. I do need a vacation."

So that settled that.

WE FOUND OUR WAY UP to the front of St. Patrick's and joined the General and the Grand Duchess and my brothers and sisters and their various companions. We filled most of the two front pews on the Gospel side of the Church.

After Father Galligan had finished reading the Gospel, I opened my notebook so I could get every word. I had already written my headline:

PRIEST DEFENDS WORKERS

"The Catholic Church has always believed in the rights of men and women to join associations which strengthen the rights of individuals and communities. This right to form organizations which enhance human life is natural and God-given. No government can take it away and no government can grant it, though governments are bound to defend it and protect.

"Anyone with eyes to see is aware of the terrible suffering of workingmen and their families in this city today. They are forced to work hours that are too long, in unhealthy places, for little money. They are treated little better than slaves. In some ways their plight is worse than that of slaves because the slave masters have some interest in keeping their property alive. The plutocrats today have no such interest. Having exploited the labor of their workers and paid them a pit-

tance in wages, they feel that their obligations are discharged.

"We all know that most of the abused and exploited workers at the McCormick plant are Catholic. We must wonder if their religious faith makes them special targets for the men who run that foul place.

"While the Catholic Church does not approve of violence and condemns all violence in the relationship between workers and employers—on both sides—it is not so blind as to believe that situations like those currently existing in our factories do not create strains and tensions which lead to violence. To repeat, we condemn violence and we condemn also those who treat workers so poorly that violence becomes almost inevitable. In conclusion, the Church also believes in justice. Many of us were born in a country where justice was a farce. We are dismayed when we see that seeming to happen here in this country."

A few wealthy people, red-faced and overweight, rose and walked out during the sermon. Many people in church, however, were grinning happily. When Father Galligan finished, our two rows, led of course by my parents, rose and applauded.

Most of the rest of the congregation did too, an astonishing event in a Catholic church in these days.

"Bishop Foley will hear of this," someone yelled from the back of the church.

"He's already read it," the priest replied.

I sighed happily. I would turn in the story the first thing in the morning and then take the train with my wife to Geneva Lake. The rest of the family would join us later in the week.

We rode up Desplaines Street on the way home. We passed the Haymarket, crowded with fruit and flower vendors even on Sunday morning.

"That's Crane's alley?" Nora asked.

"Yes, ma'am."

"And you were standing there when the bomb was thrown."

"Where did it land, Uncle Ned?"

"About where we are."

Nora made the sign of the cross and insisted that we say a decade of the Rosary. It seemed a good idea.

"How much do those things weigh?" Timmy Hardiman asked.

"They tell me they weigh five pounds. The fuse was sparkling. He was in a hurry to get rid of it."

"He must have had a good arm."

"Big fella," I said somberly.

"Timmy Hardiman plays football at Notre Dame," Josie said with a slight hint of pride.

"Does he?"

I asked the driver to turn the carriage around and take us into the Washington Street tunnel under the river. It was through that tunnel that Gus Spies and the Parsons family had come to the tiny protest meeting.

Hatred and love, death and the promise of life, I pondered sadly in the dark and dank underpass. Mystery, mystery everywhere. I prayed to the same God I had prayed to at Mass and at our little Rosary recitation that he would protect Josie and Timmy in whatever life should bring them.

Indeed I needed a vacation.

"I THINK that Nora Joyce Fitzpatrick was a shameless hussy," I said to my wife.

At least once every day, Nuala Anne moved her hand back and forth over Socra Marie's eyes. Sometimes, just to be stubborn I suspect, the little wench ignored her. However, this morning in a good mood perhaps, she followed the movement of her mother's hand with careful interest.

Then my wife clicked her fingers a couple of feet way from the child's right ear. Displeased with the noise, our little wisp of humanity glared in that direction. Nuala Anne repeated the performance on the other side. Socra Marie frowned as though she didn't like the show. Still she turned her head that way.

"Nuala," I said, "the doctors told us there was nothing wrong with her hearing or her sight."

"I just wanted to make sure that awful pneumonia thing hadn't hurt her and herself looking so grand and beautiful this morning."

"Her mother looks beautiful after a decent sleep last night."

"It was super, Dermot Michael, just super . . . Now, as to that Nora woman, I think she knew how to deal with her man, poor dear thing, and herself coming into his office more than half-naked."

"I didn't know women did that sort of thing then," I said truthfully enough.

"Give over, Dermot Michael. Sure they did. Not all of them maybe, not most of them, just like today. But some of them and himself being a bit of a gobshite, so stiff and formal."

"I don't think he was so stiff and formal that night in his study."

"He wouldn't have dared to be, and didn't he know it?"

"And you think he wrote it down for those of us who would read his manuscript a hundred years later?"

"He wrote it down because he was proud of herself and himself and didn't give a good fuck who knew it."

"Fair play to you Nuala Anne. And to them!"

"What do you think really happened that night in the Haymarket?"

"Desplaines Street," she corrected me, "and am I not calling the doctor fella now to ask if I can take the child with me on a bit of an excursion. I want to see this friggin' place."

Nuala dressed for the excursion like she was attending an afternoon tea—pale blue summer suit, nylons, shoes with modest heels, hair combed back and then piled on her head. She was now the fashionable young matron and no longer the distraught mother.

Our first stop then was in the pediatrician's office at the hospital. The young woman put Socra Marie on a scale. Nuala forgot her persona and fretted nervously. She thought our daughter had lost weight, but she had been afraid to weigh her at home because she didn't want to know.

"Well, you fat little girl!" the doctor exclaimed. "You've put on seven and three-quarters ounces!"

"That isn't much," Nuala said, resisting good news just as she had resisted the teacher's report on Nelliecoyne.

"But it is, Mrs. Coyne, it's a surprise. Usually it takes a couple of more weeks before these little ones gain any weight at all. She has a good appetite."

"Screams for food all the time, doesn't she?"

Gently and cautiously the doctor explored our daughter, marveling at how strong and healthy she was. Nuala wasn't buying any of it.

"And herself down with pneumonia only last week."

"That happens to many babies, Mrs. Coyne . . ."

"That's Dermot's mother. I'm Nuala Anne."

"Maybe because she's a little small and a little young, she'd be a bit prone to it because her immunities haven't built up yet. She could be ten pounds and still come down with pneumonia. Unless parents neglect the symptoms—which you certainly would not—we pull them through."

"They made us take oxygen home," me wife insisted.

"Purely precautionary, Nuala Anne. I won't try to kid you. There are more dangers for a premature baby than for full-term babies. It's a cliché that you should take one day, one week at a time. I know that doesn't console parents at all. However, you have one very healthy little girl here." She poked at Socra Marie's tummy and the wisp squirmed in delight. "My hunch is that she'll be just fine."

Nuala was unimpressed.

"I stew about her all the time."

"I do about my kids too . . . Would you sing that beautiful Connemara lullaby for her while I'm wrapping her up?"

Of course she would. First in Irish. Then

On the wings of the wind, o'er the dark, rolling deep
Angels are coming to watch o'er your sleep
Angels are coming to watch over you
So list to the wind coming over the sea

Hear the wind blow, hear the wind blow
Lean your head over, hear the wind blow.

The daughter closed her eyes and went to sleep.

"Thank you very much, Doctor." My wife went back to the poised young matron. "You've been very patient with us and this little one. I knew you liked that song, so didn't I bring along a disk on which I sing lullabies."

She pulled the CD out of her purse and graciously autographed it.

"You sing all these songs for her?"

"A couple of times every day."

"Now I know she'll be all right!"

"Nice show, Nuala Anne," I said as we entered my old Benz in the hospital garage.

"The poor dear thing, having to put up with a bitchy mother like me . . . And yourself getting fat on us, Socra Marie."

We had rigged up a tiny car seat for Socra Marie in the back of the car, with Nuala in attendance. When the child demanded food or a clean diaper we had to stop the car because Nuala would not remove the child from the safety of her seat for those delicate operations while the car was moving.

We then drove down Dearborn Parkway and identified the Victorian home we figured was the one where Ned and Nora and their clan lived.

Imitating their piety we stopped to say a decade of the Rosary. Socra Marie continued to sleep.

Then we drove over the Grand Avenue bridge to Desplaines Street and under the Lake Street L track, which did not exist in the days of the riot.

"That's the old Washington Street tunnel," I said. "All boarded up now. Most of the people who came to the protest rally, including Gus Spies and the Parsons, walked or rode through it.

"Hmm," Nuala said.

"Any vibrations or whatever?"

"Very faint."

"The child?"

"Haven't I been after telling you that she's not fey at all, at all, thank the good Lord."

"If we had Nellie here . . ."

"Wouldn't she be going ballistic, the poor dear!"

We found a parking place at Desplaines and Randolph. The three of us sallied out of the car into the soft spring sunlight.

We crossed the street to the Catholic Charities building at 126 Desplaines to read the plaque which had been torn off several times:

On May 4, 1886, hundreds of workers gathered here to protest police action of the previous day against strikers engaged in a nationwide campaign for an eight-hour day. Radicals addressed the crowed. When police attempted to disperse the rally, someone threw a bomb. The bomb and ensuing pistol shots killed seven policemen and four others persons. Although no evidence linked any radical to the bomb, eight of them were convicted and four were hanged. Three were pardoned. The strike collapsed after the tragedy.

"Count on your friggin' Catholic Church to speak the dangerous idea cautiously," Nuala laughed.

We waited for the traffic and then walked back across the street.

"I think this is where Ned was," I said, pointing to a small alley which had no name now, "and the speaker's stand was about here. And this parking lot was the Crane's factory."

"Why is he so close?"

"Probably because he is trying to hear what they're saying."

"Then the police came down the street toward us from just a block away with drawn guns . . . and the steeple of Old St. Patrick's down there overlooking it all."

"Right. They demanded that the tiny crowd disperse. The speakers climbed down off the wagon they were using as a stand. The police, who came up behind the crowd, herded them back of the wagon, then the man came out of the alley and threw the bomb."

"A pack of friggin' gobshites!" Nuala exploded.

The sound of her mother's voice awakened Socra Marie. She look around at the dull industrial street under the transparent blue sky and considered it very carefully.

"They were indeed, Nuala Anne."

"That's not what I mean. Who knew the police would be coming down the street?"

"Well, certainly not Mayor Carter Harrison. He told them not to."

"I don't imagine he would throw the bomb . . . Who else?"

"Captain Bonfield and Captain Ward and I imagine most of the men whom they'd gathered together from the outlying police precincts and marched out into Waldo Place."

I pointed to the map I had put together.

"So how could an Anarchist bomb thrower know exactly when they would appear, light his bomb, and run down the alley to throw it at them."

"Someone at the police station might have sneaked out and told him."

"Och, Dermot Michael, be sensible. It was dark and there were only gaslights. Your man would have had only a minute or two to run down the street, duck into the alley, tell the man with the bomb to light it, and then throw it."

"I suppose so . . ."

"The bomber didn't even know the police were

there! Why didn't all those people know it was an accident and even Neddie himself acting like a friggin' eejit!"

"So the bomb was aimed at the protesters?"

"As far as the bomber knew they were the only ones there!"

"Could be . . ."

"Hush now, little dear," she murmured to the child who was twisting and turning and trying see what was going on, "your ma's playing detective."

"Couldn't someone from the police station have slipped out on to Waldo Court here, dashed over to Jefferson Street here, cut through these driveways or alleys and either tell the bomber or throw the bomb himself. Might not one of the cops been a closet Anarchist?"

"Give over, Dermot Michael Coyne! Why would a cop want to risk killing other cops?"

"Unless Captain Bonfield wanted to provoke an incident!"

"If he knew the bomb was coming, he could have provoked an incident without killing his own men. All he had to do was to hold them back fifty meters or so and yourself missing the point."

"Which is?"

In dialogues like these Nuala abandons her loving wife role and becomes the stern taskmaster. I used to resent it. Then I suppressed my resentment. Now I laugh, albeit inwardly.

"The bomber had no idea the police were there."

"He just heaved it into the dark, brushed Ned Fitzpatrick aside and ran back down the alley to Jefferson Street."

"And over to that Washington Street tunnel and himself not knowing at all, at all whom he might have hit."

"If anyone."

"Take the child, Dermot Michael."

I did.

Socra Marie did not seem upset by the switch. She cuddled against my chest.

Nuala leaned against the wall of the building south of the alley, her eyes closed, her face pale. She was having one of her "interludes," as I called them.

"Guns and screams and pain and terror," she murmured.

It was 1886 again.

"Poor Ned is paralyzed. He wants to do something to stop it but he can't."

Could my wife have really tuned into Ned Fitzpatrick's emotional vibrations from a hundred and fourteen years ago?

Don't be silly. Of course she could not have!

Right?

She opened her eyes.

"It's fading away, Dermot. I'll be all right. Hold me please."

So I had the child in one arm and the mother in the other.

Nuala shivered.

"'Tis over now. Maybe just my hyperactive imagination. I don't know . . . Socra Marie child, your ma is just a little crazy sometimes. You mustn't mind."

The child would have none of this. She began to wail.

"Giver her back to me, Dermot Michael. I'll sing her a lullaby."

We walked back to the car.

"Sure, maybe she's just hungry? You want something to eat, little one? It'll be a milk shake this morning I'm afraid."

Whether she was hungry or not, Socra Marie was only too happy to be offered food.

I sat in the front seat of the Benz, waiting for a cop car to appear. Then it occurred to me that I could put some quarters in the traffic meter.

When I returned to the car, Nuala was changing a diaper.

"Didn't she dump a load of shite in her pants, the little brat. That'll serve me right and proper for upsetting her."

"Nuala . . ."

"What is it, Dermot Michael, and yourself sounding so mysterious?"

"You remember the day we brought this one home from the hospital?"

"I'll never forget it."

"You thought you heard thunder."

"I did."

"And Nelliecoyne told us that some men had set off a bomb down at the Haymarket."

"She did."

"But that was three o'clock in the afternoon . . ."

"And the bomb went off at 10:30 . . . Angels and Saints preserve us!"

"What could that mean!"

Nuala strapped Socra Marie back in her car seat. The child promptly went back to sleep.

"I don't know . . ."

"Shall we go home?"

"Hmn? . . . Oh, no. Herself will sleep for a couple of hours now. I want to see that cemetery place you were talking about. It isn't far, is it?"

"Not at this hour in the morning."

I drove over to the Kennedy and then turned onto the Congress to drive west to Forest Park.

"Dermot Michael . . ."

"Yes, ma'am."

"You've been around me long enough to know that these experiences are not logical . . ."

"Metaphorical, poetic, imaginative."

"Maybe something like a dream in which one thing stands for something else."

"Uh-huh."

"Why we would hear the bomb seven hours before it went off . . ."

"If you had been alive in 1886."

"'Tis true, I wasn't and neither was Nellie . . . Maybe memories were sort of floating around in the atmosphere because people were planning on making the bomb then or on throwing it."

"Could be . . . I wonder if it matters."

"It would to Ned . . ."

"Ned and Nora are in heaven, Nuala Anne."

"And themselves watching everything we do now."

The Irish believe that the dead are very near to us, especially when they're interested in what we're doing. In the World-to-Come, Ned and Nora Joyce Fitzpatrick presumably have better things to do than to watch us. I might ask my wife whether she actually was aware of their presence or just presumed they'd be lurking around. She would doubtless reply that she didn't see the difference.

"If the bomb was made that late in the afternoon of May 4, then it's unlikely that either the police or the Anarchists were responsible."

"'Tis true, Dermot Michael, you have the right of it."

We left the Congress at Harlem and headed south to Harrison and then turned right to Des Plaines Avenue, a different street than the Desplaines Street which intersected with Randolph at the old Haymarket.

"'Tis near your neighborhood, is it?"

"'Tis. Forest Park is just south of River Forest, though we try to pretend that it isn't."

At Des Plaines Avenue we entered the gate of Forest Home Cemetery or Waldheim as it was called for many years (the German for Forest Home).

"If I remember correctly what my mother told me, this was once burial grounds for the Potawatomi Indians on the high ground along the Des Plaines River which is over there on the left. When the Northwestern Railroad built a line out in this direction, the Germans, Jewish and Gentile both, built cemeteries here because they were barred from burial in the city. The mourners would ride out on the trains and carriages would pick them up at the stations. There were thirty extra cars when they buried the five men who were condemned to death after the trial."

Behind me, Nuala Anne sighed loudly.

"And them all innocent."

"It certainly seems that way."

We stopped in front of the Martyrs Monument, a fierce woman standing guard over a dead man, a kind of Anarchist Pieta.

"Ugh," Nuala murmured.

"A monument to the police who were killed stood at Randolph and Desplaines for many years. It was blown up twice in the nineteen sixties. A third version is now safe in central police headquarters."

"Who blew it up?"

"Your radicals, who else?"

"Cheap grace . . . Well, we should pray for all of them, shouldn't we, Dermot Michael Coyne?

She shifted the child to her left arm and fingered her Rosaries with her right hand. I joined in. I feared all five decades, but Nuala was content with one.

"They're all buried here?"

"All but Fielden, the English Evangelical who was giving the final talk at the protest meeting. When he was pardoned, he distanced himself from the Anarchists. Most of the wives are here too: Lucy Parsons; both of Oscar Nebbe's wives, the first of which, Metta, died from the strain while he was in prison; Nina VanZandt Spies, though there was never money for a monument for her."

"I thought she was rich."

"She spent all her money on the Anarchist cause. She died in terrible poverty, in a messy house, surrounded by cats. She left three thousand dollars that she had somehow hidden away from Lucy Parsons to a cat shelter. No money for a tombstone but at least she's here in the same graveyard with her husband."

"Terrible!"

"She must have been an incorrigible romantic."

"That's never a good idea, is it now?"

"Well, they're together not only here but in the world to come."

"'Tis true . . . Let's go home, Dermot Michael. This place is so sad."

Out on the expressway, however, she changed her mind.

"Let's see this Ogden place that your man was trying to build."

"You sure?"

"I am."

I left the Congress at Kedzie and drove south into Lawndale, an area thoroughly devastated by crime. Most of the people on the streets were either drug dealers or their clients. At Cermak Road I turned onto Ogden. In a couple of blocks, we came upon a large area that had been cleared. Gigante had laid down a few new streets and some foundations and built a boarded-up and forlorn model town house. Even in the spring sunlight with wild grass growing up in the ruins and skinny trees turning green, the site had all the appeal of a radioactive dump.

"This is supposed to have been for yuppies?" my wife asked sceptically.

"Eventually it will be. The Burlington Railroad and the Douglas Park L both are nearby. It's close to three expressways. Eventually the Boulevard system will be rehabbed. Yuppies are as far west as Ashland and even Western in some places. Kedzie is still a little far. Ten years, maybe even five. Jimmy Gigante's vision was a little premature."

"What will Seamus do with it?"

"Probably sell it to someone with capital and patience. No tag days for Seamus."

"Tomorrow you must talk to the O'Leary woman."

"Whatever you say, my love."

By the time I pulled up to our house on Southport, both the women in the back of my car were sound asleep.

Neither Nellie nor the Mick, who were playing in front of the house, seemed remotely interested in the return of their little sister from her first outdoor venture.

"I'll carry herself upstairs," I said, lifting the baby out of her car seat.

"Then come back and carry me upstairs."

— 14 —

 Geneva Lake

I left the Daily News *and walked over to the train station to meet Nora and ride up to Geneva Lake. Though I loved Chicago, I wanted to get away from it as quickly as I could.*

On Madison Street, alas, I encountered young Cyrus McCormick, the scion of the clan who now ran the company and helped to fund Captain Schaack. He was dressed in riding clothes with a riding whip in his hand. He was about my age and tall, turning fat.

He saw me from across the street and, ignoring the traffic, strode towards me.

I must stress in these notes that I was not looking for a fight. Nor was I looking forward to one. Yet one part of me, some deep Gaelic demon perhaps, was eager to face him.

"Fitzpatrick!" he shouted.

"Mr. McCormick." I bowed.

"I heard what you did at St. Patrick's Church yesterday."

"I didn't do anything, Mr. McCormick."

"You were behind it all."

"I was not."

"You ought to be horsewhipped"—he raised his

whip—"because of your support of those damned foreigners."

I evaded the first blow of his whip and hit him with a sharp left and then a solid right.

He collapsed into a readily available pile of manure.

Nursing my fingers, for effect if truth be told, more than for anything else, I continued my walk to the station. I didn't bother to tell Nora about the encounter, not because it would worry her (though it might) but because she might give me undue credit.

When my father and mother appeared on Thursday along with Josie and our daughters, the General took me aside almost immediately.

"I hear you've been horsewhipped by young Cy Mc-Cormick," he said with a grin.

"Have I now?"

"Well, that's the story he's been spreading around. He has, however, a swollen jaw it seems to me."

"I can't imagine how that might have happened."

"You disposed of that vainglorious punk with one punch?"

"No, sir."

"Two?"

"That might be a bit closer to the truth."

Later the General and I sat on the porch in front of the larger house, smoked our pipes, and drank a glass of Irish whiskey. The blue of Geneva Lake reminded me of pictures of the Mediterranean. I had promised Nora I would take her abroad after the trial and the appeal were over. The sun set slowly, painting the lake red and gold.

The General sighed contentedly.

"'Tis good to have this place and myself with only half a bed in a turf-heated cottage when I left home."

He could never quite believe his good fortune in America. "Pure luck," he would say. He meant it. He

*laughed at the pretensions of the Fields and the Mc-
Cormicks and the Pullmans, who thought they were
rich because of superior virtue.*

"What's happening in the trial?" I asked casually.

"You haven't gone into town to buy a paper?"

"I wouldn't waste a precious moment here."

"With Nora?"

"Certainly."

"As I've always said"—he sipped on his whiskey—
"I am constantly astonished at your good taste . . . You
have missed very little. It is a circus, a disgraceful circus. Your stories from Dublin and Galway four years
ago portrayed a harsh judicial system blind to justice,
but at least serious. Justice in Chicago is exposed to
the world as a farce."

"So it seems to me," I agreed.

"The tide will turn eventually. Many of the better
educated people in Chicago are already embarrassed
by Gary and Grinnell. The working people have begun to understand that the Anarchists are on their
side. In a year or two or three sympathy will shift to
the Anarchists."

"After they're dead."

He sighed again, much the way Nora sighs.

"I'm afraid so, Ned. Not necessarily all of them. Bill
Black is a fine lawyer. He knows that the jury has already made up its mind. He's making a record for an
appeal to the Illinois Supreme Court, perhaps even to
the United States Supreme Court."

"Will he win?"

"Not as long as the rich men are ready to buy jus-
tices. However, he will get a chance to make the case
in public without the endless interruptions of that fool
Gary. The best hope is Governor Oglesby, who can
commute the sentences by a grant of clemency."

"Will he?"

My father shifted uncomfortably.

"You understand that some of the things I say to you ought not to appear in the newspaper."

I laughed.

"Very well, I had occasion recently to speak to the Governor. He deplores the trial. He detests Judge Gary. He is disgusted by young Cy McCormick, who he thinks is a fool. He can barely stand men like Marshall Field and George Pullman. I came away from our conversation with the conviction—no promises mind you—that he would entertain appeals for clemency."

"Most of those men have wives and children!" I cried, "young wives and young children!"

"I understand that, Ned. So, if I may say so, does the Governor."

"I'm not sure that they would ask for clemency."

"I wonder about the same thing. While Captain Black makes a record for appeal, the defendants strive to make a record for history."

"Fools!" I exploded.

My father sighed again.

"History will listen to them, I think. And to you, Ned, for writing the truth."

"Life is more important than history. Let the dead bury their dead."

My mother's voice rang out on the twilight air.

"If youse want food, you'd better come now or we'll throw it away."

"By the way," the General said as we walked up to the cabin, "I think that young Miss VanZandt would make a good story. She is no one's fool."

"Very well."

Chicago August 1, 1886

Next summer, please God, we will spend at least a month at Geneva Lake.

Only Josie was unhappy with our brief vacation. Poor Timmy Hardiman could not join us because he had to shove lumber. She confessed to me that she might attend college at St. Mary's, across the road from Notre Dame.

"Would you object to that, Uncle Ned?"

"I would accept any decision that your aunt might make," I said cautiously.

"Oh, she doesn't mind. She thinks Timmy is a wonderfully sweet boy."

"And you?"

"Well . . . I'm not quite sure. It wouldn't hurt, however, to get to know him better, would it?"

"I am much too young, Josie, to be acting like a father for a woman your age. However, in words your aunt might use on a subject like this, 'They wouldn't be all that wrong who might say that it would be a good idea to get to know Timmy Hardiman better.'"

She grinned impishly and ran from my office.

I consoled myself with the thought that perhaps I would be better prepared when my two daughters reached the same age.

The trial drones on. Verdicts, for whatever they are worth, sometime this month.

I saw the bomb thrower the other night.

I was walking down North Avenue, returning from a brief visit to Laddy's, where the general opinion seemed to be that it was time to get the whole thing over.

I saw ahead of me on the street, not my mysterious friend, but the man who had thrown the bomb, a big man with broad shoulders and an odd gait. I followed him as quietly as I could.

I pondered swiftly what I ought to do. He was big enough to brush me aside again if I got in his way. I would have to overtake him, make him turn around and try to land some decisive blows.

I confess I gave no thought to Nora or Josie or Mary Elizabeth or Grace.

I was only a few feet behind when he turned suddenly, saw me, and then broke into a run. I followed him as he turned north on Clark Street but lost him in the darkness of Lincoln Park.

Though I had caught a glimpse of his face, I still did not know who he was. However, I knew he was from Ireland, indeed from Galway.

Back here in my office I am unaccountably shaken. The man could be dangerous. I worry now about my family. Moreover, I don't know his name. I can hardly identify him in court. I must consult with the General.

I wonder if Nora would recognize him.

August 2 1886

The General wisely says that I should do nothing unless I have another visit from my mysterious friend on the beach. The story is so wildly improbable that it would do nothing to save the Anarchists. He will assign some of his men again to protect me and the family, though he insists that it's only a precaution.

"Was he an RIC man in Galway?" he asks me tentatively. "Though why one of them would be throwing a bomb in Chicago is not obvious to me."

"Not uniformed. He seemed to be present at the fringes of crowds, just watching. More likely a Fenian spy, though I can't imagine why one of them would be involved in the Haymarket incident."

"Deep waters here, Ned. I don't think there's any danger, but we still must be careful."

"If he were acting for anyone it would be the police, which confirms my suspicion that Bonfield and Schaack planned the explosion, but lost control of the situation."

"You probably have the right of it, Ned. You'll never be able to prove it, however."

I knew that.

SOCIALITE SIDES WITH ANARCHISTS

Although she attended Mrs. Grant's Finishing School and graduated from Vassar College, Rosanina Clarke VanZandt has chosen to side with the Anarchist defendants in the trial which is dragging on at the County Courthouse on Michigan Street.

"Along with many of my friends I went to the courthouse for the fun of it," said the striking beautiful young woman. "We had decided that it was the thing to do this summer. I was expecting to see a rare collection of stupid, vicious, and criminal-looking men. I was greatly surprised to find that several of them, so far from corresponding with this description had intelligent, kindly, and good faces."

Miss VanZandt's father owns a successful pharmaceutical company. She is rumored to be in line for a large inheritance from an aunt in the East and is expected to join Society and make a good marriage. Yet her reported love for defendant August Spies puts that happy future in serious jeopardy.

She does not try to hide her feelings about Spies, whom she is assisting in the preparation of his autobiography.

"My sympathy with the persecuted and lawlessly adjudicated prisoners soon changed in a feeling of amity for Mr. Spies and from feeling of friendship there has gradually developed a strong affection."

Poor Nina. She does not know what she is risking. How can the rich and spoiled know that the life of an Anarchist's lover or even widow must be dedicated to a never-ending crusade for his memory. Lucy Parsons could tell her and perhaps warn her away. However, Lucy will see Nina VanZandt as another recruit to the cause, another soldier in the war for justice and the cause of working people.

I reflect on Metta Nebbe, living in terrible poverty

with her two children, or George Engel's aging wife, presiding over their tiny toy store while her husband suffers through this joke of a trial, of Elise Freidel, Louis Lingg's pretty immigrant girlfriend with only a smattering of English.

She sees me on Michigan Street and shows me a pair of gold cuff links.

"Ja, I give to Louis. He look fine in court, nien?"

I agree with her.

"He wear when he die, nein? Carry to tomb."

"I hope not."

"See, I have our initials carved inside heart. Together in death, ja?"

Does one this young know what death is? Peasants cannot afford to be romantics, can they?

Do these men, dedicated and mad as they are, deserve such women? Do any of us deserve the women who give their lives to us? Probably not.

Someday, not now, I will write a story about these women. I will ask Nora about it first. She knows what it is like to lose a dearly loved husband to a murderous legal system.

"SHE'S FIDGETY this morning," Nuala informs me. "Maybe too much stimulation yesterday."

Socra Marie looks distressed, restless. She's not crying and she's uninterested in food and she won't sleep. She twists and turns in the bassinet and glares at the world.

Nuala sings a couple of lullabies. Socra Marie whines in protest. Do not bother me with music this morning.

"She's in a bitchy mood like her mother," Nuala complains.

"Does she have a fever?"

"No."

"Do you want me to stay home? Ms. Shepherd can wait till tomorrow."

"Ah, no. I want to get that one out of the way. I can call you if anything happens."

I rode the L down to the Loop and then crossed the river back to the IBM Building. Not as much river traffic as in Ned's days, when Chicago was the busiest port in the world. Nevertheless, cruisers, yachts, water taxis, tour boats and gondolas plied their way on its murky waters. It was still a sewer and probably always would be. Now at least it was a picturesque sewer.

Ms. Helen Shepherd, sometime partner to Seamus

and now wife to Seamus's rival Len Shepherd, as she called herself, was in her office overlooking the river. She was a handsome svelte woman in her early forties, skillfully made up with straight brown hair, cut short, and deftly touched with frost though it was unlikely that there was any authentic gray in it. A lot of exercise and diet had gone into the maintenance of a figure which fit neatly into a brown suit. The image was youthful but mature, attractive but competent and responsible.

"I cannot imagine why Seamus would think that Mr. Shepherd and I would want to kill him," she began. "As far as I am concerned, I have no hard feelings about my time with Costelloe and Associates."

Her name had been Mary Helen Cross. She had married Goeff O'Leary, a law school classmate who by all accounts was an alcoholic bum, a description which fits too many Irish criminal lawyers of short stature. He deserted her after the birth of their first child. She ended up in Costelloe and Associates where she established her credentials as a very tough trial lawyer. It was during a high-profile P.I. trial that she and Seamus became lovers—if one was to believe the gossip.

Having lawyers in my family (relatively sober ones) I had learned to believe nothing that they had "heard on the street."

I'd always play dumb and ask what street and they'd always fall for it and say something like, "LaSalle Street, of course."

"Nor about the recent trial in which twenty million dollars was at stake."

She sighed.

"You have to understand, Mr. McGrail, that Seamus is a very competitive man, unhealthily so. He has defined Mr. Shepherd as his rival for several years."

I did not correct her about my name. I loved being called Mr. McGrail. Better that than Dr. Watson.

"So it would be natural that they would strike sparks in a courtroom. Do you think your move to Shepherd and McCabe has, ah, exacerbated the rivalry?"

"Neither from my perspective nor that of Mr. Shepherd . . . From Seamus's, knowing him as I do, it has indeed exacerbated the rivalry."

"I see."

"This particular case is quite sad, a family wiped out by a drunken driver, with only a baby girl surviving. The insurance company should have settled. They insisted on going to trial. The jury awarded forty million dollars. The company then wanted to settle for fifteen million. We held out for twenty-five. Then Seamus offered to take their case for appeal. It will be a couple of more years before the poor child gets her money."

And before you and Mr. Shepherd get half the money.

"Will he win the appeal?"

"You can never be sure with Seamus how level the playing field is."

"You mean he might bribe the appellate court judges?"

"It wouldn't be the first time . . . Would you like some coffee?"

It had taken her long enough to offer it. I declined. She didn't offer me tea.

"I suppose he bills the insurance company at a high rate?"

"Two thousand dollars an hour, but only if he wins."

"Does Seamus need the money?"

"Certainly he doesn't need it. Neither for that matter does Mr. Shepherd. Seamus, however, wants to win. He likes to take big risks and win big. He's always been that way. I'll spare you a psychoanalytic explanation."

"Do you think he seriously believes that you and Mr. Shepherd were behind the attempt to kill him?"

"I really don't know what he believes. When he gets

into a fight, he often walks close to the edge of madness. We are very angry at him, that I admit. Kill him? That's absurd, no matter what I might have said to him in a moment of anger."

She buzzed her secretary for coffee. I thought she was wearing thin around the edges.

"It was a similar case that led to your departure from Costelloe and Associates, was it not?"

"We were on the plaintiff's side then. I brought in the case. He promised me a partnership if we won. I worked hard, even though I was a single mother with a troubled child. I did all the research, drafted all the briefs, handled most of the questioning. He rarely appeared in court till the end. I admit that he delivered a powerful summation."

"He pocketed his half of the money and gave you nothing?"

"Only the usual Christmas bonus. No partnership of course."

A pretty black woman brought in a cup of coffee for Helen.

"Would you like something, Mr. Coyne?" she asked me.

"Would you ever have a cup of tea?"

"I would indeed."

Big smile. "Milk and sugar?"

"I don't pollute my tea with that stuff."

Even bigger grin.

Ms. Shepherd drummed her fingers nervously on the desk until her secretary left the office.

"That was about the time that my brief affair with Seamus came to an end . . . Actually it was such a trivial interlude that it hardly merits the name. Diane has no sense of her husband's sexual needs, which is not all that surprising given her personality. Seamus himself, incidentally, is not all that great a lover, though he thinks he is."

Did she seduce him? Probably.

Or was I thinking like a male chauvinist pig? I'd have to ask herself.

"You left the firm after the Christmas bonus?"

"I threatened to drag him into court and create a scandal. I would have charged that we had a handshake agreement on a partnership. I might have won. He merely laughed and told me to go right ahead. Mr. Shepherd advised me against it and hired me here as a full partner."

So Len Shepherd had won a woman away from Seamus Costelloe, a defeat the latter would not appreciate, even if he had dumped the woman. Shepherd, Irish and Catholic despite his name, had a reputation for collecting a string of young women lawyers as mistresses and then setting them up with partnerships in major firms when the relationship lost its spark. None of these women seem to have anything but affection for him. He was a courtly and charming fellow. However, none of these other women were hired by his firm or became candidates for marriage. It was said "on the street" that Helen had insisted on annulments of both their first marriages. Len must have been besotted by her.

"If the cases went through our Tribunal," George the Priest had assured me, "it was on the up and up. No extra fees. Maybe a few tickets for Notre Dame or Bulls games—given but not asked for. Hurried up a little? Maybe but not much. Our annulment factory is efficient and straight."

"You don't approve of annulments?"

"I think the German bishops have it right. Let the divorced and remarried receive the sacraments and be done with it. Enough of them are doing it in this country anyway."

Ms. Shepherd's charming assistant brought me in my mug of tea.

"So Seamus is quite out of his mind if he thinks we would waste our time on something as tawdry as hiring a gangster to shoot him."

"If he were out of the picture, however, it would make it more likely that the insurance company would settle, would it not?"

"And a lot of money is involved and neither of us has any love for Seamus. However, Mr. McGrail, we are not killers—tort lawyers maybe, but not killers."

She smiled lightly, as if she were joking.

"So you are not particularly amused by Seamus's threats to kill you if there is another attempt on his life?"

She did not blink.

"I'm sure he's threatened a dozen people with such a fate, a regular *Gotterdammerung* of enemies blotted from the face of the earth. No one who knows Seamus would take such foolishness seriously."

She waved her hand slightly, the only gesture of the morning, to dismiss the possibility of an ocean of blood if Seamus should die.

"The question is would Seamus take it seriously?"

"He might. You can never tell with him when he's joking and when he's serious. However, why should the potential hit men not simply pocket the money he's paid them and forget about the contracts? The only honor among such men is fear of the Boys and this is not a contract from the West Side, should there be any contract at all."

"So you and Mr. Shepherd have not taken any special precautions?"

"Neither of us are fools, Mr. McGrail. We are fully prepared to go into hiding if Seamus is shot again. Moreover, some friends we have with West Side contacts are monitoring stories about such contracts. They hear nothing. It would have been very difficult for Seamus to plan mass murder without their knowing of it."

She rose as though it were time for me to leave.

I nursed my tea.

"One last question, Ms. Shepherd: who might have tried to kill Seamus Costelloe as he was leaving his office in this very building?"

"I have no idea, Mr. McGrail. None at all. Seamus has so many enemies that it would be hard to select one of them. He might have set it up all himself and have been more seriously wounded than he intended."

I finished my tea and left. Nothing like a conversation with Mary Helen Cross O'Leary Shepherd to chill out a lovely spring day.

At home, our tiny daughter in the nursery now was still irritable.

"She doesn't have a fever," Nuala reported to me. "She won't eat, she won't sleep, she just cries. I'm really worried."

"You call the doctor?"

"Three times, poor dear woman. She says sometimes babies become nervous because they decide that they want to go back into the womb where life was much nicer. They just have to learn to cope with the fact that they can't."

The thundering herd came up the stairs, two dogs, one red-haired panting girl child.

"We went to the doggie park with Ethne and they ran and they ran and the other dogs were all scared except one mean Rottweiler who snapped at Maeveen and did they scare him!"

The dogs were panting happily too. Nothing like chasing away an obstreperous Rottweiler.

"What's the matter with baby?"

"She's fidgety and restless, won't eat, won't sleep, won't do anything," I said.

"Little brat!" Nellie leaned over the bassinet and glared at her sister.

Then she smiled and began to hum lullaby melodies, no particular lullaby, just a kind of generic tune.

Socra Marie stopped fidgeting and listened. Nellie rocked the bassinet gently. She continued to hum her nonsense tunes.

Socra Marie sighed and closed her eyes. Big sister stopped humming and seem to concentrate on her.

"She was mad at me," Nellie explained to us, "because I hadn't paid any attention to her the last couple of days. She wants us to stew over her all the time. She really is a spoiled brat. I suppose I was too at that age."

So saying, Nellie bounded back down the stairs with the hounds following her.

"You saw that?" I asked my wife

"It's scary, Dermot Michael . . . What are we to do?"

"We are going to let Nellie talk to her sister as often as she wants and thank the good Lord that she's on our staff."

Nuala Anne made a fervent sign of the cross.

"I never did that, Dermot Michael. Never, except maybe once or twice when I was in school and baby-sitting for a little brat in Carraroe. I talked real nice to her and she quieted down, just like herself . . ."

"Wasn't that nice."

We slipped out of the nursery and into Nuala's office, where I could report on the day's adventure at the IBM Building.

"She's just used to Nellie's red hair and missed it," I said confidently. "Nellie is part of her little world. She wants her around."

"And maybe the dogs too," Nuala said with a giggle.

We were both whistling in the dark, but that was all right. Our little girl was sleeping peacefully again.

Nuala listened carefully to my account of the conversation with Helen Shepherd.

"Bitch," she said. "And herself driving her poor first husband to drink!"

"Maybe," I admitted. "She's not a nice person. She's spent a lot of her life surrounded by men who are even less nice. She's survived because she has learned to protect herself with pretty tough skin."

Nuala nodded grudgingly.

"It used to be, Dermot Michael, that families protected their daughters from such gombeen men. Now women are on their own and there's no one to protect them. We even like to think we don't need protection."

It was a strange statement from a feminist like my wife. Nuala, however, never let ideology interfere with reality.

"'Tis a jungle," she continued, "and there's lots of predators out there."

"Shepherd is supposed to be a nice man."

"A lion king who doesn't eat the females in his pride!"

"Like Seamus?"

"Who knows about Seamus? Do you think he's been unfaithful to Diane?"

I paused to ponder that one.

"Probably, but not very often and not for very long. His conscience is Irish Catholic—on sex anyway."

"You know, Dermot Michael, he may even be an honest man according to his own lights. People try to cheat him, he fights back. Sometime we have to hear his side of the stories."

"I agree."

"He certainly hasn't put out all those contracts, has he now?"

"I doubt it."

"He's probably having a big laugh over it all, the poor friggin' gobshite!"

"I see the two lawyers next?"

"First thing tomorrow. They'll be having the same story for you, the nine-fingered shite hawks. They were poor helpless innocents and this inhuman monster cheated them out of their money. And they'll expect you to be enough of a friggin' eejit to believe that."

"Your man," I replied, "knew how to pick passive-aggressive associates."

"And family except for that sweetheart Sonia, who may give them all some backbone."

"You think Seamus might make a pass at her?"

"Give over, Dermot Michael Coyne, and yourself an expert on the culture of Chicago Irish Catholics. He might think about it, but he'd also think about the guilt afterwards and reckon that it wasn't worth the cost."

"What about his affair with Helen?"

"I wouldn't believe a word that bitch said!"

"Which one do you think might have put out a contract on Seamus?"

"None of the above." She sighed. "Pretty soon, Dermot Michael, we'll run out of suspects."

"Do you think that Seamus is sending us on a wild-goose chase?"

She pondered that thought carefully.

"He might be, Dermot love. He might just be and himself the only one of the whole lot who is a real gombeen man."

We fed the little nuisance and put her to bed. Then we visited the nursery and tucked in the other two, who were delighted at our attention.

Then we returned to our own bedroom, checked the child's vital signs, and went to bed. I don't know about my wife, but I was in the land of Nod immediately.

Sometime later, midnight, I thought, we heard her scream of hunger.

"Bloody shite!" Nuala exploded.

I went back to sleep grateful that technology had yet to find a way for fathers to feed their babies.

Sometime later, in the depth of night when the ghosts and goblins and the beasties are about, she demanded food once again.

My exhausted wife woke up, fed the little brat,

burped her, changed her diaper, and collapsed back into bed next to me.

"Are you asleep, Dermot Michael?"

"I am."

"I don't suppose you would want to make love at this ungodly hour."

"I would not."

"I thought not."

She snuggled up to me.

"Especially to a messy and smelly woman such as meself?"

"'Tis yourself you had in mind?"

"I half thought so?"

"Well, I guess it might be all right, now that you mention it."

A man and a woman can't make satisfying, much less ecstatic love under such circumstances, you say?

Sure, you don't know me wife at all, at all if you think that.

— 16 —

August 19, 1886

The summations are almost finished. The jury will retire this afternoon and after sham deliberations will reach a decision. Tomorrow morning they will find the defendants all guilty of murder, even Nebbe, whom Grinnell wants to release because there is not the slightest hint of evidence against him. However, the General has heard that Gary will insist on twenty-five years in prison and Oscar with a very sick wife at home. Then Gary will adjourn till October to continue sentencing. The adjournment is not out of any consideration for the Anarchists but because of the intolerable heat in the courthouse on Michigan Street. None of the wealthy people in Chicago can be expected to postpone any longer their jaunts to Wisconsin or the Indiana and Michigan Dunes.

I ate lunch with the General, who was in one of his rare melancholy moods.

"What will they think of us in the next century, lad? It's only fourteen years way, you know?"

"They'll think we're savages and barbarians who are prepared to execute innocent men after a sham trial."

"All of us?"

"*There might be a few footnotes about those who re-sisted the rush to judgment, sir. Not much else, not un-less we achieve some sort of clemency or pardon.*"

"*Bill Black has done a fine job. I think you'll like the end of his summation this afternoon. It's difficult to re-ply to Julie Grinnell when he announces as he did yes-terday, that even if these men are not killers personally, they are Anarchists and that makes them murderers.*"

"*It's too bad that they have said and written enough foolishness, sir, to lend some plausibility to that line of reasoning.*"

"*Ah, well, if it wasn't that it would be something else . . . What will they say about all our immigrants who are under attack especially by that bigot Joe Medil over at the Trib, as much as are your friends over in the Michigan Street Jail?*"

"*They might wonder why the immigrants didn't re-alize what was being done to them, even the Ger-mans, who are by far the more sophisticated of the immigrants.*"

"*You have the right of it, Ned.*" He sighed. "*As al-ways.*"

"*I don't know whether we're doing enough,*" I said, slipping into Nora's habit of sighing.

"*What else can we do?*"

On that uncertain note our lugubrious lunch ended. I hiked across the city to the River under the implaca-ble August sun. There was a huge throng of people, horses, carriages, carts, wagons waiting at the Rush Street bridge as tugs escorted a line of lumber schooners up the River to Wolf Point. The dust of the lumberyards, the smoke from factories, the sickening stench of people, animals and manure made me wish I was back at Geneva Lake. Why had I ever left it?

Chicago is the busiest port in the world. On many days during the shipping season a hundred schooners appear at the mouth of the River, which is as crowded as streets on either side of the River.

Trade in the lumber schooners is declining, despite the denial from the shipping companies and the lumberyards. The demand for milled lumber is greater than ever but the supply is vanishing. No one had bothered to think that Michigan might run out of trees.

The lumberyards, up and down the River, are dangerous places. Men die when cranes fail and tons of wood fall on them. Others collapse from the heat and the dust. Anyone with a tendency to tuberculosis might take sick at the yards and be dead before they arrive at the hospital.

As I waited for the bridge to come down, I thought of the lumber shover who had moved to the fringes of our family. He wanted to be a lawyer, not necessarily a mortal sin. Why could he not work at the General's office next summer and read the law? He was a bright and quick young man. He could pick up enough law to pass the bar examination the same year he graduated from college (which is what I did). He wouldn't risk another year in the hell of the lumberyards.

There were problems in such a solution. He didn't seem given to any excessive pride. Yet he might still resent the offer of a decent summer job. The General, master of blarney that he is, could make it look like Timmy was doing us a favor.

There remained the more serious problem of Josie. Would she feel we were putting undue pressure on her if we brought Timmy into the family business with the hint of a hint that we were bringing him into the family. There was no telling how a strong-willed young woman like Josie might react. I would ask Nora what she thought . . .

No, that wouldn't be right. I should ask Josie directly. Not for the first time did I tell myself that I was much too young to have a daughter Josie's age.

The line of schooners finally passed, followed by the noisy curses of those who had been waiting. I was *grateful for the time to think about something besides the trial.*

Inside the oven of the courtroom on Michigan Street, William Black was finishing his defense summation. The General, who had written much of it, had as usual been correct. It was a carefully reasoned argument that you could not have a conspiracy to murder unless you knew who the murderer was. Since the police had let Schnaubult, the alleged bomb thrower, slip through their fingers, Julie Grinnell could not link the defendants with him as a murderer. It was an elementary point of law on the basis of which an honorable judge would have had to dismiss the indictment.

The judge did not listen. He was busy drawing pictures of birds for the young ladies on the bench with him. Several of the jurors were asleep. The crowd in the courtroom was bored. They wanted fire. Earlier in the day Julie had told the jury that anarchy itself was murder and that it was their duty to convict the murderers.

This was legal nonsense. I assume Julie knew it. Perhaps Judge Gary knew it too. Neither of them cared. Their masters in the plutocracy and the newspapers demanded hanging. So hanging there would be.

Interestingly enough, Julie had in the morning suggested that Oscar Nebbe might be released as there was not a "preponderance of evidence" against him. The Judge seemed hostile to the suggestion.

"We will see what the jury has to say about Herr Nebbe," he observed pontifically.

There wasn't a "preponderance of evidence" against anyone. Nebbe looked less like an anarchist than any of the others. Perhaps Julie hoped that by freeing one of them he would create an illusion of judicious fairness, for which the press would praise him. I doubted that my friend Cy McCormick would be pleased.

"Everyone wants to get this over with," one of my colleagues yawned. "Save the hangings for November."

"It will take longer than that," I replied. "After the sentences, there will be appeals to the circuit courts and the Illinois Supreme Court and maybe even the United States Supreme Court. I hear there's going to be a clemency movement too. There'll be news in this trial for years to come."

"Just so long as there's no more summer trials."

I ignored the comment.

"You really think these guys didn't do it, Ned?"

"There's not a shred of evidence against them that would stand up in a fair courtroom."

"I know that. Everyone knows that. Julie's argument comes to that we know they did it anyway and we don't need evidence."

"Would you want to be convicted that way?"

"Hell, no! But I don't throw bombs at cops!"

"I was there, Hank. They didn't either."

He grunted, not caring much one way or another.

He was a working journalist. He wrote what his editors wanted him to write. He couldn't afford, if he wanted to keep his job, to ask himself too many ethical questions.

I, on the other hand, was a "gentleman journalist" with a lot of clout. Hank and the others did not enjoy the freedom I took for granted. Somehow they didn't resent me. They even praised my work. Not fair.

"What's your lead going to be?" he asked me.

"Captain Black: No proof of conspiracy!"

"That will stir the boys up. How long do you think it will take them to reach a verdict?"

"They won't let it interfere with a dinner over at the Revere House."

"Probably not . . . Well, they'll be able to tell their grandchildren that they were on the jury that convicted the Haymarket Anarchists and lived in the finest hotel in the city while they were doing it."

"In years to come that might not be a matter of pride."

I redid my headline:

JURORS NAP DURING BLACK'S SUMMATION.

I wrote the story during Judge Gary's extravagant charge to the jury. Marshall Field could not have done a better job of warning them that a failure to convict the defendants would lead to a wave of explosions all over America. Conviction, on the other hand, would destroy anarchism for fifty years.

That gave me a lead for tomorrow's story:

JUDGE URGES CONVICTION OF DEFENDANTS

At least some of my readers would know enough about law to catch the irony.

My editor did.

"Ned, you are either the bravest or the craziest reporter in Chicago."

"Perhaps both."

"As well as being the only sober one."

"That may be my problem."

"You infuriate Field and Pullman and McCormick."

"At least they read me."

"That's a point well taken . . . Still you have to live and work in this city."

"So do they."

He laughed.

Gently, as was his custom (strange in an editor), he was trying to warn me that eventually the pressure of the plutocrats might outweigh whatever appeal my writing might have and the clout of the General.

If that happened, then I'd practice law and write for the national magazines. Law is not the most honorable of professions, but it is marginally more honorable than journalism.

As I walked back to the River, sickened by the stench and the heat and the corruption, I told myself that someday Chicago would be a beautiful city. The Lake invited the city to turn it into a playground. Someday the children of that 70 percent of the city who were immigrants would run the city. Someday men like Cy McCormick would not be able to think they owned it.

Then I thought of the women—Lucy Parsons, Nina VanZandt, Metta Nebbe, even the pretty German girl with gold cuff links for Louis Lingg—except for Nina they would return to their suffocating little hovels, hot and exhausted like the rest of us, yearn for their men, hope for justice, and begin to resign themselves to lives of loneliness and the struggle to keep alive the memories of their martyred heroes.

Martyrs!

Yes surely that's what they would be called. I pulled out my notebook and wrote it down.

Finally, the Clark Street bridge opened, and we poured across it. I faced a mile and a half walk home. I was desperate to hug Nora, remove my vest and waistcoat, and relax in the garden with a single glass of Irish whiskey. Yet I lacked the energy to hurry.

Even my magical Irish Princess, I thought, could not blot out the ugliness of what this city is doing.

Later in the garden in summer garb and with a glass of lemonade—Nora said that whiskey would only depress me more—I began to relax. I was not a hero, not a crusader for justice, certainly not a martyr. Yet I was doing what I could. Please God, I hope that is enough.

Nora went into the house for another pitcher of lemonade. A touch of a breeze drifted in from the Lake. Maybe tomorrow there would be rain. I was half-asleep.

"Well, Ned," said my mysterious friend through the wooden fence around the garden, "you do know how to take your ease, don't you now?"

"You again."

"*Meself indeed. That was a disgrace in the court to-day, wasn't it?*"

"*Especially since we both know who did throw the bomb.*"

"*We couldn't prove it, could we now?*"

"*We certainly couldn't.*"

"*Did you recognize him when the idiot stumbled across your path?*"

That was the question I feared. Might the answer be my death warrant?

"*I know he's from Galway. He was on the edge of things over there, watching. I didn't know his name then and I still don't.*"

"*Ay. His name doesn't matter much. He has a lot of them. He's always on the edge of things, a great one for watching.*"

Silence.

"*You shouldn't be afraid of him, Ned. We're on your side. You're the man who saved Myles Joyce's widow and child.*"

Fenians of some sort.

"*I love them both,*" I said fervently.

"*All the better. Don't try to find him. He's not worth your trouble. I wouldn't tell you that if I thought that finding him might save their lives. We both know that it wouldn't.*"

Suddenly I understood everything as though a streak of lightning that had exploded in my brain. Then the light faded and with it my insight. It would come back, however. I would know the answer, for whatever that would be worth.

"*Why do you bother telling me these things?*"

"*Because we think we ought to.*"

Then he wasn't there anymore.

Because I was the husband of Myles Joyce's widow. And General Fitzpatrick's son.

You took your blessings where you could find them.

Nora came back with the pitcher of lemonade.

"Now that the trial is over," I said, "we might go back to the Camp."

"Won't there be more to write about?"

"The Tribune will start a campaign to raise a hundred thousand dollars to pay the jurors for their verdict."

"How terrible!"

"The public will lose interest until Judge Gary pronounces sentence. Then there will be much to write about. If we can present them and their families in a sympathetic light, it might help the campaign for clemency."

"Save some of them?"

"The General thinks so."

"Then"—she smiled as she did when making affectionate fun of her father-in-law "it must be true!"

After a pause, she asked, "You're sure they're innocent, Ned?"

"They're guilty of many things, Nora—of misreading the temper of Chicago workers, of idiotic rhetoric, of Germanic stubbornness, of lack of concern for their wives and children, of sweet innocence, of blind zeal, and a host of other crimes I could think of were it not so hot, but of murder, no. None of them are capable of murder, with the possible exception of Lingg and he didn't kill anyone."

"No more guilty than my Myles."

Nora rarely spoke of her first husband. He was in a walled-off but not forgotten part of her life. I refused to intrude into her privacy unless and until she wanted me to.

"A lot more stupid and probably not as brave, but no more guilty. Myles would have lived if he could have. They would rather die for their cause than live for their families."

We then sat there in silence until darkness slipped in over the Lake.

"I'll make you a bite of tea," she said softly.

Afterwards, when I was in my study writing in this diary, Josie bounced by.

"Young woman!"

"Yes, Uncle Neddie," she said, with an entirely false tone of obedient docility.

"Could I have a word with you?"

"I haven't done anything wrong, Uncle Ned, not a thing. At least nothing you know about."

The first time I had seen Josie she was an ill-clad, undernourished urchin with a dirty face and sad, winsome smile who acted as the royal court for her aunt who was surely an Irish queen—or would have been if England had left Ireland alone. She also seemed to know unerringly when I would ride up to Nora's cottage. She would appear on the road at exactly the same moment I would, whether to protect her aunt or to make clear her fealty I did not know at first. As time went on we conspired to provide food and clothing for Nora and then for the infant Mary Elizabeth. Nora knew of these conspiracies but pretended she did not. Josie was not only sly about protecting Nora from the truth, she was also sly about pretending that Nora didn't know whatever truth at which she had guessed.

It was difficult to link that shy, elfin little waif with the beautiful young woman she had become—until she smiled.

In my study she sat down, without being asked, something none of us would have thought of doing if we were called into the General's study.

I was not, however, the General.

"I wanted to talk about Timmy Hardiman."

"That toad!"

"Are we mad at him now?"

"Well, not really."

"I am concerned about him."

Sudden Josie was very serious.

"Is there something wrong?" she said anxiously. "Has he done something wrong?"

I am making a mess of it. I am too young to have a daughter this old.

"Certainly not. He's a fine young man."

"I don't like the idea of him working in the yards again next summer." She sighed as her aunt would.

"Neither do I, Josie. That's what I want to talk about."

"We're going to conspire!" she clapped her hands. "How wonderful! Just like in Ireland."

"I understand he wants to be a lawyer."

"You yourself said, Uncle Ned, that there are less honorable professions!"

"To do that he must study law, either in a law school or in a law office—like the General's, beginning next summer."

Her eyes flooded with tears.

"O, Uncle Ned, you're so sweet!"

"That is perhaps debatable. Regardless of what may or may not happen between you two, he would be, I am convinced, a strong asset to the office."

"Did Nora speak to you?"

"She speaks to me a lot, Josie, as you may have noticed. But not about Timmy."

"I wanted to ask you and I was afraid to and she said I should and I'm glad I didn't because it's nicer this way."

So little do I understand women!

"We could ask the General if he'd invite him in that embarrassed way of his which would make Timmy think he's doing the General a favor."

"Perfect," she exploded. "I have to tell Nora."

She bounded out of my study, then bounded back in and hugged me.

"Uncle Ned, you're a real angel. You saved Nora, and you saved me, and now you're going to save my poor dear Timmy. God sent you into the world to save people."

Then she dashed out again to seek her aunt.

I had never been called an angel before. I am certainly not a messenger for God. So far in life the people I have saved have been grace for me.

Nora would be very pleased with me.

She would say how wonderful I had been with poor dear Josie.

I was pleased with myself.

Until I began to think again about the Haymarket Martyrs.

"ISN'T HE a wonderful man, Dermot Michael?"

"Who?" I looked up from the *New York Times*.

"Uncle Ned!"

"The trouble with him, poor dear man," I replied, "is that he has so little confidence in himself. He's let the General intimidate him."

"Give over, Dermot, you're just saying things like that to tease me. You know as well as I do that he intimidates the General and just about everyone else including poor Nora."

I didn't know that at all. At all. Yet Ned Fitzpatrick's ironic and reckless integrity would scare anyone.

"Well, thank goodness I don't intimidate anyone."

"Sure didn't you intimidate me something terrible in bed last night?"

"You started it!"

"And weren't you after finishing it!"

Our flirtation with ecstasy the night before had apparently perked my wife up. She had run with the dogs, leaving me in charge of Socra Marie for a half hour. She charged up and down the stairs like she used to. She held the child in her arms and pretended to dance with her, much to the brat's apparent delight.

"You know, Dermot Michael," she said as though she were pondering a great philosophical truth, "I think this daughter of ours is developing a personality of her own."

"Ah?"

I gave up on the *New York Times* editorials. They were pompous bunk anyhow.

"WELL, she has a very strong will and a mind of her own and she wants to be the center of attention all the time and she has a great sense of humor and she knows she's beautiful and wants to be told that repeatedly."

"Sounds autobiographical."

My wife cocked her head, trying to be certain she'd understood me.

"Fair play to you, Dermot Michael! She's my daughter, isn't she?"

"No doubt about that!"

"Now let's be serious again!"

She put the daughter back in her bassinet, where the child returned to kicking her legs up and down as though she were riding an imaginary bicycle.

"About what should we be serious?"

"About poor Seamus, naturally!"

"What about him?

"Who's trying to kill him and when he tries again?"

"There's going to be another effort?"

"Oh, yes, that's the whole point. If we can stop the next effort, then the mark of death will leave him until his natural time comes around."

There were metaphysical and theological issues in that sentence I did not want to address.

"Tell me again why we're concerned about that nine-fingered shite hawk."

"How should I know, Dermot Michael? Why should we be concerned about the Haymarket riot that happened a hundred and fourteen years ago, even if it is nice to meet Ned and Nora and Josie again? I suppose because Ned thinks it's time to tell the truth and he wants us to do it for him just like we told the truth about the death of Myles Joyce?"

Ned Fitzpatrick, now happy in the World-to-Come with his wife and family, suddenly decided that the truth about the bomb should be told and nudged my wife's psychic sensitivities?

That laconic, ironic, brave and tender man surely had better things to do. What difference does history make to the blessed?

Still, what did I know?

"You don't see the mark of death . . ."

"Violent, evil death, more evil than just plain death."

"You don't see it on many people?"

"Hardly any."

"But when you do see it, you have an obligation to protect the person who is so marked?

"I do, Dermot Michael, else why would I see it?"

SHE'S DAFT YOU KNOW. SHE'S OVER THE TOP ALTO-GETHER. YOU'RE ENDANGERING YOURSELF AND YOUR WHOLE FAMILY BY ENCOURAGING THIS SHITE!

Shit!

"Mike the Cop's people are protecting him now, so he should be safe."

"There's still someone out there who wants him dead!"

"Who?"

"I think I know but still we have to talk to those two lawyer gobshites!"

"Who?"

She checked our wisp of a daughter to make sure she was still breathing, walked over to her desk and on a sheet of green note paper headed NUALA ANNE wrote in her long, firm handwriting a name and an explanation, hiding the text of her note from my eyes with her hand. Then she put it in an envelope with the same return address, sealed the envelope, and put it in her desk.

"Mind you, I'm not sure. But I don't think I'm all that far from wrong."

Which meant that the odds were that she was right. She'd done this before and I resented it because she was guessing. She had no right to guess.

"Why do I have to interview those two shite hawk lawyers if you know who took the shot at him over in the IBM Building?"

"I didn't say that I knew who took the first shot. I'm saying I have a pretty good idea who's going to take the next shot and you have to talk to McGourty and McGinty so I'll know I'm right."

"Fair play to you, Nuala Anne." I sighed. "I'm off to see them."

I raised the sleeping child out of her bassinet and kissed her good-bye.

"Take good care of your mother, Socra Marie, she's a little bit over the top these days."

The baby opened her eyes, looked at me with something like disgust, then closed them and went back to sleep.

My wife giggled. "Well, I guess she told you, poor sweet little thing!"

I left before the two of them ganged up on me.

McGourty and McGinty occupied a cubbyhole office filled with the smell of cheap cigars and cheaper cologne in the Conway Building across from the County Building half of the City Hall/County Building. There was no hint of a secretary or a staff, no computer, no fax, only a single phone on a littered desk behind which the two of them sat like a modern Irish American version of Tweedledum and Tweedledee, two short, fat, bald unsmiling trial lawyers gone to seed. Several years ago, I imagined, they would be wearing baseball hats turned backwards and Notre Dame sweatshirts. Now they wore unpressed black three-piece suits which might well have been pur-

chased five or six years ago off the same rack. Brian
McGourty and Kevin McGinty were the kind of legal
hacks who had always gone for what looked like the
main chance only to find out that it really wasn't. Now
they were ambulance chasers and low-level city hall
operators.

How could Seamus Costelloe have ever worked
with such lowlifes?

"We are not sure we ought to talk to you, Mr. Mc-
Grail," McGourty began.

"We consider Mr. Costelloe's charges to be defama-
tory," McGinty continued, "and are considering going
into the circuit court of Cook County to seek relief."

"My name is Dermot Coyne," I said, "Ms. McGrail
is my wife."

"Irregardless," they said together.

"I believe that Mr. Costelloe has warned you that
your lives will be in danger if there is another attempt
to kill him. Knowing Mr. Costelloe, I'm sure you take
those threats seriously."

"Enough to have submitted a petition to the Board
of Governors of the Chicago Bar Association to dis-
bar him."

"Yet you once worked closely with him," I said
softly, hoping that they would spill out their hatred
for him.

"Yes, we were younger and we idolized his legal
success." McGinty replied. "He invited us into his
firm. We were flattered and accepted. We understood
that we were partners in the firm and that we had a
handshake agreement on that."

In fact they were not very old, younger certainly
than Helen Shepherd. The stench of failure which
clung to them made them look old.

"We brought many personal injury cases to his attention," McGourty continued, "with our help, he
made a great deal of money on the cases. When it
came to the dispersal of funds, we were underpaid."

"We protested to him. He acknowledged that there might have been a certain inequity in the dispersal. We proposed a formal arrangement. He accepted it. Then, when he won a huge settlement from an insurance company, we asked for a share that the agreement had specified. He laughed and said that such a dispersal applied only to cases that went to trial, not to those that were settled without trial."

"I see."

"We calculate that with due consideration of interest monies that are due to us, he owes us in excess of five million dollars."

"Each . . . And we are vigorously pursuing our requests for relief in both state and federal jurisdictions. The playing field is not even. Mr. Costelloe has the resources and the influence to bribe judges at every level. Nonetheless, every time he obtains a fraudulent dismissal of our claims, we file yet another motion for relief. We will not be deflected from our pursuit of justice."

"Never!"

These two lived in their own world of legal argot and constant legal activity, unaware that they had lost touch with reality. As long as they lived they would fight Seamus with unflagging hope in the will of the wisp—an honest judge who would at last see the justice of their claims.

"Has not Mr. Costelloe sought to settle your claims?"

"Naturally." McGourty shifted in his chair as if he were brushing off a troublesome fly.

"Like all lawyers," McGinty continued, "he would rather settle than litigate, always, candidly, on his terms."

"Candidly" meant the same thing on their lips as it did on the lips of Newt Gingrich.

"He is oblivious to the value of our claims. We would accept three, even two million dollars, arguably a little less, so that we might be free of the burden of fighting him. He laughs when we mention sums like that."

These two men, I reflected, needed a good lawyer to tell them the truth. A good lawyer, however, was the last thing they wanted.

"How long will you pursue him?"

"To the grave," McGinty snapped.

"Kevin means," his colleague quickly interjected, "that we will never give up. We were faced with that question when someone shot him. If it were necessary we would pursue our actions against his estate. Candidly we presume that the lawyers for the estate would be less inclined to risk their careers by turning judges than Mr. Costelloe is."

In their own hermetically sealed world, these two losers had excellent reason to wish Seamus dead. Would they hire hit men to shoot him? Somehow it didn't seem likely that they had the energy to do that. They would continue to file motions and to chase ambulances for less prestigious lawyers than Seamus Costelloe. Beyond that they would be content that justice would finally come down on their side.

"Yet the police seem to think that you had reason to commission a contract killing of Mr. Costelloe."

"Candidly that is an outrageous allegation," McGourty exploded.

"There is no evidence of that at all."

"Our reputations are at stake."

"If these defamations continue, we are fully prepared to seek appropriate redress."

"I hardly endorse them," I said reassuringly. "I'm merely asking you for your reactions."

A thin layer of saliva appeared on McGinty's lower lip.

"We talked to the police. They were very difficult at first. We offered to take lie detector tests. That offer remains on the table. They seemed to have lost interest."

McGourty was squirming restlessly in his chair.

"Presumably they looked into our reputation for probity and decided that the complaints Mr. Costelloe made against us were absurd."

"Frankly we talked to the police about Mr. Costelloe's threats against us. They did not take our complaints seriously."

"Costelloe has threatened you?"

He had threatened everyone. This dynamic duo were the only ones to tell the police. The cops took their story no more seriously than they had seriously considered these two losers as capable of plotting a contract killing.

Which was so inept, come to think of it, that it might have been the work of losers. Amateur night.

"A thug came into this office and threatened us with horrible deaths if there was another attempt on Mr. Costelloe's life. He dismissed our protestations of innocence with a sneer."

The twosome were now considerably agitated. Seamus's goon must have been very persuasive. He must also have enjoyed scaring the daylights out of a half dozen people. I had no reason, in fact, to conclude that Seamus had not threatened a half dozen more of his enemies—or a dozen. The ones we knew about were the ones whose names the determined Sonia had been able to pry out of her future father-in-law.

"We cannot imagine"—the saliva was now drooling down McGourty's chin—"why of all his enemies, Mr. Costelloe would think that we would be involved in such nonsense. It makes no sense."

"Who would make sense?"

"Jimmy Gigante," McGinty said promptly. "Seamus took his development away from him, a development in which Jimmy put all his money . . ."

"And all his hopes. If Mr. Costelloe were out of the picture, Gigante would have some hope of reclaiming his investment."

"Yet Mr. Costelloe chooses to blame us and to threaten us. Candidly we believe that he is losing his mind."

"His behavior has become increasingly irrational."

"Not the Shepherds?"

"They hate him, of course, and with reason. But both are far too cautious to risk their reputations and perhaps even their personal freedom in such a tawdry crime. Gigante on the other hand is Italian. He would certainly have contacts in the organized crime environment who would attempt murder for hire."

"Papageorgiou?"

"Another obvious suspect." McGourty swiped at the saliva and made a worse mess of it. "He is afraid of his own shadow, to say nothing of his abominable mother. However, Greeks are known to settle feuds in this manner."

"And," McGinty continued, "to have long, long memories."

It was time, I decided to escape from the noxious smells in their office and from the even worse smell of personal failure. At one time their parents must have been proud of them when they graduated from law school, young men, as they saw it, of great promise. They must even have been proud when the famous Seamus Costelloe hired them and hoped they would marry some nice South Side Irish girls—losers like them couldn't come from the West Side. What, I wondered, did their families think of them now?

Under somber rain clouds drifting leisurely in from the prairies, I walked to the River, tracing Ned Fitzpatrick's path back towards North Avenue. The River was no longer the disorderly port of the world with schooner sails stacked up as far as 22nd Street. It was lined not with docks and lumberyards but with gracious, elegant skyscrapers. Across from Wolf Point a green glass building shaped the turn of the South Branch and acted as the gate for the River's former rush to the Lake, now forever reversed by euphemistic Water Reclamation District Canal (nee "drainage canal"). Ned had lived into the nineteen thirties; he would have seen the disappearance of the schooners, the appearance of some of the skyscrapers, and the reversal of the River's flow. He would have marveled at all this and would be delighted by the magic beauty of the riverbanks today with their lawns and curving walks and outdoor art exhibitions. My faith said that he knew in some way about all these marvels and rejoiced in them. It also said that if he were really involved in my wife's attempt to solve the mysteries of the past (an involvement which I very much doubted), he would help us in our search.

I shrugged and crossed the River at Clark Street, before an armada of pleasure boats could force the bridge up, offending drivers and pedestrians as much as it did in Ned's day.

At Hubbard Street (Michigan Street in Ned's day), the old courthouse building—built after the demolition of the Haymarket trial court but on the same lines and with some of the same stone, loomed as a quiet remembrance of the past and its injustice. It has become the headquarters of the Board of Health (now presided over by a Catholic nun), then the Traffic Court (whose corruption Ned would have understood), and now a "loft" apartment building for yuppies who do not know or care about the ghosts of the men who had been hung behind it.

"I'm talking like an old man," I told Ned's ironic but gentle spirit. "Before the rains wash me away, I'm catching a cab and going home to my wife, whom I adore as you adored Nora."

Said wife and youngest child were entertaining Sonia, the child resting comfortably in Sonia's arms.

"She's a little miracle," Sonia assured me, "which I suppose is what everyone says. You are so fortunate."

"The child is already a spoiled brat," Nuala Anne

commented, expecting refutation. "She demands adoration from everyone who walks in the house."

Fiona, a half-awake sentinel, thumped her tail against the parlor floor as a greeting to me.

"What did you find out from the two lawyers?"

"South Side Irish creeps, a pair of losers, capable only of submitting sloppy briefs filled with misspelled words."

"I do not understand these things," the always serious Sonia said. "The two kinds of Irish in Chicago look alike to me. However, Seamus says that they are from the West Side!"

"Unthinkable!"

Socra Marie decided that Sonia's arms were as good a place as any in which to return to the world of pleasant dreams. So she did. Sonia gently returned her to the bassinet. Fiona thumped her tail again.

"You understand what we Americans mean when we used the word 'loser'?" I asked.

She smiled briefly and for that instant became very pretty.

"Oh yes."

"Why does Seamus always pick losers to work with?"

She smiled again, this time permitting the smile to linger on her lips. Nuala Anne winked at me.

Outside thunder boomed and lightning seemed to crackle down Southport Avenue.

"He has worked with many who are not losers," Sonia replied. "It is only the losers who might want to kill him."

"None of them, especially the two shysters I met today, seem to have the decisiveness to contemplate murder."

"Especially successful murder," Nuala Anne said mysteriously.

"Is that not why they're so dangerous?" Sonia asked.

"Do you know any of them?" I asked.

"I have not had the pleasure of meeting them," she said formally, without a trace of irony. "However, I suspect the Greeks. They are a very violent people. Also they hate Russians because we think we are better Christians than they are."

It was hard to tell when this woman was joking.

"Could not it be someone in the family?" I asked.

"Of course," she agreed. "All is possible. My Andrew might hire an assassin though he is the most gentle man in the world. I would know if he did. The son-in-law needs money. However, Seamus is paying off his debt. Diane loves him in her own way. I do not think anyone in the family would harm him. I might be wrong of course."

"She might be capable of arranging for a hit," I said to Nuala Anne when Sonia left after the thunder shower stopped.

"Och, Dermot Michael give over! She's much too intelligent. She knows her future depends on Seamus having a long life."

That settled that.

"What next?"

"I think you should pay a visit to your man in his law office and make him tell you the truth."

"How do I do that?"

"The same way you always do. Be your sensitive, sympathetic self, the little priest listening to a confession."

So saying, she leaned over our child and sang a lullaby. In Irish.

— 18 —

ANARCHISTS LAW-ABIDING
CITIZENS: SPIES.

Special to the Chicago Daily News
By Ned Fitzpatrick

August Spies, editor of the now suppressed German
paper Arbeiter-Zeitung, said today that despite their
incendiary propaganda Anarchists in this city are
law-abiding citizens.

"Yes," he said, "we may demonstrate and protest,
but we would never take a human life. If we would
do that we are no different from the police or the
government."

But what about the broadsheets posted before the
incident at the Haymarket calling for revenge and
advising the protestors to bring their arms?

"Most of our people have no arms. No one in the
crowd did. All the weapons were fired by the police.
None of those posters were hung. I forbade it. The
prosecution have not proved that one had been dis-
played."

Mr. Spies has a gentle voice and a pleasant smile.
He speaks much like a teacher whose students
would love him while they were in his class and remember him fondly after they had graduated. Yet

there is a certain propensity to argue in his character and an inclination to be swept away by his own rhetoric.

He was a Catholic once, he says. But he saw a bored priest drink too much at a first communion celebration for young people. That priest is now a bishop and has written a book defending papal infallibility. What kind of religion would permit such a thing? He agrees with Albert Parsons that the only God is humanity.

Might it not be wrong, one wonders, to judge the Church by what one priest, even one bishop does?

A church which can do no better than that, he replies, is not a church that can understand workingmen. Yes, he knows what the priest said at St. Patrick's but most church leaders are on the side of the rich and powerful.

Beneath the sweetness of character there appears a certain Teutonic stubbornness. Does he expect he will be sentenced to death? Of course, he replies. Is not that the whole purpose of the trial, is it not a drama which the plutocrats and the police have designed to reach its fulfillment on the gallows? However, he and his friends have outsmarted them. In fact, the police and the government are on trial. The death of the defendants will be their victory and proof of guilt of the prosecutors. Out of death will come triumph.

Perhaps he is right. That will be a judgment of history. He says that he is willing to stand the judgment of history.

And Miss VanZandt?

The police have forbidden her visits because she is not a member of his family. Therefore they will marry one another. If the police will not permit that marriage in jail, then his brother will act as his proxy. He and Miss VanZandt are very much in love with one another. Then a beatific smile spreads across his face. He has at last found the true love of his life.

Has he thought what will happen to her after his death? Will she not be disowned by her family? Will she not be cast in the role of a martyr's wife for the rest of her life?

Her parents, he replies, support her decision. The aunt will perhaps cut off the inheritance. He lifts his shoulders in protest. Fortunately Miss VanZandt does not care about money.

One leaves his cell feeling that this scholarly, respectable, definitely bourgeois editor is in fact a romantic. He sees himself as a tenor in one of Signor Verdi's operas and Nina VanZandt as the soprano. They will suffer tragically but will conquer in the end.

If only life were an opera.

I do not have to note in this diary that the story I have pasted above delighted my editor, despite the pressures he is experiencing against me. I will probably remain on the staff of the Daily News *until after the executions, which will take place a year from now after the appeal has failed. Perhaps there will be clemency for some of them. Spies would be an excellent candidate for clemency because of his appearance and his voice. The love of the much admired Nina Van-Zandt might lure him away from the final aria in the libretto he has imagined for the more earthy and realistic pleasures of marriage. I doubt it, however. Miss VanZandt is not a real woman but the soprano in his opera who will mourn his passing for the rest of her life.*

I almost write the word "fool."

Yet that is not my judgment to make, is it?

I interviewed Albert Parsons today. Like Spies he is not a workingman. Rather he is an educated man, an Anarchist by political conviction and not by personal experience. He is exuberant. He waits eagerly for the death sentence which, like Spies, he defines as a great victory.

Doubts about his decision to turn himself in for trial?

None at all! I could not permit myself to be deprived of my share of our common victory. This trial and our deaths will awaken the workingmen of America. There will be a "general strike" and the whole crumbling edifice of American capitalism will come tumbling down. He will die confident of victory.

I do not tell him that I think this is mad self-delusion. He and his friends may well be hailed as martyrs. However, there will not be a general strike. The capitalists will have won at least in the short run. I do not tell him that he abandons Lucy and their children to a lonely and impoverished life. Unlike Spies, Parsons is not a tenor on the opera stage. He is rather a tragic hero in a play by Shakespeare. "Good night, sweet prince . . ."

Neither man, however, is able to imagine what the lifelong role for their women, in which they have cast them, can be like.

He lectures me on the economic wisdom of the eight-hour day. If men work less, more men will be needed to sustain the factories. That will mean more money for workers to spend. That in turn will mean prosperity, no more panics like the one fifteen years ago. Men like McCormick will no longer be able to argue that they have to cut wages. In short order poverty and misery will be eliminated.

I don't question his economic theories. He may well be right. I merely wonder whether this is Anarchy or even socialism. It sounds like a variation on American capitalism, a more humane, a more profitable, a more successful capitalism.

He laughs. "Perhaps that it's the truth, Ned. It does not matter after all what we call it. What matters is

*that the working class will no longer be powerless.
The plutocrats, the government, the police will no
longer be necessary!"*

He was far more pragmatic than his German allies.
They had spun out a theory of justice and then tried to
apply it whole to American economic life. Al had
thought out his thesis pragmatically and then applied
it, if necessary piece by piece. Both he and Germans
radiated the enthusiast's gleam in their eyes, but in Al
Parsons gleam there was also a smile.

Yet he is willing to die, expects to die, almost hopes
to die.

Do you think Judge Gary will sentence you to death?

"Certainly! That's what the trial is about! The government of Chicago and of the United States wish to
sacrifice us as the Romans wished to sacrifice Jesus.
We will be a sacrificial ritual, like the Jewish Paschal
lamb. We embrace that fate, as Jesus did."

At some time between now and the execution—
within a year unless I am mistaken—I will write this
interview as one of my stories. Perhaps it will gain
some public sympathy for Parsons, though most of the
good Christians of our city will think it blasphemy.

I ask him if he thinks he will rise from the dead as
Jesus did.

He laughs exultantly.

"Oh, yes, Ned, I do. In a manner of speaking. As
long as workingmen and-women organize and fight
with the plutocrats and especially when they begin to
win their fights we will be alive and well and fighting
with them."

I cannot gainsay that expectation. I ask him what
seems to me to be the critical question: do you believe
that your deaths will hasten the day of the victory of
the working class?

"Certainly. That's why I came back from Wauconda,
to join forces with my colleagues and friends. I do not

doubt that we will notably accelerate the triumph of laborers over the bosses."

I could ask him by how many years his death will accelerate the triumph. That would not be a fair question. Nor do I point out that the Haymarket "incident" ended the eight-hour day movement across the country. The plutocrats managed to persuade the citizenry of America that the eight-hour day was a sign of bloody anarchism.

Instead I ask him about Lucy and little Albert and Lulu.

His shoulders sag and he leans back against the wall of Cook County Jail. For a moment he is no longer the powerful orator with the deep voice that influences even those who dislike him. He becomes the frail little man with the big forehead and the vast handlebar mustache and the sad eyes that he really is.

"It is very hard on Lucy." He sighs. "She has had a difficult life, as you might imagine. She was indeed born a slave. Yet she is an indomitable fighter for workingwomen. She would never want me, indeed never permit me, to turn back from the path we have charted for ourselves."

I think of scatological words to describe what he is saying, but remain silent.

"The police arrest her every time she leaves our tiny apartment, for no other reason than to aggravate the misery in which she lives and the fear she feels for me. But they will not stop her, they cannot stop her. As long as she lives the Haymarket Martyrs will not be forgotten."

And the children?

He winces with pain.

"They are both in poor health, Ned. I worry about them every night when I try to sleep here in the Cook County Bastille. I wish there was a God I might pray to for them. I know that they will grow up proud of me."

If they grow up at all, I think to myself.

We chat a little more. He tells me that he can hardly wait till the court reconvenes and he has his opportunity to tell the whole world what he believes.

"And the whole world will be listening, Ned, the whole world will be listening!"

Doubtless it will.

I leave his cell in a daze. I think what a wonderful politician he would make if he had not rejected the political process as worthless. Certainly nothing had happened since the "incident" which would have caused him to change his mind on that subject, not even the honest testimony of Mayor Carter Harrison at the trial, one of the few defense witnesses that Judge Gary did not harass.

The Mayor will lose the next election because of his testimony. He is a shrewd and resilient fellow, however. He will be back.

I should leave the jail, which depresses me, and pay a visit to Laddy's, which does not depress me, for all its vile smell and foul talk. However, I have to speak with Louis Lingg sometime. It might as well be now.

He is a tall, dark, young man, strong and handsome, vigorous and determined. The General said of him, "He's a warrior. He'd make a fine Captain of an infantry company, say in Napoleon's Grand Army. He would not survive more than a couple of battles of course. He would die with honor and pride and we would have to search for another warrior like him. Warriors are interesting people, Ned. They love battle, they love the killing, they don't seem to mind when someone kills them. Thank God I was never a warrior."

Amen to that.

"I do not wish to speak with hired agents of the plutocrats," *he snarls at me.*

Good beginning.

I compliment him on his cuff links which his girl-

friend had shown me when she brought them to the jail.

"Ja," he melts completely, "my Elise brings them to me. You see the engraving, my initials and hers within a heart. Beautiful, no?"

I wondered how many hours Elise had to work as a maid of all work to buy such jewelry.

She certainly has good taste, I tell him. Probably better than the people for whom she works.

"Ja," he says, sinking back to his cot. "She is a very simple girl, Catholic peasant from Bavaria. Good girl. Loyal girl. I don't deserve her."

Do I see tears in this warrior's dark and normally angry eyes?

"I tell her," he goes on, "that I will wear them when they hang me. She says I must wear them to the grave, so that her heart and mine will be buried together. Brave girl."

Sentimental, romantic Bavarian Catholic girl. Also very brave. We must see that nothing happens to her after the hanging.

Do you have to hang?

"Certainly. I spit on the Judge and the lawyer and the jury. They are defectives. They do me a great honor when they permit me to die for our cause. I am not afraid of them. I am not afraid of death. I laugh at them."

On paper it looks foolish. However, when one hears Louis Lingg speak those words, one understands that his capacity to hate, no, to despise, his prosecutors knows no limits.

And Elise? I ask.

"She does not understand. Naturally. Women do not understand. If this is what I want, however, then she wants it too."

Absolute nonsense, Louis Lingg. I don't know much about women, but I know more than you do. Elise goes along with this nonsense to keep you happy. Yet she prays every night and lights candles every day that somehow you live. She will never tell you that you are a fool. You are, however.

What will happen to her when you and the cuff links are in the ground?

"She will leave Chicago immediately. I tell her not to stay for the funeral. Good, kind German people will take care of her. I tell her that she must forget me. Remember me and forget me. She must have a happy life. She will do as I say."

Will she now?

Catholic peasant women tend to be pragmatists. Pretty young woman that she is, Elise will have no trouble finding herself a steadfast and reliable husband, perhaps a farmer in Iowa or Wisconsin. She will never tell him about Louis Lingg. Yet he will always have a sacred, secret place in her heart.

Unlike the others, Lingg at least cares what happens to his love when he is dead. All these men are different from Myles Joyce and his relatives and friends. The latter did not want to die. Myles fought it to the bitter end, even on the gallows. They were not Fenian revolutionaries who wanted to die to make their point. Myles Joyce would have thought such ideas to be nonsense. He died because a brutal English government was more interested in saving face than in justice. Yet they are heroes in Ireland, perhaps in a way the Haymarket Martyrs will never be.

What do I know?

It is time for Laddy's.

Astonishingly the door is open and a gentle autumn breeze blows in. Outside the trees are turning color. A polite warning that another Chicago winter looms ahead.

"So what's the word, Neddie? Spending time down with them Anarchists on Michigan Street? Did you have fun down there?"

"The jail is not a place to have fun," I say wearily,

doffing my white bowler. "It's an antechamber to Purgatory."

I sip my Irish whiskey. Tonight I will have two of them. The admirable Nora will raise her eyes, but say nothing. I don't know what she would say if I ever came home drunk. I don't want to find out either.

"Are they going to swing?"

"One of them will get off. Jules Grinnell just wants to let him go. Judge Gary will sentence him to twenty-five years."

"Why?"

"Because he is Judge Gary and has the power to do that."

"Bastard!"

"Power is a dangerous possession. Ask Cy McCormick."

Hoots at that hated name.

"Or Captain Schaack."

More hoots, some curses this time.

"Will they swing right away?"

Ghouls looking for sights of death?

"No, there'll be appeals, maybe even to the United States Supreme Court."

"Will they do any good?"

"Delay the executions for a year. Maybe provide the opportunity for sentiment to change towards them. The verdict will stand, however."

"Why, Ned, if it's as bad as you say it is?"

"Because the judges belong to the same clubs as rich people."

Laughter around the room.

"Maybe we should invite them to join our club!"

"You wouldn't want them. They're dull people."

"It's wrong," says a middle-aged teamster, "to hang men for crimes they didn't commit, even if they are Germans."

General rumble of agreement, even from the few Germans who are in the saloon.

"They can hang anyone they want," someone else says. "It isn't fair."

"All they did was support the eight-hour day. What's the crime in that?"

As I expected it would, sentiment among Chicago workers was turning towards the Anarchists. The rich people and their hirelings had taken too long. Another year and there would be strong support for clemency. My colleagues in the press would be ambivalent. The sympathy stories about the families of the condemned men would fill their pages because people wanted to read those stories. On the other hand, the editorials would scream for blood.

No one expects consistency from the press.

What would my friends Gus Spies and Al Parsons do when they were offered the possibility of life which they were now proclaiming they didn't want.

They would be tempted.

I wondered as I walked home whether my mysterious friend would appear. I hoped he would.

However, there was so sign of him.

As usual I told Nora about the events of the day. I did not want to frighten her. On the other hand she is probably more resilient than I am.

"They're a bit daft, aren't they, Ned?"

"They don't believe everything they're saying exactly, Nora. The problem is that if they say it often enough they might come to believe it."

I am concerned about Nora. She is pregnant again. In that condition she is always radiant, glowing with joy over the life that is within her. She is convinced that the child will be a boy because everyone insists that Daddy wants a son.

"Uncle Ned," says Josie, "is outnumbered."

"He and the lad will be outnumbered, won't they?"

says Annie, our servant girl, who has made common cause with the other women in the house, especially our Gracie.

"Well," Josie replies, "at least he'll have someone to talk to. He wouldn't mope around all the time feeling sorry for himself."

So it goes.

I do not care whether it's a boy or a girl. I agree with my parents' philosophy that you take the baby as it comes and love the childeen for what it is. I cannot persuade the flock of women in my house that this is true. So I don't argue.

All I want is a healthy wife. And, secondly, a healthy child. Women die in childbirth, not as often as they do in Ireland, but still too often. Only one in fifty, my mother tells me, and fewer than that when they're cared for properly.

Somehow those odds don't seem very good.

Grace's birth was uncomplicated. She was a paragon of health from her first appearance. Her mother recovered quickly and happily. Still the odds go up, do they not?

From what Josie tells me Nora survived the birth of Mary Elizabeth better than might be expected given the cold and the hunger and her terrible grief because of Myles's death.

After Grace's birth we thought we might not have any more children. We had to wait two years before she came. Then two more years in which nothing happened. My mother suggested that perhaps Nora's hunger during those awful years might be a permanent obstacle to conception.

I hoped it would. Nora wanted more children and I suppose I did in some theoretical way. I did not, however, want my wife to be in danger.

That is foolishness, I tell God. I am sorry. I will rejoice when this child is born just as I rejoiced when

Grace was born. If it is a boy, I will suggest we name him Myles Joyce Fitzpatrick in honor of Nora's first husband.

Nora rarely mentions him. Yet I know she grieves for him and always will. I know nothing about the love between them. Except that she worshiped him totally and completely. I thought they were an odd match, an aging king of an Irish tribe and an orphaned young princess—though that was only an approximation of an Irish-language relationship which was beyond the understanding of anyone who was not part of that ancient and dying culture.

Myles's first wife had died. His children were either dead (in one or the other of the famines) or in America and Australia. Nora's parents died of a disease (perhaps influenza) which almost carried her off. Someone had to take care of her. As the king (or whatever he was) of the tribe she was his responsibility and, I suppose, his pleasure. It would be impossible not to enjoy such a beautiful young woman. However the relationship might have started, it had turned into love by the time I rode up the hill to their house with the constables who were to arrest him for a murder he patently did not commit.

His shrewd eyes must have seen my instant—and I confess lascivious—desire for his wife. I tried to hide it immediately, ashamed as I was of my agonized lust for her.

In the Dublin courtroom where they were trying him for murder in a language he did not understand, he caught my eye several times, smiled and nodded. Was he, I wondered, leaving the princess to me? Was he telling me that she was to be my love, my responsibility, my pleasure when he was gone?

I dismissed this fantasy as a product of my fevered desires. Yet Nora would later tell me that he had said to her the last time they had met, "Now, lass, I'll be leaving you. That good-looking boy with the blond hair in

*the white suit will be taking care of you. He'll be a
grand husband to you and you must be a good wife to
him, like you've been to me. I'll have none of this silly
business of rejecting him, do you hear me now?"*

She almost rejected me just the same and would
have if I hadn't threatened to come and carry her off.
Then in a burst of inspiration (for which I thank God)
I added that I wanted Josie to come with us.

Even on our first night together (on a steamship in
Kinsale) she was a graceful and generous lover. I
couldn't help but thank Myles for that—and wonder
about the mystery of how this love could have developed between them.

It is none of my business, I suppose. I will never ask.
I wonder if she compares her two husbands and how
she rates me in comparison with him. It is a stupid—
and stupidly male—way of thinking. Nora herself
would never think that way. She had two husbands.
They were very different men and that was that.

Why am I writing all of this down today? Perhaps I
have been thinking of leaving wives behind and the
possibility of wives' leaving husbands behind.

I must stop this foolish thinking and join Mrs. Fitzpatrick in our bedroom, where she waits for me, over-
flowing with joy about the prospect of new life coming
into the world.

As I should be. As I soon will be, please God.

Just as I had closed this book, Josie bounces up to
my door.

"Don't worry, Uncle Ned. Nora will be fine."

I am in no mood to argue with my fey niece.

The next morning.

The light was out in our bedroom. I entered quietly,
undressed, and slipped into bed with my, as I supposed, sleeping wife.

"You worry too much, Mr. Fitzpatrick." She sighed.
"You should leave the worries to the women in your
family. That's what women are for."

"They're for other things too, Mrs. Fitzpatrick," I said as my bare shoulder touched hers.

"That's only occasionally. They worry all the time, Mr. Fitzpatrick, to protect their men from worry."

The intensity of the moment loosened my tongue.

"I've been thinking about a name for our son . . ."

"You surprise me, Mr. Fitzpatrick. Why have you concluded that our baby will be a boy?"

"Josie said so. She usually knows things."

" 'Tis true . . . What names have you decided on, sir?"

Her knee touched mine. Or perhaps mine touched hers.

"I only propose a name. Mothers, at least Irish mothers, always make these decisions."

"You defame us, sir," she said with a giggle. Her hand touched my stomach gently. "What names do you propose?"

My power of speech was failing me.

"I had thought of only one name—Moaylmiuhre, Servant of Mary. Myles in English."

She sobbed, hugged me fiercely, and rolled on top of me. "Mr. Fitzpatrick, you are the sweetest man in all the world . . . Do you want me to turn on the light?"

"That would be nice," I gasped.

That's the least I can do for you, Myles, I whispered. In case you're listening.

"HAVEN'T I had a visitor?" my wife informed me when I came into the house. She was sitting on the floor in the middle of the parlor, helping the Mick work on a portrait of the two wolfhounds. It seemed to be very good for a two-year-old.

"Hey that's great work, Mick," I said. "You're going to be the artist in the family."

"Doggies," he insisted.

"I know," I agreed. "Really good."

The Mick beamed happily. It didn't take much to please him these days. He had suddenly, and with considerable pride, solved the mysteries of toilet training, for which we praised him greatly as a "big boy."

He had also without warning begun to speak in sentences, such as "I'm glad, Da, that we have the doggies. They'll protect the baby from dragons and dinosaurs and monsters."

Right.

These feats would show this little brat we had brought into the house to replace him in his role as the "baby."

"Who was your visitor?" I asked as my son continued to draw the "doggies," both of whom rested contentedly at the door.

"Didn't he bring me those flowers?"

"A dozen roses!"

"What did your man say, *Timeo Danaos, et dona ferentes?*"

"Virgil," I said, showing off just as she had been. "Hector Papageorgiou?"

"Your very man . . . A hairy, overgrown little boy . . . about as subtle as the Red Line L train . . . wanted to see you but was content to give his side of the story to me. Never took a dollar. His brother, a pathetic little coward, had not told Seamus the truth or us. Yes, he had financial problems. But he had taken care of them. It would have been crazy to steal from the Elegance firm. Their future was in the restaurant chain . . . Honestly, Dermot Michael, he wept when he said that."

"I'm not sure you should have let him in."

"Give over, Dermot Michael! Like I always tell you, I can take care of myself and the two girls sitting in the corner like they were debating when they would jump him and himself terrified at the sight of them. He's really a big baby. Then didn't Fifi and Maemae jump on the couch with me so I felt like Cleopatra with her tigers."

"No tigers in Africa!"

"She imported them from India."

"Fair play to you, Nuala Anne. Now was your man lying?"

"Certainly he was lying! Only I think that he may not have realized it."

"Psychopath?"

"With a soft spot in his heart, like his brother, for his dear old mother! He cried about her too!"

"Do you think he might have taken a shot at Seamus?"

"If he did it himself, he would not have even wounded him. Maybe he hired a hit man who couldn't shoot all that straight! He would never be able to carry it off either way."

"Sounds useless!"

"More concerned about his mother than his wife and kids . . . I promised him I'd relay his version of it to you."

"So we shouldn't worry about him?"

"I didn't say that, Dermot Michael. Useless and dumb people can do a lot of harm without meaning to and maybe even more when they try."

We heard a plaintive cry from upstairs.

"Socra Marie hungry," the Mick said. "Better feed her, Ma."

"Yes, I'd better. Da will be down in a couple of minutes to help you with your drawing."

Da always does what he's told.

As she was nursing the ravenous little girl, Nuala finished reading the section of Ned's diary we were working on.

"It was a boy," she said as she folded her reading glasses, "wasn't it?"

"Naturally," I said. "Josie was a witch just like you are."

"Poor dear thing."

"Josie?"

"No, that one was a survivor."

"Nora?"

"With two husbands like that, give over, Dermot Michael. Husbands like that are great crack."

"You mean Ned?"

"And himself such a kind, strong man"—she glanced up at me and grinned—"just like me own husband, poor dear man!"

"Bull shite, woman!"

She laughed happily and said to the childeen, "Da's using bad language with Ma, isn't that terrible now, *alanah?* . . . And, Dermot, why, with all the fucking they were doing, was your man surprised that his wife was pregnant?"

She held the baby over her shoulder to help her burp,

which Socra Marie did with little attempt at refinement.

"My dad tells me that in those days there was a lot more infertility than there is today. A fifth of all married couples had no children at all. The causes were poor nutrition and childhood diseases like scarlet fever. I don't suppose poor Nora ate all that well out there in Connemara."

"And meself feeling sorry for meself because this childeen is a bit of burden sometimes . . . Och, your diaper is wet, isn't it now? Well, I won't make Da change it this time."

The childeen having been diapered, fed, and burped was soon lying contentedly in her mother's lap, taking in the whole scene and quite undisturbed by the thunder that was exploding over our house.

"Do you mind if Da holds you for a while?"

She passed Socra Marie over to me. The child snuggled comfortably into my arms.

"She likes Da more than Ma," Nuala complained.

"Self-pity is not one of your vices, Nuala Anne McGrail."

"Aren't you the sweet thing now?"

"We were talking about Ned."

"Dear God, didn't the poor man stew a lot!"

"Men stew too," I said primly. "Only they're not expected to show it."

"Don't know how to show it, more like," she sniffed.

The *alanah*, as Socra Marie was now called (something like "my dear little one" though, I am told, with an untranslatable affection) had already been tested for Nuala Anne's next Christmas special which, she had ordained, would be dedicated to all premature children and their parents and the doctors and nurses that kept them alive. How could that theme miss?

The testing had consisted of Nuala Anne humming lightly various Christmas hymns to see how Socra

Marie reacted to them. Not unsurprisingly she liked "Silent Night" and the "Cantique du Noel" and disliked "Adeste Fideles."

"Now how would you think herself will do on the program?" my wife had demanded.

"Won't she steal the whole show?"

"Funny thing, I was thinking the same thing."

"Dermot," she asked as though it were a question she had been thinking of for a long time and was afraid to ask, "would it be really brilliant crack for a man like Ned to know that another husband had prepared his wife for him?"

"Indeed it would," I said promptly.

"Because he had taught her about love?"

"No."

"Because he had her now and poor Myles didn't?"

"No."

"Then why?"

"Because she was a bigger challenge to him and if he could rise to that challenge, he would have been a step closer to establishing his manhood."

"Aye," she said reflectively. "I can see that."

Then after a pause.

"Did you ever have any doubts like that, Dermot Michael?"

"If a husband can survive six years of marriage to a woman like you, Nuala love, he should have no doubts at all, at all."

She nodded in approval.

" 'Tis true."

"Have you any solutions to your man's problem?"

"Poor dear Ned?"

"The very same."

"Isn't it as clear as the little pug nose on my *alanah's* pretty face?"

"No."

"Dermot Michael, you don't think things through.

You don't use the little gray cells. You don't watch the elevator door when it opens, like the little bishop says."

I should note that what she actually said was "dink dings dru."

"I think it's Mayor Carter Harrison."

"You're having me on, Dermot Michael. I can always tell when you're doing that."

She reached for another sheet of her *NUALA ANNE* stationery and wrote a couple words, sealed it in an envelope, and put it in the same drawer in her desk with the other sealed envelope.

"Now about your man," I began.

"You mean poor Seamus Costelloe?"

"Didn't I say that?"

She grinned and kissed Socra Marie as she closed her eyes.

"Fair play to you, Dermot Michael," she said. "Well, you're brilliant altogether when you say he picked a fine lot of shite hawks to work with him . . ."

"Losers."

"Same thing. And themselves the kind of amadons who would believe his threats. Only your man on Ogden Avenue even wondered whether his goon might have visited other people. Sonia knew he did and we knew he did. None of those he threatened, however, tried to find out whether they and their families were the only intended victims."

"Shite hawks."

"Losers . . . Does that suggest anything to you?"

"Maybe they want to be afraid so they can hate your man even more."

"Brilliant, Dermot Michael Coyne . . . And?"

I thought hard, trying to unleash the little gray cells and open the elevator door.

"And so that they would be afraid so they would not stupidly try for a second chance?"

"So your man's threats might have been insurance for the person who commissioned the killer?"

"It's a little complicated for my thick skull, but yeah."

"Well, then, go find out."

"Huh?"

"Go see Seamus Costelloe and persuade him, like you always do with everyone, meself included, to let down his guard and tell you more than he intends to."

"Oh."

I pushed myself out of the easy chair, patted Maeveen on the forehead, kissed Socra Marie, and then kissed my wife.

"Och," she said after a spirited response, "didn't you make me tell you more than I intended?"

"Fat chance."

"Before you leave, remember to fuss over the Mick's pictures."

"Yes, ma'am."

As I walked down the stairs, she shouted after me, "It wouldn't be too terrible wrong to take herself up to Grand Beach for Memorial Day would it, and your parents being a doctor and a nurse?"

"We'll talk about it," I said, repeating one of her favorite lines.

Joyous, if faintly derisive laughter followed me down the steps.

"You sure know how to choose losers, Seamus Costelloe," I said to him later as I sat in his corner office at the IBM. "All shite hawks, as my wife says."

"Aren't they now," he said jovially. "They're not typical, however. Most of the people I've worked with in my career are not losers. They have no reason to want me dead. The people you saw are the losers, the kind of nebbishes who would put out a clumsy contract to a bumbling hit man."

"I'd like to see your hired goon in action. He sounds quite scary."

Seamus laughed and his whole body shook, kind of like a sinister Santa Claus.

"He's very good all right. He's the least goonish of men, an often out-of-work actor, who hangs around Steppenwolf and those places up on Lincoln Avenue. He loves the role. It's fun, he says, to scare people who need to be scared."

"None of them had figured out that you had a whole cast of nebbishes to frighten."

"That's the point of being a nebbish, Dermot. It would never occur to you that such a warning might be delivered to a crowd of other nebbishes."

"Isn't that kind of cruel?"

"To scare them? Hell, it's a lot better than blowing up their cars or breaking their legs or kidnapping their kids."

"You're sure the would-be-killer is part of that crowd?"

"Who else do I know that would hire a hit man who couldn't shoot straight!"

He laughed again.

"Diane and Sonia both are afraid that I might be wrong, that it might be someone else I haven't thought of. So I hired your friend Michael Casey to provide a little security for me. Otherwise"—he held up his hands in a gesture of dismissal—"it's a dangerous world and we take our chances."

"Any favorites among the crowd?"

His eyes narrowed and his monumental jaw tightened.

"That bastard Shepherd. He hates me. Always has since we both went to Leo High School. I played football and they cut him. He's never quite good enough for the things he attempts. I've lost track of how many times I've beaten him. He's smooth and elegant and all that shit, but he's a hollow man, Dermot. And he knows it. He's exactly the kind of guy who would hire a hit man who couldn't shoot straight to save a couple of dollars. I'm offended that he wanted a bargain basement contract on me."

More boisterous laughter, a tad too boisterous. Still, Seamus had apparently proven in Vietnam that he was not easily frightened.

"I guess I would be too."

"He knows that I have a file full of evidence that would get him disbarred."

He pulled a thick file out of a desk drawer.

"This could cost him his license and maybe some time in the slammer. He's not smart enough to realize that I couldn't use it without getting some of his shit on me."

"Couldn't you leak it to the media?"

"Everyone would know where it came from. I just hang on to the stuff to keep him honest."

"And keep him worried."

"It takes his mind off that castrating bitch when he has to go bed with her. I never slept with her, by the way. She tried hard enough, heaven knows, but I know a ball-buster when I see one."

"Why does she claim she did?"

He scratched his head.

"Who knows what crazy ideas get inside a head like hers? Maybe she thinks it's prestigious to have my scalp as one of her conquests. She sure is a prick-teaser, get it?"

More laughter as he rubbed his bald pate.

"Tell you the truth I don't think she's had all that many conquests . . . You like her tits?"

"I don't remember noticing them," I said, resolving that I would not repeat this part of the conversation to my hot-tempered spouse.

"See what I mean! No one notices them! I figure she spreads this bullshit about me to attract Lenny boy. He sees it as a big triumph to take her away from me. Well, he's welcome to her. She's as seductive as one of those big freezers over at Sears."

"So you really figure he's the top suspect?"

"Not much real payoff for any of the others, is

there? He must piss in his silk pants every time he thinks about this file."

He picked it up off his desk and tossed it in the drawer from which he took it. Then he carefully locked the door.

The door had been open when he pulled out the file to play show-and-tell with it. Part of the act.

Did I believe the act?

Not altogether.

"You think his wife would urge him to get rid of you?"

"She'd love nothing more than to go out to Holy Sepulchre Cemetery and piss on my grave with my body in It. I used to say that I'd plant a urinal for my gravestone, as a convenience for those who wanted to piss on my grave. Now with all the women lawyers around who want to castrate me, I'll have to start thinking about building a His and Hers."

Why was my wife making me talk to this vulgar man?

Because the mark was upon him.

What mark? I didn't see it.

"So you think they put out the contract?"

"Nah! They would have liked to, but I doubt they'd have the courage to do it. They sure would like to see it happen, however . . . Len has some pretty good contacts with the Boys. They'd find him someone who could shoot straight."

"Tweedledum and Tweedledee?"

"Hey, that's good, Dermot, those two guys over there in the Conway Building are really out of Wonderland! Have you ever seen any of their briefs—slop, pure slop. Erasures, handwritten inserts, misspellings, malapropisms, pompous solemnity: kind of things judges laugh at before they throw the shite into the circular file. They might just hire a hit man who couldn't shoot straight. It would fit in with their characters. I don't know why they'd bother. No money in it for them."

"Unless your estate would want to settle their pending suits."

"My trustees wouldn't be that dumb."

"It would get rid of them."

"Maybe . . . I should have seen them coming. Ambulance chasers, but dumb ambulance chasers. Occasionally they'd come up with something worth pursuing, but not very often. Even then they'd mess up the clients with idiotic promises. Hangers-on! Nuisances!"

"Why didn't you brush them off right away?"

He made a face of both embarrassment and regret.

"I kind of felt sorry for them. Dumb kids. They would have been better off in some harmless city job. They could strut around with the claim that they worked for the Mayor and wouldn't do any harm to anyone, themselves included. So I gave them a break. I should have known that once they were in my office they would hang on like leeches. I literally had to hire security guys to throw them out."

"You're saying you're a sucker for second-raters down on their luck like them and Helen?"

He frowned, pondering the question.

"Oh, hell! I guess I am. Never thought of it that way." He chuckled. "None of the lawyers you'd meet out on the street would tell you that."

I didn't ask him what street.

"I suppose that's an explanation for why I got mixed up with that vain asshole Jimmy Gigante. He's only half a loser. That Ogden Town is a brilliant idea. Ten more years and I'm going to make a lot of money out of it. But he would have run it into the ground long before there was any demand for the place. Classy idea, classy plans, asshole administrator. Never could do anything right. Spent too much money on his jewelry and too much time on admiring himself in a mirror. I would have thought he was a faggot if he hadn't been married to that gorgeous woman. What a wonderful pair of tits she has!"

I almost said that such talk might be all right in a locker room at a country club, but not in my presence. However, the better course would be to ignore him and not report his precise words to my Nuala Anne.

"What did he do for example?"

"Well he decided to spend a half million dollars for trees. They cost a lot of money, you know. He figures that the Mayor likes trees and, if he sees we're putting in trees, he'll like us. We can say they'll be mature trees when our people move in."

"And after the trees, wrought-iron fences!"

"You think you're kidding? He already had them picked out! Anyway, it takes a lot more than trees and wrought iron to build up clout at City Hall, especially when you have a reputation as a lousy administrator."

"He probably wanted to do something."

"Sure he did, the little prick. I say to him, look, Jimmy, let's concentrate on land clearance and the sewers. The city is hot to do that kind of work. Let's get it done now. Who knows, the way this prosperity is going, maybe we got customers in five years. Then we're ready for them."

"And he says that he hates to work with the sewer people, they're so vulgar. So I see that he's never going to cut wood for us, so I take over as boss and let him be general manager. That means I make all the decisions. I could have just fired him. I should have just fired him. But, see, the fucker has kids that will have to go to college. So I give him a job. He goes ahead and without telling me puts up a model home. It's a gorgeous place and I read about it in the papers. I also get the bills which I've got to pay because there isn't any money left in the Ogden Town accounts. So I tell Jimmy the Giant that he's history."

"So he tries to get rid of you?"

"Like I say, I wouldn't be surprised. He's a Guinea after all. Sometimes they do things that way."

"From northern Italy."

"Dermot, a Guinea is a Guinea. I don't care where he's from."

"But if he's using an Outfit gun, why can't the gun shoot straight?"

"Some of the made guys can't shoot straight. So the Boys lease them out to customers who don't know any better."

This didn't sound very plausible. The word on the street—whatever street in the "old neighborhood" where the elders in the Mob put out the word—was that it wasn't one of theirs. Seamus must know that too.

"Did you check that out on the street?"

"I asked my friends over on Taylor Street. They say they don't know nothing about it, which only means that the big guys aren't saying anything."

"I see."

I'd ask both John Culhane and Mike Casey about that.

"I made the same mistake with that damn Greek pisser. I like his idea. Real class. They're making money hand over fist. He wants to build a couple of more restaurants. He's got a cash flow problem. I look at the books, everything seems copacetic. So I say let's go and spread some more fucking Elegance around the fucking suburbs. They need it."

"You don't find out about the brother till later?"

"I should have checked this guy Hector out with my Greek contacts. He's one of the all-time great losers in the city. Give him some money and he'll buy race-horses, shack up with a new mistress, put a payment down on a home in Santa Barbara, take a trip to China—all first class. He's bleeding us dry and covers up because he's a loser all right but a damn clever loser. Arrogant prick too. Thinks he's smarter than I am."

"And you find out?"

"I begin to smell trouble. So I have one of my accountants look at things. He tells me Hector Papageorgiou is a swindler and a damn clever one. He's been taking me like Grant took Richmond, though, hell, I'm smart enough to know that Grant never took Richmond, right?"

"Right, they occupied the city peacefully only after Lee surrendered."

THE WOMAN WOULDN'T APPROVE OF YOUR SHOWING OFF THAT WAY.

I'm not going to tell her.

"Yeah, you're right. You a Civil War buff too?"

"Might write a novel on it someday."

SEE!

"Great idea! . . . Anyway I say to these two pricks, I could get indictments against both of you. Put you in jail for maybe ten years, and this prick Nick begins to wail about what this would do to his poor old mother. I tell him I don't care about what happens to his mother. I want my money. I'll settle for the complete ownership of the chain. He weeps and moans and begs, but I finally pick up the phone to call the Feds and he signs the papers. I get him out of there right away because I don't trust that mother of his because she's leading him around by his balls."

"You've met the brother?"

"Big, overgrown mama's boy. Superannuated college kid, long hair, torn jeans, pierced ears. Clever, very clever, not quite clever enough. Took my accountants a couple of weeks to figure out how he was siphoning money out of the corporation."

"How was he doing it?"

"Making fake payments to the suppliers, not a whole lot at any one time. You steal a hundred dollars a day from a company it starts to mount up."

"You paid them for their share of the company when you bought it out?"

"Yeah, I didn't want the twats to run off and start a

rival firm. Half million I guess. It will take a couple of years to make back all I lost, but then the profit will be pure gravy. I kept the staffs on by giving them big raises. They're worth it. Should have given them long ago. Nick told me he had . . . Dermot, he's a miserable little pisser!"

"They sound to me like top-of-the-line suspects."

"What do they get out of it? There's no way anyone will lend them the money to buy Elegance back. All the Greeks in the city know what Hector tried to do. My Greek friends say if he does it to them they put out a contract on him. They're finished."

"You know the mother?"

He sighed loudly.

"I should have checked all this stuff out. Believe me from now on I don't spend any money on classy ideas till I know the people who have them are classy people . . . she's an ugly little bitch with burning eyes. Scary. You know, I still can't believe she fucks over Nick the way she does. Never again!"

Seamus had diarrhea of the mouth. He was spilling out all kinds of shite, overwhelming me with it, putting his spin on everything. Some of it may even have been true. As he told the story, he was a generous, warm-hearted personal injury lawyer who had been taken in by clever losers. Somehow I didn't quite see that image of him. More likely he was an insatiable shark. His genes drove him to gobble up smaller fish who thought they could play in his part of the ocean. He didn't need the money, but the sheer pleasure of eating his hapless victims drove him to the hunt.

At any rate that was one plausible construction one could put on his story. Even if it were true, it didn't justify an attempt to kill him.

"I suppose you're wondering about my family?" he asked with a knowing wink. "Cops say when some asshole gets put down always look for a family member, right?"

"So I'm told."

"Yeah, I think the same thing, but who? Diane? Fuck, if she's going to put me down, she does it years ago. Much easier to sue for divorce. No way she doesn't get a big settlement? Right? Revenge? Diane is not the revenge type. All she wants is money to buy shoes and that kind of shit. So? I give her the money. Why not? I don't give her as much as she wants, but I give her enough. She's not too bright. But hell I didn't marry her because she's bright. Generally speaking I'm faithful to her. I think she'd be genuinely sorry if I croaked, get me?"

"I think so."

"Then you take Lourdes. She's not very bright either. Reads romance novels and watches television all day. Still she takes pretty good care of her kids. She marries this guy who is a hotshot trader. Makes a lot of money in a hurry for the guys he works for. Goes out on his own, get me? Loses his nerve when it's his own money he's playing with. Wiped out and then some. So I make a deal with him. I pay off his debts, not all at once, but in installments. His customers are happy to get anything. I persuade his old company to take him back by promising to back him. What happens? He's a hotshot again. He owes me, but I'm not making a big deal out of that."

"But if you should die . . . ?"

"Everything is tied up in trust funds, mostly for my grandkids. There's no percentage for any of them to put me down. Why fuck with the pot of gold at the end of the rainbow, get me?"

"And Andy?

"The kid wants to be a trial lawyer like his old man, make even more money. He's not quick enough. Prepares carefully, works hard, lots of attention to detail, then fucks up in the courtroom, get me? Wants to kill himself, I mean seriously. I tell him he's lucky he's not a voracious shark like me. Try estate law I tell him, you've got the mind for it. You'll make a lot of dough and you'll enjoy life, get me? Then he meets this Sonia babe and she tells him the same thing. He's so hot to get her to spread her legs for him, he goes along. Sure enough. Now he's happy. Thinks he's better off than I am and he's right. Sonia will keep him in line. She's one tough babe, too tough for me, but then I'm not the one who's going to get my hands inside her bra and pull off her pants, am I?"

"Presumably not."

He laughed and rolled his eyes.

"I'm too Irish to mess around with incest, Dermot, especially with a ball-buster. I really don't go for aggressive women ... Yeah, but she's still a classy broad."

"You check her out?"

"Oh, yeh," He grinned complacently. "I'm a little more careful about my family than about my peripheral investments, get me? I'm suspicious of her from day one. Andy would look like a pretty good catch to a refugee. So we check her out really good. Can't find a thing. She's clean, nothing more than she pretends to be, a hardworking Russian nurse from somewhere in Siberia. Ambitious for all those things we take for granted. Loves Andy in her own way. She's tough. I respect her. She respects me. I'm part of the deal she's making. Diane and Lourdes don't like her at first, but now they're in cahoots with her, you know how women are. You ask me, I think we're lucky to find someone like that for the family. Fuck, I'm talking to you and paying Mike Casey because she insists. Mister, she says to me, you're more fun than trust funds ..."

So that's the end of my conversation with Seamus Costelloe, a brilliant, complicated, vulgar man, with *perhaps* a heart of gold. Our ethnic group is not without a lot of men and women like him.

I rode down the elevator, trying to figure out how I

was going to summarize the conversation for my wife, in terms that would do me credit as a reasonably able Dr. Watson.

"How did it go?"

Mike Casey, a thin, handsome Irishman with snow-white hair and laughing eyes was leaning against the wall of the *Sun-Times* Building across from the IBM Building.

"You cover these clients personally, Commissioner?" I asked.

"Not very often. This guy is an interesting specimen, a throwback in a way. The playing field is not quite level whenever he plays, but no one has ever gotten anything on him."

"I don't know how it went," I admitted. "He is unbearably vulgar and a disgusting male chauvinist. Yet, as herself says, he's got a right to live out his appointed years."

"That's what I think too."

"Your guys find out anything about the shooting?"

"Only that the hit man, in addition to being a bad shot, is pretty stupid. He took a lot of crazy chances riding up in the elevator and then trying to escape down the stairs. We got a couple of good camera shots of him from the security cameras."

"What did he look like?"

"Standard-issue Hollywood hit man in black. Clumsy, not smooth at all. Bill Clinton mask, dressed in black. Only an idiot would try to make a hit in this building at night. He must have worked pretty hard at getting by the security guards, who have been fired by the way. Smart but dumb."

"Amateur night?"

"You'd better believe it . . . How's the kid doing?"

"Putting on weight by the ton!"

As I walked north on Wabash Avenue, I flipped on my cell phone to call Nuala. Before I could push her code number, the phone rang.

"Dermot," I said.

"Dermot love," she said calmly, "I'm back at the hospital. Our little daughter is sick again. The doctors are looking at her now."

"What's the matter!"

"I don't know. She's lethargic. Won't eat, won't sleep, won't react to us. She just lies there like she's getting ready to die."

Nuala was in total control. That scared the hell out of me. If she had put on that rare persona of the forty-year-old materfamilias who could absorb any tragedy, she must be expecting the worst.

"I'll be right up!"

"Be careful, Dermot Michael, don't take any chances."

—20—

October 1886

The trial resumes tomorrow. Judge Gary will give the guilty men a chance to plead their case. He'd better be prepared for a long time of listening. Al Parsons's talk will last eight hours. He let me read it yesterday. It is a brilliant argument for social justice. It will have no effect on the Judge or most of the Chicago journalists. However, there will be reporters here from around the world. They'll quote it at great length. I'm sure it will become a classic of labor rhetoric. How successful he would have been if he had chosen electoral politics!

Al is ecstatic. It is for this moment, he tells me, that he has waited all his life. It makes everything worth the effort and suffering. He will die happy after tomorrow.

He won't die immediately. Bill Black has a powerful brief for an appeal. I read it yesterday in the General's office. The money people will try to bribe the appellate judges to refuse to hear the appeal and to execute these criminals immediately so as to send a message to Anarchists all over the world. The judges will reject the appeal eventually. However, they are much more concerned about appearances than Judge Gary. The men in the jail will have at least another year of life. Anything could happen in a year. We might obtain a positive response to a clemency petition for all of them. I am not terribly hopeful, but more hopeful than I was during the summer.

Timmy Hardiman works at the General's office on the weekends, hardly believing that his work is deemed essential to the smooth functioning of the office. The General tells me confidentially, "That lad is a lot better law clerk than you were at his age."

"That's not necessarily a compliment to him."

Josie claims, not seriously, that Timmy is more in love with the law office than he is with her. She is terribly proud of having picked him out of the crowd.

"Don't you dare tell her any different!" Nora warns me with a smile, knowing full well that I won't.

There was a Catholic charity ball last night for our own upper crust. My parents insist that it was much nicer than the "Protestant balls" as they call them, though they are always invited. "Them folks don't know how to have any fun," my mother insists. "They're sober and somber and serious all the time."

"Like your son," my wife says mischievously.

They all laugh, as they always do when the subject is my seriousness.

The General rides up on his white charger in my defense.

"Ned is the funniest man in this room if you read what he writes carefully. It's the straight face which confuses people."

I hope he's right.

Nora's pregnancy is not quite obvious yet. She was easily the most beautiful woman at the ball.

The Catholics at the party are of mixed minds about the Anarchists. Most of them congratulate me on my writing. Some of them buy the opinion of their betters that Anarchy by itself is a crime and the defendants must be executed to protect the civility of our city. Others say that the trial has been a damned disgrace and *that Judge Gary will give our city a bad name all over the world.*

A lawyer comments, "We'll have to stage another fire to win respect back."

I remember that earlier in the day an arrogant fop of an English journalist complains to me about the "uncivilized and repulsive style of American justice." I tell him that I covered the judicial murder of the Maamtrasna defendants four years ago and continue to be astonished at how the English lose all their storied sense of the sacredness of law when they cross the Irish sea.

I don't tell the guests at the ball that conversation because it is the lead for my story in tomorrow's Daily News.

November 1888

There was a festive atmosphere in the courtroom today. Everyone was greeting their old friends from summer days. Judge Gary had three empty-headed, giggling young women on the bench with him. The defendants were talking to their desperately hoping wives and sweethearts. The foreign press and the American reporters were chatting amiably. Captains Bonfield and Schaack are strutting around in their dress uniforms, looking much like generals in the Union Army.

I stand in a corner of the courtroom by myself, in my usual pose of forlorn cynicism. I suspect that I will last on the job until after the execution of the defendants or, please God, decrees of clemency for them. Then the powers at the Daily News *will decide that they've had quite enough of me.*

I will probably rejoice in that fate. I can put aside my courtroom pose, if by then it hasn't become part of my character.

Nora assures me that she will not tolerate that.

Louis Lingg is the first of the defendants to speak. He is nothing if not uncompromising. His raw defiance electrifies the courtroom. He has told me that he did not make the Haymarket bomb but he has made bombs. I wonder if perhaps the prosecution might not have a case against him that they were too inept to make. I noted that he wore the gold cuff links which Elise had given him.

COURT OF JUSTICE! WITH THE same irony with which you have regarded my efforts to win, in this "free land of America," a livelihood such as humankind is worthy to enjoy, do you now, after condemning me to death, concede me the liberty of making a final speech.

I accept your concession; but it is only for the purpose of exposing the injustice, the calumnies, and the outrages which have been heaped upon me.

You have accused me of murder, and convicted me: what proof have you brought that I am guilty?

In the first place, you have brought this fellow Seliger to testify against me. Him I have helped to make bombs, and you have further proven that with the assistance of another, I took those bombs to No. 58 Clybourn Avenue, but what you have not proven—even with the assistance of your bought "squealer," Seliger, who would appear to have acted such a prominent part in the affair—is that any of those bombs were taken to the Haymarket.

A couple of chemists also have been brought here as specialists, yet they could only state that the metal of which the Haymarket bomb was made bore a certain resemblance to those bombs of mine, and your Mr. Ingham has vainly endeavored to deny that the bombs were quite different. He had to admit that there was a difference of a full half inch in their diameters, although he suppressed the fact that there was also a difference of a quarter of an inch in the thickness of the shell. This is the kind of evidence upon which you have convicted me.

It is not murder, however, of which you have convicted me. The judge has stated that much only this morning in his resumé of the case, and Grinnell has repeatedly asserted that we were being tried, not for murder, but for Anarchy, so that the condemnation is that I am an Anarchist!

You have charged me with despising "law and order." What does your "law and order" amount to? Its representatives are the police, and they have thieves in their ranks. Here sits Captain Schaack. He has himself admitted to me that my hat and books have been stolen from him in his office—stolen by policemen. These are your defenders of property rights!

The detectives again, who arrested me, forced their way into my room like housebreakers, under false pretenses, giving the name of a carpenter, Lorenz, of Burlington Street. They have sworn that I was alone in my room, therein perjuring themselves. You have not subpoenaed this lady, Mrs. Klein, who was present, and could have sworn that the aforesaid detectives broke into my room under false pretenses, and that their testimonies are perjured

But let us go further. In Schaack we have a captain of the police, and he also has perjured himself. He has sworn that I admitted to him being present at the Monday night meeting, whereas I distinctly informed him that I was at a carpenters' meeting at Zepf's Hall. He has sworn again that I told him that I also learned to make bombs from Herr Most's book. That also is a perjury.

Let us go still a step higher among these representatives of law and order. Grinnell and his associates have permitted perjury, and I say that they have done it knowingly. The proof has been adduced by my counsel, and with my own eyes I have seen Grinnell point out to Gilmer, eight days before he came upon the stand, the persons of the men whom he was to swear against.

While I, as I have stated above, believe in force for the sake of winning for myself and fellow workmen a livelihood such as men ought to have, Grinnell, on the other hand, through his police and other rogues, has suborned perjury in order to murder seven men, of whom I am one.

Grinnell had the pitiful courage here in the court-room, where I could not defend myself, to call me a coward! The scoundrel! A fellow who has leagued himself with a parcel of base, hireling knaves, to bring me to the gallows. Why? For no earthly reason save a contemptible selfish desire to "rise in the world" to "make money."

This wretch—who, by means of the perjuries of other wretches is going to murder seven men—is the fellow who calls me "coward"! And yet you blame me for despising such "defenders of the law"! Such unspeakable hypocrites!

The Judge himself was forced to admit that the State's Attorney had not been able to connect me with the bomb throwing. The latter knows how to get around it, however. He charges me with being a "conspirator." How does he prove it? Simply by declaring the International Working People's Association to be a "conspiracy." I was a member of that body, so he has the charge securely fastened on me. Excellent! Nothing is too difficult for the genius of a State's Attorney!

It is hardly incumbent upon me to review the relations which I occupy to my companions in misfortune. I can say truly and openly that I am not as intimate with my fellow prisoners as I am with Captain Schaack.

The universal misery, the ravages of the capitalistic hyena have brought us together in our agitation, not as persons, but as workers in the same cause. Such is the "conspiracy" of which you have convicted me.

I protest against the conviction, against the decision of the court. I do not recognize your law, jumbled together as it is by the nobodies of bygone centuries, and I do not recognize the decision of the court. My own counsel have conclusively proven from the decisions of equally high courts that a new trial must be granted us. The State's Attorney quotes three times as many decisions from perhaps still higher courts to prove the opposite, and I am convinced that if, in another trial, these decisions should be supported by twenty-one volumes, they will adduce one hundred in support of the contrary, if it is Anarchists who are to be tried. And not even under such a law—a law that a schoolboy must despise—not even by such methods have they been able to "legally" convict us.

They have suborned perjury to boot.

I tell you frankly and openly, I am for force. I have already told Captain Schaack, "If they use cannons against us, we shall use dynamite against them."

I repeat that I am the enemy of the "order" of today, and I repeat that, with all my powers, so long as breath remains in me, I shall combat it. I declare again, frankly and openly, that I am in favor of using force. I have told Captain Schaack, and I stand by it, "If you cannonade us, we shall dynamite you." You laugh! You think, "You'll throw no more bombs;" but let me assure you I die happy on the gallows, so confident am I that the hundreds of thousands to whom I have spoken will remember my words. When you shall have hanged us, then—mark my words—they will do the bomb throwing! In this hope do I say to you: I despise you, I despise your order, your laws, your force-propped authority. Hang me for it!

As usual the General was correct: Louis Lingg was a warrior, more likely of the kind to be found in the Confederate Army. Or the Prussian.

A minority of the spectators in the courtroom ap-

plauded. Judge Gary pounded for order, temporarily ignoring the young women who shared the bench with him.

"We will see what we can do to oblige your request, Mr. Lingg," he sneered.

The next defendant to speak was Adolph Fischer. Born in Bremen, he is a tall, strong man in his late twenties who has lived in Chicago for only three years. Like Parsons and Schwab he is a typographer. Like Spies he worked at the Arbeiter-Zeitung. He also edited a small weekly with George Engel called Der Anarchist, whose motto was "We hate authority." He designed the original broadsheet for the Haymarket meeting, which urged the crowd to come armed. When Spies told him to eliminate it, he readily agreed. The prosecution had used the original broadsheet as evidence. Judge Gary had prevented the defense from arguing that the final version had no reference to arms. He is typical of all of the defendants except Lou Lingg in that he cannot understand why people think his violent rhetoric could cause violence. He spoke briefly and with a strong German accent, which did not help with those in the city who hated and feared all foreigners:

I protest against my being sentenced to death because I have committed no crime. I was tried for murder but I was convicted of Anarchy. I protest against being sentenced to death because I have not been found guilty of murder. However, if I am to die on account of being an Anarchist, on account of my love for liberty, fraternity and equality, I will not remonstrate.

THE CROWD WAS SOMEHOW DISAPPOINTED *that he did not speak longer. The condemned men owed to the courtroom a longer period of entertainment.*

Judge Gary adjourned the court for lunch and departed with his bevy of female attendants. I scribbled out the first few paragraphs of my story:

YOUNG ANARCHIST DEFIES JUDGE GARY

Like a Confederate officer facing a Union court-martial which had already decided his fate, Louis Lingg, the youngest of the accused Anarchists, defied Judge Gary to hang him. The vigor of Lingg's defiance stirred the Judge out of his sotto voce conversations with the bevy of young woman who routinely share the judicial bench with him.

Wearing the gold cuff links that his adoring young friend had given him, Lingg was attractive in his courage if not prudent in his expression.

Chief of Police Pemberton, who is able to maintain only minimum control over his captains, stopped me on the way out of court.

"I think you ought to know, Ned, that Captain Schaack is so pleased with the outcome of this trial that he has suggested to me we create our own Anarchist groups."

"What!"

"He wants detectives to form secret Anarchist organizations which will flood the city with propaganda. He says that will sustain public fear and enhance the power of the Police Department. He hinted that money would become available to finance such schemes."

"Marshall Field and Cy McCormick?"

"Doubtless . . . I said I would not stand for that. He seemed to withdraw the suggestion. However, I suspect that he will proceed regardless of what I say."

"Unless someone in the press writes about it?"

"That would at least postpone the realization of his schemes."

"I understand, Chief"

"Mind you, don't quote me."

I smiled.

"Certainly not."

Another headline took shape in my head:

SCHAACK WANTS POLICE TO CONTINUE ANARCHY

When I was retired from the Daily News *in a year or so, who would public officials confide their secrets to? Well, that was their problem. It was time for me to begin thinking about a respectable career.*

In the afternoon Engel and Fischer spoke, both in strong Germanic accents. Despite the consistency of their Anarchist theories and the logic of their argumentation, they did little either for Anarchy or their own cases. They lacked the passion of Lingg and the charm of Gus Spies. Tomorrow we will hear from Al Parsons, sounding perhaps like a cowboy as he speaks in his nasal Texas twang.

Elise rushed up to me as I was leaving the court.

"Was he not splendid today, Mr. Fitzpatrick? Did he not speak with courage and conviction?"

"Like a splendid young warrior, Elise."

"I am so proud of him. Did you see my cuff links?"

"I did, Elise. They made his defiance all the more elegant."

"Ja, I am very proud!"

I recounted for Nora the events of the day.

"We must protect that young woman, Ned."

"I have been thinking the same thing."

"If Lucy Parsons and her friends make her part of their group, they will control her life as long as she lives."

My Nora didn't miss much. She did read the Chicago Daily News *every day.*

"They will indeed."

"One could not object to that so long as that's what Elise wants."

"Elise is only a year or two older than our Josie. She has no idea what she wants."

Nora chuckled.

"Josie thinks she knows what she wants, though

what she thinks changes every week. If I understand you correctly this Lingg person wants her to escape from the world of the explosion and the trial. He has a place of refuge for her in Iowa?"

"It would seem so."

"Do you know where?"

"Approximately. I can find the exact names and place easily enough."

"Then you should find out if those people are appropriate for Elise, establish contact with them, and inform them when it's time for her to join them."

"Yes, ma'am."

She paid no attention to my irony.

"When the time comes, immediately after the execution I presume, we will put her on the train to Iowa and a new life."

"We?"

"Of course. Josie and I with perhaps your assistance."

"I will try my best to assist you."

"Young Myles here"—she patted her swelling belly—"will have joined us by then. Annie or your mother can watch him for a couple of hours. We should have no trouble putting Elise on the train. However, we should meet her several times between now and then to reassure her that she can trust us."

"That would be wise."

"We should put her on the train immediately after the execution, should we not?"

"I think so. That's what Lingg apparently expects us to do. He wants to die without having her on his conscience. If she becomes part of the funeral ceremonies, she might find it impossible to leave Chicago."

"If she is not an Anarchist, she must leave immediately then."

"She's not an Anarchist, Nora. She is a very young woman smitten by love for a gallant and handsome young warrior."

"Poor thing," my Nora said, dabbing at her eyes.

We were both silent for a moment.

"Ned . . ."

"Yes?"

"We must stay in touch with her once she is in Iowa, must we not?"

I had not thought of that detail.

"Certainly."

She sighed.

"Poor things."

She wept in my arms. I wished I could weep with her.

October 8

George Engel is the oldest of the defendants, a man with hair turning white, probably in his middle fifties. His white-haired wife, hunched over as if burdened with care and worry, listened nervously as he spoke in heavily accented German. He is a toy store owner who was at home playing cards when the bomb went off. I think of him as an aging elf who might work in Santa's workshop except that he rarely smiles as Santa's elves are supposed to smile. There is not a shred of evidence which connects him to the explosion, other than that with Fischer he is coeditor of Der Anarchist.

This is the first occasion of my standing before an American court, and on this occasion it is murder of which I am accused. And for what reasons do I stand here? For what reasons am I accused of murder? The same that caused me to leave Germany—the poverty, the misery of the working classes.

And here, too, in this "free republic," in the richest country of the world, there are numerous proletarians for whom no table is set; who, as outcasts of society, stray joylessly through life. I have seen human beings gather their daily food from the garbage heaps of the streets, to quiet therewith their gnawing hunger.

I have read of occurrences in the daily papers which prove to me that here, too, in this great "free land," people are doomed to die of starvation. This brought me to reflection, and to the question: What are the peculiar causes that could bring about such a condition of society? I then began to give our political institutions more attention than formerly. My discoveries brought to me the knowledge that the same society evils exist here that exist in Germany. This is the explanation of what induced me to study the social question, to become a socialist. And I proceeded with all the means at my command to make myself familiar with the new doctrine.

When, in 1878, I came here from Philadelphia, I strove to better my condition, believing it would be less difficult to establish a means of livelihood here than in Philadelphia, where I had tried in vain to make a living. But here, too, I found myself disappointed. I began to understand that it made no difference to the proletarian, whether he lived in New York, Philadelphia, or Chicago.

In the factory where I worked I became acquainted with a man who pointed out to me the causes that brought about the difficult and fruitless battles of the workingmen for the means of existence. He explained to me, by the logic of scientific socialism, how mistaken I was in believing that I could make an independent living by the toil of my hands, so long as machinery, raw material, etc., were guaranteed to the capitalists as private property by the State.

I took part in politics with the earnestness of a good citizen; but I was soon to find that the teachings of a "free ballot box" are a myth, and that I had again been duped. I came to the opinion that as long as workingmen are economically enslaved they cannot be politically free. It became clear to me that the working classes would never bring about a form of society guaranteeing work, bread and a happy life by means of the ballot.

Before I had lost my faith in the ballot box, the following occurrences transpired, which proved to me that the politicians of this country were through and through corrupt. When, in the fourteenth ward, in which I lived and had the right to vote, the Social Democratic party had grown to such dimensions as to make it dangerous for the Republican and Democratic parties, the latter forthwith united and took a stand against the Social Democrats. This, of course, was natural for are not their interests identical? And as the Social Democrats nevertheless elected their candidates, they were beaten out of the fruits of their victory by the corrupt schemes of the old political parties. The ballot box was stolen and the votes so "corrected" that it became possible for the opposition to proclaim their candidates elected. The workingmen sought to obtain justice through the courts, but it was all in vain. The trial cost them fifteen hundred dollars, but their rights they never obtained.

Soon enough I found that political corruption had burrowed through the ranks of the Social Democrats. I left this party and joined the International Working People's Association, that was just being organized. The members of that body have the firm conviction that the workingman can free himself from the tyranny of capitalism only through force—just as all advances of which history speaks have been brought about through force alone. We see from the history of this country that the first colonists won their liberty only through force; that through force slavery was abolished, and just as the man who agitated against slavery in this country had to ascend to the gallows, so also must we. He who speaks for the workingman to-day must hang. . . .

The State's Attorney said here that "Anarchy" was "on trial."

Anarchism and socialism are as much alike, in my opinion, as one egg is to another. They differ only in their tactics. The Anarchists have abandoned the way of liberating humanity which socialists would take to accomplish this. I say: Believe no more in the ballot, and use all other means at your command. Because we have done so we stand arraigned here today—because we have pointed out to the people the proper way. The Anarchists are being hunted and persecuted for this in every clime, but in the face of it all anarchism is gaining more and more adherents, and if you cut off our opportunities of open agitation, then will all the work be done secretly. If the State's Attorney thinks he can root out socialism by hanging seven of our men and condemning the other to fifteen years' servitude, he is laboring under the wrong impression. . . .

When hundreds of workingmen have been destroyed in mines in consequence of faulty preparations, for the repairing of which the owners were too stingy, the capitalistic papers have scarcely noticed it. See with what satisfaction and cruelty they make their report, when here and there workingmen have been fired upon, while striking for a few cents' increase in their wages, that they might earn only a scanty subsistence.

Can anyone feel any respect for a government that accords rights only to the privileged classes, and none to the workers? We have seen but recently how the coal-barons combined to form a conspiracy to raise the price of coal, while at the same time reducing the already low wages of their men. Are they accused of conspiracy on that account? But when workingmen dare ask an increase in their wages, the militia and the police are sent out to shoot them down.

For such a government as this I can feel no respect, and I will combat them despite their power, despite their police, despite their spies.

I hate and combat, not the individual capitalist, but

the system that gives him those privileges. My greatest wish is that workingmen may recognize who are their friends and who are their enemies.

As to my conviction, brought about as it was through capitalistic influence, I have not a word to say.

THE IMPACT OF THIS CALM, logical argument was lost in the courtroom because of Engel's thick accent and hubbub of the crowd. I was furious. This man is making the final statement of his life. The least they could do would be generous enough listen to his anguish.

Then Gus Spies rose to speak. He smiled briefly at his wife and began in his mild reasonable voice, a speech which was also mild and reasonable, if you didn't listen too closely to what he was saying.

ANARCHISM DOES NOT MEAN BLOODSHED; *does not mean robbery, arson, etc. These monstrosities are, on the contrary, the characteristic features of capitalism. Anarchism means peace and tranquility to all. Anarchism, or socialism, means the reorganization of society upon scientific principles and the abolition of causes which produce vice and crime. Capitalism first produces these social diseases and then seeks to cure them by punishment. . . .*

Now, if we cannot be directly implicated with this affair, connected with the throwing of the bomb, where is the law that says "that these men shall be picked out to suffer"? Show me that law if you have it. If the position of this court is correct, then half of this city—half of the population of this city ought to be hanged, because they are responsible the same as we are for that act on May 4. And if not half the population of Chicago is hanged, then show me the law that says "eight men shall be picked out and hanged as scapegoats!" You have no such law. Your decision, your ver-

dict, our conviction is nothing but an arbitrary will of this lawless court.

It is true there is no precedent in jurisprudence in this case. It is true we have called upon the people to arm themselves. It is true that we have told them time and again that the great day of change was coming. It was not our desire to have bloodshed. We are not beasts. We would not be socialists if we were beasts. It is because of our sensitiveness that we have gone into this movement for the emancipation of the oppressed and suffering. . . .

This seems to be the ground upon which the verdict is to be sustained. But when a long train of abuses and usurpations pursuing invariably the same object evinces a design to reduce the people under absolute despotism, it is their right, their duty, to throw off such government and provide new guards for their future safety.

This is a quotation from the Declaration of Independence. Have we broken any laws by showing to the people how these abuses, that have occurred for the last twenty years, are invariably pursuing one object, viz: to establish an oligarchy in this country as strong and powerful and monstrous as never before has existed in any country?

I can well understand why that man Grinnell did not urge upon the grand jury to charge us with treason. I can well understand it. You cannot try and convict a man for treason who has upheld the Constitution against those who try to trample it under their feet. It would not have been as easy a job to do that, Mr. Grinnell, as to charge "these men" with murder.

Now, these are my ideas. They constitute a part of myself. I cannot divest myself of them, nor would I, if I could. And if you think that you can crush out these ideas that are gaining ground more and more every day, if you think you can crush them out by sending us to the gallows—if you would once more have people to suffer the penalty of death because they have dared to tell the truth—and I defy you to show us where we have told a lie—I say, if death is the penalty for proclaiming the truth, then I will proudly and defiantly pay the costly price! Call your hangman. Truth crucified in Socrates, in Christ, in Giordano Bruno, in Hus, in Galileo, still lives—they and others whose number is legion have preceded us on this path. We are ready to follow!

MOST OF THE CROWD LISTENED, *though not Judge Gary who was busy entertaining his ever-present bevy of womanly admirers. Spies's English was presentable and his voice calm and reasoned. The logic of all the arguments is similar. We break no laws. We are appalled by the condition of workers. We have banded together to improve their lot. Eventually we will drive you out of power. We will die if we must for our cause. The mix of unruffled tone, pleas of innocence, threats of revolution, and willingness for martyrdom was not quite as logical as it seemed. However it did not much matter. The Anarchists were delivering their message to the world and for posterity. The whole trial was about these statements even if few in the court paid much attention.*

October 9

Parsons spoke today for four hours. Judge Gary would not permit him a respite, so Al went on in a voice that was increasingly forced and tired. At first the courtroom crowd listened closely. He was a brilliant orator. They were impressed with the clarity and sense of his description of American society. Then they began to lose attention and drift away. Even the silly women on the bench made their excuses to the Judge and slipped away.

*Most of the local press departed too. They had all
the quotes they needed. The foreigners stayed to listen
because they knew this oration was an important historical event. They wanted to be able to say that they
had been there when Albert Parsons delivered his
eight-hour epitaph.*

*My own feeling was that he might have been much
more effective in four hours or even two. He was Hamlet delaying the end of the drama. On the other hand
he was willing to pay the price of his own death to
earn the stage. He was entitled to as much time as he
wanted.*

October 10, 1886.

*The statements of the defendants ended this after-
noon. Finally Judge Gary's moment in history came,
the scene he had been anticipating since the beginning
of the trial. The canoodling young women were dismissed from the bench.*

*He sorted the papers on his desk, put on his glasses,
brushed back his hair with an elegant gesture, and
donned his most solemn face.*

*He sentenced poor Oscar Nebbe, against whom
even Julie Grinnell had found no evidence, to twenty-
five years in prison and ordered his immediate re-
moval to the state prison in Joliet. Then adjusting his
glasses again and brushing back his hair again, he
sentenced the others.*

*"I hereby order and decree that each of the other
defendants, between the hours of ten o'clock in the
forenoon and two o'clock in the afternoon on the third
day of December next, in the manner provided by the
statute of this State, be hung by his neck until he is
dead. May God have mercy on your souls, even as humans may not and cannot."*

No one in the court was surprised. The Judge's mo-

ment of glory had become an anticlimax. Nina Spies cried out in horror. Belated cheers and applause swept the courtroom.

The drama was not over, only the second act. But for the moment it seemed like it was over.

My lead was obvious and perhaps cheap:

DEATH BEFORE CHRISTMAS!

— 21 —

 SOCRA MARIE lies motionless in her neonatal bassinet. She did not protest the tubes in her mouth and nose, nor show her usual interest in the world around her.

"She won't eat," Nuala explained, as she caressed the baby's arm. "She won't cry. She won't cuddle in me arms. She won't even shit, if you can imagine that. It's like she's getting ready to die. All the fight has gone out of her, poor little thing."

It sounded bad to me. The tiny infant looked so forlorn, so detached, so ready to conclude that the decision to come into the world was a bad one.

"Did she turn blue?"

"She did not," Nuala said, dry-eyed and self-possessed. "They put them tubes into her as a precaution."

"What happened?"

"Wasn't I taking a nap and didn't I wake up with a start because I was expecting her to cry and herself lying in bed with her eyes open and not making a sound. So I brought her over here."

"What do they say?"

I put my arm around her; she leaned against me and sighed. She was, incidentally, wearing her Galway Hooker sweatshirt, which seemed to be her uniform for the hospital. She would explain to everyone that a "Hooker" was a fishing boat.

Outside the rain was pelting the windows and the wind was howling off the Lake.

"She's breathing all right and doesn't have a fever but she's not very responsive. I asked them about the cerebral palsy thing and they say they don't think so."

"What do they suspect?"

Nuala sighed loudly. "They think it might be some of the medication she's on, so they took her off it to see what happens. They say she's not dying and herself looking like it to me."

"That's all they did?" I demanded, my temper rising and my fist clenching.

"They say they have to try that first. Nothing else unless she deteriorates. She looks pretty deteriorated to me, Dermot Michael."

"She'll be all right," I said, trying to sound like I believed it.

"That's what they say, but look at her, Dermot Michael. She doesn't want to live anymore."

"Maybe she's just bored. Why don't we sing her some songs."

"Why don't we do your lullaby?"

A family joke is that the only cradle song I know is Brahms's "Lullaby."

So we sang it together, soft and gentle and meself watching the monitor over her bed. Nothing changed.

"I think she's a little more responsive," said the nurse who had joined us. "She definitely heard you singing."

"Do you really think so?" Nuala asked skeptically.

"She'll be all right," said the young woman. "It's just something temporary. She has to get that medication out of her bloodstream."

"Please God."

The day dragged on and slowly faded into a fretful night. Nuala called home several times.

"Everyone's acting up, the little bastards, driving poor Ethne crazy."

"The crises are catching up with them."

"Sure, 'tis good that's not happening to us."

We laughed, hollow, weary laughter.

"What did herself say?"

"That one will be the death of me. One minute she hovers over the little one like she's the mother and the next moment she's not interested."

"The way little girls are."

"'Tis true . . . She says to me today as I rush off to the hospital, 'I wish that baby would stop being silly.'"

"Really?"

"And I say to her, 'Nelliecoyne, your little sister is very sick' and doesn't she say to me, 'Ma, you know she's going to be all right.' And off she goes to play with her little friends."

"Maybe I should go home and sort things out?"

"Och, no, Dermot Michael, I need you here. Why don't we say the Rosary?"

We did, all fifteen decades. And then again. Finally Nuala drifted off to sleep, the Rosary still in her fingers.

What will happen to us if we lose her, I wondered. If she had died when she was born, that would have been terrible. Now we'd had her for four months. She had become for us a very real person, with her own personality (as we imagined) and her own characteristics we had grown to know and love. She was a fighter, not the kind of child which would give up on us and just die.

They said that maybe it was just that her medication needed to be changed. What did they know?

We should be grateful that God had given her to us for just a little while. That's what we should believe. And we would believe. Still the pain of loss would be with us a long time.

The really bad sign was that Nuala seemed to have given up hope. Like her daughter, Nuala was a fighter, a woman of wit and will and grim determination. If she felt like quitting, maybe that was a sign that the battle was almost over.

I called Ethne. The kids were both in bed and perhaps sleeping. They had been bickering with her and one another all day. The dogs had been banished to the basement, a punishment for misbehavior. They were down there now howling.

"Let them howl, Ethne."

"Me very thought."

Then it was my turn to sleep. I dreamed about the St. Ignatius women's basketball team. This time there was no curly-haired little point guard streaking down the floor.

Ill omen, I thought when I woke.

YOU'RE A REAL EEJIT IF YOU BELIEVE IN DREAMS.

"Go way, I don't have time for you."

THINK OF ALL THOSE PEOPLE IN NED'S STORIES AND STOP FEELING SORRY FOR YOURSELF.

I went back to sleep. No dreams that I can remember.

I woke up with a start.

"Any change?" I asked.

"None, Dermot Michael. It's like she's lost interest in living. I tried to nurse her and she paid no attention. Would you watch her while I go to the bathroom?"

"I will."

I continued to wallow in self-pity. Outside, lightning was cutting the sky above the Lake.

Suddenly, there was a fierce wail, a child in mortal agony.

Not ours, please God.

It was ours.

Socra Marie was raising bloody hell, kicking and waving her arms and shouting her lungs out.

I looked around. No nurse.

Was this displeasure good or bad?

Not knowing what to do, I tried the lullaby bit.

She didn't stop crying exactly but calmed down a little.

I tried a second round. She screwed up her tiny face and bellowed.

"Dermot Michael," Nuala cried, "whatever in the world are you doing to the poor child!"

"Singing, which doesn't do much good. I think she wants to eat."

"Well, hadn't I better feed her!"

She unhooked the pipes, lifted the baby out of the bed, opened her blouse and bra, and offered her nipple to Socra Marie.

The kid began to suck like it was going out of fashion.

"Well, 'tis about time, ya little brat. What have you been doing to us?"

The young resident and the nurse appeared behind us. We hadn't noticed that when Nuala unhooked the lines, bells had started to ring.

"She seems her old aggressive self again." Dr. Foley smiled. "It must have been the medication!"

"One hungry little girl," the nurse said approvingly.

"And," I added, life suddenly meaningful again, "one very angry little girl."

"And herself showing it," Nuala whispered, "by just dumping a new load of shite."

The smell of strong excrement enveloped us. Socra Marie paused in her pursuit of food, made a displeased face, and decided that for the moment food was more important than being wiped clean.

The doctor suggested we keep her in the hospital until noon to make sure she was all right. We agreed instantly.

So as the sun peeked over the rim of the Lake and decided that it was all right to stay the day, our daughter had been fed, burped, cleaned, and sung back to sleep. She had clearly decided to give this world of ours another chance. Nuala made sure that she heard us and saw us.

They tried different medication about which she'd made a face, but which she swallowed. Then she went

to sleep, pleased with herself no doubt that she had reminded us of our obligations to her and feeling quite
generous that she had given us another chance.

I phoned home.

"Coyne residence, Nellie speaking."

This was a new game.

"Hi, Nellie. It's your da."

"Hi, Da, how's the baby?"

So grown-up!

"Much better. We'll be home later in the day."

"I gotta hurry, Da, Ethne says we gotta go to
school. Bye."

"Herself?" Nuala asked, worn but happy.

"She had to hurry because Ethne said they had to go
to school. Bye, Da."

"I think, Dermot Michael, we may have been a pair
of friggin' eejits. The people here weren't worried.
Nellie wasn't worried. We were."

I put my arm around her again.

"We were very calm under stress."

"More like resigned."

The pediatrician appeared later and looked the child
over.

"My, haven't you become the pudgy little one,
Socra Marie. Did we make a mistake on the medicine?
I promise that we'll try not to do it again."

The childeen seemed skeptical.

"I wish we could promise you," she said to us, "that
there won't be any similar incidents. I don't think there
will be, but you never know for sure. I can tell you,
however, that all things considered, you have one very
healthy daughter."

"God knows, she's still alive," Nuala said cautiously.

"Very much alive. Still has that strong will to live
that I noticed four months ago."

So we took her home that afternoon.

The sun was shining brightly in the blue sky when
we pulled up across from St. Josaphat church. Ethne,

the two kids, and the wolfhounds, apparently back in good repute, were waiting on the porch. The humans cheered as we got out of the car and the dogs barked enthusiastically.

"She's fine," Nellie said as she looked at her sister in Nuala's arms. "She's always going to be fine."

I took the dogs for a run in the doggy park and then came home and played trucks with the Mick. We sent Ethne back to her apartment to get some rest and finish the paper that was due the next day. Nuala fed the child again and the two of them took a nap.

After feeding the kids and putting them to bed, we ate a pasta supper and settled down in the parlor.

"So what happened with Seamus yesterday?"

"I'll repeat it all, omitting only the routine obscenity, vulgarity, and male chauvinism."

"That's good crack, Dermot Michael. I wouldn't want me innocent ears to be shocked."

When I was finished, Nuala looked very thoughtful.

"I don't know why we're supposed to save him, Dermot Michael. I suppose God wants us to. Sometimes he doesn't seem worth saving and then other times he does. Is he a predator or a kind man with a heart of gold underneath all that shite? I think he's probably both, not that that helps us much."

"You still think you know who put out the contract?"

"Not to say 'think' Dermot love, I *know* who tried the first time. Course I can't prove it. The question is whether that person will try again. Or whether it will be someone else. And when."

"Hmm," I said as if I had the foggiest notion what she was talking about.

"He doesn't seem to realize what the pattern means, does he now?"

"The people that hate him are all passive-aggressive, wouldn't you say? Losers who nurse resentments and want to get even, but don't know how."

"'Tis true."

"Even the person who paid the hit man or was the hit man himself wanted desperately to settle a score with poor Seamus but he wasn't able to do it effectively. Probably at some level didn't want to kill him."

"Sounds like you have the right of it."

"Lost his nerve or her nerve at the last minute."

"Could be."

"And now would never try it again because he—or she—has decided that it's better to hate him while he's still alive than after he's dead."

"So you think there are two killers, Nuala Anne?"

"I wouldn't be surprised."

"Is that what's in your envelope?"

"Only the name of the second killer, the one we have to stop."

"Oh. I see."

"Do you now?"

"No, Nuala love. I don't know what the fuck you're talking about."

"Well, I suppose it's all right to go to Grand Beach this weekend, so long as we tell Commander Culhane and Commissioner Casey where we are."

"Not worried about the kid?"

"She's got to get used to the ride to Grand Beach, doesn't she now?"

That meant that we would have to pack a ton of toys for the other kids and enough clothes for Nuala to spend the summer.

And also Ned's manuscript.

—22—

Sept 14, 1887.

    There has been little enough to report in the last ten months. The Defense Committee, made up of many prominent people, has pushed its appeal to the Illinois Supreme Court. The Committee would have been much larger if that bastard Marshall Field had not bitterly opposed it. The brief that Bill Black had prepared (in my father's office naturally and with the help this summer of the resourceful Timmy Hardiman) was powerfully written and would have easily triumphed in an unbiased court of law.

However, the Illinois Supreme Court is not unbiased. Messrs. Field and McCormick must have spent a lot of money to persuade the court to rule today in the person of Justice Benjamin D. Magruder, speaking for the whole court, that there was "nothing erroneous, vicious or defective" in the record, proceedings, or judgment.

Mr. Justice Magruder has carved himself a place in history. I wonder how much Field paid him.

The Defense Committee is presenting an emergency petition to the United States Supreme Court. My father has persuaded General Ben Butler, the great war hero, to act for the Committee.

I doubt that the United States Supreme Court will overturn the verdict.

The Defense Committee will then convert itself into the Clemency Committee and try to persuade Governor Oglesby to grant clemency—twenty-five years in prison being clement compared to the gallows. The Governor is willing to grant clemency to anyone who applies. It would be a marvelous rebuke to Field, McCormick, Pullman, and Palmer if everyone received clemency. I don't think we can manage that. Schwab and Fielden, both men with wives and children will certainly request and receive clemency. Lingg, Fischer and Engel, the hardest of the radicals, refuse to think about it, though Lingg continues to speak to me about spiriting the lovely Elise away from Chicago. We will certainly do that. Nora and Josie have already befriended her. If I may be permitted a word of pride about these two women, when they befriend you, you are truly befriended.

Spies is strongly inclined to ask for clemency. The charms of the lovely Nina are hard to resist. Yet operatic tenors don't have happy endings. Parsons? You want Hamlet or Macbeth or Lear to live happily ever after? Don't be absurd.

Yet he is the most important of all. He is the leader of the group, the least anarchist of the lot, a man who can make an important contribution to the future of the labor movement when poor Terrence Powderly of the Knights of Labor fades from the scene.

"Think of it, Al," I tell him. "In a few years clemency will turn into a pardon. That will be the ultimate victory over Marshall Field and his ilk. You'll have won not only the trial but the war and you'll live to fight another day, the acknowledged hero of American labor, the man who fought Cyrus McCormick, Marshall Field, Potter Palmer, George Pullman, Joe Medil, a crooked police force, a corrupt Illinois court system and won."

"We have already won, Ned," he says, with a slow Texas smile. "Give me liberty or give me death!"

"Stop saying that! You're not Patrick Henry! You're someone better than that braggart. We need you. Your family needs you. The world needs you."

All of which I believed, at least when I was saying it.

"You'd make a good organizer, Ned." He chuckles.

"That's not the point," I shout.

"I know what the point is," he says slowly. "Believe me, Ned, I am thinking about it. I will think about it. I can imagine how angry old Marsh Field will be if I'm still around to haunt his dreams."

FIELD LOSES IN SUPREME COURT!

October 29, 1887

Marshall Field, the world-famous Chicago merchant, has won most of the battles in which he has engaged as the behind-the-scenes impresario of the Haymarket Trial. Yesterday he lost one battle, however temporarily. Despite Mr. Field's determined efforts, the United States Supreme Court agreed to hear an emergency plea from the Haymarket Defense Committee. Chief Justice Morrison R. Waite permitted a motion for a writ of error in an open court because of "the urgency of the case and its importance." The Chief Justice warned that the petition would not be accepted unless it involved Federal questions. No less a barrister than General Ben Butler will lead the Defense Committee's attempts to persuade the court that there are many Federal questions of basic human rights at issue.

Mr. Field is reported to be furious at this setback, the first he has encountered since the Haymarket incident itself. Realists on the Defense Committee are not hopeful that the court will rule for the Anarchists. As famed Chicago journalist Pete Dunne once remarked, the Supreme Court follows the elec-

tion returns. That a court would order a new trial for
the eight Anarchists who will die in less than two
weeks, would be a revolutionary development in
American society. Yet for the Anarchists, men who
are not afraid of death, that the court would listen to
their story is in itself a major victory.

My editor shook his head when he read the copy.

*"You are ruining your career, Ned. I have to publish
this. It will stir up a firestorm. But the big guys will
catch up with you."*

*"Come on," I said, "we both know that by Christ-
mas I am finished at this paper."*

*"I hope that's not true," he said sadly. "What will
you do?"*

"Find another way to bother them."

*Under no circumstances will I leave Chicago. It is
my city and my family's city as much as it is Marshall
Field's and Cy McCormick's. I've already drafted on-
commission articles for several New York magazines,
including one for* Harper's *about the Chicago Police
Department. The General will always have room for
me in his office, despite the much touted brilliance of
Timmy Hardiman.*

*I should note that we have a new child in the house,
one Myles Joyce Fitzpatrick, a healthy, handsome, and
apparently happy young man, in the last respect quite
different from his morose and ironic father.*

*Timmy and Josie continue their cautious courtship,
studying each other warily, like two wily lawyers in a
courtroom. They debated this last summer whether
Timmy should return to Notre Dame to earn his degree
or work at the General's law office. He saw no point in
the extra year of school. Josie argued that he would
disappoint his parents, who had sacrificed so much for
him, if he did not graduate and that, additionally, he
would disappoint her.*

The General, always the discreet diplomat (when he

wanted to be), hinted that a desk would be waiting for Tim whenever he returned. "You could probably have Ned's desk if you wanted it. He didn't graduate from college."

For a moment Josie was furious at him for what she perceived as a lack of respect for me. I had in fact graduated from college though I had never bothered to pick up the degree. Then she caught the General's wink and laughed like she was supposed to. So Tim came to Chicago on the train every weekend this autumn as we prepared for the last battle.

I don't doubt that they will marry but only when both are sure of the terms of the contract, a very different courtship than the one between me and Josie's aunt.

Even now we two are not clear on the terms of that contract and never will be.

I made this observation to Nora one night while we were sitting in front of the fireplace, sipping from small glasses of Irish whiskey.

"As Himself said, Ned, in His father's kingdom there are many mansions."

"I wouldn't want to trade places," I continued, "though I admire their carefulness."

"Josie of course is a wonderful young woman and Timmy a fine, fine young man. They will be happy, I'm sure."

"I agree."

We stared at the fire in silence.

"Well," my wife renewed the conversation, "Timmy Hardiman is a fine young man and they'll have a happy marriage, but after ten years of working hard and successfully on the marriage, he won't be anywhere near what the kindest, sweetest, most tender man in the world was when I first saw him in Maamtrasna during that terrible time."

I couldn't find my voice.

Finally, I said in choked tones, "Thank you, Nora my beloved."

" 'Tis only the truth, Ned. 'Tis time you begin to be-lieve it."

"I'm on notice," I said.

We both laughed.

Now I wonder. Surely those who love me see me the way Nora does. Do they deceive themselves, however? Does love blind them to my failings?

The obvious answer is that they are the only ones whose evaluation matters. If one must choose between their opinion and Marshall Field's evaluation of me, then who cares what the latter thinks?

And I end tonight with fervent prayers for Al Parsons and Gus Spies and their women. Thank God that, through no particular virtue of mine, Nora and I are not in the same position.

— 23 —

 COURT DENIES WRIT! FIELD HAPPY!

November 1, 1887

Chief Justice Waite of the United States Supreme Court announced today that the court had denied a petition for a writ of error in the Haymarket Trial. There was no evidence of major error which might be appropriately considered as a matter for Federal intervention.

Chicago merchant Marshall Field who has taken a personal, and it is said, a financial interest in the outcome of the trial was delighted. "It's about time we punish those criminals," he told a group of reporters. In one more week we'll have eight dead corpses hanging in the yard between the courthouse and the jail. The good people of Chicago will then be able to sleep peacefully at night."

A reporter asked whether the good people of Chicago would also be safe from raids by Mr. Field's good friend and protégé Captain Schaack of the Chicago Avenue Police Station, who enters their homes without warrants and without warning.

Mr. Field stormed away without responding.

Depending on the Clemency Committee's ability to persuade Governor Oglesby that the alleged Haymarket killers do not deserve to die, there may be fewer than eight bodies on November 11.

It is reported reliably that two men, Samuel Fielden and Michael Schwab, have already written letters of appeal, though it is not known whether they have reached the Governor's desk. Sources close to the defendants say that August Spies is seriously considering such a plea because of the pathos of the entreaties of his new wife, Nina VanZandt Spies. Only George Engel, Louis Lingg, and Adolph Fischer seemed determined to die next week. Despite his frequent repetition of Patrick Henry's "Give me liberty or give me death" slogan, Albert Parsons's intentions are not known.

I am convinced that the prospect of fighting on for the cause of labor in this world, as well as concern for his wife and sickly children, incline Al Parsons to seek clemency. However, Lucy Parsons is vehemently against such a petition. She argues that it would undercut the splendid drama of the trial and the lessons Al taught the world in his two-day speech. She loves him passionately, of that there can be no doubt. She would argue, however, that it is precisely that love which forces her to resist a humiliating plea to the Governor.

"They will always say that he did not have the courage to die a martyr's death," she tells me.

It would destroy the story, would it not, if Hamlet and Ophelia lived happily ever after.

It is not my responsibility to judge that faith, though many of my colleagues say, quite falsely, that she wants to be rid of Al because she has another lover.

Elise Freidel does not want her man to die either. However, she does not plead with him because she knows it will be to no avail. She accepts his wishes because that is what the lover of a warrior must do.

Nina VanZandt, with her parents' admiring support, begs Gus Spies to choose for life. She is sure that he will be out of jail in a couple of years and can continue his journalistic efforts to improve the condition of working people. There will be plenty of time then to begin the family Nina wants.

She seems to think that her pleas have been successful. When she encountered me on Michigan Street this afternoon, she told me, tears pouring down her beautiful face, that Augustus had agreed to write a letter to the Governor. She thanked me for my efforts to persuade him to do so.

For Gus the conflict must be terrible. Sensitive, generous man that he is, he is surely torn by his wife's agony. On the other hand, he must be loyal to his friends and colleagues, who have already disowned Fielden and Schwab.

He will write the letter, I think, and perhaps even send it to Governor Oglesby. But will he resist the fury of Fischer and Engel and perhaps of Al Parsons?

I don't know.

I stopped at Laddy's this afternoon to see how the workingmen were responding to the coming executions. Their sentiments, never hostile to the Anarchists, have changed greatly in the last year.

"No one proved anything against them."

"Don't they give a damn about their wives and kids?"

"Who the hell gave Marshall Field the right to say that these men should die?"

"Will they try to hang Sam Gompers next?"

Samuel Gompers is the president of the Cigar Makers Union and also the head of the new American Federation of Labor. He patently is no more an anarchist than Marshall Field himself. He represents the kind of respectable crafts unionism that my friends at Laddy's like. Gompers, a shrewd Jew from New York, is probably marking the path to success which American labor must follow. No bomb talk from him. However, he knows America and these German immigrants do not.

"What's going to happen, Ned? You're in the center of it. Do they like your white suit?"

"My wife likes it." I laugh. "She's the only one who matters."

It is also a useful symbol, though of what I'm not sure.

They all laugh.

"Yeah, but what will happen?"

"On execution day the honest workingmen and -women of Chicago will storm the jail and release the prisoners. They will hack Captain Schaack to death with bloody knives, they will lynch Marshall Field in front of his own store, they will burn the Board of Trade to the ground, they will form a commune to govern Chicago with Al Parsons as mayor and Louie Lingg as chief of police."

They were silent for a moment, thinking perhaps that they should do these things.

"You're having us on, aren't you, Neddie?"

"I am," I admitted.

"You think we should do these things?"

"No," I said. "I think Sam Gompers's way is better." *Did I really? Maybe.*

"Are they really afraid we might?"

"The rich people are terrified. Captain Schaack and Captain Bonfield know better but they're stoking those fears. There are plans to fill downtown with troops, there will be a heavy guard at the Board of Trade. Your potential Anarchists who might like to see Marsh Field swaying in the wind, better stay away from the troops. They will be as trigger-happy as the cops were the night of the so-called riot."

"What will happen?"

"You'll hear the wailing of wives and children and sweethearts. You'll read the celebrations in the papers. The Tribune will think it's in heaven."

"Nothing more."

"Nothing more except a big funeral over in Wicker Park and a sad burial in Waldheim Cemetery."

"They deserve better than that, Ned."

"They do indeed. Alas, they have done the wrong thing for the right reasons."

My burly friend did not appear tonight as I walked home. Would I ever hear from him again? Maybe his messages were an attempt to deceive me.

"Two drinks of Irish whiskey tonight is it, Mr. Fitzpatrick?" my wife said when I kissed her at the door of our house.

"Both small ones," I said. "You know, Mrs. Fitzpatrick, I often wonder what would happen if I came home after three drinks of Irish whiskey."

"Wouldn't they have to carry you in and wouldn't we put you right into bed?"

November 2, 1887

SPIES SEEKS CLEMENCY! COLLEAGUES UPSET!

August Spies, editor of the suppressed newspaper *Arbeiter-Zeitung* today wrote a letter to Governor Oglesby for the clemency the Governor seems prepared to offer to the convicted Anarchists who seek it.

Spies will be an interesting test for the Governor. He is intelligent and personally charming, his paper, before Chicago policed closed it, was a platform for strong Anarchist rhetoric, though it never explicitly advocated violence, much less bomb throwing.

Spies has vigorously denied that he has ever broken a law.

The two men who have already received clemency, Michael Schwab and Sam Fielden, are both husbands and fathers of small children. It may be wondered how life in prison will enable them to devote much time to their wives and offspring. However, life is better than death, especially since many believe that in a few years a pardon for the Anarchists is likely, a final repudiation of Marshall Field and his hirelings, Captain Schaack and Judge Gary.

Spies has no children and his marriage to the beautiful Nina VanZandt is at this time only a technical union. If Governor Oglesby does grant clemency to Spies, he will be offending Marshall Field, who desperately wants to see seven corpses next week. He will also signal that clemency might be possible even for Albert Parsons, the acknowledged leader of the convicted men, who also is married and has two small and sickly children.

However, it is not certain how long Spies will persist in his application. Rumors both inside and outside the jail assert that Spies is under strong pressure from prisoners Engel and Adolph Fischer and Anarchist sympathizers to withdraw his application, which they contend is an admission of cowardice.

I stopped by Louis Lingg's cell on the way out of the jail. He was stretched on his cot, hands behind his head, resting contentedly, as though he had not a concern in the world, the young warrior preparing to go into his last battle.

"Surely, Ned, you are not trying to talk me into applying for clemency!"

"I would if I could, Lou."

"Well, I may have something to say on the whole issue in a day or two, but you can rely on it: I would not
accept clemency if they forced it upon me. You told me
that I would enjoy a happy life with Elise. You know
that's not true. I would drive the poor little thing mad.
I don't belong in the domestic world. I belong in battle, battle to the death."

"The Prussian Army could doubtless use your skills."

"I don't believe in the Prussian Army. I believe in
spitting in the face of all authority. Women are wonderful creatures but not for the likes of me."

"Aren't they more than wonderful creatures, Lou?
They're companions, allies, confidants, friends. Don't
we owe them respect as equals?"

"Women equal to men? Now you sound like Lucy
Parsons. That's absurd, Ned. They are incapable of
true idealism, true sacrifice for the good of humanity.
They would unman us all, if we permitted it."

"Or would they make us perhaps more human?"

"They would make us morally flabby. Your pleas to
Gus and Al are always based on concern for women
and children. Such pleas may be effective with weak
men like Schwab and Fielden. Not with the men who
make history. Did Napoleon worry about what
would happen to Josephine when he marched on
Russia?"

His wife when he marched on Russia was the Aus-
trian princess Maria Luisa. I did not, however, play
the pedant.

"You think I'm appealing to the weakness of your
colleagues?"

"No, to their softness. There is no room for that in
men who are warriors."

"I suppose not."

I briefly wondered what he meant when he said that
he might have something to say on the whole issue in a
day or two. Lou Lingg was a very dangerous man.

"You're sure you will take care of Elise?"

"We've made contact with your friends in Iowa. They will welcome her gladly. We will get her out of town before the funeral and remain in contact with her during the years to come."

He nodded.

"I know I can rely on you."

The warrior making sure that someone would provide for his woman when he was gone.

"We don't think she belongs as a permanent member of the Association of Martyrs' Widows."

"Lucy Parsons is a bitch," he said calmly. *"She'd ruin Elise's life like she will ruin the life of that Van-Zandt woman. Spies is wise in seeking clemency to protect his wife from Lucy."*

"Good-bye, Ned"—he stretched his long, lean frame from the cot and shook my hand—*"you're one of the few decent human beings in this city."*

"I'll see you again, Lou. I'll be at the hanging."

He laughed.

"Don't bet on it, Ned!"

I wondered what that meant.

Bill Black was at my father's office.

"Oglesby," the General said to me, *"is a man with a conscience. He knows that the trial was a farce. He'll commute the sentences of everyone who applies, even Parsons and Lingg. He may also grant a commutation to all of them, even if they don't want it."*

"That will break Al Parsons's heart. He's looking forward to his final words from the gallows."

"Will Spies stick to it?" Black asked me.

"I doubt it," I replied. *"Nina loves him. He is fond of her, but it is the opinion of his fellow Anarchists that matters."*

"Well maybe we can save them all despite themselves."

It was a crazy game we were playing. The Anar-

*chists wanted, with greater or lesser degrees of en-
thusiasm, to die. We on the Clemency Committee
wanted to prevent them from doing what they wanted
to do.*

*Life in prison for Lou Lingg? He'd kill someone in
jail rather than face that. If we obtained pardons for
them in the next couple of years as both Dad and the
General thought we would, he'd be a walking time
bomb on the street.*

CLERGY PREACH TO DOOMED MEN

Although all the remaining doomed Anarchists
have resolutely denied that they believe in God,
veritable battalions of clergy have descended on the
County Jail to plead with them to do penance for
their sins.

Ignoring the plea of the condemned men that they
be spared clerical ministrations, officials have permitted the clergy to wander up and down the aisle of
the County Jail, where the condemned men are held,
to warn of the dangers of hellfire.

The reactions of those who will die next week are
varied. Engel and Fischer curse them in German.
August Spies, who has submitted his plea for
clemency but has not decided yet whether to withdraw it, argues with them, almost as though he were
a Jesuit priest. Louis Lingg laughs at them with a
deep powerful laugh which makes the bars of the
jail rattle. Albert Parsons preaches to them. One
wonders if the preachers want to be rebuffed just as
the doomed men want to die. The ministers can tell
their congregations the Sunday after the execution
that they did their best to redeem the wayward souls
of the condemned killers.

Father Galligan of St. Patrick's has visited August
Spies twice for brief periods of time. Apparently

they had a very civilized conversation. They agreed that if, towards the end, Spies wants a priest he need only send word through a guard and he would be there any hour of the day or night.

Spies probably would have made a good Jesuit.

─ 24 ─

 BULLETIN
SPIES RECANTS

November 6

August Spies, former editor of the *Arbeiter-Zeitung*, has withdrawn his application of clemency. It is understood that Governor Oglesby had intended to commute the death sentences of the convicted Anarchists to life in prison, if they had petitioned for clemency. It is also understood that the Governor judged Spies's letter the best reasoned and most moving of the three letters he received.

Spies chose death over life because his Anarchist colleagues both inside and outside of County Jail told him he was a coward, a man who permitted a woman to deprive him of his courage. Previous applications from Samuel Fielden and Michael Schwab were treated more tolerantly because they were never considered to be real Anarchists. The charges against them were even more ridiculous, Anarchists thought, than the charges against the others.

Spies wrote a touching letter to Governor Oglebsy offering his life as a substitute for the lives of all the others currently waiting execution in

Cook County Jail. The letter is considered legally worthless.

There is still hope for the five remaining convicts. The Clemency Committee is trying to persuade the Governor to commute the sentences of all the condemned men even if they do not ask for commutation. Doubtless August Spies's wife Nina VanZant Spies is praying for that outcome.

The text of his letter to the Governor shows the temperament of a great romantic tenor:

Chicago, Nov. 6, 1887

The fact that some of us have appealed to you for justice (under the pardoning prerogative) while others have not, should not enter into consideration in the decision of our cases. Some of my friends have asked you for an absolute pardon. They feel the injustice done them so intensely that they cannot conciliate the idea of a commutation of sentence with the consciousness of innocence. The others (among them myself), while possessed of the same feeling of indignation, can perhaps more calmly and dispassionately look upon the matter as it stands. They do not disregard the fact that through a systematic course of lying, perverting, distorting, and slandering, the press has succeeded in creating a sentiment of bitterness and hatred among a great portion of the populace that one man, no matter how powerful, how courageous and just he be, cannot possibly overcome. They hold that to overcome that sentiment or the influence thereof would almost be a psychological impossibility. Not wishing, therefore, to place your excellency in a still more embarrassing position between the blind fanaticism of a misinformed public on the one hand and justice on the other, they concluded to submit their case to you unconditionally.

I implore you not to let this difference of action have any weight with you in determining our fate. During our trial the desire of the prosecution to slaughter me and to let my codefendants off with slighter punishment was quite apparent and manifest. It seemed to me then, and to a great many others, that the prosecution would be satisfied with one life—namely, mine. Grinnell in his argument intimated this very plainly.

I care not to protest my innocence of any crime, and of the one I am accused of in particular. I have done that, and I leave the rest to the judgment of history. But to you I wish to address myself now, as the alleged archconspirator (leaving the fact that I have never belonged to any kind of a conspiracy out of the question altogether); if a sacrifice of life must be, will not my life suffice? The State's Attorney of Cook County asked for no more. Take this, then; take my life. I offer it to you that you may satisfy the fury of a semi-barbaric mob, and save the lives of my comrades. I know that every one of my comrades is as willing to die and perhaps more so than I am. It is not for their sakes that I make this offer, but in the name of humanity and progress, in the interest of a peaceable, if possible, development of the social forces that are destined to lift our race upon a higher and better plane of civilization.

In the name of the traditions of our country I beg you to prevent a sevenfold murder upon men whose only crime is that they are idealists; that they long for a better future for all. If legal murder there must be, let one, let mine suffice.

August Spies

Spies is a fool! It was all settled, all arranged. Why did he let the other fools intimidate him? Does he not understand that Nina, despite her intelligence and apparently endless wardrobe, is a fragile young woman, generous but not old enough or experienced enough to face tragedy with maturity and poise. She does not belong in the company of passionate haters and crusaders like Lucy Parsons, a woman with a heart so hard that she wants her husband to die! That culture will destroy her soul!

However, tenors have to sing their final song, don't they!

I spoke to Al Parsons after the news of Spies's letter spread.

"I don't know, Ned, I don't know. I think they should have left him alone. I can't tell them what to do."

"The hell you can't!"

He glanced at me with a momentary flash of rage in his eyes. Then he laughed.

"I suppose you're right . . . What I meant is that I thought I had to respect their freedom."

"To violate Gus's freedom?"

He lifted his arms in a weak gesture.

"Ned, I can't let Sam and Adolph and Lou and now Gus die alone, can I? They'll never be able to die gallantly without me. You know that, don't you?"

"If the Governor commutes the sentences of all of you, will you hang yourselves?"

"We'll accept it with relief."

Not a line that Hamlet or Macbeth or Lear would have uttered.

Al Parsons did not want to die. However, more than anything else he wanted to preserve Lucy's respect for him. Love is a strange business.

November 9, 1887

I write these words in the morning after Mass and before I walk down once more to Michigan Street. I have been attending Mass every morning for the Anarchists and their families. It is about the only useful thing left for me to do.

The General and Bill Black are in Springfield at the Governor's side. Nora and Josie have taken Elsie to her refuge in Iowa. They will give her the envelope with three hundred dollars that are earnest money for any future help she may need. Annie and the children are with my mother. The house is empty.

Marshall Field and Cy McCormick have traveled to Springfield too. That might help our cause, so great is the Governor's distaste for both men.

The foreign reporters are having a field day. They compare the Haymarket affair to a three ring circus. One of them writes that the Chicago Tribune *runs the city and that the people at the Trib more than anyone else are responsible for the hanging of innocent men.*

That is true perhaps but it does not give enough credit to the local plutocrats.

It will all be over in a few days. There will be a massive funeral, which will scare the timid of Chicago all over again. Then a Pardon Committee will emerge out of the Clemency Committee, just as the latter emerged out of the Defense Committee. The Anarchists and their allies, led by Lucy Parsons, will form an organization to raise a monument. Life will go on.

All we've done is save Elise.

I hope.

BOMBS FOUND IN LINGG'S CELL!

Late this afternoon guards at the County Jail and Chicago Police found three pipe bombs under the cot in the cell of convicted Anarchist Louis Lingg. There was enough explosive power in the bomb, according to Captain Schaack of the Chicago Avenue Police Station, to destroy the entire cellblock housing the Anarchist prisoners.

"Lingg," Captain Schaack said, "intended to destroy himself and all his colleagues and many of the jail staff in a massive explosion before the sentence of the court could be carried out."

Police theorized that Lingg's Anarchist friends, including his girlfriend, Elise Freidel, smuggled the parts of the bomb into the cell and Lingg worked on the bombs at night.

On the face of it, this theory seems absurd. Can the guards at the County Jail be that incompetent, one must wonder. Whence came the idea to search under the bed in Lingg's cell? There can be no doubt that

Lingg is the sort of man who might attempt such a blow to the Chicago establishment. Indeed he would relish it. That he was able to arrange it, however, seems most unlikely.

Police are said to be searching for Miss Freidel, who has reportedly left Chicago.

Anarchist sympathizers throughout the city deny that there was any plot to blow up the jail. Timothy Hardiman, one of the lawyers defending Lingg, reported that the police will not let him see either Lingg or the alleged explosives.

"They've separated Lou from the other prisoners," Hardiman said. "I think they might kill him."

Some will wonder if this is not just one more of Captain Schaack's strange theories which have appeared frequently during the Haymarket affair. It certainly serves Captain Schaack's purpose of preventing clemency for all the condemned men.

When did young Timmy Hardiman become a lawyer for the defense? When I appointed him. I am still a partner in the General's firm. In all the confusion about the supposed plot, no one paid any attention to a new lawyer on the scene. Young Timmy played his part well, all too well. He's learned the tricks of the trade early.

I was able to visit the other prisoners at the end of the day. To a man they ridiculed the idea of a plot. To a man they also said, "The police will kill him now. Horribly."

"Why?"

"Because they hate him so much. He treats them with contempt."

That prediction seemed so outrageous that I did not quote it in the paper. Timmy's naive and innocent comment was enough.

I promise God tonight that no matter what happens tomorrow and the next day, I will drive Schaack and his friend Bonfield from public life.

My family will not be back until the morning. I am very lonely.

November 10

LINGG'S DEATH CALLED SUICIDE!

Police and guards at Cook County Jail said at noon today that the death of convicted Anarchist Louis Lingg in his jail cell early this morning was suicide. They say that the blasting cap which Mr. Lingg ignited inside his mouth had been smuggled in by his girlfriend Elise Freidel inside a slice of cake she brought him last night.

This is the same Miss Freidel for whom the police were searching yesterday. They reported at that time that she had left the city, which raises an interesting question about the alleged slice of cake.

Considerable skepticism exists around the courthouse and the jail. Mr. Lingg was capable of a dramatic gesture. Yet he must have known that an exploding blasting cap would have blown out half of his face and that he would live several hours in agony. Those that know Mr. Lingg said a dramatic gesture from him would have been much cleaner and more elegant.

They argue that Lingg's violent death will make it impossible for Governor Ogelsby to grant general commutation to all the Anarchists tomorrow morning.

"I demand a complete investigation," said Timothy Hardiman, a member of Mr. Lingg's legal team. "There was widespread suspicion that the police would murder him before the hanging and make it horrible. That's just what happened."

This time Timmy Hardiman did not need my urging or my scripting.

"You did fine, Timmy," I said. "I predict a wonderful career for you. But it's back to Notre Dame for you now before some of my colleagues begin to wonder where this brilliant young attorney appeared from.

"Yes, Uncle Ned," he said with a wide grin and departed for the Michigan Central station.

I renewed my pledge to drive Schaack from power.

Later.

My family is home now, tired but triumphant from their adventures. Both Nora and Josie report that the Iowa people with whom Elise has found refuge are kind and wonderful. She had not heard of Lingg's death and probably would not hear about it for many months. They had promised they would visit her often.

"She wept and wept when we left, poor little thing," said Nora, tears streaming down her own face.

"When did this Timothy Hardiman pass his bar examination?" Josie demanded with mock displeasure. "Uncle Ned, you'll get him disbarred before he gets barred."

Despite the sadness of the day, we laughed at that wondrous Irish Bull. We needed a laugh.

Still later.

A telegram from the General.

Clemency for Schwab and Fielden approved and wired to jail. Stop. Will talk to Governor tomorrow morning about general commutation. Stop. Prospects bleak. Stop. Hire this Timothy Hardiman. Stop. Ed Fitzpatrick, Commanding.

The man is always able to laugh. Yet tomorrow will be a very long day.

"YOUR FRIEND, Ned," my wife complained, "has forgotten about our mystery."

"Our mystery?"

"Who threw the bomb!"

"He's had other things on his mind."

"Obviously Captain Schaack killed poor Louis Lingg."

"Why?"

"Out of pure spite and to prevent a more general commutation."

"An evil man."

"Our friend Ned will get him, never fear . . . so how do you like lying on the floor in your diaper, little one? This is Grand Beach and it's summer and it's hot so we're all being comfortable. And your ma's going down the beach for her first swim in a long time, isn't she now? And your da and your big sister are going to watch you real carefully, aren't they?"

"Yes, Ma," Nellie said with the air of someone whose patience is routinely trampled upon.

"And the Mick is going to play with his trucks, isn't he now?"

"Yes, Ma. I hope when the baby grows up she will want to play with the trucks too."

The Mick rushed over and kissed his little sister with a show of sincerity that was admirable.

"Be careful, Nuala Anne," I warned her. "The Lake is still cold."

"Sure, 'tis a lot warmer than Galway Bay."

My wife was alive again, the hoyden she was when I first met her and especially when she went to Galway, where her exploits at Camogli were legendary.

One of the neighbors had asked her this morning how she was feeling.

"Well, not too bad," Nuala had responded, using the proper Irish response.

The Irish are, I should explain very cautious in such matters, perhaps because they fear that God will punish them for claiming too much and perhaps because they love indirection and understatement. Sometimes.

"She's grand altogether," I said to the neighbor.

"Didn't I say that?" my puzzled wife had asked.

"Da, the little brat just shit in her pants," Nellie informed me.

"I can smell it, dear. And don't say shit. It's a vulgar word."

"Ma says it all the time."

"When people born in Ireland say it, then it's not a vulgar word."

Nellie didn't argue with that truth.

So we wiped and cleaned and powdered the small one and wrapped her up in a clean diaper.

Then we hummed Brahms's "Lullaby" together.

Socra Marie looked up at me and smiled.

"She smiled at you, Da," Nellie whispered as though we had witnessed a sacred event.

"No she didn't, Nellie. It just looked that way. She's too young to know what a smile is."

"It was a smile . . . She did it again! Isn't she pretty when she smiles!"

"It certainly looks like a smile," I admitted.

"We won't tell Ma," Nellie warned me.

"No way."

Ma reappeared from the beach, shivering inside a thick terry cloth robe.

"Wasn't it grand altogether! Not cold, at all, at all! . . . How's my little sweetheart!"

She swept Socra Marie into the air and kissed her. The kid grinned happily.

"Dermot Michael! Did you see what she did?"

"Shit in her pants again?"

"She *smiled* at me, didn't you, love."

"She's not old enough to smile."

"Still she smiled at me, didn't she, Nellie?"

"I didn't see anything."

"The two of youse are blind! Look! Both of youse saw that! A real smile!"

"Accidental contraction of the facial muscles which if we positively reinforce she'll do all the time."

"Isn't she pretty, Nellie, when she smiles!"

"Yes, Ma."

"Isn't she pretty, Mick, when she smiles!"

The son actually looked at his little sister smiling and smiled back.

"See, Dermot Michael! You're outvoted!"

"So what else is new."

She placed the child back on the blanket. Socra Marie promptly closed her eyes and shut down for her morning nap.

"Why don't ya go out on the dune and play?" she asked the small fry.

They shouted enthusiastically and rushed for the door.

"Don't ya even think of opening the gates, ya hear?"

"Yes, Ma!"

We had left the hounds at the kennel for the weekend because there wasn't room in the Mercedes for them and the three kids and all the toys, without which one dares not even think of going to the beach. They looked woebegone when we left. I knew from past experience that they would forget about us and play with the vet's kids and intimidate all the other dogs boarding there. We would have to buy a bigger vehicle before the Fourth of July. And a house. We couldn't impose our huge family on my parents any longer.

I was much too young to have such a large family.

"I'm going to go upstairs and get out of me cold swimsuit," Nuala Anne informed me.

"I'll help you," I offered gallantly.

"I won't be needing any help. We have serious talking to do about your man, don't we? 'Tis time for more stewing, isn't it?"

She didn't wait for an answer. My man in this case was obviously Seamus Costelloe.

She bounded down the stairs almost immediately in denim shorts and a checkered blouse. I devoured her with my eyes as she charged into the parlor.

"You been watching the kids outside, Dermot Michael Coyne?"

"Woman, I have."

"And me smiling little girl?" She leaned over Socra Marie to make sure she was still breathing.

"Woman, I have."

"And, Dermot Michael, stop staring at me that way. It melts me altogether."

"I reserve my right as a husband to consider my spouse with lustful intent."

She sighed as if in abject resignation.

"Well, I suppose we'll all need a nap this afternoon, won't we now?"

She sat next to me on the couch, close enough so I could touch her superb thigh. I postponed that delight for a couple of minutes.

"That will be as may be," I said, firing one of her pet phrases back at her.

"Now," she said, businesslike and serious, "tell me what you found out about our suspects."

"They all own weapons, registered weapons that is, even our pathetic little ambulance chasers. They own twenty-five caliber pistols they claim to use for target practice. As does Helen Cross O'Leary Shepherd."

"The same weapon that nicked your man?"

"The same kind of weapon, yes. They actually let the police look at their guns, which hadn't been fired for some time. Of course, they could have another twenty-five that they tossed into the Chicago River after they had winged Seamus."

"And them respectable Shepherd folks?"

"They have a veritable arsenal of weapons, revolvers, rifles, shotguns, an automatic weapon or two. Len Shepherd is a collector. They claim never to use them except for target practice."

"Which doesn't mean that the woman couldn't have taken one of them small things and used it that night, does it now?"

"It does not . . . You don't think it was a contract shooting?"

She made a skeptical face.

"Like you say, Dermot, 'tis amateur night."

"And why would it be the woman?"

"I don't like her."

"You haven't met her."

"I don't need to . . . And your Greek friends?"

"Nicholas has an old rifle, Enfield .303, that he says his father used in the war. He doesn't say which war."

"That's all?"

"That's all he admits. I wouldn't be surprised if he or his brother had enough guns stashed away to start a minor uprising."

"And Jimmy the Giant?"

"He has registered one massive .45 revolver, enough to kill a charging tiger. If he had used that against Seamus it would have blown him out of the building."

"So they all have guns or at least access to guns?"

"Not clear that any one of them has much experience if any in using them."

"The Costelloes?"

"Chauvinist vulgarian that he is, your man is a firm supporter of gun control. So is all the family."

"That's not much help, is it now? . . . Dermot Michael Coyne! Whatever in the world are you doing?"

"Exercising me spousal right to caress me wife's lovely leg!"

"Despite what it might do to her hormones?"

"No, because of what it might be doing to her hormones."

"The children might come rushing in."

"I'll stop."

"It's no great crack riding a nursing mother." She sighed.

The Irish when they want to be obscene refer to intercourse as "ride." When they wish to avoid obscenity they call it "fock."

"You got it wrong, Nuala Anne McGrail. It's the greatest crack riding a nursing mother."

"Why?" she demanded, her interest in this apparent perversity stirred up.

I had better come up with a good explanation.

"Everything's so elemental—milk, semen, life, woman as a vessel of pleasure and a vessel of nourishment."

I thought that was a pretty good off-the-cuff answer.

"Oh."

"You satisfy my daughter's need for food and my need for sexual release," I continued, pushing my luck.

"I'm just a thing to be used by you and by that little brat on the blanket?"

"You are a person to be reveled in by the two of us."

"Well, we can't do it now anyway."

"I can wait for the nap," I said, squeezing her thigh. "I'm just preparing you."

"I don't need much preparation at all, at all, Dermot love . . . Now let's talk about alibis."

"They all have them as you might expect. The Shepherds were attending a play at the new Goodman Theater with another couple. They went over to Shaw's Crab House for dinner afterwards. The other couple swear they were with them till midnight."

"Uhm . . ." Her fingers rested on my thigh, turnabout as always being fair play.

"The Greeks were at a confirmation party for one of their relatives, scores of witnesses."

"Uhm . . ."

"McGourty and McGinty were playing poker with several other ambulance chaser lawyers."

"Uhm . . ."

"And Jimmy the Giant was in bed with his wife."

"Lucky woman," she said cynically.

"Who knows?"

"And the Costelloe family?

"All allege to have been in similar domestic situations . . . I'm afraid that none of this is much help."

"Ah, well, now, doesn't it raise some interesting possibilities." She sighed. "There's still too many loose ends. Doesn't it get more and more complicated, Dermot Michael? Won't I have to amend my prediction, just a little bit? . . . What does Seamus have on your man?"

Me man this time was probably Leonard Shepherd.

"Enough to destroy his reputation. Not enough probably to put him in jail, because all the briberies of judges about which Seamus has gathered evidence are beyond the statute of limitations. He might be liable for a ton of civil actions."

"Remind me why Seamus gathered evidence against your man?" She rested her head against my shoulder, her hair, still wet from the lake, fell on my face.

"To forestall any attempt to take him down that Len

Shepherd, egged on by his wife, might have tried to engineer."

"Seamus is smarter than your man?'

"Much, much smarter."

"Dermot," she whispered, "I love you more than I've ever loved you before. It breaks me heart, how much I love you."

I held her tight. All I could manage was the very unpoetic, "I love you too, Nuala."

"'Tis strange, isn't it now, Dermot Michael?"

"'Tis," I said, not having any idea what was strange.

"Two young people meet one night, filled with hormones and loneliness. They decide that they're meant for one another, though it takes the lad a while to realize it. They kiss and play with each other a lot. Then they decide that it's time to marry. They want to have children of course. So they do. Before they know it there are three little rugrats around the house, each one totally different from the other, a housekeeper and a nanny about whom they have to stew . . ."

"And two huge dogs . . ."

"'Tis true"—she giggled—"don't stop caressing me, Dermot, don't I love it altogether . . . And all kinds of other worries to stew about too . . . Would they not have run out of the pub that foggy night if they knew what marriage would be like?"

Good question. And I had better answer it right.

"Marriage is great crack, Nuala Anne," I insisted, as I unbuttoned her blouse. "Especially to you!"

Then Socra Marie, perhaps wakened by a cry from outside, erupted in a roar of protest.

"Och, me dear little one," Nuala said as she sprang from the couch, pulling her disarrayed clothes back together, "wasn't your da getting ready to ride me when them terrible children woke you up. Now settle down and relax and we'll give everyone a bit of lunch and then think about our afternoon naps. Hush, now, your ma is with you. Everything is all right."

She faded into a lullaby in Irish and I, hoping for the promise of a late spring nap on the side of a lake, turned to Ned Fitzpatrick's agonized story.

— 26 —

November 11, 1897

    I found two messages when Nora and I returned from Mass at Immaculate Conception Church on North Park. One was a telegram from the General.

Failure Stop Returning home Stop.

I choked up. Nora wept when I showed it to her. The other was a scrawled note from Lucy Parsons.

Mr. Fitzpatrick,

They would not permit the children and me to visit Albert last night. Other families were also barred. We will try again this morning.

                                Lucy Parsons.

    I drank a cup of tea, ate a piece of toast, and dashed down to Michigan Street. Police and soldiers were everywhere, the latter with rifles and fixed bayonets. The guards didn't want to let me into the jail, despite my press credentials. Fortunately for me, Chief Pemberton, in full uniform, appeared and waved me in.

"They will not let the families see the condemned men!" I shouted.

"I know, Ned. I know," he said soothingly. "Everyone's frightened. We have guards at the homes of everyone associated with the trial. Mounted troops in front of the Board of Trade. The city is under siege."

"Why?"

"There is a rumor that twenty thousand armed Anarchists will storm the jail, release the prisoners, and blow up the courthouse and the jail."

"Do you believe that?"

We walked into the first floor of the jail, which was filled with armed soldiers, milling about with apparently no clear idea of what they were supposed to do. The General will be horrified, I thought, at the use to which his troops have been put.

"Certainly not. Sheriff Matson, who is in charge of the execution, believes it, however. The bombs they found in Lingg's cell have terrified them all."

"Do you think there were really bombs there?"

He shrugged. "Schaack said there were."

"And has frightened the whole city!"

"I'm afraid that's what he wanted to do."

"He has kept the families away from the condemned men!"

"He says they would smuggle in more bombs."

"Do you believe that?"

He hesitated and sighed sadly.

"Certainly not, Ned. It's all illusory, like everything Schaack does. Sometimes I think he deceives even himself with his Anarchist stories."

I did not ask him, because I already knew the answer, why a mere Captain of Police could run the whole city of Chicago, eclipsing even his usual ally, Captain Bonfield.

The answer was that he had Marshall Field's money behind him.

"They've been reciting poetry and singing hymns all night," the Chief said as he showed me into the hanging yard, a roofed-over alley separating the jail from the courthouse.

"They all seem ready to die, eager even . . . it will be between eleven o'clock and twelve o'clock."

I was filled with rage, grief, and a sense of utter powerlessness. Unlike most of the crowd, I had witnessed an unjust murder by mass hanging once before. I did not want to endure the experience again. Yet it was my job to do so.

There were a couple of hundred people jammed into the yard. They were restrained from crushing against the gallows at one end of the yard by a cordon of armed police, Captain Schaack in charge.

Rumors raced up and down the yard like a prairie fire. Governor Oglesby had pardoned all of them. He had revoked the clemency of Schwab and Fielden. Spies had asked once more for clemency. Parsons had hung himself in his cell.

The appeal and the terror of a mass execution is that the victims are human beings just like us. One moment they are alive, breathing, thinking of their wives and children. The next moment they are pitiable corpses with broken necks, hanging at the end of nooses. To soften the terror of the experience, the sense that one could just as well be standing on the gallows with them, attempts are made to dehumanize them, to set them apart from the fortunate ones who are only watching.

Thus when Parsons, Spies, Engel, and Fischer appeared a little before noon, singing the "Marseillaise" they were clad in rough white shrouds and their heads completely covered by hoods. Each of them had a noose around his neck. Their legs were bound by straps and their arms bound by handcuffs. No egregious blunders would be permitted like those at Galway Jail when Myles Joyce and his fellows were hung.

They were lined up on the gallows and the nooses attached to the overhanging ropes.

"The time will come when our silence will be more powerful than the voices you are throttling today," Spies shouted.

I wonder if he and Nina had been permitted a last farewell.

Engel, Santa's gray-haired little elf, shouted "Hooray for Anarchy!"

Fischer also shouted, "Hooray for Anarchy!" And then added, "This is the happiest moment of my life!"

Parsons had the last word, of course.

"Will I be allowed to speak, O men of America? Let me speak, Sheriff Matson! Let the voice of the people be heard!"

He was about to continue when the trap fell.

There were a few cheers. Most of the crowd were silent, in horror or shame, or sickness I do not know. I suffered all those emotions but did not vomit, as much as I wanted to.

They had died, I tried to tell myself once I had fought myself out into the chill autumn air on Michigan Street, like brave men. Their part in the drama was over. Their story would go on and their brave deaths would be a high point in it.

The headline for my first story would read,

GALLOWS TRAP SILENCES PARSONS—
FOR NOW

However before the day was over I had another story to write.

SCHAACK ARRESTS PARSONS WIDOW
AND CHILDREN
REMOVES THEIR CLOTHES IN SEARCH
FOR BOMBS

CAPTAIN MICHAEL SCHAACK, WHO HAS been ruling Chicago like a military dictator, not only prevented the families of the condemned Anarchists from visiting their loved ones last night, he also barred them this morning. He even arrested Lucy Parsons, wife of Alfred Parsons, and her two children this morning when they tried for a last visit with Mr. Parsons. He then ordered that the woman and two children be taken to the Chicago Avenue Police Station, where their clothes were removed and they were searched for explosives at about the same time as the gallows trap was sprung on their husband and father. Naturally the searchers found no explosives.

Captain Schaack, who usually sees no need for explanations, insisted that this was merely a precaution against alleged Anarchist plots to blow up the Cook County Jail.

It is obvious now that there were no such plots. They existed only in Captain Schaack's mind. Apparently there is no barbarity to which he will not sink in his passion for public attention.

Mrs. Nina VanZandt Spies, together with her loyal parents, also attempted to visit Mrs. Spies's husband for the last time but were turned away by the police. Later, when it became known that the execution had been carried out, hysterical cries were heard from the VanZandt mansion.

Mrs. Spies at least was spared the indignity of being probed by the none too gentle hands of Captain Schaack's police matrons.

"DID HE REALLY DO THIS?" my editor asked.

"Of course he really did it. You and the other editors have created a monster. He will never stop until you are prepared to stop him."

"Maybe you're right, Ned," he agreed solemnly.

Someday stopping Schaack might sell newspapers.

Nora and I sat somberly in front of the fireplace that evening. We both sipped two glasses of Irish whiskey.

"I shall have nightmares tonight, Ned," she said. "I suppose you will too."

"I'm sure I will."

"You shouldn't have been there."

"Yes, I should have."

"You're right as always." She sighed. "God will take care of those men, even if they think they didn't believe in Him."

"I'm sure He will."

"You will go to the wakes and the funerals?"

"Yes, of course."

"And then?"

"I will resign before they can fire me."

November 12

My first stop as I made the round of the homes of the victims today was the Parsonses' apartment at 1120 West Grand Avenue, a third-floor walk-up in the poorest of neighborhoods. I arrived just as the body of Alfred Parsons was being delivered to his home.

WHEN THE STREET DOOR WAS opened, Mrs. Parsons was observed at the head of the stairs, dressed in a long black wrapper. Apparently she had rested little during last night for her eyes were swollen with much weeping. She was greatly excited when she realized that they were about to bring up her dead husband, and she immediately commenced weeping again. A committee went to her and endeavored to calm her, but she grew more agitated until they almost forced her into her apartment and locked the door. She would not listen to their entreaties, and one was left to see that she did herself no harm, while the others carried up the coffin and deposited it on two chairs in the little sitting room. The top of the casket was removed and the calm, pale features exposed.

All the time they were taking off the lid, Mrs. Parsons was struggling in the room adjoining and calling the name of her husband. Little Albert and Lulu, the fatherless children, stood together, crying and unnoticed in the corner of the room. When the chamber door was unlocked, the widow rushed out and threw herself bodily on the coffin. An hysterical cry escaped her lips, and the poor woman fell on the floor in a dead faint before her friends could catch her.

I REALIZED THAT I HAD been harsh on Lucy Parsons. She wanted her husband to be true to his vision, she wanted him to speak out with his life itself to tell the story of oppression and injustice to working people. She knew he would die when she suggested he return to Chicago from Wauconda, Wisconsin. She would not permit him to apply for clemency. Yet she loved him and would miss him forever. It is not up to someone like me to sort out such a tangle of emotions. I should have been kinder.

She collapsed into my arms when I tried to console her. "Ned," she sobbed, "you were always on our side!"

I'm not really sure that I was.

My next stop on this day of wakes was at 630 North Milwaukee Avenue in the Wicker Park district, where so many of the German immigrants, rich and poor alike live, where some of the most beautiful homes built since the fire exist but a stone's throw from some of the most miserable hovels. The wake for Engel and Lingg took place in the back room of Engel's toy store.

In my story I wrote:

The door of the little cigar and toy store which Mrs. Engel had managed since the arrest of her husband was draped in mourning. A red-faced man with white mustache stood on a box in the center of the door and separated those going in from those going out.

*In the back room lay the bodies of Louis Lingg, the
suicide, and Engel. They were in their coffins and no
one was permitted to take more than one look as he
passed along.*

*Hardly one out of twenty who go into the Engel
store to view the remains speak their minds in English.
The babble on the sidewalk was sometimes loud
enough to be heard far down the avenue. People came
from all directions, men, women and children. Every
street car from across the bridge and from the ex-
tremes of Milwaukee Avenue deposited several people
who rushed and pushed and swore to get a place in
line . . . Now and then a detective from the central station or from Chicago Avenue loomed up, but he came
and went so as not to attract attention. If the men knew
that Bonfield's spies heard every excited threat that
they are uttering over the dead bodies of their heroes
there might be trouble. Often a very excited man would
raise his hand and utter fearful oaths in German. Often the names of Bonfield and Schaack could be distinguished in their rantings.*

*These men and women are not Anarchists. They are
friends and neighbors and Germans and workers who
do not want to tear the city apart but are angry at what
they see as a blatant miscarriage of simple justice. At
least twenty thousand of them passed through his sad
and simple little toy store today. One of Santa's
bravest elves is dead, murdered as these people see it.*

BECAUSE THEY RECOGNIZED WHO I was, the people at the
bier permitted me more than a single, quick look at
Lou Lingg's body. He was not wearing Elise's gold
cuff links.

Out on Milwaukee Avenue I was hot with rage despite the damp and cool November air. Schaack had
stolen the cuff links that were supposed to be buried in
the ground with Lou Lingg. Whatever it takes and no
matter how long it takes, I told myself, Schaack would

pay for being a ghoul, a grave robber, a thief of the innocent love of a poor peasant girl from Germany.

Over our second Irish whiskey that night, Nora asked me, "How are you going to undo Schaack and Bonfield, Ned?"

"I don't know Nora. I must wait for the proper opportunity. When the tide turns, as it will, there will be plenty of opportunity. Somehow we must collect the evidence against them all. Perhaps one of the Chicago papers will reconsider what happened. Otherwise, I will write an article for Harper's. I may do both."

She nodded, wise woman that she is, knowing that I was too sick with grief and rage to think clearly on what had to be done.

November 13

The Daily News *asked me to cover the funeral. Why not, I was riding out there anyway.*

The cortege began up in Wicker Park, picking up bodies one by one, then worked its way over to Grand Avenue to add the Parsons casket to the five other hearses.

As the rain poured down on us we crossed under the Chicago River in the Desplaines Street Tunnel and then to the railroad station. There were thirty cars waiting to take us out to Waldheim. The grief and the rage in the air were thick, like heavy curtains hanging from the sky. The rain beating against the roofs of carriages sounds like a heavenly dirge.

The procession was constrained to cross the river at Desplaines Street Tunnel, just a few blocks above the Haymarket, because it was forbidden to pass through the central business district. Mayor Roche, who had succeeded Mayor Harrison, perhaps because Harrison had spoken for the defense during the trial, had feared, perhaps with some reason, that the cortege might turn angry as it passed near the fashionable downtown clubs. In one of them, Marshall Field and his cronies were sipping their brandies and smoking their cigars in a celebration of their triumph over the hated Anarchists and laying plans for further triumph over the immigrants in the city.

At the Wisconsin Central station at the end of Wells Street, thirty cars waited on the tracks for the special train out to Forest Park. Timmy Hardiman greeted me with an umbrella to lead me to the compartment in which my mother and father, two of my sisters and one of my brothers, Nora, and Josie were waiting for us.

Despite the grimness of the day, I could not help but note that Timmy was already considered a member of the family.

Beware lad, once this family gets a hold on you, it will be hard to escape.

All the women were dressed in black. My father and Tim wore black armbands on their dark suits. Even I for once had given up my white suit and was dressed in funereal black.

Normally, if one gathers that large a portion of my family together, the result is a riot of fun and laughter. Not on this day, however. At my mother's suggestion we said the Rosary all the way out to Forest Park.

"They may not have been Catholics," she said, "but God loves them as much as He loves us. Maybe more."

My mother constantly wandered near the limits of heresy, God bless her. Sensitive to what this situation might mean to Nora, she kept her strong arm around my wife throughout the train ride.

Gradually the rain diminished and then stopped, just as we pulled into the small station on Des Plaines Avenue in Forest Park.

"There'll be much confusion as they move the caskets to the hearses and the crowds to the waiting carriages," my father observed. "We should wait here till the confusion is over. We really don't belong with them. In their present mood they might resent us."

"Not if they recognize Ned, Grandpa General," the irrepressible Josie said. "Too bad he didn't wear his white suit."

Desperate for something to break the tension, the family laughed more at that sally than it merited.

Naturally, the General had contracted for a special carriage for his family. Naturally, one had to look at it carefully to know that it was special.

We stood at the back of the crowd, astonishingly anonymous for the General's family. The wives and children around the gravesites were crying loudly. We could hardly hear the funeral oration by Captain Black. However, we could pick out his theme. He had not known any of the five men before the trial. He had taken on the case because of his conviction that everyone had the right to a proper legal defense. He had come to know them during the trial and to admire them. While he did not agree with their philosophy and sometimes winced at their rhetoric, he had learned to respect their integrity and their goodness. There was not a mean or violent strain in any of them. They were completely innocent, the victims of an irresponsible and vicious criminal procedure of which Chicago would always be ashamed. They had sacrificed their lives for their beliefs. In some ways their courage had reminded him of that of Jesus.

"Hmf," said my father.

"Hush," said my mother.

We walked by the mourners, expressing our sympathies. Both Nina Spies and Lucy Parsons embraced me. Under other circumstances there would be many comments about this from my family, not the least from Josie.

However, we rode back in silence.

I jotted down my story on the return trip.

BLACK COMPARES DEAD MEN TO JESUS.

One might as well end on a strong note.
For the moment, it's over.

February 1, 1888

It wasn't over for very long.

Last night, Nora and I were reading in the parlor and Josie was playing the piano, an activity at which she had become very skilled.

The doorbell rang. We had excused Annie early for an evening with her young man.

"I'll get it." Josie bounced up from the piano bench.

"She'll always be grateful to you, Ned," Nora remarked. "She'll never be able to do enough for you."

"Nonsense," I said, knowing full well it was true.

She appeared a few moments later with a tall, handsome man.

"Mayor Carter Harrison to see you, Uncle Ned. I knew it was him because he was riding his white horse."

The Mayor strode into the room, shook my hand vigorously and kissed Nora's hand.

"And this charming and witty young woman, I believe, is your niece Josephine."

"My real name is Josie, Josephine is my nickname."

"Unless I am mistaken, Miss, ah . . ."

"Philbin," I filled in the name.

"I have seen you at certain events with young Master Timothy Hardiman."

"I remember the name, but I can't quite recall the face."

"Josie, I think you and I had better withdraw. His Honor and your Uncle Ned have serious matters to discuss."

"Not at all, not at all, Mrs. Fitzpatrick. The matter is very simple indeed. Despite your generosity I don't

*deserve the title anymore. In truth I would like it back
for at least one more term. In order to further that goal
I have bought today the Chicago Times. In particular I
want to report on police corruption. I have hired Mr.
James West to be editor and Mr. Joseph Dunlop to be
city editor. I assume, Ned, that you share my respect
for those two men?"*

"Best editors in the city."

*"The three of us discussed other staff today. We de-
cided unanimously that the first one we wanted to hire
was Edmund James Fitzpatrick Jr."*

"SEAMUS," MY wife asked bluntly, "do you always work so late at night in your office at the IBM Building?"

"Sometimes, Ms. Holmes, ma'am," he said with a broad grin. "That's not a crime, is it?"

"How would someone know that you would be coming out of your office at that hour on the night you were shot?"

"Well, I usually don't stay there after eleven."

Your man had been issued a preemptory summons to appear at our house in the 2300 block on Southport Avenue. It was strictly a business meeting. The dogs were in the yard, the older kids in the basement with Ethne, Socra Marie upstairs in her bassinet under the watchful eye of Danuta, who was pursuing whatever dust had dared to settle in the upstairs rooms. My wife had donned a light brown, summer business suit from her days at Arthur Andersen. She had insisted that I note it still fit her, in a tone of voice which hinted that she knew I wouldn't believe her.

"Have you been working late there often recently?"

He lifted a hand as if in self-defense.

"We have a major case scheduled for trial in a couple of weeks. With all that wedding noise and mess at the house . . ."

"You were, however, waiting for someone there that night?"

He squirmed uneasily.

"I told the police I wasn't."

"Come, Seamus, I don't care what you told the police. Someone phoned you and promised you something special if you waited in the office. Who was it?"

"The voice was disguised. I didn't recognize it."

"Man or woman?"

"I'm not sure. Man probably."

"And he promised you . . . ?"

"I'd rather not say . . ."

"Come on, Seamus, I'm not the police."

In such dialogues as this, the brogue disappeared and Nuala talked like a Yank.

"If I tell you something that might be illegal, you'd be obstructing justice if you didn't tell the police."

"All right, I'll tell you. The phone caller promised you more information for the dossier you're keeping on the Shepherds."

If Seamus Costelloe had been holding a drink he would have dropped it. For a moment I thought he might flee the house. Failing that I expected a sign of the cross.

"How did you know that?"

She'd been guessing. My wife is a pretty good guesser. Now she knew for sure.

"I know, that's all that matters. The caller had information about tilting the playing field in a recent high-profile trial."

Still guessing.

Maybe.

"All right. The man on the phone said he'd come by about ten-thirty. I said I'd wait till eleven. If he didn't come I'd go home. He didn't. I left the office, locked the door, and turned around and there was this person with the Clinton mask and the cloak and the gun. He missed. I ran towards the elevator and he winged me. Then he turned and ran to the stairs, just like I told the cops. I went back into the office and called 911."

"You insist that you didn't recognize the person?'

"How do you recognize someone with a mask and a black coat?"

"Man or woman?"

"I thought it was a man."

"You're not telling me everything, Seamus."

"Absolutely everything."

Nuala was unhappy when he left.

"I don't like this at all, at all, Dermot Michael," she said. "There's a lot of bad people out there."

" 'Tis true." I sighed, imitating her as I often do, sometimes unintentionally.

"Your man's a grand friggin' fool, Dermot Michael."

"Is he now?"

"He is."

"You think that the killer will try again?"

She looked at me in surprise.

"Not that killer, if you take me meaning."

I didn't.

— 28 —

 March 4, 1888

"*You weren't out of work long, were you, Ned?*"

It was my Irish friend from the past, hat pulled down over his face, waiting for me as I came out of Laddy's into the snowbanks on North Avenue.

"*I thought you had disappeared forever.*"

"*Ah, no, just for the time. 'Twas a shame those poor men had to swing. You and your da gave it a good effort.*"

"*You could have stopped it,*" I snapped.

"*No, Ned. We couldn't have stopped it. Not at all, at all.*"

We plowed on through the snow in silence.

"*Still, we have something that might help you.*"

"*Oh?*" I said still angry at the damnable Irish love of indirection and mystery, perhaps the only quality in my wife that I find it hard to tolerate.

"*'Tis about your good friend Michael Schaack.*"

"*Is it now?*"

"*'Tis . . . There's a certain house over on Grand Avenue, not all that far from the police station, where he keeps his treasures.*"

"*Treasures?*"

"*All the things he's stolen from prisoners, the pay-*"

offs from the saloonkeepers and the whores, list of names of people he blackmails, some letters from Marshall Field and Joe Medil, grand stuff. He also has been known to entertain women there."

"Indeed . . . What's the exact address?"

That was too blunt for an Irish person.

" 'Tis on the three hundred block on West Grand, not far from the jail either."

"Is it?" I said.

" 'Tis . . . Just beyond Orleans."

"Near the river?"

"On the right-hand side of the street. You can't miss it. An old cottage, ready to collapse."

"I'll try not to miss it."

"There's a funny thing."

"Ah?"

"Doesn't your man have one just like it?"

"Captain Bonfield?"

"The very same, Black Jack himself, not mind you that either knows about the other one."

"They wouldn't tell each other, would they now?"

"They would not."

"Same general area?"

"Not exactly."

We turned off on Dearborn and sloshed down the street.

"You wouldn't be far away from the truth if you looked over by the Desplaines Street Police Station."

"Ah?"

"Round the corner from where the bomb went off."

"Washington Street?"

"The very place."

"Just west of Desplaines?"

"You have the right of it, Ned."

"Another cottage?"

"No, a snug little house with a wrought-iron fence. Nice place to invite women, if you take me meaning."

"Perhaps my friends and I might have a look at them."

"That might not be all that bad an idea, Ned. I'll take me leave of you now. We'll not be seeing each other again, not in this world anyway."

I was so excited by the news that I slipped and fell down the steps leading to my front door and landed in a big snowdrift.

"Ned, whatever did you do to yourself?"

Nora had been waiting for me in a thick quilted robe in front of a blazing fire. A decanter of whiskey and two glasses waited on a table next to the couch.

"Fell in a snowdrift," I said embracing her.

"Ned," she protested without much sincerity, *"you're getting snow all over my robe!"*

"The way to prevent that is to take off your robe."

"Ned!"

I kicked off my boots, hung up my coat, and snuggled with her on the couch. She poured me a glass of Irish whiskey.

" 'Tis only your second tonight, Mr. Fitzpatrick? If it were your third, I wouldn't be safe with you."

"You're not safe with me now, woman!"

I opened the top button on her vest.

"Well," she replied with a little gasp, *"a man has to keep warm on a cold March evening."*

She bundled me inside her vast robe. It was indeed warm there. I opened a second button.

"You found out news about Bonfield and Schaack?"

Long ago I had given up trying to know how she reads me so well, especially since she's not fey like Josie.

I told her about my mysterious friend.

"What do you want to do to those men, Ned? Send them to jail?"

I hadn't thought much about that issue. All I cared about was trapping them.

"*It will be enough to get them off the police force, take away their power, so they can never abuse innocent people again.*"

Then our conversation ended.

The next morning (today) I brought the news down to the Chicago Times building at Wells and Washington, built after the fire specifically to be a headquarters for a newspaper. We shared the building with the Freie Presse, a German-language paper which huddled under our protection when the police were shutting down everything German in Chicago.

West and Dunlop, my bosses, were delighted.

"*Those could be gold mines!*"

"*What do we do?*"

"*We find a judge who will issue us secret search warrants,*" I said, "*and then demand that Pemberton live up to his promise to assign officers of unquestioned integrity to conduct the searches in our presence. We have to be sure that we are acting legally.*"

In early afternoon five of us were slogging down Grand Avenue towards the frozen river—the three of us from the Times and two stalwart plainclothes detectives. The sun had emerged from a long period of hiding and quickly turned our snowdrifts into rushing tides of water, seeking the Lake, the River, anyplace to run.

The cottage which was alleged to be the site of Schaack's illegal treasure trove was so decrepit that one could easily imagine it swept into the river by the rushing thaw. The police officers pried open the door. A dank, sickeningly sweet smell assailed us as we entered, the smell of sexual orgy and of spilled wine.

"*This will do for Mike,*" one of the cops said in a rich Kerry brogue, "*the focking bastard!*"

It would indeed. The three rooms of the house were littered with jewelry, bottles of wine and whiskey, women's clothes appropriate for a bordello, obscene posters, and huge packs of money—at a glance as much as a hundred thousand dollars in cash.

Some of the wine bottles had frozen and broken open. Schaack probably wasn't worried. There was plenty more where that came from.

The five of us stared in amazement at the vile corruption which surrounded us like the stench from the Union Stockyard.

"Well, lads, let's get to work," Jim West said. "We'll list all the material here and then get an order to seal the place. Joe, would you start a fire? We don't want to burn this place down, but there's no point in freezing to death."

I worked my way through a mountain of jewelry that was piled up on the floor just inside the door, bracelets, necklaces, rings of every kind—diamond, emerald, ruby, sapphire, wedding bands. No piece of jewelry, however small or inexpensive, was beneath Michael Schaack's avarice.

WE AT THE Times HAD been hounding them for several weeks.

"Bonfield proclaims to the world that the gamblers are gone and the dens of vice are closed but the Times knows of scores of places open to the public."

"Bonfield still would shrug his shoulders and say, 'There is no gambling in Chicago' and march off to look for some respectable German citizen whom he might arrest and call an Anarchist."

POLICE ENGAGED TO BUILD, REPAIR, AND DECORATE HOMES OF BONFIELD AND SCHAACK

MARSHALL FIELD DENIES FINANCIAL SUPPORT FOR SCHAACK'S ANTI-ANARCHIST CAMPAIGN.

Now we had more sensational evidence. They were finished.

Joe Dunlop found a boy wandering down the street and sent him over to the Times building. He came back with four more reporters and a couple of artists. We'd have great pictures of Schaack's prizes.

Then I found the prize that I had expected to find. I closed my eyes and waited till the churning in my stomach stopped.

I took out my notebook and began to write.

GHOUL SCHAACK STOLE LINGG'S CUFF LINKS

Police Captain Michael Schaack removed the gold cuff links that alleged Anarchist murderer Louis Lingg was wearing when he committed suicide in the County Jail the day before he was to be executed. The cuff links had been given to Lingg by his immigrant girlfriend, Elise Freidel, for him to wear when he made his speech before sentencing and when he was executed. Miss Freidel, who had spent all her meager savings to purchase the cuff links, had caused to be engraved on them the initials E.F. and L.L. inside a heart. She told people that they would be buried with Mr. Lingg as a token of their love, which death could not destroy.

These very cuff links, with the inscription, were found today by investigators from the Police Department and the Times in a bawdy house treasure trove that Captain Schaack maintains at Grand Avenue and the River.

We will never know in this world whether Louis Lingg, a defiant warrior, committed suicide or was murdered in the County Jail. We do know, however, that after his death, Captain Schaack did steal the only treasure Lingg had in the world.

"J_IM_," I CALLED WEST OVER to the jewel mountain. "*My first story on this.*"

He glanced at it.

"*Great God in heaven, Ned!*"

"*Precisely.*"

"*Those are the cuff links?*"

"*Look at the inscription.*"

"*Tony,*" he cried to one of our artists, "*a quick drawing of these cuff links!*"

As I stared at the two pathetic little pieces of gold, my eyes filled up with tears.

"*Lou,*" I prayed silently, "*I'm sure that you're in heaven, much to your own surprise. I hope you know that we have found Elise's gift.*"

"*Take your story over to the paper,*" West ordered, "*and Tony's drawing. Tell them to get out an Extra. Then put a team together and go after Bonfield's place. We have to document all of this before they find out what we're doing.*"

It took most of the afternoon to assemble a team of reporters, artists, and cops to raid Captain Bonfield's hideaway. I managed to scribble a note to my father and send it by messenger.

Chief Pemberton himself managed to accompany us.

Captain Bonfield was a much more orderly man than his colleague. The little house on Washington Street was clean and neat. Someone had stacked wood and kindling by the fireplace. The walls were lined with bureaus, cabinets, chests, and closets—all filled with money and jewelry. In the file cabinets we found letters from the plutocrats of the city in which they praised Bonfield for maintaining order in the city and enclosed large sums of money to help him in his work.

We also discovered, discreetly tucked away in closets, women's clothes appropriate for an aristocratic *bawdy house, obscene photographs and paintings, and vicious-looking instruments of torture.*

I jotted down my headline.

BONFIELD TREASURE HOUSE NEATER
THAN SCHAACK'S BUT TORTURE INSTRU-
MENTS FOUND

"He's finished," Pemberton muttered. "We might not be able to put him in jail, but he'll never serve as a police officer again."

"It's about time," I replied.

Then I came upon the biggest treasure of them all— a file about threats on Bonfield's life.

From the Fenians.

The threats were on a crude letterhead which purported to belong to the "Army of the People of Ireland," one of the fifty or so Irish nationalist groups in the city.

My fingers trembled as I went through the file. The letters informed Captain Bonfield that he had been indicted by a court of the People of Ireland for the murder of three soldiers of the Army in Chicago. A later one informed him that he had been convicted. And a yet later one told him that he had been sentenced to death, a sentence which would be carried out at a time and place chosen by the Army High Command.

I continued to examine the file. One scrap of paper noted the payment of two hundred dollars to Bonfield to permit the killing of a certain Jack Mulhern, a traitor to the cause of Ireland, by officers of the Army of the People of Ireland.

I vaguely remember a shoot-out between the police and Irish nationalists just after I had returned with Nora. The police had tried to apprehend these men after they had killed another Irish nationalist. The men had resisted arrest and had died in the gunfight.

Why had Bonfield taken money to permit the killing and then shot it out with the killers? Or had something

gone wrong? Had police not in Black Jack's pay made
a mistake? And why would Bonfield compulsively keep
such neat records?

Then I came upon a yellowed photograph of a
group of seven very dangerous-looking Irishmen in
black coats and hats and with black mustaches and
beards. The face of one of them was circled with a
thick pencil mark.

It was the man who had lurked at the edges of the
crowd during Myles Joyce's execution, the man who
had thrown the bomb from Crane's alley.

He had been aiming at Captain Ward, who he must
have thought was Captain Bonfield. Instead he hit
poor Degen.

Attached to the photograph was a letter from an officer in the Royal Irish Constabulary.

Dear Captain Bonfield,

The so-called Army of the People of Ireland are nothing more
than a raggedy group of incompetent ruffians, more interested in
theft and murder of rivals than Irish independence from the Crown.
They can, however, be dangerous in some circumstances.

According to your request we have made inquiries from our
agents. They report that the man in the picture, known as Captain
Mayo, has been assigned to kill you. We recommend that you take
serious precautions. However, we suspect that this Captain Mayo
will never make it to America, much less to Chicago.

I remain yours sincerely etc,

Thomas Cowan
Inspector.

So here was the explanation of the Haymarket
bomb. It was a clumsy attempt at revenge against
Black Jack Bonfield.

Why a bomb?

Perhaps to divert attention to someone else. If Bonfield had died someone might have found this file and tried to hunt down Captain Mayo.

Incompetent ruffians indeed!

I thought quickly. This file would have no impact now. It would get lost in the scandal that our stories would create. Better that it be kept for a later occasion, when it could be used to obtain pardons for the remaining Haymarket prisoners—Nebbe, Fielden, and Schwab.

I folded it into my overcoat pocket.

It was after ten when I returned to my home.

Nora was waiting for me in the parlor, as always. Tonight she was waiting for me fully dressed, which was the usual manner.

"Ned," she said as she kissed me, "you look destroyed."

"Sorry to be so late," I murmured as I collapsed in the chair by the fireplace.

"You said you might be."

"Everything all right?"

"The childeen is suffering from a new tooth, the girls are sound asleep. Annie wanted to spend the evening with her beau but was afraid to ask me. So I told her to go ahead, of course. Josie is writing a letter to her Timmy . . . We read your extra when it came down the street . . ."

"What did you think?"

"I cried, as I'm sure you did . . . Would you like a tiny drop of Irish whiskey?"

"Would you ever have a cup of tea?"

"Of course!"

As we were drinking the tea, I showed her the picture in the file I had taken from Bonfield's house.

"Do you know that man, Nora?"

She pondered the picture carefully.

"I do, Ned. It's that terrible man Sean-Tom Og Joyce. He was my Myles's third cousin four times removed."

"Was he a farmer?"

"*Weren't we all, Ned? His father, Sean-Tom Mor had a little place way up in the hills. The son was kind of a layabout, didn't do much except talk. They said he was one of the ribbon men who killed an agent on the other side of the mountain. He tried to give the impression that he was high up in the Fenians, but no one really believed him.*"

"*I remember him in Galway when Myles was in prison there. He hung about at the edge of the crowd. He was such a big man, I couldn't miss him.*"

"*That would be him all right, pretending he was taking care of things for the Fenians. He's dead now.*"

"*Dead!*"

"*The last letter Josie had from Mary, her sister, said that he was found in a ditch by the road up the mountain with a bullet through his head.*"

Did that, I wondered, have anything to do with the botched attack on Captain Bonfield?

"*He threw the Haymarket bomb, Nora.*"

"*Merciful God,*" she made the sign of the cross. "*He didn't!*"

"*I'm sure of it . . . Read this file.*"

Very carefully she went through the file.

"*You recognized him that night from the size of him?*"

"*From the way he carried himself, the shape of his shoulders, the air of recklessness . . . I don't know what it was. It took me a long time to remember where I'd seen him before.*"

"*And then it was too late . . .*"

"*It was always too late, Nora. Who would have believed my story, especially when they had all the killers.*"

"*Now they're dead and so is he.*" She sighed. "*How terrible!*"

I buried my head in my hands.

"*I keep asking myself if there wasn't something else I could have done.*"

"There was not, Ned," she said firmly in her rarely used tone of voice which was designed to settle questions. Which it always did.

"I guess not."

"What are you going to do with this file?"

"Save it till the day that a governor is thinking about a pardon so that he'll know the truth."

She nodded approvingly.

"That day will surely come, Ned," she said.

I gave her Lou Lingg's cuff links. When the weather improved we would ride out to Waldheim and bury them in the earth next to his tomb.

As I scratch these notes at the end of a hectic day, my eyes heavy and my heart aching, I hope she's right.

I wonder what Schaack and Bonfield will do tomorrow to fight back.

— 29 —

March 5, 1888

I found out early in the morning what the two captains would do. They would try to close the Chicago Times just as they had closed the Arbeiter Zeitung and the other labor papers.

I had mounted my horse for the ride down to Washington and Wells when my brother Packy came galloping up, his red hair blowing in the fresh breeze off the lake.

"The old fella says they're going to close the *Times* today and put the editors in jail. You're to come to his office. We'll get a couple of writs. Then you return to the paper and open it up again while we're getting West and Dunlop out of jail."

"He enjoys the smell of battle, does he?"

"Loves it! And like Ma says it's safer than real war because the other side are such amadons."

We rode downtown and over to Randolph and Wells, where we could see the Times Building. It was surrounded by cops, probably from the Chicago Avenue station. While we watched, a dozen or so of them dragged Jim and Joe out of the building and threw them into a police wagon.

"We better get out of here," Packy insisted. "The old fella doesn't want you to fall into Schaack's power."

"Good idea," I said fervently.

The General was in his element. He strode around the office like a commanding officer on the morning of battle, barking orders feverishly.

"Packy, go over to City Hall and tell that quaking coward Pemberton that I want to see him now or I will swear out a warrant for his arrest . . . Thomas, we need some members of the First Illinois—in uniform. Get them for me . . . Ned, maybe there's still some law left in your dream-ravaged head. See if you can write me a writ of habeas corpus to get your bosses out of jail and a writ enjoining the Police Department to cease and desist in its occupation of the Chicago Times building. Also draft a suit against the City of Chicago and the Chicago Police Department, holding them liable for all the damages done to the people of the city by the crimes of Bonfield and Schaack."

"Yes, sir," I snapped, like I was about to salute him.

For a moment he permitted a smile to flicker across his face, a smile which said, "We both know that we're frauds, Ned, but don't let on to others."

He had no legal right to mobilize the militia. Nor was there any grounds for a suit against the city and the police for the crimes of Bonfield and Schaack. Neither technicality, both of which he knew, bothered him in the slightest.

I was busy finishing the pleas for the writs when the hapless Chief Pemberton appeared in our office, head bowed, voice anxious.

"I'm sorry, General, I knew nothing about it."

"Pemberton"—my parent, booted feet on his desk, stared up at him over his unlighted cigar—"you never know nothing about anything. You're the chief of police. I hold you responsible for what the police have done. You must do the following instantly. You must appoint trusted men to replace Bonfield and Schaack in their stations, you must direct that these two scoundrels be arrested immediately and brought be-

fore you. You will inform them that they have been sus-pended indefinitely. If they attempt to contest this deci-sion, they will be immediately indicted and imprisoned. You will also order them to immediately withdraw such renegade police who may remain in the Chicago Times building in blatant disregard of the Bill of Rights of our Republic."

"But, General . . ."

"Wake up, Pemberton! The game is over. The other papers may not like the Times but like all rogues, edi-tors and publishers stand together. The police may suppress small, German-language papers. They dare not touch a major Chicago journal. Marshall Field cannot repeal the Bill of Rights, no matter how much money he spends on crooked cops. Moreover, neither West nor Dunlop is an immigrant with a German ac-cent. They both belong to the best clubs. Do you really think their friends will tolerate this outrage? It is fin-ished, done with, over. Get rid of them today before they can pull you down! Now get out of here and do your duty!"

The quaking police chief left hurriedly.

My parent cocked his eye at me to see how I was re-acting to his extraordinary performance.

"Sir, here is the plea for a writ of habeas corpus."

He glanced over it quickly.

"Damn it, Ned, you would have made a fine lawyer."

"You forget, sir, that I did pass the bar exam."

"And then went off and filled your head with roman-tic dreams, one of which, fortunately for you and for all of us, you brought home."

"Thank you, sir."

The General's compliments tend to be both indirect and graceful, very Irish.

Precisely at noon, we strode into the County Court-house on Illinois Street, like the Ostrogoths entering Rome. The six officers of the First Illinois were un-

*armed, save for the swords which came with their
dress uniforms. The judge into whose courtroom we
barged woke from a noontime snooze and stared at us
like we were figures out of the Apocalypse. Several of
my press colleagues, perhaps waiting for court action,
though hardly expecting anything quite so dramatic,
scurried in after us, notebooks at the ready.*

*"We have three pleas here." The General pounded
on the judge's bench. "We demand immediate relief!
We demand that the editors of the Chicago Times be released from durance vile. Immediately! We also demand that the Chicago Police Department vacate the
Chicago Times building. Immediately! We expect, Your
Honor, that you will deal with these matters. Immediately!"*

"Yes, sir," said the frightened jurist.

*Without any command being given, we executed an
about-face, and strode out of the courtroom and out of
the court into the mud and slush of Illinois Street.*

*The press fired questions at the General, which he
dismissed with a wave of his hand.*

*Back at my parent's office, we feasted on the roast
beef meal he had ordered from O'Boyle's, drinking
several toasts to one another in excellent red wine.*

Vicksburg, after all, had fallen.

*About one-thirty some of our scouts reported that
the police had abandoned the Times building.*

*"OK, Ned," he ordered, "go over there and get
some practice editing a newspaper."*

"Yes, sir!"

Again the fleeting smile.

*The editorial room was in chaos. My colleagues
cheered enthusiastically when I appeared with six
determined-looking "boys in blue."*

*"Richmond has fallen," I announced. "Let's get this
paper out."*

I wrote the lead editorial.

CROOKED COPS FINISHED!

The careers of Captain Bonfield, an apparent torturer, and of Captain Schaack, a proven ghoul, are now finished. Under indefinite suspension on the tardy orders of Chief Pemberton, their official days are numbered. Their brutal assumption of authority, their clubbing exploits, their receipt of presents from courtesans, gamblers, and saloonkeepers, their protection of disreputables, subservience to the rich and the powerful will soon be a thing of the past. It will be a glorious event for the city of Chicago. People do not want to be terrorized; they want to be protected in their lives and liberty and property. They have had enough of these two crooked cops and their methods.

One is forced to remember the major role they played in the prosecution of the Haymarket Anarchists and ask again if justice was done at that trial.

"Ned," asked one of the young reporters, "do you want to do a piece about the scene in the courthouse today?"

I laughed.

"I might not be able to do it justice. You do it."

The headline announced:

GENERAL FITZPATRICK TAKES CHARGE. LIBERATES THE TIMES

Later in the day, after the first edition was coming off the presses, my father appeared with West and Dunlop. They approved everything I had done and promptly offered me the job of assistant editor. I declined with gratitude. The "boys in blue" were dismissed.

We walked back to the General's office.

"I suppose you wonder, Ned, why I can get away for

a few hours with the pretense that I am the military governor of Chicago."

"No, sir."

"No?" he seemed surprised.

"Not at all, sir. If one plays that role with enough vigor and confidence one creates an illusion that quite overcomes disbelief. It requires nothing but nerve, self-assurance, and imagination. No one in our family is deficient in any of those characteristics."

My father merely laughed.

ANDREW COSTELLOE and Sonia Burnovsky were married at St. Clement's Church in the Lincoln Park District on the second Saturday in June. Nuala Anne insisted that we attend. Moreover, against all my advice she also insisted that Socra Marie accompany us.

"We'll go only to the Mass, not the dinner," she insisted. "The child is all grown-up now and knows how to behave. If she cries I'll take her to the back of the church."

In fact she wanted to show off how healthy and bright our little wisp of humanity had become.

Socra Marie was in fact in fine fettle. She was getting bigger, not a lot bigger yet, but still bigger. She was alert and responsive and quite conscious of her environment. The pediatrician said that she was showing early signs of considerable intelligence.

"How do they know that?" My wife had responded with her usual skepticism when the subject was the intelligence of her children.

She was also now unmistakably pretty and not merely in the prejudiced view of her parents. Her head still suffered from the somewhat triangular shape which is characteristic of the heads of preemies. Her neck was not quite up to holding the head in its proper place. The first problem was obscured by the cap in which Nuala dressed her when we went out. The second was hardly noticeable and could be attributed to her interest in everything around her. The cap permitted a few rings of curly hair to peep out.

We were not out of danger yet. It would take her two years to catch up. A lot could still go wrong. She behaved very well during the wedding, listening attentively but sleepily to the Russian music and staring at the young Russian priest in his glorious robes. Then, during the Catholic priest's homily, which was remarkably well done, she dozed off and slept through the rest of the ceremony.

It was one of those hot early-summer days when the glare seems especially strong and heat assaults you like a mugger's breath. St. Clement's, beautiful Romanesque church that it is, cannot be air-conditioned. After Mass one stands around in the back of the church waiting anxiously for the bride and groom to appear and then depart among cheers and showers of politically correct birdseed (since rice has been found to harm our feathered friends). That signals a liberation from the heat as one drives in an air-conditioned car to the air-conditioned boredom of a reception. There one nibbles on unsatisfying hors d'oeuvres and drinks a little too much to kill the pain of small talk about one's wife's singing, usually with someone who suffers from hideous bad breath. Then one sits through inane toasts delivered by folks who think they are funny and are not. One envies the spouse who has had to take the baby home.

I had been pondering this triumph of chaos over ordered creation in back of the church after Mass when, with his usual vast grin, Seamus Costelloe approached me.

"How you doing, Dermot? The little girl looks great!"

"She's coming along all right."

Which, I thought, was a little better than "not too bad."

"My new daughter-in-law is really a knockout, isn't she? Great tits! Andy is really lucky. Great pussy too, I bet."

"A real Slavic princess," I said, hoping that the tone indicated my disapproval of such inappropriate comments about a new member of his family.

Waste of time. Seamus was incurably vulgar. Any male with normal hormones could not help but notice the size and shape of Sonia's breasts. Good taste, respect, propriety demanded that they not be the subject of chauvinist conversation.

I didn't say that. But I thought it for the sake of political correctness in my conscience.

YOU CHECK HER OUT AS MUCH AS HE DOES.

It's too hot a day to deal with you.

I searched for Nuala Anne. She was some distance away, the center of a gaggle of young matrons who were clucking over our daughter.

"So," I asked Seamus the questions my wife had instructed me to ask him, "when did you figure out that it was Helen who shot you coming out of your office? When did you remember the smell of her perfume? What is it, Opium or something like that?"

I had told her that it would be a terrible way to ruin a wedding. She replied that if he wanted to see his first grandchild he'd better start telling the truth.

Seamus reacted like I had done a cut-back block on him. His chest caved in, his shoulders dropped, his red face turned white, his wide smile disappeared, his mouth fell open.

"How did you know that?"

"It's pretty evident," I replied.

It hadn't been evident at all. Nuala had told me to gamble and we'd won. Well, she'd won.

"It was easy for her to do it, Dermot Michael," Nuala had informed me. "Her offices like his are in the IBM Building. She excused herself for a minute from the meal at Shaw's Crab House, let herself in through the garage parking lot, took the mask and the cloak out of her car, rode up the elevator, took her shot at Seamus, and missed his vital organs, fortunately for both of them. Then she ran down the stairs a couple of floors, took an elevator to the garage, opened the door with her key, threw her disguise in one of the trash cans, let herself out of the garage, and returned to the table at Shaw's Crab House with an apology for an upset stomach. It took less time than it does to tell about it."

"How do you know all this?"

"Dermot, you know that I know things. Seamus did fool around with her and she hated him for it. She hated him even more because he was a threat to the respectability of her marriage. Besides, she is the only one who knows her way around the IBM Building to be able to pull off that kind of caper. Once you begin to think that it wasn't a contract killing, she's the obvious choice."

"And you speculate about how she did it?"

"No, Dermot Michael Coyne, I don't speculate. I figure it out."

"I see . . . Brilliant!"

"Och, it's elementary, isn't it now!"

We were lying in bed, exhausted and happy after a satisfying romp. Our life was slowly returning to its ordinary patterns.

"I figured something else out too."

"And that is?"

"That your man knows who shot him. He realized it in the hospital, after he sent his goon out to scare people. Didn't you think he was lying to you?"

"How did he know?"

"Maybe the smell of her perfume. He remembered it from the times he played around with her. Men don't remember scent too well . . . You never notice when I change mine. Yet the memory finally came alive in your man's thick skull and he knew."

"You figured that out?"

"No, Dermot Michael," she said, impatiently poking my arm, "I speculated."

"I thought you didn't speculate."

"Only sometimes."

"What do we do about it?"

"You ask him tomorrow at the wedding . . . Och, isn't the little brat hungry again . . . It's all right, little princess, Ma is right here."

As Seamus Costelloe leaned weakly against the gray stone wall of the church, I recited Nuala Anne's theory as though it were an obvious matter.

"I feel guilty about it all," Seamus said, his voice dull, his eyes downcast. "I never should have done it. I knew it was a sin all along, but it was so damn much fun. I finally confessed it to a priest and he said I had to end the relationship, which was hard to do, but I did it. She wanted me to divorce Diane and I couldn't do that. I love Diane. Helen was only fun. She pretended that's all it was too. I should have known better. I dumped her from the job. She just wasn't very good at it. I figured she wouldn't sue me because that would ruin her chances with Len. She was sleeping with him, I'm convinced, while we were still fooling around."

"Sleeping with both of you?"

The babble of wedding conversation was going on all around us. We drifted away from the church to the curb where we were more or less alone, except that is for my wife's eyes, which were watching us closely while accepting the compliments to Socra Marie, who seemed to be enjoying the adoration. An elderly woman with a thick cane seemed especially taken with the little wisp of humanity.

"I didn't sleep with her," Seamus said, now looking very sick. "I fooled around with her. It's fun fooling around with a ball-breaking feminist, even if she has small tits. I had to hurt her a little bit to make her come, but she enjoyed every second of it."

I felt sick too. Why were we bothering to try to save the life of this louse?

"I confessed the whole thing. The priest said I was a savage, a barbarian. Thing is that's how I felt when I was doing it and enjoyed it so much. I know I'm disgusting. I made a vow to Our Lady of Lourdes I'd never do anything like that again, my daughter is named Lourdes you know. I've always had a great devotion to Our Lady of Lourdes."

Piety and sadism all wrapped up into one sick bundle.

"Never did it before," he continued. "Never do it again."

"It's not my job to judge you, Seamus."

"So when I finally remembered the smell, I had my goon walk up behind her on LaSalle Street. He told her that if she ever did anything like that again, we'd turn her over to a crowd of blacks who would gang rape her to death. They'd tape the whole process and show it in men's clubs. That'll do the trick."

"How horrible!"

"Yeah, well, I had to prevent her from having another try, didn't I?"

"Couldn't you do that by sending her the whole file you have on her husband?"

"She'd figure I'd made a copy of it. I got some pretty good pictures of her in the file too. I don't look at them anymore. Not once. But they're really great."

His sick smiled faded away.

"Maybe you should burn the whole thing."

"Hey, I never thought of that! Yeah, that's a good idea. Our Lady of Lourdes would approve of that. Maybe ease my conscience a little. Great idea, Dermot. Thanks for suggesting it."

"Be my guest."

"Yeah," he said, trying to square his shoulders and go back to the role of the Father of the Groom. "I'll never do it again and I'll do penance for the rest of my life . . . You'll think I'm a pervert, Dermot. Maybe I am . . . I don't know . . . It was such great fun."

I heard Nuala shout, "Dermot! The car . . ."

Out of the corner of my eye I saw a car moving slowly east on Deming Place. George W. Bush was driving it. As he came up to us, he pointed an automatic weapon out of the open window.

I knocked Seamus to the ground and fell next to him. A baby shrieked in protest. Da shouldn't fall on the ground.

Bullets snarled over us like a flight of angry wasps, ricocheting off the stone walls of the church. Mr. Bush jumped on the gas. The car plowed down the narrow street and collided with a car that was backing out of a parking place. Mike Reilly's men swarmed around.

Mr. Bush jumped out of the car and ran towards us, trying to fire the weapon. It jammed on him. He shook it and hit it as he ran. Then I tackled him and clobbered him on the ground. He was a big strong guy, this George W. Bush. We wrestled desperately for the Mac 10. He wasn't going to get it. If he did, it was jammed.

One does not take chances, however.

Someone was pounding Bush's arms with a massive cane. He screamed and gave up the fight.

"Friggin' Greek!" My wife yelled at him.

Who else?

In the distance, Socra Marie was screaming her head off. Ma and Da ought not to be doing these things.

Too true, small one.

The cops pulled the Bush mask off his head. Beneath it was a big, bearded face with long hair. Tears of rage and pain poured down his face.

Hector Papageorgiou, I presume.

I looked back at the crowd in front of the church. Many of them were on the ground. Sonia Costelloe was leaning against the portal of the church, a red splotch on the side of her wedding dress.

Seamus Costelloe had risen from the ground and was moving towards her and Andy. He was sobbing.

"It's all my fault!" he sobbed.

— 31 —

June 24, 1893

"Come in, Ned." Governor John Peter Altgeld rose from his desk and held out his hand. *"I have reread all your reports and have found them most helpful in this work on which I am engaged."*

"Thank you, Governor," I said respectfully. *"May I present my wife, Nora Joyce Fitzpatrick."*

"I believe I have met you before, Mrs. Fitzpatrick, at some of the balls in Chicago. You are most welcome."

His tone implied that only a blind man would forget my wife, which was certainly true.

"Nora will confirm some of the details of the story I have been led to believe you want to hear."

"Excellent."

Everyone expected that the long-awaited pardon of the surviving Haymarket prisoners would occur shortly after Altgeld was elected governor. The studious, somewhat frail German Lutheran, with the neatly trimmed spade beard, was a Democrat and had no use for Marshall Field and Cy McCormick, to say nothing of the unspeakable Joe Medil at the Tribune. Yet he had delayed. The whole matter, he had told his allies, had to be explored carefully.

The World's Fair has started. The White Stockings

are still the world's champions in baseball, the L tracks are going up around the area the papers are calling the Loop.

"He should examine it carefully," the General had said. "He will be speaking to the ages."

"I quite agree," I said.

"That's why he wants to see you."

"Why me? Everything I think about the case is already in print."

"Not quite everything."

"The Galway file?"

"It is time for it, Ned. I told John that you had information about the one subject about which he remains in doubt."

"Who threw the bomb?"

"He is inclined to think that it was an individual seeking revenge against the police."

"He's right, though in a way he cannot imagine."

"He seeks a little more certainty. I told him you could provide it."

"If he is willing to believe the fantastical."

"He is, Ned. Believe me, he is . . . Will you take the train down to Springfield and show him the Galway file?"

"Certainly."

His circuitous approach to the request was unnecessary. However, it was very Irish.

"Good!"

"Nora will come with me."

The General digested that for a moment.

"Capital idea!"

"I have written a draft for my pardon," the Governor said as we sat at his desk. "It examines in detail five issues." He picked up the first page of a document and began to read.

FIRST—That the jury which tried the case was a packed jury selected to convict.

SECOND—That according to the law as laid down by the Supreme Court, both prior to and again since the trial of this case, the jurors, according to their own answers, were not competent jurors and the trial was therefore not a legal trial.

THIRD—That the defendants were not proven to be guilty of the crime charged in the indictment.

FOURTH—That as to the defendant Nebbe, the state's attorney had declared at the close of the evidence that there was no case against him, and yet he has been kept in prison all these years.

FIFTH—That the trial judge was either so prejudiced against the defendants, or else so determined to win the applause of a certain class in the community that he could not and did not grant a fair trial.

"I ASSUME, NED, FROM YOUR writings that you agree with all these arguments."

"I do indeed, sir."

"My only problem is why the bomb was thrown. The prosecution, as I note later in my proclamation, never discovered who threw the bomb at the policeman. I myself believe that it was the revenge of someone who had been abused by the police . . ."

"You're quite right, sir. The bomb hit Matt Degen but was aimed at Captain Ward who was near him. I remember in the police station when the priest was anointing Matt, Captain Ward muttered over and over again, that if Matt had not absorbed the explosion, it would have hit him."

"Someone was trying to kill Captain Ward?"

"No, sir, someone was trying to kill Captain Bonfield. He assumed from the insignia of rank on Captain Ward that he was Bonfield. He was a careless killer, sir. Very careless."

"Do you know his name, Ned?"

"Yes, sir. He was called Sean-Tom Og Joyce."

"He was my first husband Myles's third cousin, four

times removed, your lordship," Nora explained. "He's dead now."

The Governor frowned at this relationship which, not unreasonably, he could not comprehend.

"Dead?"

I intervened before Nora called him "your lordship" again.

"We call this the 'Galway file,' Governor. I discovered it while we were searching Captain Bonfield's house. I saved it for a day like this."

I gave him the file, which included the page of Mary's letter to Josie in which she told of the death of Sean-Tom Og Joyce. He looked through it very carefully. Then we told him the story.

He returned the file to me and sat back in his chair.

"It certainly confirms my suspicions," he said slowly.

"It's a fantastical story, sir."

He smiled, a warm smile that one would expect from a man whose name was "old gold."

"Ned, madam, you two are certainly among the most intelligent and honest people in the state of Illinois. You have no reason to concoct such a story. Naturally I believe it. Thank you for making my work easier."

"It may not be politically expedient, sir, to issue that document."

"That's what many of my staff say, but, damn it, Ned," he pounded his desk, "It's the RIGHT thing to do!"

"Ned," my wife said solemnly as we left the executive mansion, "we have just spoken with one of the great Americans of our time."

"As always, my dear, you are right."

I add to this record the portion of the document about the trial which may be pertinent.

The state has never discovered who it was that threw the bomb which killed the policemen, and the evidence does not show any connection whatever between the defendants and the man who did throw it. The trial judge, in overruling the motion for a new hearing, and again, recently in a magazine article, used this language:

"The conviction has not gone on the grounds that they did have actually any personal participation in the particular act which caused the death of Degen, but the conviction proceeds upon the ground that they had generally, by speech and print, advised large classes of the people, not particular individuals, but large classes, to commit murder, and had left the commission, the time and place and when, to the individual will and whim, or caprice, or whatever it may be, of each individual man who listened to their advice, and that in consequence of that advice, in pursuance of that advice, and influenced by that advice, somebody not known did throw the bomb that caused Degen's death. Now, if this is not a correct principle of the law, then the defendants, of course, are entitled to a new trial. This case is without precedent; there is no example in the law books of a case of this sort."

The Judge certainly told the truth when he stated that this case was without a precedent, and that no example could be found in the law books to sustain the law as above laid down. For, in all the centuries during which government has been maintained among men, and crime has been punished, no judge in a civilized country has ever laid down such a rule before. The petitioners claim that it was laid down in this case simply because the prosecution, not having discovered the real criminal, would otherwise not have been able to convict anybody; that this course was then taken to appease the fury of the public, and that the judgment was allowed to stand for the same reason. I will not discuss this. But taking the law as above laid down, it was necessary under it to prove, and that beyond a reasonable doubt, that the person committing the violent deed had at least heard or read the advice given to masses, for until he either heard or read it he did not receive it, and if he did not receive it, he did not commit the violent act in pursuance of that advice; and it is here that the case for the State fails; with all his apparent eagerness to force conviction in court, and his efforts in defending his course since the trial, the Judge, speaking on this point in his magazine article, makes this statement: "It is probably true that Rudolph Schnaubult threw the bomb," which statement is a mere surmise and is all that is known about it, and is certainly not sufficient to convict eight men on. In fact, until the State proves from whose hands the bomb came, it is impossible to show any connection between the man who threw it and these defendants.

It is further shown that the mass of matter contained in the record and quoted at length in the Judge's magazine article, showing the use of seditious and incendiary language, amounts to but little when its source is considered. The two papers in which articles appeared at intervals during the years were obscure little sheets having scarcely any circulation and the articles themselves were written at times of great public excitement when an element in the community claimed to have been outraged; and the same is true of the speeches made by the defendants and others; the apparently seditious utterances were such as are always heard when men imagine that they have been wronged or are excited or partially intoxicated; and the talk of a gigantic anarchistic conspiracy is not believed by the then chief of police, as will be shown hereafter, and it is not entitled to serious notice, in view of the fact that, while Chicago had nearly a million inhabitants, the meetings held on the lakefront on Sundays during the summer by these agitators rarely had fifty people present, and most of these went from mere curiosity, while the meetings held indoors during the winter were still smaller. The meetings held from time to time by the masses of the laboring people must not be confounded with the meetings above named, although in times of excitement and trouble much violent talk was indulged in by irresponsible parties, which was forgotten when the excitement was over.

I also think it pertinent to add his opinion of Judge Joseph Gray because it confirms that what I have written in this account about the Judge is not my own prejudice.

It is further charged with much bitterness by those who speak for the prisoners that the record of the case shows that the Judge conducted the trial with malicious ferocity and forced eight men to be tried together; that in cross-examining the State's witnesses he confined counsel for the defense to the specific points touched on by the State, while in the cross-examination of the defendants' witnesses he permitted the State's Attorney to go into all manner of subjects entirely foreign to the matters on which the witnesses were examined in chief; also that every ruling throughout the long trial on any contested point was in favor of the State, and further, that page after page of the record contains insinuating remarks of the Judge, made in the hearing of the jury, and with the evident intent of bringing the jury to his way of thinking; that these speeches, coming from the court, were much more damag-

ing than any speeches from the State's Attorney could possibly have been; that the State's Attorney often took his cue from the Judge's remarks; that the Judge's magazine article recently published, although written nearly six years after the trial, is yet full of venom; that, pretending to simply review the case, he had to drag into his article a letter written by an excited woman to a newspaper after the trial was over, and which therefore had nothing whatever to do with the case and was included simply to create a prejudice against the woman, as well as against the dead and the living, and that, not content with this, he in the same article makes an insinuating attack on one of the lawyers for the defense, not for anything done at the trial, but because more than a year after the trial when some of the defendants had been hung, he ventured to express a few kind, if erroneous, sentiments over the graves of his dead clients, whom he at least believed to be innocent. It is urged that such ferocity or subserviencey is without a parallel in all history; that even Jeffries in England contented himself with hanging his victims, and did not stop to berate them after they were dead. These charges are of a personal character, and while they seem to be sustained by the record of the trial and the papers before me and tend to show that the trial was not fair, I do not care to discuss this feature of the case any farther, because it is not necessary. I am convinced that it is clearly my duty to act in this case for the reasons already given, and I, therefore, grant an absolute pardon to Samuel Fielden, Oscar Neebe, and Michael Schwab this 26th day of June,
1893.
JOHN P. ALTGELD,
Governor of Illinois.

HOME IN CHICAGO

June 26, 1893

Special to the *Chicago Times*
By Ned Fitzpatrick

Shortly after 4:00 this afternoon, E.S. Dreyer, who had chaired the Grand Jury which indicted the Haymarket defendants but who has championed their cause through the years, handed Governor John Peter Altgeld's "absolute pardon" to Warden R.L. Allen of the State Penitentiary at Joliet in the presence of Samuel Fielden, Oscar Nebbe, and Michael Schwab. Nebbe, whose young wife and the mother of his two children died while he was in prison, said to Dreyer, "I have to thank you for this and I believe that this is justice, even though it comes tardily."

Warden Allen treated the survivors to a dinner, promised them the best suit of clothes money could buy and a "sterling recommendation" for their work ethic. He also advised them to steer clear of anarchism when they returned home.

The men left for Chicago at 6:15 and arrived shortly after eight o'clock. Each returned to his home with emotions that one can barely imagine.

The story does not really have a happy ending. Five innocent men are dead. Nor is the story over, as the dedication tomorrow of the Martyrs Shrine at Waldheim Cemetery proves.

Perhaps it will never be over.

None of the pardoned men were present at the dedication of the shrine to the Haymarket Martyrs. Young Albert Parsons Jr, looking weak and confused, did the actual dedication just as Matt Degen's son dedicated the policeman's statute at the Haymarket. History will always see the police and the Martyrs as opponents, though in fact they shared a common enemy. Nora and I went to the ceremony. I was astonished at the deterioration of Nina Spies. The beautiful and fashionable young socialite has become a haggard, haunted woman though she has yet to reach her thirtieth year. Is she paying the price for youthful folly or will she always be a dedicated mourner? Perhaps both.

There was great rejoicing over the pardon because it in effect declares the martyrs innocent. Yet as someone said it does not bring them back to life. Nor does it bring back from the dead Oscar Nebbe's wife, who died of worry and heartache during his imprisonment.

A few people did recognize me though I was not wearing my white suit. They thanked me for my efforts for the pardon, though I had done very little.

"It is over," Nora said on the train ride back to the Wisconsin Central station, "not for them surely. Not ever for them, but for us."

"Yes," I agreed, "it is over for us."

I have permitted personal matters to intrude into this story. I should not end without reference to them, should anyone read this document and wonder.

I continue to write for magazines and sometimes for the Chicago Times. I also appear on occasion in the General's law offices. Josie and Timmy are happily married, the adoring parents of Nora Ann, and expecting a second child. We have another son, Edmund. It is ten years now since I brought the boy's mother back from Ireland. I am over thirty and my wife is twenty-nine. She is more beautiful than ever and I am more in love with her than ever. Her intelligence, determination, and grace have made her what she was destined to be, a West of Ireland Gaelic queen.

Apparently she still loves me. She permits me to share her bed, which also astonishes me. I said this to

*her one night. She snuggled close to me and laughed.
"Don't be absurd, Mr. Fitzpatrick. You own the bed
and everything else in this house, including me, thanks
be to God."*

*I do not quite understand, but it is perhaps not nec-
essary that I do so.*

32

NUALA SAT on the floor, playing with her younger daughter, a very primitive form of patty cake, which seemed to intrigue the small one.

I was reading the notes from the two dated envelopes she had given me.

The first one read,

> Isn't it obvious altogether? The lads, or some early form of them, were trying to settle a score with the Chicago cops, probably with Captain Bonfield. Eeejits that they are they missed him.

The second one read,

> This one is slightly revised. The woman shot him the first time. She's the only one who would know her way around the building. I don't think she'll try again because in the end she really didn't want to kill him. The danger for the next time is from the Greeks, most likely from Hector, who sounds really crazy. He probably figures that if someone takes another shot at Seamus, the contracts will be carried out. His brother is killed, maybe with his family. Hector hides out till the heat is off. Then collects the rights to the whole escrow. It's crazy, but he's pretty crazy.

"Brilliant," I admitted.

She didn't respond with "Elementary."

"I warned Mike Casey that the next attempt would be by the Greeks. They did their best to keep an eye on him. None of us realized how crazy he was. I don't know what else we could do."

"Thank God Sonia was only nicked with a piece of the church. And no one else was hurt."

"She is so brave, Dermot Michael. She insisted that she was all right and came back to the wedding reception. She told me that she would probably have died of an infection if it had happened in Russia."

"And everyone else was only scared, except our daughter, who was very angry at us."

"Och didn't the woman whose cane I took, calm her down quickly enough . . . Wasn't she a nice lady, *alanah*?"

"So they have Hector on an attempted murder charge and Helen walks?"

"It's not our task to put her in jail, and herself being almost as badly confused as your man."

"What a bundle of emotional mess he is."

"The Marquis de Sade and Our Lady of Lourdes, Dermot Michael. Only a Catholic could put that together. Can you imagine what his mother was like?"

"I'd rather not."

"Well, he's burned the file and sent the ashes to her. Whether she believes him or not is another matter. I think he should get off the elevator if she gets on."

"For fear she might try to kill him again?"

"Give over, Dermot Michael! She tried that once and couldn't do it. She probably still loves him. She might try to have another go at seducing him . . . and wasn't that threat of gang rape right out of *Justine*?"

"I didn't know you read the Marquis."

"Only the first part. It was boring!"

I'd take her word for it.

"The mysteries were similar, were they not, Dermot love?"

"How so?"

"Two ways. First of all, dumb people did stupid things and messed up what they did. Secondly, nothing at all was what it first seemed. I knew she shot Seamus as soon as I heard she did target practice. She knew her way around your IBM Building and was confident that she could kill him herself and didn't need a hit man. So it was not a hit man who couldn't shoot straight but a woman scorned who could shoot straight, but finally didn't want to. Otherwise your man would be dead."

"And Governor Altgeld," I added, getting it at last, "figured out that it was someone who had a grudge against the police and had nothing to do with the Anarchists? Ned and Nora merely confirmed his suspicions."

"And didn't the poor Anarchists just happen to be there and took the blame for it?"

"A terrible tragedy for everyone."

"'Tis true. God will have to explain someday, Dermot Michael, I suppose, though all of them understand now, even poor Lucy and poor Nina."

"That's what we believe," I agreed.

"We don't have the Galway file, do we?" she said, snatching our delighted daughter up in her arms.

"We don't."

"You'll need it for the book?"

"We could make do without it, but it would finally end the doubts about Haymarket."

"Och, Ned was careful about the diaries he turned over to rectories. We'll go over there and demand that his rivirence let us into that storeroom of his."

"We will," I said, taking secret delight in the fact that my wife would finally discover that her brother-in-law was a slob. She would doubtless dismiss it all on the grounds that the "poor priesteen" works so hard.

"And Seamus has hired," my wife enthused, "both Jimmy the Giant and Nick to work for him and has even got some simple cases for McGinty and McGourty."

"I'm sure Our Lady of Lourdes is pleased with him."

Nuala Anne sang two stanzas of the Lourdes hymn.

"There are only two Absolutes in the world, Dermot, a Swedish vodka and God's love. Who are we to budget his forgiveness."

"'Tis true," I said with a loud sigh.

"Do you think I'm at all like Nora Joyce?" she said in a massive change of the subject.

"Well, I was really impressed that Ned brought her to Springfield to meet Governor Altgeld."

"The poor man had no choice, did he now? That doesn't answer my question."

"Well, you can't say that I own everything in the house, including you, thanks be to God."

"Of course you do," she said impatiently.

I hadn't noticed that.

"She wasn't fey like you. That came on the Philbin side of the family."

"That's not what I mean at all, at all!"

"Are you a Gaelic princess with intelligence and determination and grace?"

"I know that! I want to know if you think I support you the way she supported poor Ned and himself feeling inferior to this father when even the old fella knew it was the other way around!"

I essayed a very careful answer because I knew it was important.

"Well, Nuala Anne, times have changed and styles of supporting a husband have changed, though perhaps not all that much. I'd judge that when it comes to the essentials you two are very much alike."

She sighed in relief.

"I was afraid that I wasn't at all like her."

"I'll buy you a big quilted robe for Christmas."

She pounded my calf and said to our daughter, "Da is being fresh again!"

33

ON CHRISTMAS Day, Socra Marie decided she would crawl, causing great amusement to her family. She seemed to view entertaining us as her main goal in life, beyond sleeping, eating, and defecating.

I have this theory about children. They come into the world with a certain genetic endowment, certain memories from the time in the womb, and perhaps certain expectations. They check out how the world reacts to this package and then adjust their behavior to fit the reaction, relying on certain possibilities that are part of the package.

This is all probably nonsense. Yet it helps to explain our younger daughter. She is still a very determined young woman, aggressively hanging on to life.

However, she has also decided that the most effective way to do that is to charm the reality in which she finds herself. She has learned the two magic words— "Ma" and "Da"—and uses them indiscriminately of her parents, her siblings, Ethne and Danuta, and even the dogs. Everyone seems to be delighted by this, so she continues with a happy grin.

The doctors tell us that she is already substantially beyond full-term babies of her age in intelligence.

"Do we want a friggin' genius, Dermot Michael?" Nuala complains with notable lack of sincerity.

We are not out of the woods yet. Something could still go wrong, though Nuala dismisses that with a wave of her hand. She insists that she knew from the beginning that the little wisp would be fine. When I ask her if it's her real self or her fey self that knows it, she replies impatiently that her fey self IS her real self, which I ought to know anyway.

I don't doubt her confidence, but earthling that I am I will relax after the second birthday.

She appeared on the *Nuala Anne at Christmas* program in which Nuala sang songs of hope from many religions and dedicated the show to all premature babies and their parents and the doctors and nurses who take care of them. She had already promised that the profits from the show and her next record would go to more research on the subject.

She also used the quote about the only two absolutes.

For reasons I don't fully understand and don't want to, the children, without much coaching, know just how to act when they're on TV in their brief scene with their mother. This year the two kids joined herself in singing "Silent Night" to their little sister, Nellie right on key and the Mick not too far off key. The latter fortunately was in his "adoration" phase of the cycle and not in his "I hate her" phase.

Socra Marie smiled and chortled and goo-gooed to the whole world, I dare say causing millions of tears to fall. Maybe billions.

A lot of them from me.

"Dermot Michael," my wife said to me after the taping was over, "would you ever think we might let the dogs join us next year?"

"It's a brilliant idea, altogether!" I lied.

We took all three of them to see the Christmas tree and the window displays at Marshall Field's, but only after I assured Nuala Anne that Ole Marsh's family no longer owned it.

All three rugrats were impressed, each in their own

way. Nellie studied each window very carefully and reviewed it for us. The Mick reported that the Nutcracker had become a Prince, which he thought was a very good idea. Socra Marie, secure in the sack around her mother's breasts, laughed and cooed and pointed in delight, especially at the Christmas tree, which she called "Da!"

A couple in their forties approached us, short, grim-eyed people with thin lines for lips.

"Is that a premature child?" The woman demanded in the tone of a prosecuting attorney.

"She is," Nuala said proudly, "she was born fifteen weeks early and she's ten months old."

"We believe," the husband growled, "you're socially irresponsible for keeping that child alive. It will have no quality of life."

"It will be a constant drain on the public schools, the health-care system, and on the American taxpayer," the woman added.

"You should have treated it like a miscarriage," the husband concluded.

The two of them waited eagerly for our defense.

Socra Marie who had been smiling at them sensed that these were not nice people and began to wail. The other two, not understanding the exact words, still knew that their little sister was under attack. Thunderclouds appeared on their foreheads and on their mother's.

"She'll go to the Catholic schools," I said, stupefied by their arrogance.

"I might have known you were Catholics!" the woman snarled. "Keeping this thing alive is the sort of thing Catholics do."

Socra Marie was now screaming at them. Nuala lifted her out of the sack and sang to her in Irish. Then she turned to the couple, who were clearly enjoying the prospect of a screaming match.

"Sure, aren't you entitled to your opinion," she said gently as she patted the still angry little wisp of humanity. "And we respect your right to express it. But you're wrong!"

She turned and walked in the opposite direction, singing once again as her bedraggled family trailed along after her. I turned on the couple, who looked like they were about to follow us and pointed my finger in sharp warning at them. Unlike most people they had good sense to be frightened by me.

"Och, Dermot Michael," my wife said as she eased our daughter back into the pouch, "haven't I grown up something terrible? I actually acted like an adult, didn't I now?"

"Like a grand duchess dismissing a fly."

On Christmas Day the dogs were present with the four of us, as Socra Marie tried to crawl. She would lift up her rear end, move her hands forward, and then fall on her face as the rest of her body tried and then refused to cooperate.

We'd all laugh. She'd roll over and grin at us and then try again.

She was too young for a twenty-five-week child to crawl. No one, however, had told her that.

Finally, thanks be to God, (I think) she got it and moved ahead, one body length toward Fiona, who warily moved back. The wisp of humanity looked up at us, a party to a great conspiracy, then tried again. Fiona barked softly and moved back once more.

"Da," said our daughter, pointing at Fiona.

"We won't have to stew about her anymore, will we now, Dermot Michael?"

"I hope not."

We would have to worry for another year. She was still tiny and tired easily.

O YE OF LITTLE FAITH!

The Devil quoting scripture.

The third attempt at a crawl wasn't magic. The little tyke ran out of steam. We, however, applauded and she cooed contentedly as Nuala picked her up, held her close, and sang one of those Irish lullabies. She followed up with "Stille Nacht" and we all hummed with her.

— NOTE —

THIS STORY is a fictionalized account of the Haymarket controversy. The major players in the Haymarket case are all real. The Fitzpatricks are fictional. I agree with Governor Altgeld that none of the accused was involved in the bomb throwing and that probably it was a work of revenge. The revenge scenario I suggest in the story is, as Ned tells the governor, fantastical. However, given the situation in Chicago in 1886, it is by no means an impossible scenario. It is also possible that the bomb was intended to explode among the protestors. Finally it is also possible that the bomb was thrown by an *agent provocateur*.

The behavior of the police, the courts, and the press in Chicago in those days is a disgrace to the city. Perhaps the heroism of John Peter Altgeld, also a Chicagoan (and one of the very few of us ever elected governor in this Chicago-hating state). He was viciously denounced on all sides. The immigrant-hating *Tribune* (which manages often to be on the wrong side of history) declared that he had never become an American. He was not reelected in 1896, though in a national Republican sweep, in Illinois he ran substantially ahead of William Jennings Bryan, the Democratic presidential candidate. Marshall Field led a conspiracy to deprive him of the value of his real estate and forced him into bankruptcy. However, his friend and ally Clarence Darrow took him into his law partnership. He died, before his time, in 1902, as Nora says, one of the great men of American political life.

Oscar Nebbe remarried and had two more children. He opened a shoe store in Chicago. Samuel Fielden, with a surprise inheritance, bought a ranch in the west. Michael Schwab named his daughter, born after his release, Johanna Altgeld Schwab. He worked for two years as a compositor for the *Arbeiter-Zeitung*, but then drifted away from the Anarchists. How, after all, can you be an object of a martyr cult when you are still alive. His wife was reunited with her brother, Rudolph Schnaubult, only very late in life in Argentina, where he had migrated. There was never any proof that he threw the bomb.

Nina Spies died in 1936 in abject poverty, a woman whom others avoided because of her smell. She shared an old house on Monroe Street with cats, dogs, chickens, and even a horse. Her aunt had disinherited her, her parents died, she earned a meager living for many years as a translator, but became increasingly strange. Still, at the end of her life, she still had $3000, which she left to an animal shelter. Lucy Parsons, who preached at her funeral, became furious at Nina when she learned that this money had not been left to the cause.

Lucy's children died young. The police harassed her for many years. She died at the age of ninety in 1942 in a fire which destroyed her house and killed her partner since 1910, George Markshall. She was part of every organizing drive and march in Chicago until the late nineteen thirties. Her extensive library was not destroyed in the fire but disappeared, according to some confiscated by the "red squad" of the Chicago Police Department.

The monument to the Anarchist Martyrs still stands in Forest Home (as it is now called) Cemetery. The monument to the police was blown up twice in the nineteen sixties and now stands inside the Chicago Police Department headquarters. As Ned remarks, the ordinary police and the Martyrs shared a common enemy—the police leadership of the time. The monument was criticized when it first appeared on the grounds that the cop seemed "too Irish."

As Ned predicted, Chicago is now a union town. Even the police have a union.

The *Chicago Times* still lives though as the *Sun-Times*, the name representing an ironic merger with the *Chicago Sun*, a left-wing paper founded by Marshall Field III.

Mayor Carter Harrison, after five two-year terms, was assassinated by a disappointed office-seeker the day after the 1893 World's Fair ended. His son, Carter II, also served five terms.

The sign on the Catholic charities building I quote disappeared (through vandalism) long before Nuala and Dermot visited the Haymarket.

St. Patrick's parish—now called "Old St. Patrick's" is alive and well.

The Chicago White Stockings morphed into the Chicago Cubs, a major league baseball franchise in Chicago till 1945. Between 1906 and 1945, they won two world series and ten national league pennants. The White Stockings, despite their name, are no relation to the Chicago White Sox.

Chicago is obsessed with the name of Desplaines— there is a suburb, a river, and two streets, the latter (Des Plaines Avenue), many miles apart, appear in this story. No copy editor would tolerate this abundance unless it were true. Oh, yes we pronounce it like Displanes. Also Goethe Street, which does not appear in this story and was surely named to please the German immigrants, is called Gaythe.

The conversation between Nuala and Dr. Foley is, I believe, an accurate description of the Catholic teaching about extraordinary means to preserve life. Perhaps a Catholic couple would be more likely to take a chance on a very premature child.

Not all such risks work out, hence the warnings that Dr. Foley gives them. The NICUs do wonderful work, but more research is needed before attempts to prolong life at its beginning can be free of most risks.

AG
Feast of the Immaculate Conception
December 2000, the last year of the Second Millennium

Turn the page for an exclusive look at
ANDREW M. GREELEY's
NEW NOVEL

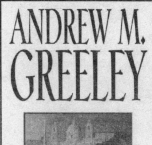

ANDREW M. GREELEY

SECOND SPRING
A Love Story

A Chronicle of the O'Malleys in the Twentieth Century from the
Bestselling Author of *September Song*

0-765-30236-5

SECOND SPRING
A Love Story

Arriving in hardcover April 2003

FORGE®

www.tor.com • www.agreeley.com

❧ Chuck ❧
1978

"You might," the naked woman said to me, "make model airplanes."

"Ah," I said, as I caressed her firm, sweaty belly, an essential of afterplay as I had learned long ago.

"You always wanted to make them when you were a kid."

The full moon illumined the dome of St. Peter's in the distance and bathed us in its glow, as though it were doing us a favor. Over there the cardinals were doubtless spending a restless night in the uncomfortable beds in their stuffy rooms. None of them had a bedmate like Rosemarie with whom to play, worse luck for them and for the Church.

"You said . . . Don't stop, Chucky Ducky, I like that . . . You said that you were too poor to buy the kits."

"I did not!" I insisted, as I kissed her tenderly.

"You did." She sighed. "You don't have to stop that either."

My lips roamed her flesh, not demanding now, but reassuring, praising, celebrating.

"I did not!"

There had been a time, long years ago, when I would have tried a second romp of lovemaking in a situation like the present one.

"Or you could take up collecting sports cards. You told all of us that you couldn't afford that either."

"I never said that!"

"You did too!" She giggled as I tickled her.

"I guess I'm in my midlife identity crisis," I admitted.

"You can't be, Chucky Ducky darling." She snuggled close to me. "You haven't got beyond your late adolescent identity crisis."

One of the valiant Rosemarie's favorite themes was that I was still a charming little boy, like the little redhead in the stories she wrote.

"Mind you," she whispered, "I like you as an adolescent boy."

"Oh?"

"Only an adolescent boy would be so nicely obsessed with every part of a woman's anatomy."

That would be a line in her next story. I wondered how the *New Yorker* would handle the spectacular lovemaking that preceded the line.

"A man could become impotent at the possibility that his bedtime amusements would become public knowledge."

"Ha! . . . I don't know about you, Chucky Ducky, but I'm going to sleep now."

She pillowed her head on my stomach.

"Chucky love," she sighed, now well across the border into the land of Nod, "you're wonderful. We really defied death this time, didn't we?"

That would be in the story too. I had become a character in a series of *New Yorker* stories—a little redhaired punk as an occasional satyr.

Rosemarie Helen Clancy O'Malley had found her midlife identity as a writer. Her poor husband had found his identity as a character in fiction. On that happy note I reprised in my imagination some of the more pleasurable moments of our romp and sank into peace and satisfied sleep.

✌ *Rosemarie* ✌

1978

I stirred my second cup of tea in the Hassler breakfast room, on the top of the hotel, and watched the Dome steam in the morning sun.

Instead of wondering about the outcome of the conclave, I worried about my poor husband.

In bed he was indeed the delightful adolescent who had learned a lot of tricks and a lot more of wisdom in pleasuring a woman. Our sex life wasn't always great, no one's is. But it was mostly good and often great, sometimes almost transcendent.

Our romp of the night before had left me in a state of pleasurable and self-satisfied complacency. It had started off routinely enough and then suddenly we both warmed to the task and it expanded to the edge of the transcendent, perhaps because the future of our Church was at stake in the conclave, a Church to which we were irrevocably committed despite its flaws.

I rejoiced in my condition as a woman animal, rational indeed to some extent, like a self-satisfied lioness lounging on her back in the sands of the Kahalari. Someone had rolled my nightgown into a ball and thrown it across the room. I refused to leave before we found it. Both of us blamed the other, but I was fibbing as Chuck knew very well.

Out of bed he was a mope, a sad sack, an old man long before his time.

He rarely touched his cameras. I had to insist that he bring the Nikon along for our trip to Lucerne and Vienna. He had not wanted to fly to Rome when we heard of the Pope's death. He had lost interest in recording great events and saw no reason to produce a portrait of the next Pope. I insisted again. He agreed, as he always does when I insist.

"You can quote me in a story," he said with a laugh, "that I had learned long ago that it was bootless to resist the orders of the monster regiment of women."

I had given up long ago any effort to convince him that he was not only quoting John Knox out of context but actually misquoting him.

He had stopped reading his beloved economic journals. He did not enjoy his children, not even the darling little Siobhan, currently being spoiled rotten by her Grandma April. He was not especially interested in his three grandchildren, two of them redheads like himself and Siobhan. Adoration from the next couple of generations did not much interest him. He is clever enough to cover that up, so the kids and grandkids adore him all the more.

He has stopped reading the papers since our unfortunate expedition to the White House to photograph Jimmy Carter. Nor did he vote for Gerry Ford. "It is not fair, my beloved, to say that he cannot walk and chew gum at the same time. However, you add the obligation to talk while he walks and chews gum and you befuddle him."

When President Ford assured everyone that the people of Poland were able to choose their own government, Chuck writhed. "Thomas Jefferson, where are you when we really need you!"

Yet when we went to the White House to do a portrait of Ford, we couldn't help but like the man. We spoke of Michigan and New Buffalo and Grand Beach and the Tabor Hill wines which we drank and which he served at state dinners. He was a genuinely nice man.

"You would like to spend time with him," I said on the plane back to Chicago. "Unlike Johnson or Nixon."

"And Jack Kennedy?"

I considered that.

"Sometimes those Boston guys, God be good to both of them, were like chalk scratching against the blackboard. They were fun, but you weren't altogether sure they were human. Gerry Ford you know is human."

Poor dear man.

Chuck tried to give up on exercise, but I wouldn't stand for that. However, he made little effort to beat me at tennis and gave up on his efforts to learn windsurfing. "Ridiculous for someone as old as I am," he protested.

That was the problem. On the coming September 17, my darling little redhead punk, would turn fifty. The strands of white in his wire brush red hair were increasing. He would not cover them as I promptly did when any gray appeared in my hair. Chuck was getting old, he thought. Life was slipping away and was pointless anyway.

He still made love with me, but I was almost always the aggressor. He was very good at the art of ravishing me, better than ever perhaps. It made him happy for a little while.

As I sipped my tea and worried about him, his lips touched the back of my neck, sending a shiver down my spine and causing my nipples to firm. No man should have that much power over a woman, right?

Wrong!

"You weren't the woman in my bed last night, were you?"

"Certainly not!"

"I didn't think so. Whoever she was, she had no modesty at all."

"Couldn't have been me. I'm Irish."

"Right."

"You were straightening up the room for the house-keeper?"

"I couldn't leave it a mess for the poor Giovanina."

"You made the bed?"

"Well . . ."

"Chucky, this is a high-class hotel. She'll remake the bed anyway."

"Yeah, well . . ."

My husband is, to put it mildly, fastidious. I'm a pretty good housekeeper—for someone whose origins are Irish. Chuck makes Missus, our Polish defender of order in the house, seem slovenly.

Also he keeps obsessively neat files, each one carefully labeled in his neat, precise printing. On the other hand he dresses like a slob—this morning in tattered jeans and a Notre Dame tee shirt which had seen better days thirty years ago. Out of place in the breakfast room of the Hassler? My poor Chucky looked like someone who came in every morning to walk the dog.

"*Por favore,* cornflakes?" he asked the pretty waitress with a pathos that would have been appropriate for an orphan in a Dickens novel.

"Certainly, *signor,*" she said with a big smile.

The little bitch thinks he's cute.

When she returned with the cereal and a big pitcher of cream, Chuck murmured, "*Mille grazie,* Paola."

Of course, he knew her name. For a couple of days the Hassler was his precinct. Like a good precinct captain, he had to know the names of everyone. Some traits are so ingrained that even a midlife identity crisis couldn't demolish them.

"You notice the major change in Catholic doctrine the last couple of days?" he asked.

I poured him a refill of his tea.

"How can they change doctrine when the Pope, poor dear man, is dead?"

"They did just the same. They wouldn't let women in slacks or shorts into the wake in San Pietro. Then they permitted slacks, then even shorts if they were not too short, then they gave up on that judgment call. Bare shoulders and spaghetti straps are still sinful, however. Nonetheless, I think there has been a real corruption of Catholic truth."

"It's because everyone is on vacation. Even the poor Pope was on vacation when he died."

"Did him a world of good, didn't it?"

"Chucky, that is a very old joke."

"I am a very old man . . . Paola, *ancora una volta?*"

"Si, signor." Paola rushed away.

"The little bitch thinks you're adorable."

"Women do. Cute little old guy."

It was not just the advent of his fiftieth birthday which bothered my Chuck. His real problem had been caused by John Kennedy and Pope John XXIII almost twenty years ago. Both men had believed that change in our country and our Church were possible and necessary. Jack Kennedy had invited Chuck to be part of his project when he sent us to Germany as ambassador. Pope John had launched an Ecumenical Council that had created great hope among the parish clergy and the laity for change in the Church.

John Kennedy had died. Chuck served under Lyndon Johnson till it became clear that Kennedy's successor had decided to escalate the war in Vietnam. He turned down an appointment as UN representative and walked out of the Oval Office, to return in 1968 as one of the "Senior Advisers to the President" who had gathered together to tell Johnson that it was time to get out of the war.

(He had called former Secretary of State Dean Acheson "Dean" and that frosty man had called him "Charles.")

One of our children disappeared into the dropout underground during the war and another had his foot

blown off by an American mine. Richard Nixon became president and Chuck, who had marched at Selma
(because I had insisted), dropped out of politics.

Paul VI had appointed us to the commission which
was supposed to find grounds for changing the birth
control teaching. Then when we recommended a
change and the reasons for it, he ignored us and caved
in to the curial reactionaries. Chuck gave up his hope
that the Church could really reform itself—though he
continued to be a practicing Catholic and even a lector
at Mass. Chucky navigating the syntax of St. Paul was
a comic delight.

If Kennedy and the Pope had left things alone, my
husband would be a distinguished photographer with a
worldwide reputation and no sense that he had failed.
You can only experience disillusion when someone sets
you up with illusions. At our silver anniversary celebration a couple of years ago, he had smiled brightly and
seemed to enjoy every moment of it. I cried all day because I knew that I had never deserved a husband like
Chuck. He had prevented me from becoming an incur-
able drunk. Now he was in trouble and there was nothing I could do to help him.

The young radicals of the late sixties had fallen all
over each other in "selling out." The blacks, or African-
Americans as some of them insisted that they be called,
had retreated into self-segregation. Disco music became popular as a retreat from rock and roll but not
from drugs. Black musicians hated it. I love to dance.
Chucky hates it, but he's learned to be presentable on
the dance floor to please me (which is very generous). I
dragged him off to a disco dance hall one night. We
lasted maybe ten minutes. We were too old and I
couldn't stand the smell—a mix, I thought of sweat,
urine, and pot. He wanted to go back to take pictures. I
said that he might be beat up by some pothead.

Besides, disco wasn't radical and didn't represent
anything except maybe the survival of the psychedelic

drug culture (though without rock and roll), which was maybe what the sixties were all about anyway.

We liberals had rid the country of Nixon and defeated Ford by less than one percentage point, so inept was our candidate. There were no causes around. Why bother if all your hopes were to turn to dust?

"What did you think of our supper with Msgr. Adolfo last night?" I asked him when Paola had delivered the third helping of cornflakes, rolling her eyes at me.

I rolled my eyes back.

"Trastevere is a nice place," he said as he spilled a spoonful of cornflakes on his tee shirt. "Great old church, nifty restaurant. You can take me there anytime you want."

I paid the bills on these trips with my credit cards because my husband, as obsessive as he was about neatness, has never been able to cope with finances. He would have put us in a pensione somewhere instead of the most expensive hotel in Rome and would have worried for days if he knew how much our suite in the Hassler cost. Deep down in the murky subbasements of his character, he was still afraid that the Great Depression would return.

"And his opinions on what your friends over there are going to do?"

The cardinals were no friends of ours, but that's the way we Chicagoans talk.

"I wonder if it matters." Chuck sighed. He considered another dish of cornflakes and reluctantly decided against it.

"*Ancora, signor*?" Paola asked.

"*Basta.*" Chuck grinned at her.

"*Si, signor.*" she grinned back. "More toast, *signora*?"

I shook my head and smiled, just to let her know I didn't think she was flirting with my cute little husband.

Msgr. Raimundo "Rae" Adolfo was like a character from a Fellini film, sleek and handsome with thick, jet-black hair, a neatly chiseled face, even white teeth, flashing black eyes, and just the faintest hint of cynicism in his quick smile. He did something for the secretary of state who was kind of the Vatican prime minister. He had adopted us for some reason and insisted that Chuck must do a portrait of the new pope.

"Well, that depends on who it is," Chuck said as he was gulping down his pasta.

Adolfo shrugged, as he often did, a sign of a man who had seen everything and would be surprised by nothing.

"It will be very close," he sighed. "The whole project of the Vatican Council is at stake. My former boss, Cardinal Benelli, in his intervention just before the conclave said that collegiality is the most important issue, whether the Pope is willing to share power with the other bishops. You could see the tight jaws of his old enemies in the Curia."

"They really think they can repeal the Council?" I asked, deftly turning over my wineglass.

I'm quite good at that. I've had enough practice.

"Not explicitly. However, they can ignore it and return to governing the Church the way they did before 1960. They forced the long delay between the Pope's burial and the opening of the conclave so they would rally around a candidate. Pericle Felici, who opposes everything, has been on the phone every day. They will all vote for Siri of Genoa, who is very conservative and also authoritarian. They are saying that the last Pope was weak and we need a strong man now. Siri is very tough."

"And the good guys don't fight back?" Chucky said as he looked in dismay at his empty pasta dish. I shook my head as a sign that he'd had enough.

"For once," Adolfo sighed again, "they organize themselves. Leo Suenens does not go back to Brussels as he pretends but rather remains in northern Italy. He too knows how to use the phone, as does Benelli. They are ready, I think."

"Pope Paul ended the Council when he issued the birth control encyclical," Chuck insisted, his voice bitter.

Only two events made my poor husband bitter, the escalation of the Vietnam War in 1965 and the birth control encyclical in 1968.

Adolfo would not permit himself to discuss that subject.

"Yet much remains, Carlo. If Siri wins, you will realize just how much."

"He wouldn't put the Mass back in Latin, would he?"

"Slowly and gradually he would restrict the number of times it might be done in English. They're not opposed necessarily to a vernacular liturgy, only to the decline, as they see it, of papal power."

We were both silent for a moment. Above us a lovely full moon looked down benignly on the glittering mosaics of the Church of Santa Maria in Trastevere. In a city of such beauty, how could there still exist such ugly realities as corruption and power lust?

"Who's our guy?" Chuck asked.

Adolfo hesitated.

"You must understand," he said finally, "that there are very few Italian cardinals left who are capable of being Pope . . . Illness, ah, peculiarities, age. There is talk of Albino Luciani from Venice. He is a good man, a simple *padre di compagna,* a priest of the land, what you Americans would call a good parish priest. He walks the streets of Venice talking to people. He smiles and is witty and would never overturn a vote of his priests' council. However, it is said that he is not sophisticated. One also hears that he has very poor health."

"The best we can do?"

"I'm afraid so. Some of the Curia will support him,

as will the Europeans and the Americans. You can never tell what will happen inside the conclave, however. One must pray."

"Indeed one must," I said.

Adolfo lifted the bottle of Frascati, noted my overturned glass, and offered some to Chuck. He declined with a lifted finger. Adolfo poured a small portion for himself. Two very abstemious Americans, he must have thought.

I don't look like a drunk you see, not at all. I haven't had a drink in almost twenty years and don't propose ever to have one again. I almost ruined my marriage and my life. Chuck saved me along with a couple of first-rate psychiatrists, including a little witch with immense and kind gray eyes named Maggie Ward. If you've been sexually abused by your father and routinely beaten by your mother, drink is one way to escape.

"It is said that he has an open mind on that issue which is so important to you . . ."

"And to all the Catholic married people in the world," I interrupted.

The monsignor smiled briefly, his teeth flashing in the candlelight on the table.

"Of course . . . You remember when the so called test-tube baby was born in England? Everyone here condemned it naturally. Luciani began his very mild comment by congratulating the couple on the birth of their child."

"How dare he!" I said ironically.

Adolfo smiled again. He enjoyed me. Most men do, though I have a hard time admitting that to myself.

"This man Suenens has a lot of clout?" Chuck asked.

"That is one way of putting it, Carlo. He was one of the great men of the Council. He was the Great Elector of the late Pope Paul, who would have made him secretary of state if the Curia had not threatened to resign. They would not have of course . . ."

"Paul was never strong on courage against those guys, was he?"

Msgr. Adolfo sighed very loudly.

"I'm afraid not . . . Later he ostracized Suenens because he called for more collegiality between bishops and the Pope."

"I thought Pope Paul supported that."

"He did, but his feelings were hurt by Suenens's criticism."

I expected Chuck to argue that a Pope can't afford to have such sensitive feelings. However, he said nothing.

"So we pray tomorrow for this Albino Luciani," I said, filling the silence.

"We pray fervently, Rosamaria. So much is at stake."

"You think he will win?"

He hesitated.

"How do you Americans say it? I don't want to jinx the outcome?"

At my insistence we walked back to the Hassler. We needed exercise. Chuck put his arm around my waist, just high enough so that his fingers were close to my breasts. A full moon sometimes does that to a man. I would be ravished before the night was over. To make sure of that outcome, I leaned against his arm.

A couple of Italian men made lascivious comments about me. I ignored them. Chuck didn't hear them.

"You remember what Father Ed said to us?" I said.

Ed was Chuck's brother, six years younger than he was, three years younger than Peg, who was my age and my lifelong coconspirator. He had been the secretary of our crazy Cardinal O'Neill and, by his own admission, had barely kept his vocation and his sanity. Chuck gives me credit for persuading him to resign from the job.

"Ed talks all the time" Chuck replied. "Always has since you signed on as his confidant."

Father Ed's name is Edward Michael. He likes to be called Michael or Ed. Chuck insists that he is Ed just as he insists that I am Rosemarie, though for everyone else in the family I am Rosie.

I like being called Rosemarie, it makes me feel elegant. And sexy.

"About the revolution not ending when the bishops went home."

"Oh yeah . . . Well, he said that the bishops thought that they'd had a nice little quiet revolution during the Council and they went home feeling quite euphoric about what they had done. However, the enthusiasm spread to the lower clergy and to the laity and within ten years they . . ."

"We . . ."

"All right, WE had swept away just about everything in the Church we didn't like or seemed silly— birth control, masturbation, divorce, married priests, women priests, priests and nuns leaving their vocations, Confession before Communion, Mass every single Sunday. Yet we remained Catholic, vociferously so . . . That the conversation?"

"Yes."

"And he said that the bishops really didn't understand this change or that no one could ever turn it around?"

"Not even a Pope?"

"Paul VI sure tried in 1968."

"And failed?"

"You win, Rosemarie, you always do."

"Chucky, you should not play with my boobs in public!"

"I don't think the Pope has made a rule against that!"

However, his fingers retreated a bit. Not too far, however. My hormones began to rage. No way he was going to fall asleep as soon as we returned to our suite.

"Do you think our children will worry about these problems?"

"No, I guess not."

"Yet they'll still cheer for the Pope whenever they're in Rome. And you know why?"

"Because they're Catholic," he admitted. "Always will be, can't ever be anything else."

"Right! We must remember to call your mother and see how Siobhan and Moire Meg are doing."

"Don't miss us at all."

We climbed up the Spanish Steps, though Chuck pretended to be too old to try such a venture. I insisted.

I kissed him passionately as we rode up in the elevator.

He undressed me as we talked to our daughters on the phone, two exuberant and loving young women, both of whom insisted that we should have a good time during our vacation.

"Chucky and Rosie," Rosary freshman Moire Meg instructed us, "you totally need to have a good time."

We did the rest of that night anyway. Our worries about the future of the Church drifted far away.